GECKO

BY
JACK PRIEST

A BOOTLEG BOOK

A BOOTLEG BOOK
Published by
Bootleg Press
82431A NE Halsey
Portland, Oregon 97232

Bootleg Books may be purchased for educational, business, or sales promotional use. For information please e-mail, Kelly Irish at: wwwkellyirish@bootlegpress.com.

First Bootleg Press Trade Paperback Edition

10 9 8 7 6 5 4 3 2 1

Bootleg Press is a registered trademark.

ISBN: 0974524646

Cover by Compass Graphics

Printed in the United States of America

November 2003

//

For Richard Laymon

Reading a horror story should frighten you.
It should have you on the edge of your seat.
It should keep you up at night.
But most of all, it should be fun.

Every single one of Richard's books were like that.
His work was so good, it made me weep.

GECKO

CHAPTER ONE

IT RAINED JUST BEFORE DAWN the day Jim Monday's mind was invaded. The streets in Long Beach's fashionable Belmont Shore section were slick and wet. Dew glistened from the palm fronds. A cool breeze drifted in off the ocean. A late morning chill hung in the air.

"Where am I?" He heard the words in his head as if they were his own thoughts, but they weren't. He stepped around a puddle, stopped at the crosswalk.

"Where am I?" He heard it again, looked up, shaken. The light was still red.

"Did you hear a word I said?" David asked. David Askew was both his lawyer and his best friend.

"I'm sorry, I didn't. My mind was wandering," Jim said.

"Okay, I'll ask it again. Do you think there's any chance you can talk her out of this?"

"I tried, but she's in love with him." He spat the words as he glared across the street at the corner building of Cobb and Cobb, Attorneys at Law. In minutes he would be in the second floor office of Frank Cobb, the younger, signing half his life away.

"Are you going to be civil?" David asked.

"If she's alone, yes. If Kohler's there, I don't know. I'm afraid I might hit the bastard."

"You better not."

"I know, but it tears me inside out."

"Just don't hit him," David said.

Jim glanced upward as the words were leaving his friend's lips and his eyes locked onto Dr. Bernd Kohler, the man who had taken his wife away. Even from across the street, Jim could read the stare.

Hatred, pure and evil.

"Calm down," David said. "Keep your head and we'll get through this."

The light changed, they stepped into the street and started to cross, Jim fighting to control his anger.

"Jump Back!" the voice in his head screamed and Jim Monday was taken back to a country he'd spent half a lifetime trying to forget. A place where when men yelled words like, *Take cover, Drop, Hit the deck*, or *Jump Back*, you obeyed, or you died.

Jim jumped back.

And his life turned into a slow motion horror show as a gray Buick Regal screamed around the corner, picked up David on its grille, smashing his body the way a handballer smashes the ball, sending the human missile flying twenty feet through the air, where it careened onto the sidewalk, stopping only when it blasted into the Spanish bay window of Cobb and Cobb, sending shards of glass hailing down, covering the body with red rainbow sparkles as the sun gleamed off the bloody glass.

It happened so fast and so slow.

"Where am I?" He heard the voice again as he looked up to see the scowl on Kohler's face. And he saw green as the scowl changed into a snarl. It was as if his whole world had shifted to green. Killing green. The green jungles of so long ago. The kill or be killed jungles.

"What's happening?" The voice wouldn't stop.

Jim pushed it from his mind as he faced away from Kohler and moved toward the broken body of his friend, fighting to shake the numbness as he started across the street. He wanted to cry out, but couldn't. Then he heard the thick German accent he had come to loath.

"Out of my way, I'm a doctor."

Jim turned and saw Bernd Kohler, shoving through the crowd, his shoulder length, gray hair flying in the breeze, glowing in the sun. Julia was trailing in his wake, wearing an expensive summer dress, one of her many designer creations.

They approached David's body at the same time, wife, husband and lover. Kohler bent over the body and Jim Monday's mind clicked out of shock. He watched as Kohler reached for David's lifeless pulse. Then clarity struck him. Kohler watching from above. The hatred in his eyes and all of a sudden the green came back. Kohler seemed to be covered in it. An evil green. The man's mouth was open wide, snarling words with green tinged teeth.

And now Monday new. It was if his subconscious had painted the world green, making it obvious to him. Kohler had been waiting for the car. The doctor had tried to kill him, but had killed his best friend instead.

Rage roared through Jim Monday, ripped him raw. He saw the man for what he was. A cold killer after his money and his wife. Again he was back in the green jungles that he had fought so hard to forget. He turned from a reasoning man into a crazed kid soldier and he saw the enemy.

"*I can't think like this.*" Another thought that wasn't his, but agony and anger forced it away.

He reached out to Kohler from behind, grabbed his silver hair in a tight fist, jerked the doctor to his feet. Kohler screamed as Jim spun him around. He screamed again when Jim smashed him in the face with a stiff left, catching the doctor halfway between the right cheek and his aquiline nose.

Then he delivered a punishing blow to the doctor's solar plexus, knocking the wind out of him. He was pulling his balled fist back for the killing blow, when a huge black arm snaked around his neck and another, with a mammoth hand attached, grabbed his fighting arm and locked onto it like a vice latched onto a piece of copper tubing, one mistake and the tube snaps.

The other officer, also black, wrapped a hand around Jim's right wrist, the one still holding Kohler aloft.

"Let him go," a deep bass voice commanded.

Jim was powerless.

The two strong policemen had reacted with lightning speed to Jim's attack on Kohler, saving the doctor's life and saving Jim from a murder charge. There was no point in resisting. He relaxed his hand, relaxed his rage and sagged into the strong arms of a strong cop. The policemen, intent on restraining him, had forgotten about Kohler. When Jim let go of the doctor's hair, he collapsed on the sidewalk with a bone cracking sound.

"Shit," the base voice said, "that had to hurt."

Jim hoped so.

He felt his arms being pulled behind his back. He heard, more than felt, the click of the handcuffs. Then there were sirens and more police telling everyone to get back, but none of it made sense to Jim's fogged mind. He was marginally aware of being pulled away from the awful scene of David's bloody body and the sight of his wife cradling the gasping doctor in her arms. He thought she might have been crying. He couldn't be sure.

"Lower your head," someone commanded and Jim felt a slight pressure against the base of his skull, guiding him into the back of the police car.

"This is not right." The voice in his head again, but Jim Monday was in no condition to wonder about strange voices. The burly policeman started to close the back door of the cruiser and the voice screamed, *"I can't take anymore."* Jim Monday started to pass out.

"No! Don't turn out the lights! Don't make it dark!" the voice screamed and with an effort driven by fear and rage, Jim rocked onto his back, pulling his knees to his chest. He screamed, thrust his legs forward, feet connecting with the door inches before it closed, catching one of the cops by surprise, busting him in the chest, like a powerful steam engine, knocking him back and onto his backside the way cowboy heroes did to cowboy bad guys all those years ago.

"Jesus!" the other voice said, "are you all right, Washington?"

"Get the son of a bitch, Walker," the cop named Washington boomed. And Officer Walker yanked Jim out of the car, slamming him onto the pavement.

"Put him back in the car," Washington said.

Walker picked Jim up as if he weighed no more than a feather pillow.

"Careful," Washington added, "don't break anything."

Walker wasn't careful. He tossed him into the backseat with too much force. Jim screamed as a sharp crack sent pain stabbing up his right arm.

"Don't you listen, Walker? I said careful."

"Sorry," Walker said, but he didn't sound very sincere to Jim.

"Now what are you guys going to do?" a young officer said, addressing the two black policemen.

"What else can we do? We take him in," Washington said.

"Like that? Aren't you in enough trouble? The last thing you need is another brutality case."

"Washington didn't bust him up. I did," Walker said.

"Yeah, but Washington's in charge."

"How do we handle this mess, Lieutenant?" a fair-haired, uniformed sergeant asked.

"Not lieutenant anymore," Washington said. "You're in charge, Sam. You out rank me now. It's you're show. You tell me what to do."

"It doesn't seem right."

"It's the way it is. What do you want me to do?"

"Take your prisoner by Community Hospital. Get him fixed up. Then bring him in and get a statement. We'll handle everything here."

"All right, Sam."

"And Lieutenant?"

"Yeah, Sam."

"If it means anything, I think you got a raw deal, all the boys do. That son-of-a-bitch had it coming. We think you were too easy on him."

"Thanks." Washington moved toward the passenger side of the car. "You drive," he told Walker.

"But you always drive?" Walker slid behind the wheel.

"Not today."

"Keys." Walker held out his hand. Washington fished into his pocket, handed them over.

They were a half mile from the hospital when Washington said, "Turn right."

"Huh?"

"Just do it."

Walker turned into an alley and parked.

"It's daylight, Hugh."

"I'm not gonna hurt him. I just wanna ask a few questions before he gets himself lawyered up."

"In the six months we've been partners I've never mentioned your brutality case, but I hear that's what you did with the child molester."

"That's what I did."

"I hear you almost killed him."

"Yeah, I beat him to a pulp, then kneed his balls so hard, he'll never be able to get it up again."

"Why?" Walker asked.

"The fear in that little girl's eyes tore me up. That baby-raper was going to use her and kill her. I wanted to make sure he never got the chance again."

"So you weren't thinking clearly?" Walker shut off the engine.

"My mind was working fine." He got out of the car, stretching as he looked up and down the alley. It looked to Jim as if he was trying to cover the fact that he was checking to see if anybody was watching.

"Don't hurt him," Walker said as Washington climbed into the back.

"I won't, I just wanna ask him a few questions."

Jim pushed himself as far from the big man as possible, but there was nowhere he could go. His retreat was blocked by the locked door.

"Don't hurt me anymore," the voice in his head pleaded.

"Quiet! I'm not a coward." Jim thought it must be his subconscious and he didn't understand, because he'd never plead, never beg.

"I didn't say anything," Washington said. "And I don't think you're a coward. I just want to talk a little before we get to the hospital."

"You scare out a lot of confessions this way?" Jim asked.

"Some."

"They stand up in court?"

"Some. I'm a big man, big boned. Frightens some people."

"I killed a couple of baby-rapers once," Jim said, ignoring Washington's statement. "I caught them right after they raped a young mother and her little girl." He was looking through Washington, speaking like he was in a trance. "I shot them both in the balls. Then I blew off their knee caps and sat and watched them scream and bleed to death. That's what got me caught, watching them die. I could've killed them quick and got away, but I didn't and it cost me four long years."

"Jesus." Walker crossed himself.

"And you know what," Jim continued, "even though it was the worst four years of my life, if I had it to do over again, I'd kill them slow again."

"What have we got here?" Walker said.

He didn't get an answer. The men in the back were quiet, staring at each other. The silence was interrupted by the sound of a gunshot and the pinging of shattering safety glass as a bullet lanced through the rear window.

"Go, go, go!" Washington shouted, but Walker didn't need any urging. He started the car in an instant, pulling the gear shift into drive with his foot already on the floor. The new Ford cruiser shot out from the curb with its rear wheels spinning.

A second shot rang out, ricocheting off the rear bumper, but before the gunman could fire a third, Walker had the car sliding around the corner. One hand on the wheel, the other on the mike.

"Officer's under fire. Alley behind Tenth, east of Park, turning north onto St. Joseph."

Walker stomped on the brakes as soon as they were out of sight and no longer a target. He leapt out of the car with his gun drawn, instinctively opening the back door. Monday and Washington scrambled out. Washington also had his gun drawn. There was the sound of a siren off in the distance.

The two policemen ignored Monday as they ran, hoping to get a shot at their attacker, but by the time they reached the corner, the alley was empty. They turned and walked back to the car, only to discover their prisoner gone.

"We're in for it now," Washington said.

"Come on, get in," Walker said. "He couldn't have gotten very far."

"Over here." Both officers turned toward the voice.

"There, I think, between those two houses." Walker pointed to an area between two houses covered in green bushes, a perfect hiding place for a child playing hide and seek.

"I need some help here, I don't think I can get up by myself," Jim called out.

"You didn't think you could hide from us for long did you?" Washington helped Jim up.

"I wasn't hiding from you."

"Then who?"

"The shooter, the man trying to kill me."

"What makes you think it was you he was after?" Washington said as the sirens got closer.

"Someone tried to run me down on Second Street, but they got the wrong man. Makes me think the shooter was trying for me. Unless of course you guys get shot at all the time."

Two police cars came skidding around the corner onto St. Joseph, one from the alley, the other from the north, boxing them in.

"For Godsakes get these cuffs off. I think my arm is broken and besides, I'm not going anywhere."

"Turn around," Washington said. Jim obeyed and Washington unlocked the handcuffs. "Now don't go making me sorry I did that."

"Are you crazy, Washington?" Walker said. "Didn't you hear what he said about killing and going to jail? Now you go and take the bracelets off. You think that's smart?"

"Maybe it is, maybe it isn't, but I think I can trust him."

"Holy shit, Washington, look at your car. Looks like someone put a bullet through the back window," an approaching officer said.

"Went in but didn't go out, looks like," a second uniform said.

"Doesn't look like it hit anything inside. Must have gone out one of the open windows."

"Driver's window. You driving, Washington?"

"No, Walker."

"Damn, Walker," one of the young cops said, "you're one lucky policeman, must've missed by inches."

"Motherfuck!" Walker crossed himself again.

"Okay, boys," Washington said, "show's over, let's clear out! The natives are getting restless."

Doors were opening and curious people were starting to fill the street.

"Yep, time to move," Walker said. "We got a casualty to get to Community."

"Okay, take your man to the hospital. We'll clean up here and calm the common folk," the first uniform said.

"I think we can leave the cuffs off." Washington opened the rear door for Jim, waited while he climbed in, then closed it. The two police officers got in front and once again started for the hospital.

At the hospital, Washington and Walker were called upon to keep order between a battling couple. She had given her husband a broken nose, he'd given her a black eye. So they turned their prisoner over to the staff in the emergency room while they kept the peace. By the time the officers had calmed the quarreling couple, Jim was fixed up and ready to go.

"Sorry about that," Washington said.

"Not a problem," Jim said.

"So I guess we better go to admin and see about the bill."

"I paid it," Jim said.

"You're not supposed to have to do that."

"Yeah, well you were busy and I can afford it."

"How much did it set you back?"

"Not much. Besides, they did a good job." He held his right arm up, showing it off. It was in a cast from the wrist almost to the elbow. He was lucky, he thought, he could still drive and dress himself.

"Now we go to the station." Washington's tone was more subdued. Jim thought he probably didn't get too many prisoners paying their own hospital bill after the police had roughed them up.

"All right, I'd like to get this over with," Jim said.

"That's right, you're a big man," Walker said as he came into earshot from the other side of the emergency room. "You've done time. For murder, isn't that what you said? So why did they let out after only four years if you killed two people?"

"The war was over. They let us come home."

"Where did you do your time?" Washington said.

"In a small camp south of Hanoi."

"The child molesters you killed were Viet Cong?"

"Yes."

"And you could have gotten away if you would have killed 'em quick and quiet?"

"Probably."

"Why didn't you?" Walker asked.

"I was a little upset."

"Boy, you and me are gonna get along fine." Washington said. "It's a shame we gotta take you in, but that man you half killed is gonna press charges, sure as I'm my momma's son."

"I understand."

"You know," Washington said, "we've been through so much together and we don't even know your name."

"Jim Monday." Jim held out his left hand as the right was in the cast.

"Hugh Washington." The big cop took the hand with his own left, "and this is my partner, Ron Walker."

"The Jim Monday?" Walker said.

"I didn't think anybody still remembered."

"How could a guy like me forget. I learned all about you in boot camp." Now Walker was being respectful too. "You were like a god to us. I campaigned for you. I got all my friends to vote for you."

"What are you talking about?" Washington said.

"This is Monopoly Jim Monday, Silver Star, Navy Cross and the Congressional Medal of Honor. He used to be our congressman."

"That was a long time ago," Jim said.

"Did you really get that name the way they say you did?" Walker asked.

"I really did."

"I don't understand."

"They called him Monopoly Jim because he loved to play the game. In Vietnam he had this set and when he wasn't in the field, he played. They say that if he couldn't find anybody to play with, that he played himself. That true?"

"Yes."

"They told us you only did two things in Vietnam, Monopoly and kill. They said that you didn't go for the girls, you didn't drink, you didn't take R & R. They said you didn't even like to eat. They said you were one crazy motherfucker."

"I was." He had spent a long time trying to forget, but now it was all coming back. The long days, the longer nights. He joined the Marine Corps to get out of school and they turned him into a killing machine, probably because they'd discovered he had an aptitude for it. However it changed him, made it so he was unable to communicate in a normal way. So he played the game.

"They said you played imaginary Monopoly when you were a POW to stay sane. They said you didn't break under torture, you didn't sign anything and you never gave an inch. They said it was because of the Monopoly you played in your head."

"I still play, only now it's for real. I buy and sell real estate." He remembered the nights of the imaginary game. They couldn't crack him because his mind was somewhere else. They could never understand that. He lived on Boardwalk and Park Place. He rode the Reading Railroad, paid Luxury Tax and tried to stay out of Jail. He played the game in his head and after a while they figured he was crazy and they left him alone. He used to wonder why they didn't kill him and be done with it, but sometime about ten years ago he stopped wondering.

"I know who you are now," Washington said. "You're the Jim Monday that owns half of Long Beach. You own the building I live in. You're my landlord."

"Probably."

"Are you still crazy?" Walker asked.

"No, now I'm a rich." Jim smiled, secretly pleased somebody still remembered him.

"We still have to take you in, sir," Hugh Washington said. "Small matter of assault and battery." His words brought back with frightening clarity the picture of David, dead and covered in glass. This wasn't just a friendly conversation with two policemen. He was being arrested for attacking Bernd Kohler, a man he believed had tried to kill him. Twice. That meant that he would probably try again. Maybe he had someone waiting at the house, or the apartment. He needed someplace safe. He needed it quickly, he needed it now and he needed a little time to plan. He needed to get even, but he couldn't go running around with guns blazing. He wasn't a kid anymore. It had been almost four decades since his war, he was five years shy of sixty and he'd always considered sixty old.

But still, almost over the hill or not, he had to find out what he was up against.

"It doesn't seem right bringing you in like a criminal."

"It's okay, Walker, I don't want any special treatment, never have."

"You want us to call someone? Your lawyer maybe, so you can make bail as soon as possible?" Washington asked.

"I don't have a lawyer anymore. He was just murdered on Second Street. He was my best friend."

"I'm sorry," Washington said.

"That's okay, you couldn't have known."

"What do you want us to do, sir?" Walker asked.

"Take me in. Book me. Let me spend a couple of days in a cell. I need the time alone, to think. When I get everything straight in my head, I'll make bail."

"It doesn't seem right, a man like you in jail," Walker said.

"A few days behind bars isn't going to bother me much. For a man like me it would almost be like a resort hotel. I'll be safe from whoever is trying to kill me. I'll be able to think. I'll be able to grieve, alone. I need the solitude."

"There's no solitude in our jail, Mr. Monday. It's full of drunks, drug addicts and punks."

"That's okay, Walker, for me that would be solitude. I don't want any favors except one."

"What's that?"

"Forget about me. Pretend we never had this conversation. Just book me like you would anybody else. In forty-eight hours the public defender will come to see me and find out I'm not a charity case. Then I'll make bail. That's all I ask."

"That's what you want, you got it," Walker said.

"Don't sound right to me," Washington said, "but if you want us to forget about you, well then I already forgot."

CHAPTER TWO

DONNA TUHIWAI OPENED HER EYES and lay still. She was back in the dream. This time she didn't ask questions. She didn't want to be forced away. She would keep her thoughts to herself. She would observe, nothing more. She would watch the dream like a television. She would be good. Then maybe the dream would let her go and she would wake up.

She studied the man on the bench in front of her. Rumpled clothes, like they had been slept in. Unshaven face, deep hooded eyes, weak chin, thick mustache, hollow cheeks, balding head with a scabbing cut over the right ear, like he'd fallen down recently. Not a nice face.

His clothes were spotty and stained, dark pants, open flannel shirt and a black tee shirt underneath. On the front of the tee shirt, sticking out and glaring at her through the open flannel, was the caricature of a one-eyed pirate and the word, *Raiders.*

"That's one of those American Football teams," She thought aloud.

"Who said that?" She heard a man's voice, but didn't answer.

"I didn't say nothing, buddy," the rumpled man said.

"Than who did?" The man's voice again.

"Just you and me in here and I didn't say nothing." The rumpled man scratched under his left arm.

"You sure?" the man's voice said.

"You hard of hearing? I told you, I didn't say nothing."

"Okay, sorry, I must have imagined it. I've had a bad night and I'm having an even worse morning."

"I'm not exactly having a picnic here myself."

"What did you do?" the man's voice asked.

"So now you're talking to me. All night you been sitting there staring off into space. People coming and going and you don't say a word and now you want to talk. Well la de da Mr. Big Shot, maybe I don't want to talk to you."

"Then don't."

"I know who you are, Mr. Monday, Mr. Jim Monday. I know who you are and I know what you did."

The rumpled man was looking right at her, but he called her Jim Monday. *"Why?"*

"What?"

"I said, I know who you are."

"I thought you said something else."

"Well I didn't. I said, I know who you are. You're a rich bastard. You're in deep trouble and I'm glad."

"Why, what did I ever do to you?"

"You made your money off the backs of the working class. You keep your workers down by paying low wages, so you can sit in your big house and drive hundred thousand dollar cars, while your employees can barely afford twenty-year-old Chevys."

"I live in a rather small house, I drive a five-year-old Ford. and I don't have any employees."

"You're a millionaire big shot."

"I may be wealthy, but I'm no big shot."

"Oh yes you are. The way people talk about you, you'd think you shit gold."

"Think what you want, I don't need the conversation anyway." Donna felt herself lean back and then it went dark.

"Don't turn out the lights!" She screamed the thought and instantly it was light again and she saw the rumpled man glaring at her. Then her eyes involuntarily roved around the room. She saw benches, a toilet without a seat, a sink, bars. She was in a jail somewhere. She was dreaming that she was in jail.

"Voices, I'm hearing voices." She instinctively knew she was hearing the man who had been talking with the rumpled man, only now he wasn't talking, she was hearing him in her head.

"Me, you're hearing me!" It was her dream. If the voice could hear her, than she could talk to it. Maybe it wouldn't send her away this time.

* * *

Jim closed his eyes and tried to clear his head.

"No, please don't send me away again. Please don't turn out the lights."

He opened his eyes.

"Thank you."

"Something wrong?" the drunk sitting across from him said.

"You ought to try minding your own business." Jim had had just about all he could take from the man.

"Big man."

Jim stood.

"Sorry." The drunk cowered back, pushing himself against the wall.

"That's your last word." Jim stared down at him. He wasn't usually like this. He'd spent the better part of his life learning to roll with the punches. It was like all the years since Viet Nam were being washed away.

The drunk nodded, fear in his eyes.

"Did you have to talk to him that way? It wasn't very nice."

Jim tried to clear his head.

"No, I'll be good. Please don't send me away."

He stopped trying to fight the voice. *"What are you?"* he thought.

"I am Donna Tuhiwai. I am asleep in the Park Side Motel, in Fungarei and this is all a bad dream."

"Great, I'm going crazy," he said.

The drunk started to say something, but checked himself. Apparently he had no desire to tangle with a crazy man.

"It's my dream. I can hear you fine if you just think the words."

"This is not happening," Jim thought. He knocked on his cast, heard and felt the knock, therefore this was happening. It was real.

"*I am Donna Tuhiwai, I am asleep in the Park Side Motel, in Fungarei and I am dreaming,*" the voice repeated.

"*Where is Fungarei.*"

"*Come on, it's the biggest city in the North.*"

"*Never heard of it.*"

"*What pakeha doesn't know that we pronounce "w-h" with an "f-u" sound. Whangarei then, now don't tell me you don't know where that is.*"

"*No, I don't.*"

"*Who are you, Jim Monday?*"

"*Right now I don't know.*"

"*Where are you?*"

"*Jail, but you probably know that.*"

"*What Jail?*"

"*Long Beach City Jail.*"

"*Long Beach? Where? In California? In America?*

"I am going crazy." Jim got off the bench, started to pace the cell.

"*If you talk out loud, you just make that man curious. And even though this is only a dream, I don't think I like him.*"

"This is no dream." And to underscore his thought, he knocked on his cast again.

"*It can't be real.*" Donna thought.

"*It is for me.*" Jim couldn't put his finger on it, but the fact that she was in the same boat as him, sort of made the situation easier to take.

"*Then where does that leave me?*" Donna thought. There was anxiety in her thought-voice. She seemed young.

"*I don't know, where are you?*"

"*New Zealand.*"

"*You're kidding?*" Jim was stunned.

"*No.*"

"*Let me think this through.*"

"Does that mean you're going to send me away again?"

"I don't know. When I push your thoughts out of my head, is that when you go away?"

"I think so."

"Where do you go?"

"I don't know. It's dark. I don't like it."

"Okay, I won't force you away, but you have to let me think." He sat back down.

"I won't think a word."

Jim fought the panic threatening to rise. Somehow he was receiving a woman's thoughts from halfway around the world. Unless, of course, it was some kind of an elaborate hoax, but that didn't make sense. Who would do such a thing? Who could do such a thing?

He got up, started pacing again, five steps across the cell, five back. It was some kind of telepathy, he reasoned. It couldn't be anything else. Somehow he was tuned into this woman's mind. He remembered hearing a story, when he was a kid, about a woman who spoke Chinese under hypnosis. She was supposedly picking up the thoughts of a peasant woman in China. Everybody thought she was faking. She probably was. But this, this was real. He was hearing another person's thoughts like they were his own. It was frightening and fascinating and it was something he had to keep to himself. One word of something like this and it was the nuthouse for Jim Monday.

And it would also be the nuthouse if he went around saying his wife's lover was trying to kill him. He was sure of what he had seen in Kohler's eyes, but it was possible for the doctor to hate him and not want him dead. He made a giant leap based on nothing more than his own feelings for the man. Maybe Kohler was innocent.

Even the rifle shot through the back window of the police car could be explained. Plenty of people hate the police. It could have been a drug dealer or someone high on drugs, who saw a squad car and took a shot at it for kicks, or maybe Washington or Walker had enemies, maybe somebody they once arrested. The rifle shot couldn't have been for him. He was being paranoid.

But paranoid or not, David was dead and he was in jail, charged with assault and battery. How stupid, letting his emotions control him like that. Kohler was probably going to sue and he would have to pay, whatever the amount. The last thing he wanted to do was to go into court against Julia's lover. No matter how much he despised the man, he still loved her. If they wanted more money because he attacked the son of a bitch, he would just pay it.

"That's dumb," Donna thought.

"It's how I feel. If she wants money, she can have it. I can make more."

"I don't know much about your situation, but from what I just picked up, it looks to me like your wife and her lover are playing you for a fool."

"That may be, but I just want it over. I want to get on with my life."

"Jim Monday."

Jim started at the sound of his name, looked up and saw a uniformed officer and a young man in his late twenties or early thirties, dressed in an expensive suit, caring a black leather briefcase that matched his shoes.

"I'm Monday," Jim said.

"I'm your attorney," the man said as the officer was unlocking the cage. "We need to talk." There was something about him Jim didn't like.

"My lawyer was killed about eight hours ago."

"All I know is that our firm got a call about you, then I was told to come down here and bail you out."

"Who hired you?"

"I don't know, but when old Mr. Cobb tells me to jump, I jump."

"What about the assault and battery business?"

"Dr. Kohler isn't interested in pressing charges, but there's a small matter of getting the city to go along. You did assault a respected member of the community in front of dozens of witnesses, including, may I add, two police officers. If the city wants to go to the wall on this, we could have problems."

"So where do we go from here?"

"It'll take them about an hour to process your bail, meanwhile I'd like to talk to you, in private," he said, indicating the man on the other bench with his eyes. "The city of Long Beach has been kind enough to furnish us a private room."

"Okay, let's go." Jim left the cell, following the uniformed officer and the young attorney out of the lock up area, through another set of doors, up a flight of stairs and down a well lit corridor.

"You can talk in here." The officer stopped before an oak door. He poked his head into the room, then added, "Wait a sec." He went inside, came back with a chair, set in next to the door. "I'll be right here if you need me."

The young lawyer motioned with an arm extended, Sir Galahad style, for Jim to enter. He did and the attorney followed, closing the door after himself.

"It's not much," the lawyer said.

Jim nodded.

The room was furnished with a folding table in the center, the kind usually found in campaign headquarters or at rummage sales. Around the table were three chairs, government chairs, bureaucratic chairs, one on the side closest to the door, facing the window and two opposite, facing the door. The lawyer laid his briefcase on the table.

"Looks like one of those interrogation rooms you see on TV," Jim said.

"Not quite, but close. They use these for what we're doing, attorney and client chats."

"And interrogation," Jim said.

"Maybe." The lawyer held out his right hand. "My name is Jeff Turnbull. I'm going to try and get you out of this mess."

Jim shook Turnbull's right hand with his left, while holding up his right, letting the lawyer see the cast.

"Police do that?" Turnbull asked.

"I deserved it."

"Let me be the judge of that." Turnbull took the chair closest to the door. Jim sat, facing the door, with his back to the window. "I have here," Turnbull went on, opening his briefcase, "a legal pad and a pencil." He lay a yellow legal sized tablet in front of Jim, handed him a pencil.

"What am I supposed to do with this.

"I'd like you to make a quick outline of what happened on Second Street this morning and the events that led to your arrest."

"What's to write? A hit and run driver ran down my best friend. I went berserk and attacked the doctor that was probably trying to save his life."

"Probably?" Turnbull's eyes turned to slits.

"Was trying to save his life." Jim flipped through the blank pages of the legal tablet, picked up the pencil, fiddled with it for a second, dropped it on the tablet.

"Write it down."

"Why?" Jim met Turnbull's slitted gaze.

"You'd be surprised what comes to people when they put their thoughts onto paper. You might have seen something that caused you to act the way you did. Something that might have justified your actions. Something we can use to get you out of here."

"I saw and old, beat up gray, 1980 Buick Regal, balding tires, chrome rims, tinted windows, driver's window down, dented front fender, strike and kill David Askew. Although the driver's window was halfway down, I didn't get a look at the driver. I remember the vehicle because I've always had a teenage-like interest in cars. I notice cars like horny men notice beautiful women. Not that I don't notice beautiful women. I don't think I'll remember much more if I write it down."

"Humor me."

"No."

"I'm trying to help you."

"I'm sorry, you're right." Jim picked up the pencil. "Fortunately I'm left handed."

"Fortunately," Turnbull echoed.

Jim bent over the paper, tried to put his thoughts in order, but before he had a chance there was a light knock on the door.

"Can I come in?" a tall man, with a body builder's shape, trying to bust out of a yellow sport coat said. Jim couldn't believe how ridiculous the man looked with his shoulder length, surfer-blond hair and paisley tie. The man had a nose three times too big for his face.

"That's the driver!" Donna thought.

"Are you sure?" Jim thought.

"You notice cars, I notice people."

"Are you sure?" Jim repeated his thought.

"Look at him! How many people look like that? Of course I'm sure."

The big man moved past Jim, picked up the empty chair and took it to the other side of the table, where he took a seat next to Jeff Turnbull.

"Hi, I'm Richard Monroe, I'm going to help get you out of here," the bodybuilder said.

"Help kill you is more like what he really means," Donna thought.

"You can't be sure," Jim thought back, but he felt her conviction. He believed her.

"You better do something, or the only place you'll be going is the morgue. Yell, scream your head off."

"No." Jim picked up the pencil, flipped open the legal pad as if he were going to write something.

"What did you say your name was?" Jim asked, making conversation, hoping to distract the big man.

"Richard Monroe."

"You're an attorney also?"

"Yes sir, work for Cobb and Cobb, just like Mr. Turnbill."

"Turnbull, the man's name is Turnbull, not Turnbill," Donna screamed the thought.

"I know." Jim repositioned the pencil in his left hand with the eraser against the heel of the palm and the pointed end sticking out between the two middle fingers. Then he balled his hand into a fist with the sharpened pencil sticking out like a deadly spike. He took a deep breath, held it, then jacked his arm forward, driving the pencil into the big man's left eye and on up into his brain.

Death was instantaneous.

"What the—" Turnbull screamed, but Jim cut it short by bringing his right forearm down on the left side of Turnbull's head, striking the temple with the hard cast. Turnbull fell forward. Dead.

Though it had been almost forty years since he had killed, he'd killed a lot back then. Apparently he still remember how. He stood and backed away. The two men were slumped down, heads on the table. The big one oozed blood out of his right eye. The thick red liquid didn't quite cover the orange eraser. A grotesque sight. Turnbull looked like he was peaceably asleep.

"Are they dead?"

"Big nose certainly is."

"How about the other one?"

Jim bent, touched the two fingers of his left hand to Turnbull's neck, on the carotid artery.

"Dead," he thought.

"Shoot through!" Donna thought.

"I don't understand?"

"Shoot through, before you get caught."

"I don't understand the expression."

"It means get the hell out of here. Take off!"

"And go where? There's a policeman on the other side of the door."

"I forgot. Say, how come he didn't come in when that weasel screamed?"

"Good question."

"Better check."

"Yeah." He grabbed the doorknob with a shaky left hand. His sweaty palm slid over it without opening the door. It had been a long time since he had sweat fear. He gripped the knob harder and turned it. The latch clicked and echoed throughout the room, causing the fine hair on the back of his hands and neck to tingle out a warning. He felt sweat

under his arms as he swung the door open and poked his head into the hall.

The policeman was sitting back in his chair. He looked like he was asleep. Jim stepped into the hall and for a second time, in less than five minutes, he pressed the index and middle finger of his left hand against a carotid artery in a vain search for a sign of life. He found none.

"Dead," he thought.

"Now what?" Donna asked.

"Don't know," Jim thought back. But he knew he was going to have to do something, and quickly, so he acted. He stepped out of the interrogation room, grabbed the back of the chair with his good left hand and wrapped his bad right arm around the front of the dead police officer and dragged him into the small room.

He started back for the door, then stopped. Where could he go. Once the bodies were discovered they would go to both his house and the beach apartment. He put his hands into his pockets. No wallet, no money, no credit cards, they took them away when they booked him. He could hardly go to the officer on duty and ask for his property back.

He turned to the dead men.

"You're not going to search the bodies?"

"Got any better ideas?"

"No."

In the inside jacket pocket of the dead Turnbull he found a wallet which held just under six hundred dollars, a driver's license along with several credit cards, all in the name of Patrick Langley. He also found five business cards in the name of Jeff Turnbull, Attorney at Law.

He took the money, credit cards and driver's license, leaving only the phony business cards. Any time the police spent trying to worry over who Turnbull really was, was time not spent trying to catch and crucify Jim Monday.

Next he opened Big Nose's sportcoat and fished inside for a wallet. There was none. Great, he thought, one of those who keeps it in his pants. He lifted the coat off the dead man's buttocks and smiled as he saw the telltale bulge in the left hip pocket. This man wasn't used to wearing a suit. He slid his fingers into the pocket, pulled out the wallet.

Pay dirt, three thousand dollars in hundreds, plus another hundred in twenties. Thirty one hundred dollars. No credit cards. No driver's license, only a business card in the name Richard Monroe, Attorney at Law. A false name for a dead man. Another problem for the police.

He gave Turnbull-Langley another look. They were about the same size. He took off his coat and laid it on the floor. Then he pulled the well dressed dead man away from the table.

"What are you doing?"

"I'm going to undress him."

"Oh my God. Why?"

"My clothes look like they've been slept in and I need a shave. How far do you think I'd get walking out of here looking like this? But dressed in Turnbull's clothes I've got a chance. His suit doesn't look like it's spent the night in jail, my clothes do."

Without further thought, he took off the dead man's coat. He felt a slight tingle run up his spine as he unbuttoned the vest and removed it. His hands trembled and he fought shaking fingers as he took off the tie and the white shirt.

"Now the hard part," he said under his breath.

He pulled the dead man out of the chair, laid him out on the floor. He untied and removed the leather shoes, leaving the socks. Then he loosened the belt, pulled off the trousers.

For a couple seconds he studied the dead man, wondering if he had children who would be crying tonight. He shrugged off the thought and undressed, leaving his clothes in a pile on the floor. He took another look at the bodies, then he put on the dead man's suit. Everything fit, the jacket even covered his cast, but he grimaced as he put on the shoes, they were at least a size too small and they hurt. But his Nike trainers hardly went with the suit, so he stuffed his feet into the expensive leather.

"You forgot the tie."

"I hate ties."

"You've gone this far, put it on," she thought and he obeyed.

"Time to go," he thought and once again he started for the door.

"Wait a minute. What about the policeman's gun?"

"They have metal detectors in police stations and jails, to keep guns out."

"Oh." Then she added a thought, *"Do they check you when you leave?"*

"I don't know, but I'm not going to take the chance. I'm going to leave the gun."

"Then, let's go," she thought.

Jim opened the door, looked down a long corridor with several tall oak doors opposite each other, anyone of which could open and disgorge a policeman or policemen who could cut off his escape.

He stepped into the hallway and made his hurting feet move along the tiled floor. Sweat rolled down the back of his neck and still another chill crept up his spine. He tried to control his breathing by sucking air deep into his gut. He concentrated on swinging his arms in a casual, but purposeful manner. A man with a mission, but not in a hurry. A man with time, but not too much. He needn't have bothered, because he reached the end of the hallway without incident. No police, no lawyers, no clerks, no one.

He held onto the rail as he went down the stairs, gritting his teeth against the pain the cramped shoes were causing. He had to turn right at the bottom, into another corridor, this one filled with people. He plunged ahead, passing them without acknowledging them. He might as well have been alone. The many voices and languages of the hustling police station all carried on as if he were invisible, just another attorney doing his job. The corridor opened onto a large room full of uniformed policemen, talking, drinking coffee, writing, laughing, doing their jobs. They paid him no attention as he waded among them, a fish among sharks.

A large room, many desks, two possible ways out. Which one to take? He had to decide. He couldn't ask. Then luck attacked like lightning strikes. He saw his wife, on the far side of the room, talking to an elderly man in a cheap suit and a loud Hawaiian print tie. He stopped, saw her shake the man's hand, turn and go through door number one.

He followed her into another hallway, moving faster in an effort to catch up. In spite of his trouble, she'd come for him. Maybe she'd finally seen Kohler for what he really was. Maybe she wanted him back. Maybe everything was going to be all right, after all.

He followed her out of the police station.

"Julia," he called, but the striking woman turning her head to meet his gaze wasn't his wife. Even though she had been crying, her smile was too quick, too real. Julia hadn't smiled like that in a long time."

"Hello, Jimmy," Roma, his wife's twin, said as she smiled at him through her tears.

CHAPTER THREE

AFTER BOOKING JIM MONDAY, writing the report and dealing with the motor pool about the damaged car, Washington and Walker were forty-five minutes over shift. Walker wanted to go home and Washington, after lighting his third cigarette for the day, wanted to go to work.

He wanted the Askew case. He wouldn't get it, because he wasn't a homicide detective any more and there probably wasn't going to be a case. Hit and run—open and shut. That's what they were calling it. But it didn't feel right. People didn't speed around corners in Belmont Shore during the middle of the day. Too many cars, too many people. It felt wrong.

Whoever was driving that Buick wasn't out for the Southern California sun or the specialty shops. He was out for murder. That car came out of nowhere, struck Askew, made a quick right on a residential street and was gone in a flash. It wasn't accidental and Washington wanted the case.

"There is no case, so you can stop worrying about it," Walker said.

"I wasn't worrying about it."

"You were worrying about it."

Walker was amazing, Washington thought, he'd only been his partner for six months and he could read him better than his wife, better than his daughter, better than any partner he'd ever had. Maybe it was because they were a lot alike, both from poor backgrounds, both overeducated and they both loved police work better than life.

"Fess up, you think it was murder and you want the case. Admit it," Walker chided.

"Yeah, I think it was murder and if I didn't at first, the bullet through the back window would have changed my mind. Hell, it would have changed anybody's. And the Buick—that had to be a set up. That SOB was waiting. He saw his target, stepped on the gas, got him and vanished. Yeah, it feels like murder to me and I'll bet it feels like murder to you."

"Easy counselor, I went to law school, too. You don't have to convince me. Use your logic on somebody who can do something about it."

"Nobody wants to hear."

"Then it's over."

"If I was still in Homicide, we could work it in."

"What do you mean we, kimosabe? This Injun has a wife and two little girls at home, who don't see enough of him as it is."

"Maybe you should have stayed a lawyer."

"Least I tried it, you didn't even take the bar."

Silently Washington agreed. He'd gone into the academy five days after he'd graduated from law school. Jane was pregnant. He had to get married. He had to provide a home. He told himself he'd take the bar next year, when they got a little ahead, but next year just never seemed to roll around.

"How come you gave it up?" Washington knew Walker had quit a prestigious Century City law firm.

"I didn't like getting rich, white collar crooks off the hook. What I really wanted to do was put them behind bars. So I quit and became a cop. Now I do what I like. I was lucky, the money helped."

Walker was an enigma to Washington. His parents had been killed in a small plane crash when he was sixteen. He was an only child, with grandparents in California. He came west to live with them and inherited twenty-one million dollars on his twenty-first birthday, a million for each year he'd been alive. He didn't have to work, he could live comfortably off the interest.

"The guy in the Buick is guilty," Washington said.

"That he is," Walker agreed.

"He should be put away."

"That he should."

"We could do it."

"The suits will get mad," Walker said.

"Are you with me on this?"

"They'll get real mad."

"Are you with me, or what?"

"I'm with you."

"Because you're right, they'll get real mad."

"I'm with you."

"And if we do make a case, they'll take it away from us and give it to Homicide."

"I'm with you."

"I won't want to stop, even if they take it away. It's the way I am."

"I said, I'm with you. I'm with you till we, not some dick in Homicide, we, us, you and me, masked man, the two of us, find the son of a bitch in the Buick and put him away."

"Spoken like a true rebel. Now let's get out of here and get to work."

They went to the locker room and changed into street clothes without saying a word. Washington was lost in thought. He was back on the trail of a murderer. He wondered about Walker—because bucking the system would be like swimming out into unknown waters for him. Walker had always been a by-the-book cop, but Washington knew he wanted to make the bust. He wanted to move up to where Washington had been. He wanted to be where the action was. He wanted Homicide.

After changing they headed for the street.

"Your car or mine?" Walker asked.

"Yours I think. Mine is a little under the weather."

"Noooo," Walker said, stretching out the word, "say it isn't so."

"You're not making fun of *Power Glide*?" Washington said. It was no secret in the department that Washington held a rather juvenile attachment to *Power Glide*, his 1959 Chevy Impala.

"Never," Walker said.

"Come on, it's a great car." Washington reached to his shirt pocket for his cigarettes. He started to lift them out, then stopped himself and let the pack slide back into its nest.

"It never runs," Walker said through a wide grin.

"Yes it does," Washington said.

"We'll take my car." Walker laughed, closing off that part of the conversation as he lead Washington to a new white Mercedes.

"One ten El Jardin Drive," Washington said.

"And that is?"

"Jim Monday's address."

"How'd you get that?"

"Off his driver's license. I have a great memory."

"Too bad it spends most of its time in the fifties."

"I just wish I could have lived back then. The cars were simple. The music was better. You didn't have to lock your doors. What can I say? They were better times."

"Before or after Mrs. Brown's little girl was allowed to go to that white school, or Rosa Parks rode that bus?"

"Yeah, there was a bad side to those times. I guess I tend to forget."

"Why are we going to Monday's?" Walker started the car.

"Because we have to start somewhere." Washington's voice trailed off as he let his head sink back into the plush leather headrest. He closed his eyes.

"But if Monday was the intended victim and not Askew, aren't we looking in the wrong place?"

"We only have Monday's word. For all we know he set up the whole thing." Washington kept his eyes closed.

"But the shot in the alley?" Walker said.

"We don't know for sure that was related. We think it was, but we don't know for sure."

"So we're going to treat Monday like a suspect?"

"We're going to treat everybody like a suspect." Washington opened his eyes. "The trail to our killer starts at Monday's. I feel it and I'm usually right about these things."

"Okay, boss, if you say the trail starts at Monday's, it starts at Monday's."

Washington smiled. Before his trouble his comrades regarded him as nothing short of brilliant. They called him the department's Canadian Mountie, a nickname he loved, because like the mythical mountie, he did always get his man.

Ten minutes later they turned off of Anaheim onto El Jardin.

"Wow, nice area." Washington whistled and seconds later he whistled again. "And a nice house. You know, Walker, you could afford a place like this if you wanted."

"Actually I live about two blocks from here."

"Really? Nice house? Like this?"

"Yeah."

"Sometimes I forget about all your money."

"I try not to let it get in the way."

"I'll try to keep it out of the way too." Washington laughed.

"How you want to do this?"

"Pull up in the driveway like we belong," Washington said and Walker obeyed, turning his car into the circular driveway, bringing it to a stop by the front door.

"Now what?"

"We go inside and have a look." Washington fished into his jacket pocket, withdrew a set of keys. He turned to Walker, raised them above his head with his left hand and jiggled them.

"You stole his keys?

"A good scout is always prepared."

"You don't mean we're going to enter the premises?"

"I do."

"Without a warrant?"

"I thought you wanted to move up and get out of the uniform, maybe even make Homicide?"

"I'm not going to this way. Christ, we could wind up in jail if we get caught."

"Highly unlikely."

"That we'll get caught?"

"That we would wind up in jail. A slap on the wrists, maybe, but jail? I don't think so."

"I don't feel right about this."

"You want to wait in the car?"

"No, I'm with you."

"Because if you want to wait, I won't mind. I'll understand."

"I said, I'm with you."

"It's okay, you know, if you don't go in."

"I said I was with you and if we don't do something pretty damn quick, someone is going to get the wrong idea about us. They have a neighborhood watch here."

"Bad guys don't usually drive right up to the front door in a spanking new Mercedes."

"Some of these old gals got nothing better to do than to wait by the telephone with their gnarled fingers ready to dial 911. If we're going to go in, let's get it over with."

"Come on, Tonto." Washington opened the passenger door, slid out of the car. "It's starting to get dark and I'd like to be home in time for the evening news."

Walker jumped out of the car, followed Washington to the porch. Washington rang the bell.

"No answer. Looks like nobody's home." He tried one of the keys. It didn't work. "Wrong key, must be the apartment in Huntington Beach." He tried another. The locked turned. "Had to be the one, only two others and they're car keys." He opened the door and went in. Walker followed, closing the door after himself.

"Oh lord, look at this place, it's been trashed," Walker said as they crossed a tile entry way and entered the living room. Directly across from the entry way, behind a plush living room suite, was a large television. It had loose wires sticking out from behind

"They took the DVD player," Washington said. "TV must have been too big."

"Yeah."

"Look at this." Washington pointed to a surge protector plugged into the wall by the desk. "Got his computer."

The two men quickly went through the house, careful not to leave any prints. Every book in the library was open, pages torn out and thrown on the floor. Every drawer in the house was open and broken. Clothes were ripped and strewn on the floor. Kitchen drawers had been overturned onto the tile, then broken on top of their crushed and destroyed contents.

"This was destruction for destruction's sake, not a search, not a robbery," Washington said.

"They took the computer and the DVD," Walker said.

"But that's not what this was about. Someone doesn't like Monday. They came to destroy his home and his things. They took the DVD and the computer as an afterthought.

"Or maybe they wanted to see what he had on his hard drive," Walker said.

"There is that," Washington said.

"Do we call this in?" Walker said.

"We were never here, so how can we call it in?"

"Yeah, yeah, I wasn't thinking," Walker said.

"Okay, let's get out of here."

"Don't need to say that twice." Walker turned and headed for the door. By the time Washington was on the front porch, Walker was in the car with the engine running. He'd be a good man for a bank job, Washington thought.

Walker whipped it into drive.

"Easy," Washington said, "leave slow, like we belong."

Walker clenched his teeth and Washington knew he was fighting the temptation to stomp on the accelerator as he eased the car round the driveway.

"Where do we go from here?" Walker asked as they turned off of El Jardin and back onto Anaheim Street.

"Home."

"That's it?"

"For tonight. Tomorrow I'm going to call in sick. I'll visit the apartment, then I'll talk to some of his friends."

"What about me?"

"You can go to work as usual. I wouldn't expect you to get anymore involved in this than you have. You've got your career to think of."

"Yeah and what about your career?"

"Mine is over. I'll never get off the street. You know it. I know it. Everybody knows it."

"I'll call in sick tomorrow," Walker said through pursed lips.

"You don't have to do that."

"I said I was with you and I meant it. I'm with you."

"Okay, then go home, rest, enjoy your wife and kids. Pick me up at eight."

"Want me to take you back to the station?"

"No, home's closer. I'll leave the car at the station and take the bus to work in the morning."

They rode in silence for a few minutes, then Walker said, "Tell me what happened to you."

"Why?"

"I'm your partner. I want to know."

"It doesn't concern you," Washington said.

"It sure does. Three years ago you were busted down from the suits. Since then you can't keep a partner longer than six months. You're moody, not very dependable and a lot of the time you're just not any fun. If I'm going to stick my neck out with you, I've got a right to know."

"I said you didn't have to come along."

"And I said I was with you, but I want to know. Why did you nearly kill that child molester?"

"It wasn't just the baby-raper," Washington said, "that was just the end of a long, hard time for me." He paused, "Are you sure you want to hear this?"

"Yeah."

"It started three years ago, the end of June, two weeks into my daughter's summer vacation. She was fifteen. Did you know I was married?"

"I heard you were separated."

"Yeah, we're separated," Washington said. Then he went on with his story. "It was one of those hot days, you know the kind, you sweat like there is no tomorrow, so I came home around noon to change. I'd been out in the field all morning and my clothes were wet as a rag.

"Jane was at work and Glenna, that's my daughter, was supposed to be spending the day with a girlfriend, but she wasn't. She'd lied so she could spend the day with a boy. You know how girls can be.

"I knew something was wrong as soon as I got to the door. It wasn't locked and the stereo was blasting away. Jane always locked up. She was a stickler about it. And we never played the stereo that loud. So, I went into the house quiet like, but I coulda made all the noise in the world and nobody woulda heard over the Rolling Stones. It was *Midnight Rambler* and Mick was screaming through the speakers, '*Rape her in anger,*' and his song about rape almost covered the sound of Glenna screaming from our bedroom.

"I pulled my piece, ran down the hall and burst into the room. I found my daughter, my beautiful fifteen year old daughter, beat up and bleeding, on my bed, and this big, muscular punk was just climbing off her,"

"Jesus," Walker said.

"I let him get as far as the floor before I emptied my piece into him. Then I untied Glenna and she dashed from the room and everything was quiet as it could be with the Rolling Stones tearing the house down and then Mick hit the chorus again, '*Rape her in anger,*' he was singing and I went a little crazy. I reached into the nightstand, where I keep a loaded forty-five auto and I went out into the living room and shot the stereo. It was like I was killing the song.

"Now the house is stone-cold-dead-silent, except I hear Glenna sobbing in her room. And, guess what? I hear this moan coming from my bedroom, so I go in to see what's what and son of a bitch, if that bastard wasn't still alive."

"You're kidding?"

"No, he was lying in a lake of his own blood, trying to hold on to his guts and whining like a dog hit by a car and that's probably how he felt. I must have looked like a big black god to him, cuz he looked up at me and said out of his bloody mouth, 'Help me.'

"I blew his face off. Then I went out to the living room and called it in."

"Jesus," Walker said again, "what did they do to you?"

"I called it into Homicide. Fifteen minutes later, Jimmy Gordon, my partner and two other guys, Sammy Powers and Steve Hodges, show up. Jimmy tells me to pack some things for myself, Jane and Glenna. 'Go to the school, pick up your wife, take a couple of weeks. Let us handle it,' he says. And that's what I did."

"What did they do?"

"I never asked. However, I did see in the *Press Telegram* the next day that a white male in his early twenties had been found in a condemned house, beaten, tortured and killed. The result of a drug deal gone bad, the paper said."

"I didn't know."

"Nobody does," Washington said. "That was the start of everything going wrong. Jane blamed me for what happened. She thought if I would have been closer to Glenna, she wouldn't have lied to us that day. It was just the way she had to deal with it. And I blamed her. I thought if she wouldn't have been working, it wouldn't have happened. She moved out six months later."

"That's too bad," Walker said.

"Yeah. Things starting going downhill after the divorce. I couldn't concentrate on my work. I was pissing off the people around me, coming in late, leaving early, drinking, then came the baby-raper.

"I was off duty at the time, at the Cerritos Mall. A couple of years had passed and I was just starting to get things back together. I went to the mall to get a pair of running shoes. I was going to get back in shape, quit the drinking. It was time to get my life straight again.

"I had just pulled into a parking place when I see this man grab a little girl and throw her into his van. I threw old *Power Glide* into reverse and backed down the aisle till I was behind the van. I jumped out of the car and tried to open the van door. Naturally the perp wasn't interested in opening up, so I yell, 'Police, I'm gonna count to three and then I start shooting.'

"That did it, he opened the door pronto and I could see that the little girl was crying. In just that few seconds the bastard had got the girl's dress off and his pants down. I mean he was one jackrabbit-fast motherfucker and he really pissed me off, so I pulled him out of the van and pistol whipped him so bad that his face will never be the same. Then I started kicking him in the nuts till I was damn sure they were fucked up beyond repair.

"I was about to shoot him, when some guy jumped out of the crowd that had gathered and ripped the gun from my hand. I guess if it wouldn't have been for that good Samaritan, I'd have done a second degree murder. Anyway there were enough witnesses to make sure it could never be hushed up. They busted me back to sergeant and put me back on the street again. It could have been worse."

"We're here." Walker pulled up the driveway to Washington's small apartment.

"Call you in the morning." Washington got out of the car.

He watched Walker's taillights as he reached for, then rejected, a cigarette. He shook his head and stumbled into his apartment, more asleep than awake. He fell into bed without taking his clothes off.

He didn't see the small green gecko scurry between his feet, then dash under the bed.

CHAPTER FOUR

"HELLO ROMA," JIM MONDAY SAID as she rushed into his arms, no longer trying to hold back the tears. "What are you doing here?"

"I came as soon as I heard you'd been arrested, but they said there was no bail set. They said I'd have to come back later."

"I know," he said.

"Oh, Jimmy, I thought you were so close. How could she do it?" She tightened her hold on him. "What are you going to do?"

"We have to leave here."

"My car's over there." She pointed.

They walked, arm in arm, away from the police station and crossed the street. Roma led Jim to her car. A red Porsche Targa. She handed him the keys, like she used to do before he married her sister. The she got in the passenger side. Roma hadn't locked the doors, something his wife never would have forgotten to do.

"It's horrible about David," she said. "He was such a nice man."

"I loved him like a brother." Jim keyed the ignition, started the car.

"I know you did," Roma said.

"Listen, I have to talk to somebody. I need to try and understand what's happening. He checked the rearview, pulled over to the side of the road and parked.

"Why are we stopping?"

"So I can explain," he said. Then he relived the horror, telling her about the gray Buick Regal. About how it looked like it might have been murder. About how he broke his arm. About someone shooting at him in the police car. About the lawyers that weren't lawyers. About how he recognized one as the driver of the gray Regal. About how he killed them both. About how he found the dead policeman outside the room. About how he dragged him in. And about how he walked out of the police station. He didn't tell her about the voice in his head.

"What are you going to do?" she asked.

"I don't know."

"You can't go home and you can't go to the apartment. The police will be waiting."

"I didn't think of that." He knew she believed him unquestionably. Julia would have asked a million questions, doubting every answer.

"You can go to my place," she said.

"I think the white car back there is following us." Donna interrupted his thoughts before he could answer. He looked in the rearview and saw a white

Ford parked a block behind. There were no other cars parked on the busy street.

Are you sure?" he thought back. He was getting used to silently talking to her.

"Yes, it's been following us since we left the police station and it parked when you did."

"Roma, I think we're being followed. He started the car and eased back into the traffic.

"Police?" She turned to look behind.

"I don't think so."

The Ford accelerated.

"They have a gun!" Roma screamed.

Jim turned, saw a cannon-like shotgun sticking out of the passenger window.

He stomped on the clutch, dropped the Porsche back into first. The rear wheels started spinning as he cut off a FedEx van in the left lane as he made a screeching left turn against the light. He heard the shotgun go off, felt the car jerk. Then he heard the crash as the Ford plowed into the van. He grabbed a glance into the rearview in time to see it bounce off.

"They're still coming!" she said.

"They can't keep up with us." He checked the mirror. "Shit! We got smoke coming from the back." Then the car started missing.

"They must have hit the engine," she said.

"Must've." He, slammed on the brakes. "Come on. We've got to run for it!"

They jumped out of the car as the dented Ford came screaming up behind them. The driver stood on his own brakes, but he wasn't quick enough and the Ford slammed into the rear of the Porsche.

"Let's go." Jim grabbed her by the hand, led her, running between two houses.

The way to the alley behind was blocked by a white, two foot fence. The gate was locked, but they didn't know it, because they jumped the fence and headed into the alley. They had a fifty yard head start on their pursuers.

"Quick, through the gate!" Jim pushed Roma through a wire fence gate just as they heard the boom of the shotgun. They dashed through a backyard, ran along the side of an old wooden house, burst out onto a residential street.

"Which way?" Roma said.

"Cross the street." Jim led her across, up the driveway of another house, into another backyard. "No gate," he said. "I'll boost you over." He laced his fingers together, made a stirrup for Roma to step into. "Come on, quick."

She stepped into his fingers and he bit his lip against the pain shooting up his broken arm as he boosted her up. She pulled herself over as Jim grabbed onto the top of the fence and struggled, trying to pull himself up. It had been a long time since he had to physically exert himself and he was out of shape. He didn't think he was going to make it.

"There they are!"

The voice sent a lightning bolt of straight fear through Jim, forcing him to draw from a hidden reservoir of strength. He pulled himself up and over the fence as the shotgun blasted again. He felt, as well as heard, the pellets flying over his head.

"Run," he wheezed, grabbing Roma's hand. They took off down the alley, but this time it was Roma who was doing the helping.

"Come on, Jimmy, Come on," she pleaded, and he fought to keep going.

"There," he said, and Roma opened a gate into still another backyard.

They dashed through and she screamed as a German Shepherd sank its teeth into her forearm, dragging her onto the lawn.

"No." Jim slammed his cast down on the dog's head, killing it. Then he helped her up. "The house," he said, and they limped across the yard, opened and entered the back door of a pleasant, peaceful-looking home. The back window blew out right after Jim slammed the door.

"What's going on?" an elderly lady screamed.

"Take her into the bathroom." Jim was still wheezing. "Lock the door, get down and don't come out till I come back."

"Where?" Roma said to the lady.

"This way!" The woman might have been old, but she wasn't stupid.

Jim opened the front door, then dashed around the side of the house just as the back door burst open. He ran up the driveway and into the backyard. He reentered the back door as the two men erupted through the front, back onto the residential street.

"Where did they go?" one voice asked.

"Don't know," a second voice answered.

Then they heard sirens off in the distance.

"Time to get out of here," first voice said.

"Ditch the gun."

First voice tossed the shotgun into the old lady's living room, then closed the door.

Jim picked up the shotgun and started for the front door, opened it in time to see them calmly walking away.

"*Don't!*" Donna shouted the thought at him.

"*Why not?*"

"*You've been lucky. Don't press it. You'll just wind up back in jail.*"

"*You're right.*" He tossed the shotgun onto a sofa that had seen better days and called out. "It's okay, you can come out now." He sat on an overstuffed chair, as old as the sofa, to catch his breath.

"Are you all right?" Roma asked, coming into the living room.

"Yeah, the sirens chased them away."

"You're Jim Monday. I recognized you the second you came in the back door. I voted for you. All four times."

"Thanks, not many did that last time."

"I'm Edna Lambert."

"Pleased to meet you, This is my sister-in-law, Roma."

"You want me to call 911?" She picked up a telephone.

"No, please don't," Jim said. "I'm in trouble. I need to think. I need some rest."

"No matter what it is, young man, you can count on me."

"Maybe not after you hear what I have to say."

"Try me."

"For starters, I killed your dog. It bit Roma."

"Good for you, I never liked that dog. It was my dead husband's and you want to know a secret? I never really liked him either. Two years the man's been dead and they've been just about the happiest years of my life. The only thing dragging me down was that damn dog. I'd have killed him myself, if I could have brought myself to do it."

"Why didn't you call the pound?" Roma asked, looking at her arm. Miraculously the bite hadn't broken the skin.

"Well, that would be just about the same as killing him, wouldn't it?"

"You could have left the gate open and let him wander away." Roma didn't seem to want to let it go.

"Don't think I didn't try that. Damn dog wouldn't leave."

"The police are after me for murder," Jim interrupted.

"Well, you didn't do it."

"How do you know?"

"If you did, you wouldn't be telling me about it."

Jim smiled and he found himself retelling the last twenty-four hours for the second time that morning.

"What are you going to do now?" Edna Lambert asked when he finished

"That's a good question, Mrs. Lambert," Roma said.

"Call me Edna."

"Thank you, I will," Julia said.

"And I repeat," Edna said, "what are you going to do now, Jim?"

"I don't know. I'm convinced Kohler is behind this somehow, but I'll be damned if I can figure out why, unless he figures with me dead, he can marry Julia and get all of my money. But he's loaded, at least that's the impression he gives and besides, he's getting half of it as it is. So on the surface it doesn't make much sense. But he was waiting at that window and I saw that look in his eyes."

"I know you're hurting because Julia left you for Dr. Kohler, but really, Jim, I think you're way off base," Roma said.

"I don't. It sounds right to me. I'll bet you dollars to donuts that that doctor is bankrupt," Edna said.

"But he still gets half my money."

"I can give you at least three reasons why he might want to kill you," the old woman said.

"Okay go."

"One, maybe half your money isn't enough. Two, maybe your wife still has some feeling for you, maybe her mind isn't all the way made up. With you dead her choice is clear. And three, maybe Dr. Kohler just plain and simple hates the thought of you being alive. Some men can't live with the thought that their woman has been with someone else. And I just thought of a fourth reason. His name."

"His name?" Roma said.

"Kohler, it sounds like killer." She crossed her arms and looked Jim straight in the eyes.

"I think you're right," he said.

"Which reason?" Roma said.

"All of the above. He's the one. I'm certain, now more than ever."

"I'm glad I helped clear that up." Edna smiled.

"It's not cleared up. I refuse to believe my sister is in love with a killer. There has to be another explanation," Roma said.

"Maybe there is," Jim said, "but until we find it, I'm going to assume Kohler is behind this. I can't come up with anything else." He heard the sirens in the distance, getting closer and suddenly stop.

"Sounds like they've found my car," Roma said.

"They'll have your name in seconds. It won't take them long to figure out your relation to me," Jim said.

"What are we going to do?"

"I think we should check into one of those motels on the beach for the day. Maybe later we can take a bus to the airport and rent a car. I can't think much beyond that."

"You're not going to any motel. You might be recognized," Edna said.

"I've been out of public life for a long time, nobody's going to recognize me."

"I did and besides, from what you told me, I suspect your picture will be on the front page of the *Press Telegram*, maybe even the *Times*. No, you won't stay at any motel. You'll stay here. And you won't rent a car either. I have a perfectly good car in the garage, you can use it."

"Mrs. Lambert," Jim started to protest.

"Edna, I said to call me Edna and I insist. You can stay here and you can use my car. I want to help."

"I don't know what to say."

"And that's not all. I have some money." She shuffled across the room, opened the top drawer of a China cabinet. She withdrew an envelope. "There's a thousand dollars here. I want you to have it. And something else," she said as her hand went back into the drawer and came out with a revolver, "you might need this as well. It's a thirty-eight police special. It's loaded. And I have extra ammunition."

She came toward Jim, with her hands out, envelope in one, pistol in the other.

"Here, take them."

"But your money, why?" Jim asked.

"My son was on that helicopter."

She didn't have to say which helicopter. Jim knew and for an instant he was reliving it. He'd been on one of his solo scouting missions, when he'd heard the firefight. A Special Forces squad was pinned down and pretty cut up. They'd called for a chopper, but at the rate things were going, none of them would be alive by the time it set down. Jim's raging presence, shooting at the VC from their flank, gave the Special Forces guys new life and they managed to drive the VC back, giving the chopper a brief window to land. Jim was helping the last of the wounded onto the plane when the VC charged. Instead of diving into the chopper, he turned and charged the VC, slicing through them like a wraith, giving the chopper the cover it needed to get away. Once airborne the chopper opened up on the VC, mowing them down like new cut grass as Jim disappeared into the jungle. Safe to fight another day, but three hours later he came across that village, that woman, her girl and the two VC rapists. And then the war was over for Jim Monday.

"You went to a POW camp for all those years and my boy came home to me," Edna said. "I can never thank you enough."

Jim saw her genuine smile and the tears welling up in her eyes. He took the envelope and slid it into the inside jacket pocket of Turnbull's coat. Then he took the pistol from her and opened his arms. Edna fell into his embrace, hugged him like a mother about to lose her son to a war.

"I think I better take the pistol," Roma said.

"But why?" Edna released her hold on Jim.

"Woman's pistol champion, NRA, State of California, three years in a row, second in the nationals last year. She hits what she aims at," Jim said.

"Do you have an old handbag?" Roma asked. "I left mine in the car."

"Yes, I do." Edna scurried from the room, returning seconds later with a small designer purse. "Will this do?"

"Fine." Roma took the purse, dropped the pistol into it. "Now a sharp knife, a steak knife will do."

"I have my Swiss Army knife." Edna went back to the top drawer, withdrew a red pocket knife. "I keep it sharp." She handed it to Roma.

"Good." Roma cut a small hole into one side of the leather purse. "Now I can fire the gun while it's still in the bag, sort of a special surprise in case we run into those big nasties again, because I really don't like running away."

The door burst open. Two men filled the opening. Jim pushed Roma aside, snatched the purse from her, shoved his hand in it, grabbed the gun, started pulling the trigger. The pistol shots boomed throughout the living room, sonic booms to his ears, as he emptied the weapon, sticking each man with three shots in the chest.

"Two dead nasties," Roma said, shaken. "I've never killed anybody before. I thought I could do it, but I couldn't. How did you know?"

"Killing isn't easy, "Jim said. "Most people can't do it, and the ones that do, usually regret it for the rest of their lives."

"But you can do it?"

"It wasn't easy at first. Now it's instinct. I kill to survive. I don't question it. I just do it."

"It seems so cold."

"It was the war."

"I'm sorry, I forgot." Her voice trailed off and she had a glassy look in her eyes.

"Roma, listen to me!" Edna said in a stern, motherly voice. "You can't go into shock now. Do you hear me. Stay with us."

Jim went to Roma and put an arm around her shoulders.

"No time for that. Pull the dead man inside," Edna said. Jim released her and turned to look at the two men lying on the floor. Both were on their backs, eyes open in death, both chest shot. Heart stoppers. One was half in the house, half out. Jim pulled him inside, shut the door.

"We have to go. The police will be here any second." Edna took Roma by the hand, led her through the kitchen, the laundry room and out into the backyard. Jim followed.

"Wait here. I forgot my keys." Edna rushed back into the house, came back a full minute later, a large purse in one hand, the shotgun in the other. "Sorry I took so long," she said. "I got those boy's guns in my purse. Figured we might need them."

She was smiling as she went to the front of a single car garage. She keyed a padlock, unlocked it and opened the door.

"Come on, get in," she said. "Let's get out of here. I'll drive."

Jim stared at the car.

"I know it doesn't look like much, but it will take you anywhere you want to go." It was a two door, faded green and rust covered 1972 Dodge Charger.

"You sure that runs," Jim said.

"Time's wasting," Edna said. "Let's get a move on."

Jim opened the passenger door, helped Roma into the back, before getting in the front. Edna climbed behind the wheel, put in the clutch and started the car.

"Four on the floor," she said, as she backed down the drive way. She put it in first and slowly drove to the corner, made a right onto Cherry Avenue, where she had to pull over, because of the sirens of two approaching police cars.

"Looks like we left in the nick of time," she said as the cruisers screamed by. Then she eased the car back into traffic and headed toward Signal Hill and the freeway. "Where to now?" she added, holding the wheel with white knuckles.

"Tampico," Roma said from the back.

"Don't know it," Edna said.

"It's up north," Roma said, "on the coast, past Eureka."

"That's over five hundred miles," Jim said. "Why there?"

"Julia went there with Dr. Kohler. They left first thing this morning. He has a house there. I had the phone number and address in my purse, but I think we can find them. She said it was a big house, on Mountain Sea Road, overlooking the ocean. How hard could it be?"

"Why?" Jim asked.

"She wanted to get away."

"With him?"

"Yes, with him."

"No offense," he turned to Edna, "but when you said this car would take me anywhere I wanted to go, you didn't have five or six hundred miles in mind, did you?"

"No, I didn't." She clutched the wheel.

"We need another car. Edna, when you get to Spring Street, turn right. We'll rent a car at the airport."

It was noon and sprinkling when Edna parked in the overnight parking garage at the Long Beach Airport. They started to get out of the car when she spoke up.

"You two wait here. I'll rent the car and come back. We can't be carrying a shotgun through the terminal, now can we?"

"You're right," he said.

Twenty minutes later she beeped the horn of a new Ford Explorer. She stopped the SUV in front of her Charger, put it in park, but left the engine running and got out.

"Let's move it," she said. Then she added, "I always wanted to say that."

Jim tossed the shotgun in the back.

"Shotgun, I call shotgun." Edna was laughing as she got in the front seat on the passenger side. "I always wanted to say that, too."

"Tampico, here we come," Jim said as Roma got in the back.

Ten minutes later they were on the freeway. An hour later they were leaving the Grapevine and moving onto the long straight road that is Highway 5. After another hour both Roma and Edna were lulled to sleep by the rolling wheels and the warm sun and Jim was fighting to stay awake.

"I can appreciate that you've got heaps of problems, but can we take a bit of time to worry about mine now?" Donna interrupted his thoughts.

"I forgot about you."

"It doesn't look like I'm going anywhere."

"No, I guess it doesn't."

"I'm somebody too, at least I was until this started. The last thing I remember is driving up from Auckland with my parents for my brother's wedding. We checked into a motel, because it was late and they wanted to surprise him in the morning. I went to sleep. Then I woke up in your head. I hear what you hear, see what you see, feel what you feel."

"Pain or emotions?" Jim asked.

"Both and it's creepy. It's like I'm involved in some kind of super movie, but it's not a movie. It's your life and I'm just along for the ride. But it's better than I thought it would be."

"What?"

"At least there's something, it's not just all over. The essence of me, my mind, is still intact. I have my memories. It could be a lot worse."

"What are you talking about?"

"Don't you know?"

"No."

"Death. I'm dead. That's the only answer. I died and somehow my soul got trapped in you."

"Give me a break."

"Do you have another answer?"

"Yeah, a real simple one."

"What?"

"I'm going crazy, Looney Toons, I'm losing my fucking mind."

"You don't have to swear."

"Now I know I'm losing my fucking mind."

"Really, if I have to be here, can we watch the language? I can take a lot if I have to, but I draw the line at swearing."

"Okay," Jim smiled, "but if you're right and you are dead, then you don't have a problem."

"What do you mean?"

"All your problems are solved. You're dead. It's all over."

"But I'm here?"

"That's right, you're here and we're just going to have to accept it for now. You're here, trapped in my life. Mine, not yours. So if we accept your thesis, then my problems, at least for now, are the only ones that count."

"That's cruel."

"Look Donna, you may be dead, but I'm not. I'm alive and right now I'm trying to stay that way. I'm fifty-five years old. I'm out of shape. I'm scared. The police are after me. People keep trying to kill me. I miss my wife. I miss my life. I miss David. I really miss David."

"Okay, you're right. I'll put my problems away and we'll find out who's trying to kill you and stop them."

"I don't need your help."

"Two heads are better than one."

"I make the decisions."

"Of course, it's your body."

"You won't keep interrupting me?"
"Only if it's important."
"Fair enough."

"Jim," Roma said, yawning herself awake, "how are you doing?"

"It's 1:00 now, I can make it to the Collinga turn off by 3:00. We can stay at the Inn at Harris Ranch. We'll get some rest, have dinner, spend the night in comfortable beds and get an early start tomorrow."

They drove on in silence and Roma fell back asleep, leaving Jim to concentrate on the never ending white line and the painting of the pretty girl on the rear of the tanker truck ten car lengths ahead. She was holding a glass of fresh white milk, sitting atop the words, *Milk drinkers make better lovers.*

The women woke when Jim took the off ramp.

"Where are we?" Edna asked.

"Halfway to San Francisco," Jim answered as he backed into a parking space. They checked into the hotel, using Edna's credit card, taking two rooms, one for the women, one for him.

"We're going to need some things," Edna said after they got their keys. "You know, a change of clothes, toothbrushes, toothpaste, Jim needs a razor and I need solution for my contact lenses. And since I'm not the least bit tired, I'll go and get them while you two rest."

"I'm going to get a wake up call for six, for dinner, any takers?" Jim asked. Both women nodded their assent. "Fine, I'll see you then. Right now I have to get these shoes off, my feet are killing me, and I need to get some sleep."

Jim and Roma each went to adjoining rooms, while Edna took the car into town.

CHAPTER FIVE

THE CLOCK RADIO WOKE HIM at six, halfway through Bob Dylan's *Like a Rolling Stone*. Washington shut it off, stripped, shaved, showered, put on clean clothes and gave himself a final once over in front of the bathroom mirror. Satisfied and awake, he went to the kitchen and, while waiting for the coffeemaker to work its magic, he called Walker.

"Walker here," came his partner's early morning rasp.

"You don't have to go today. I can handle it," Washington said.

"I said I was with you and I meant it. I'm in it all the way. I've already called in."

"Okay, see you at 8:00."

Walker rang the bell an hour and ten minutes later. He was five minutes early. Walker was never late.

"We're going out Pacific Coast Highway to Huntington Beach. Monday has a place at Beach Side, you know, those places by the pier."

Walker backed out of the apartment complex, pointed the car out of Belmont Heights, a section of Long Beach just north of the Shore, and toward the Pacific Coast Highway. Fifteen minutes later they pulled up in front of the security gate to the Ocean Front Condos. Walker parked in the red.

"Can't park here." The security guard scowled. He was a young man with a military bearing and pasty white skin, despite the fact that he worked at the beach. He was wearing a starched white guard uniform with a forty-five automatic on his belt, along with a pair of handcuffs and a night stick. His shoes and leathers were spit shined to a high gloss and Washington quickly identified him as a cop wanna be.

"Police." Washington flashing his badge and the scowl of contempt turned into a smile of respect. Washington knew how to handle men like this. "We need your help." That got them every time.

"Sure, anything." The guard beamed.

"You got an occupant here, a Jim Monday. You noticed anything unusual about him?"

"One thirteen? Nice guy, not much trouble, but like all the rest, he thinks I work for him. Wants me to keep an eye out for his place because he's gone a lot."

"Why do you think that is?" Washington knew that it was because he lived somewhere else. Monday only used the condo when he felt like spending a few days at the beach.

"Gee, I dunno."

"Think he might be using it as a hidy hole? In case we get too close, or in case one of his drug deals goes bad?"

"I knew there was something funny about him," the guard said.

"You know, Bill, can I call you Bill?" Washington read the name tag over the guard's breast pocket.

"Sure."

"The problem with people like him is the American Civil Liberties Union."

"I hate them," the guard said.

"They want to undo every bust we make."

"They're all commies," the guard said.

"Ain't it the truth. They cause us nothing but problems. No matter how dirty someone is, we can never get a warrant."

"I couldn't let you in even if I wanted. I don't have the keys."

"I have a key. All I have to do now is get past you," Washington smiled.

"What are we waiting for?" the guard said. "This way." The two policemen followed him around a walkway that led down to the beach and around to the ocean-front side of the condos. "There it is. Next to the pool," the guard shouted back over his shoulder. In his enthusiasm he was almost running.

"What a deal," Washington said. "The ocean in front and the pool on the side. I can't believe it."

"That I can believe," Walker said in a hushed tone, so the guard couldn't hear, "but what I can't believe is how eager that dummy is to be part of a real cop operation. I bet he asks for our autographs on the way out."

"How do you want to do this?" the guard asked when the policemen caught up to him at Monday's condo. He was painting like faithful lapdog.

"How about you unlock the door and we go in?" Washington tossed him the keys.

"I can go in, too?"

"I don't see why not," Washington said. "We have to stick together. That's the way I see it."

"Yeah, me too." The guard's hands shook with anticipation as he opened the door. It was the last thing he ever did.

A 767 roared overhead, taking off from John Wayne Airport, but even the noise from its powerful jet engines couldn't drown out the gunshots that exploded from the center of Jim Monday's condo. The first shot took the security guard's face apart as it lifted him up and threw him out of the doorway.

A wave crashed and the second shot smashed into Walker's elbow, spinning him around like a ballerina, throwing him into the brick wall that was Hugh Washington. Their heads collided, skin and skulls smashing together in a dancing concert of frenzy and fear, sending the two men crashing to the sidewalk in a silent fall, their struggles drowned out by the jet and the sea.

Hugh Washington was conscious of Walker's heavy body on top of him. He had a pain in his ribs, where his partner's holstered pistol dug into his side. He had a pain in his shoulder, where his left arm was wrenched behind his back. He had a pain in the right side of his face, where the back of Walker's head had smashed into him. And he had a pain in his heart, because he hadn't been ready for this. He had been so stupid, so careless.

He used his free right arm to roll out from under Walker's bleeding body. He groaned as the pressure on his captured left was released and muscle and bone screamed relief as he grabbed for his weapon.

He wrapped scraped and bleeding fingers around the butt of the pistol, had it half way out of the holster, when out of the corner of his eyes he saw the blue barrel of a forty-five automatic come slicing through the bright sky and then everything went dark.

"I know you can hear me, Washington, so stop playing like you're asleep. I'm not going anywhere. I have as long as it takes."

"Head hurts." Washington forced his eyes open, only to squint against the light. He raised a bandaged right hand to a bandaged forehead.

"Nasty gash where you were clobbered, the hand's only skinned."

"Where am I?" he whispered through a sore throat.

"Hope Hospital, Costa Mesa, and lucky to be alive."

"Need water," he rasped.

"Are you okay?"

"Need water."

"Can you talk?"

"Not without water."

"What did you think you were doing?"

"Come on Captain," Washington said, "no water, no talk."

"Sometimes I wish you still worked for me and sometimes I'm glad you don't." Captain John Hart picked up a plastic glass, filled it from a plastic pitcher. "Now is one of the times that I'm glad you don't." He reached behind Washington's head with his left hand, helped him up, offering him the water with his right.

Washington drank greedily.

"Take it easy."

"Why?"

"I don't know, it's what they say in the movies."

He finished the water and Hart eased him back onto the pillow.

"You know, Hugh, when I assigned you to a case, I always forgot about it." John Hart brushed baby-fine hair out of his eyes. "You're like a bulldog, once you get your teeth into something, you worry it until it gives up what you want."

Washington grunted and stared into the man's cool blue eyes. John Hart had always been an enigma to Washington. With his long hair, blue eyes and baby face, he looked more like a twenty-five year old college student than the forty-five year old captain of detectives that he was. He jogged five miles daily, but he smoked. He scorned religion, but believed in God. He loathed politicians, but loved politics. He wore his views, about everything from government to sport, on his sleeve, but nobody could get into his head.

"Sometimes I like you, John and sometimes I don't," Washington said, mimicking his former boss. "I think this is going to be one of the times I don't. Why don't you just get it over with?"

"I should lay into you, scream my head off. I should sink you so deep in jail that you'd never get out. Hell, I should shoot you myself. But I'm too sophisticated to scream. You haven't broken any laws. And I got too much respect for what you once were to shoot you."

Hugh Washington closed his eyes.

"Are you listening to me?"

"I'm listening." He wanted to shut out the captain's voice, but he couldn't. He knew what was coming.

"You got a security guard killed and your partner badly shot up."

"How is he?"

"He'll live, no thanks to you. What in the world did you think you were doing?"

Washington didn't answer.

"Good, don't say anything. I don't want to hear it. I don't want to know. You went to Monday's house without a warrant or a backup and Monday kills an innocent man and wounds your partner, not to mention putting you out of commission. Why am I not surprised?"

"It wasn't Monday," Washington said.

"Oh, who was it?"

"I didn't see."

"Then how do you know it wasn't him?"

"He's in jail."

"No, he's not. It may surprise you to know that he broke out early this morning. He killed two attorneys and a good cop in the process."

"Ah shit."

"You can say that again. If you had followed procedure and told us about the condo, we would have had him this morning, that poor security guard would still be alive and your partner wouldn't be down the hall sucking oxygen."

"Sorry."

"Tell it to Walker, I don't want to hear it. All I want from you is what you know."

"I don't know anything."

"Yeah, then how come you knew about the Huntington Beach condo?"

"I looked it up on the internet," he lied.

"How did you get the key?"

"I didn't, the guard had it," he lied again.

"I can check."

"Then do it."

"All right, all right, no need to get hot under the collar."

"Whatever you say, John."

"After all, I just came by to see how you were doing. Unofficial."

"And?"

"You were the best once. You've been digging, don't deny it. I know you."

Washington didn't say anything.

"As long as I'm here, I'd like your take on this thing. Why do you think he did it and where do you think he might go?"

"I don't have the foggiest. And I don't believe Monday killed anyone."

"You're wrong," the captain said. The room was quiet for a few seconds as the two men stared at each other, then the captain added, "I came here offering an olive branch and you're holding back. I want some answers and if you ever want to get back into a uniform, much less back in Homicide, you'll tell me what I want to know."

"I don't know anything, John. Really I don't."

"That's your final word?"

"It's God's own truth," Hugh Washington said.

"Well, I have a final word for you. As soon as you check out of here, go straight to your captain. I have a feeling that he'll want your badge and gun. You're through Washington."

"So you were lying about me getting back in uniform or maybe back in Homicide. You only said it to get something out of me? I was finished with the department no matter if I knew anything or not, wasn't I?"

"Fuck you," his former friend said, showing his back and walking out the door.

So, Washington thought, it's finally happened. He was no longer a cop. Where to go from here? What next? His law degree might be a help, a shame he never took the bar. There must be something out there for him. Security consultant maybe—not bad, or security guard—pretty bad. But before he did anything, he resolved, he would get to the bottom of the Jim Monday business. He would show them that Hugh Washington still had what it takes. Then after he presented them with the killer and they were begging him to come back on the force, he'd tell them to shove it.

He smiled at the thought, knowing he wouldn't ever tell them that. If they wanted him back, he'd go. Being a cop is all he ever was, all he ever wanted to be. And there was only one way for him to get back. Find Jim Monday.

He looked around the room. It was an ordinary hospital room, two beds, a nightstand next to each one, the second bed was vacant. There was a television mounted on the wall, two utilitarian chairs for visitors, two dinner trays on wheels, one bathroom and one closet. He lowered the safety bar and climbed out of bed. His head throbbed. He steadied himself as he shuffled his aching body toward the closet, where he found his clothes. His shirt, slacks and jacket were neatly hanging. His underwear and socks, neatly folded on the overhead shelf. His shoes, neatly placed on the floor. His tie seemed to have gone missing.

He stepped back from the closet, did a couple of knee bends and groaned. Concentrating, he straightened his knees and tried to touch the floor. He groaned again, louder, but he wanted to see how damaged he was. He discovered sore muscles, but other than his banged up head and skinned hand, he appeared to be okay.

He went into the bathroom, splashed water on his face and studied the bandage on his forehead in the mirror. For the next few days he would stand out in a crowd. Frowning, he took off his hospital gown and studied his body, finding a large blue bruise by the lower left part of his rib cage, where Walker's gun had dug into his side. He touched it and winced. It was painful, but it wouldn't slow him down or restrict him in anyway.

He padded naked out of the bathroom. It was time to go. He went to the closet and put on his clothes, wincing again as he bent to get into his underwear and still again as he bent to put on his slacks. His belt was missing, too. He put on his white shirt, grit his teeth and held on to the wall. He sat in one of the chairs, put on his shoes and socks, feeling like a child, as he struggled with his bandaged hand to tie his shoelaces.

Then he rang for a nurse. Seconds later a young woman with a wide smile, showing plenty of teeth and wearing a white nurse's uniform entered the room. She attempted a frown when she saw the big man dressed, but she wasn't able to pull it off, because even a frown on her toothy face looked like a smile.

"Mr. Washington," she tried to scold him through grinning teeth and twinkling blue eyes, "where do you think you're going?"

"I'm checking out."

"But you can't. You're not well."

"I'm sorry, I have things to do."

"I know, I was listening at the door. He's not a nice man."

"Apparently not." Washington returned her smile.

"You'll need the rest of your things," she said.

He followed her with his eyes as she seemed to glide to the nightstand next to the bed. She opened the top drawer, took out his badge, wallet, belt and tie. His weapon wasn't there and he didn't ask about it. She handed him the belt and he put it on. Then he slipped the badge and wallet into his pocket.

"You'll need help with the tie," she said, looking at his bandaged hand.

"I'd appreciate it."

"Stand up straight." She wrapped it around his neck. "Didn't your mother ever teach you posture?"

Hugh laughed, stood erect.

"There," she said, "finished, a perfect Windsor." Then with both her tiny hands, she grabbed the tie in two balled fists and forced Washington to look straight into her eyes. She didn't blink when she said. "You are going to find out who killed those people and show that jerk up for what he is, aren't you?"

"That's just what I'm going to do." He smiled.

"Behind you." She jumped back, startled, releasing the tie.

Washington spun around and saw a gecko scurry up the wall and disappear behind the television set.

"It's only a gecko."

"I know." She regained her composure, "It's just that we don't have them in California."

"It must be somebody's pet. A kid, visiting his mother or father probably snuck it in and it got away."

"Probably," she said.

"Some places they're regarded as a good luck sign."

"And some places they're a portent of evil," she said.

"My luck has been too bad to get any worse. I'll accept it as a good luck sign," he said.

"Me too." She smiled wide, showing off her teeth.

"Now I'd like to talk to my partner, if that's possible?"

"He's in ICU."

"What's he doing in intensive care?"

"He's okay. He was shot, remember? It's standard procedure."

"Can I see him?"

"Sure, down the hall, turn left. Follow the signs."

"Thanks." He started to go.

"Hugh Washington," she said.

He turned. "Yes?"

"After you catch your killer, come back and buy me dinner. Okay?"

"Count on it."

He went through the swinging doors of the ICU and approached the nurse's station.

"I'm looking for Ron Walker," he asked the nurse on duty.

"Five-eleven, that way." She pointed. "You'll have to wait, only two visitors at a time. He's already one over."

"Is it okay if I go in now?" He showed her his badge.

"Five-eleven, that way." She pointed again. "I'm sorry. You look more like a patient than you do a policeman."

"I feel more like a patient," he said. Then added. "How is he?"

"He'll be out of ICU tonight."

"That's good."

"But his arm will never be the same."

"Oh no."

"He was lucky," she said.

"I hope he sees it that way."

"I think he does. He's taking it very well."

"Thanks for telling me." He returned her smile, then pointed, "Five-eleven, that way."

"That's right." She pointed for the third time.

He followed her finger and found Walker in his room, an IV in his arm, feeding him a clear, gluey looking substance.

"They've got you hooked up like an astronaut," he said, looking at the monitors.

"Yeah," Walker said. "I keep checking the heart rate to make sure I'm still alive."

"I'm Hugh Washington," he said to the pretty woman and the two young girls. "You must be the lovely Carol I've heard so much about." Smiling at the two girls, he added, "And you two pretty ladies must be Denise and Dianne."

"We meet at last," Carol Walker said. "I only wish it could have been under better circumstances."

"I'm sorry I got him into this," Washington said. "It was my fault. I was pigheaded and bent the rules and this is the result."

"It's not your fault. You didn't put a gun to Ron's head. It's just bad luck. You pay your money and you take your chances."

"Honey, could I talk to Hugh alone for a few minutes?"

"Come on girls, let's see if we can find the cafeteria." She kissed her husband. "We'll be back in about forty-five minutes."

"Thanks," Walker said.

"I love you," she said, leading the girls out of the room.

"I love you too," he called after her.

"I'm sorry it wound up this way, Walker," Washington said after she was gone. "I really didn't count on Monday being a killer. Go figure."

"He's not. I know it. Not him."

"You heard about what happened?"

"I know Monday escaped. That a cop and two lawyers are dead, but I still don't think he's a killer," Walker said.

"Rich guy like that, hard for me to believe, but everything seems to be pointing to him."

"You said yourself that it looked like whoever killed Askew was waiting, that you thought it was murder."

"I could have been wrong."

"Not you."

"Even I make mistakes."

"Then what about those shots in the alley?"

"Could be coincidence."

"And the Pope could be a Methodist, but he's not."

"Look, Walker, I know you admire the guy."

"I don't admire him, I respect him and everything I've learned about him tells me he wouldn't kill anyone. Not unless he had a very good reason."

"Maybe he had a reason," Washington said.

"Not for killing a cop to escape from city jail."

"Maybe getting out of jail was all the reason he needed."

"The man spent four years in a North Vietnamese POW camp and he didn't crack. A few days in our jail would be like the Hilton to him and you don't kill to get out of the Hilton."

"People change."

"You're forgetting that he didn't have to be there. He asked for it. He wanted the time to get his head straight, remember?"

"Yeah," Washington said, thinking. "You're right."

"Somebody is setting him up and doing a damn good job."

"Could be." Washington rubbed his jaw.

"Listen, Hugh, I'm finished with the department, my arm will never be right. I know that. Carol and I have just been talking about it. When I get out of here I'm going to set up my own practice. There could be a place for you there."

"I'm not finished yet."

"You will be if you keep pursuing this thing. It's not your case. In fact, I'll bet that's what that bastard Hart was doing here. He didn't come to see how we were getting on, did he? He came to tell you to lay off. Didn't he?"

"He told me to lay off."

"Are you going to?"

"No."

"See, you're finished too. You're all alone now. I can't help you, but what I can do is make sure you have a job when this thing is all over. If you want to go back to school and cram for the bar, then there will be a place for you in my firm. If not, then you can do our PI work."

"You're counting your chickens before they're hatched."

"No, I'm not. I can never go back on the streets again, even if my arm healed right, Carol couldn't live with it. I have money. A lot. I can buy my own building if I want. I can hire hotshots right out of law school and I can advertise. I can be all over TV and radio. I can be in your car, your living room and your newspaper. I'll do fine. We'll do fine."

"Why do you want me?"

"Because you're the best. You'll be able to find out if our clients are honest with us. You'll be able to track down the missing husband or the missing bank account or the missing cash, because you look where no one else thinks of looking, because there isn't a man on this planet as good as you at what you do. To be successful, really successful, and quickly, I need quick results. I need you."

"And what about Jim Monday?"

"He's my first client, only he doesn't know it, yet. And your first job is to clear him. Find out who killed David Askew, help me keep our client out of jail. Do we have a deal?"

"We do."

"And Hugh, in case you're wondering if I can afford this, you know about the money I inherited."

"Yeah."

"It grew. It grew a lot."

"So why be a cop?

"My father always said that you had a responsibility to give something back. And I liked it."

"I did too."

"You get out of here and clear Monday and while you're doing that, I'll find us a nice big office with a view. It's about time Long Beach had some good attorneys for a change."

"Okay." He turned to leave, then at the door he turned back. "Just how much money you got?"

"About seventy-five million dollars."

Washington whistled. Then he stopped to avoid stepping on the gecko that scurried across the floor and disappeared under the bathroom door. Must be a plague of the things, he thought, then he put it out of his mind.

CHAPTER SIX

JIM MONDAY SLIPPED his shoes off, massaged his tired and sore feet, then stretched out on the bed, fully clothed, too tired to undress. He closed his eyes, was about to fall into a dark sleep, when he heard the tapping on the connecting door.

He sighed, got up and opened it. Roma was on the other side.

"I'm sorry, I thought I could sleep alone," she said, "but I can't, not with you in the next room."

"Are you okay?" he asked.

"I don't know if this is right, but I know it's what I need," she said, as her fingers moved to unbutton her blouse, allowing him to see the skimpy bra and the ample cleavage. He couldn't help comparing her with Julia. They were alike, but different. Julia was demure and modest. Roma was brazen and direct. Julia, even after years of marriage, would never undress in front of him. Roma was doing it.

She balled her hands into the blouse, pulled it from the tight fitting Levi's, took it off, dropped it on the floor. She looked him in the eyes, stretched her arms behind her back and undid the clasp while shrugging her shoulders forward. The bra fell at her feet.

"I need you, Jimmy. Even if we're both sorry tomorrow. Even if it's only for tonight."

"My God, what's going on here?" Donna thought. *"She's getting naked right in front of us."* Then she moaned in his head. *"What's this, what's happening, I've never felt like this. My lord, this is what it feels like for a man. This is what it feels like when it gets hard. Oh, oh, oh!"*

The aerobics and the daily jogging paid off in small ways. Roma's breasts were more firm, more pointed, more youthful than Julia's and her waist, a touch thinner than her twin's.

She half smiled, turned and drew the curtains, plunging the room into a surreal twilight. The curtains were designed to keep out the light, but enough came through to bask the room in late evening bronze, reminding Jim of a red sunset on a Southeast Asian beach.

He was swimming in a sea of confusion. She had his wife's fluid movements, the same strong back, the same dishwater blond hair. For an instant he was at ease with the familiarity, but the ease left when she turned to face him again. A shiver rippled through him as she worked the top button on her Levi's. She popped the button open, then she stopped and smiled at him.

"You should have visited me in Florida." She crossed her arms in front of her breasts.

"You know I don't fly," he said. He never admitted to being afraid. He preferred to say he didn't fly.

"I didn't back then. I might not have gone had I known," she said.

"Editorial writer for the *Miami Herald*, the job was too good to refuse. You had to go. I couldn't hold you back."

"So you married my sister instead."

"You were gone. I thought I'd never see you again. I fell in love with Julia."

"Did you fall out of love with me?"

"No."

"Why didn't you tell me about your fear of flying?"

"I was ashamed. I broke down on the flight back from Vietnam, went crazy, shouting, screaming. It took several men to restrain me. Until that moment I thought I came through it okay, but only hours from home I fell apart." He paused to catch his breath. "For years it was all I could think about, going home. Then when it finally happened, I snapped."

"And you don't know why?" She relaxed her arms, once again baring her breasts, but her voice was so full of concern that Jim knew she wasn't conscious of her nudity. Her only care was for him.

"No. I was okay after we touched down, but I was so humiliated, that I swore I'd never get on another plane. I don't know if it would happen again, but I can't afford to take the chance."

"I'm sorry. Did you ever consider professional help?"

"No, but I should have," he said. "I know that now." He looked back into her gaze. Admitting he was wrong about something, anything, was hard for him. He sought her approval and understanding. "I've missed out on a lot. There's a whole world out there and it's been denied me, because I've been afraid to get on an airplane. I should have gotten help right away, instead I tried to bury the problem, always finding excuses to stay put."

"And now?" She met his eyes.

"And now, if we get out of this in one piece, I'm going straight to the nearest head doctor and get my head shrunk." He laughed and she laughed with him.

"I was terrified when you shot those two men." She moved to the armchair opposite the bed and sat down. "It was the most afraid I've ever been, but I knew if you didn't do it, they would kill us. I wanted to run away, but I was too scared to move," she said.

"Everybody's afraid. The only difference between a hero and a coward is that for a few seconds the hero is able to overcome his fear. Then he goes back to being afraid again, like anybody else."

"Were you afraid like that in Vietnam?"

"Everyday."

"And in the POW camp, were you afraid then?"

"Everyday."

"But you overcame you fear."

"No, I learned to live with it, but I never overcame it."

"What's the most afraid you ever were? Was it when you were in combat or in the camp?" She seemed to be obsessed with the idea of fear.

"Oh my God! She jumped out of the chair. "It's a spider," She hopped onto the bed, a mass of goosebumps and jiggling breasts. "Spider," she said again, pointing to a common garden spider making its way across the bureau next to the chair she had just jiggled out of.

"Stay here." He laughed, got off the bed, went into the bathroom and got a water glass.

"Aren't you going to kill it?"

"What for? It doesn't mean us harm." He smiled at her, made a show of sneaking up on the spider and, with a flourish, covered it with the glass. "Now we need a piece of paper," he said. "Check the nightstand."

"Lots easier to kill it." She scooted across the bed, opened the drawer, took out a tablet of hotel stationery, tore off a sheet and handed it to him.

"I never kill spiders. They eat the bad bugs."

"What bad bugs?"

"Mosquitoes, fleas, flies—the bad bugs." He slid the paper under the glass and, with the spider safely enclosed, picked it up, one hand on the glass, the other holding the paper securely underneath. "Would you get the door?"

She hopped off the bed, opened the door and watched as he pulled the paper away, flinging the spider out into the night.

"Good riddance." She took her place in the armchair once again.

He smiled and closed the door.

"You didn't answer my question," she said.

"What question?"

"What's the most afraid you ever were?"

He was quiet for a few seconds, then said. "When I was little, I used to play cowboys and Indians with the neighborhood kids. I was always the sheriff and David was always the Indian chief. The goal was to capture and tie up the enemy. Usually to the clothesline."

"Clothesline?" she interrupted.

"Yeah, the clothesline. You don't see them like you used to now that everybody has a dryer, but in the neighborhood where we grew up we all had them, two poles cemented into the ground with a tee on top and four lines running between."

"I know what a clothesline is, I just can't imaging tying someone to the line."

"Not the line, the poles. There were generally five or six kids per side, but there could be as many as ten. We would travel the block in twos or threes, searching out the enemy. If we could find and overpower them, we would take them to David's or my backyard and tie them up. Once bound you were out of action for the rest of the game, or until you were freed by your side."

"Wouldn't your team just untie you right away?" She asked.

"If they could, but once you had captives you left a guard."

"Oh."

"The last day of summer, before we entered the sixth grade, we were playing the game. We were down by five, with one to go. Two boys were tied to the poles, three more were tied hands and feet, wriggling on the grass like giant worms. I was one of the three. It was a hot September day, probably in the high nineties, so a lot of us were playing without shirts. As you can imagine, it gets pretty hot laying on the grass, baking in the sun."

"Didn't you get sunburned?" She asked."

"A little," he said, as his mind took him back.

* * *

Jerry Delawarean and his younger brother, Little Bobby, were tied to the clothesline poles. Little Bobby was crying, he was only seven and not used to the game. Ricky Stewart, John Morgan and himself, were tied with their hands behind their backs. Their feet were tied too.

"Shut up Bobby." His brother was the only one that didn't call him Little Bobby.

"I don't wanna play anymore. I wanna go home."

"You been bugging us to play and we finally let you and now ya wanna quit," his brother said.

"I didn't wanna get tied up," he wailed.

"What did the little shit think was gonna happen?" John Morgan said. He was the only kid on the block that swore. "He's too little to capture anybody by himself and too slow to get away, 'course he was gonna get caught first thing. Happened to me too when I was a kid, but I didn't whine about it when I got caught." John Morgan, at twelve, was the oldest kid in the game and it took three kids to capture and hold him. Even with the no hitting rule, there were no two he couldn't get away from.

"Where did Beanie go?" Ricky asked. Beanie was Donny Greenwood, called Beanie because he was Jewish and had to wear a yarmulke to temple on Saturdays. "He's supposed to be guarding us."

"Out looking for Rex probably," John said. Rex Russell was the last cowboy in play.

"I bet Rex has got 'em all captured," Ricky said. Only on a rare occasion did a game come down to the guard. Guards weren't supposed to leave their posts, but they always did.

"Naw, if he did, he'd come let us go."

"Not Rex," Little Bobby said, sniffling, "he'd go home and leave us here till dark."

"He's right," John said, "that son of a bitch would leave us here till dark. We'll burn red as beets."

"My mom's gonna be pissed off," Ricky said. That was the first time Jim heard Ricky swear.

"We gotta get outta here," Little Bobby said, looking at his brother.

"Okay, okay," Jerry said, "can anybody get loose?"

"I think I can," Jim said.

They all turned their eyes on Jim. If anybody could slip out of the ropes, he could. He was the skinniest and most agile. They watched as he twisted and turned, grunted and groaned, but after fifteen minutes of sweating and struggling he was no closer to loosening his bonds than when he had started.

"I can't get loose." He was breathing hard.

"You're turning red, Jimmy," Little Bobby said. Jim had fair skin and sunburned easily. He should have kept his shirt on. Rolling around in the grass made him itch like crazy and now he was starting to feel the burn. He tried again to squeeze his hands through the rope, but still he couldn't.

"I'm gonna get into the shade." He rolled across the yard to the shade offered by the garage. Once out of the sun he relaxed and caught his breath. He still itched, but at least he wouldn't burn anymore.

"Jimmy, maybe if you sit up by the corner of the garage, you can cut through your ropes," Jerry said.

Jim scooted over to the corner of the stucco garage and sat up with his back next to where two walls met and he started rubbing his hands up and down in an attempt to fray the ropes.

"Black widow," Little Bobby screamed.

Jim stopped his rubbing, his companions were silent. "Where?" he asked, quietly.

"By your leg."

Jim looked down and saw it. Big, black, marble shaped and it was crawling up onto his leg.

"Don't move," Jerry said, a tremor in his voice.

"Yeah, stay real still and maybe it'll go away," Ricky said.

"I'd roll over and squash it," John said.

"No, don't do that, you might piss it off and it'll bite," Ricky said, getting used to swearing.

"Not if it's fucking squashed," John swore.

Jim froze, hoping his Levi's were too thick for it to bite through, but not sure. He felt the sweat rolling of his sunburned back as it climbed up and sat on his knee. His comrades were mute, holding their breath, eyes glued to the spider.

It sat there for several minutes, holding the boys spellbound. They were quiet, keen and aware. The only sounds, their shallow breathing and the breeze rustling through the tall tree in the corner of the yard. Jim was paralyzed.

The spider began to move back the way it had come.

"When it gets on the grass, roll away from it," Jerry said.

"Yeah, get away from it," Ricky echoed. "That's what I'd do."

"Roll over and squash it. Smash it dead," John offered.

As if hearing John, the spider stopped and climbed back up on the knee, sat for a second, like it was surveying the situation, then started a trek up Jim's pant leg.

"Do something!" Little Bobby squealed, his tears forgotten.

The spider stopped and sat atop Jim's groin.

"It's on his dick," John Morgan said. "Better do something quick."

Jim's bladder gave way.

"He pissed himself," John Morgan said and Jim knew, scared as he was, he would never live it down.

The hot urine welling up around the spider startled it and it scooted away from the source of the wet in a sideways movement coming to rest above Jim's bare belly button.

"That's bad," Little Bobby said.

"Shoulda rolled over and squashed it," John said.

Jim remained paralyzed, with his back against the garage and once again the boys turned silent, waiting with bated breath and wide eyes. The spider remained rock still, rising and falling with Jim's quivering breath.

"Help!" Little Bobby belted out, his cry piercing the silence like a white hot knife.

"Help! Help!" Ricky and Jerry chimed in.

"Help!" John Morgan's loud voice added to the cadence.

"What's going on?" David's mother screamed, coming out the back door.

"Black widow, on Jimmy!" John Morgan said.

Cynthia Askew started toward Jimmy just as he felt a pinching sensation in his abdomen. David's mother swatted the spider off his belly, then squashed it with her foot. Jim passed out. Three days later he came home from the hospital. He spent the next five years overcoming his fear of spiders.

* * *

He told Roma the whole story, omitting only the part about wetting his pants.

"You and your sister are the only people alive that know about that," he said, after he finished the telling. "It's always been my deepest secret."

"Why?"

"I was paralyzed with fear, no one likes to admit that."

"What about the boys?" she asked.

"Except for David, who was killed yesterday, the cowboys have been dead forever. Jerry and his brother, Little Bobby, were killed in high school when the car Jerry was driving was hit by a drunk driver. John Morgan stepped on a land mine just outside Saigon. Ricky Stewart died of leukemia on his fourteenth birthday. David's mother has been dead for years. I told Julia one night when we were swapping secrets, I don't know why I told you, because you asked, I guess, or maybe because I've always loved you."

"But you overcame your fear of spiders. You should be proud of that."

"I just wanted to forget about that horrible afternoon, being afraid every time I saw a spider was no way to forget. Once I got used to not being afraid of them, I started to like them. Now I go out of my way to help them. I'd never kill one. Not now."

"I've always loved you too," she said.

All of a sudden he was extremely aware of Roma's bared breasts. "I've never been with anyone but Julia," he said.

"I suspected as much," she said.

"How did you know?"

"I don't know. I guess a woman just knows these things, but I'll confess I don't understand why. Were you afraid of girls?"

"No. I was a good Catholic boy. I was a virgin at eighteen when I went into the service, still a virgin when I was sent to Vietnam, where God knows I had plenty of opportunity, but I couldn't bring myself to go a prostitute, so I remained a virgin till I was captured. Not many girls in a POW camp. I was twenty-three when I got home and pretty fucked up. By the time I got it together, I was halfway through my thirties, too old and too embarrassed to start dating, so I just put it out of my mind and concentrated on making money. Then I met you and fell in love, but you went away with me still celibate."

"Julia never told me."

"Julia never knew."

"How?"

"The first time we did it she was too drunk to notice my fumbling around. After that first night I was an expert."

"She was pretty experienced," Roma said.

"She once told me she made a lot of men very happy, in her own shy way," Jim said.

"That's my sister. I love her dearly, but she always was a little slut." Roma laughed. "She was always faithful to you though. After she got married she stopped her catting around."

"Till she met Kohler," Jim said.

She sat still in the armchair and eyed him.

"Take your pants off," she said with a sly grin.

"No," he said.

"I'll bet you'd take them off for Julia."

"You're not her."

"Pretend I am." She smiled wider.

"I don't know if I can," he said.

"Don't be a prude, take them off," Donna thought.

"Stay out of this," He thought back.

"Take 'em off!" Roma commanded.

"Do it!" Donna commanded.

He stared at Roma's rising and falling breasts and he felt Donna inside him.

"I can feel it getting hard," Donna thought.

"I told you to stay out of this." He wondered if it was possible to forget about Donna for a while.

"Come on, Jimmy, slip them off," Roma chided.

He moved his gaze up to her eyes and was trapped in her exotic stare. He pulled down the zipper, slipped the pants off, taking the underwear along for the ride.

"Julia said you were big." She eyed his erection.

"Wow, look at it, sticking up hard as a rock. I can feel it. It's so great. No wonder men get so horny." Donna's excitement caused Jim to shiver and he blushed.

"Now the tie." Roma laughed and he whipped it off, then the vest, followed by the shirt. Jim ignored the buttons, lifting it over his head and tossing it on the floor with the rest of his clothes, leaving himself naked, except for his socks and his cast. He lay back against the headboard and met her eyes.

"Socks off," she kidded.

He was speechless, but not powerless. He took off the socks, tossed them after the rest of his clothes.

"Now it's my turn." She stood up, keeping Jim locked in her stare and finished unbuttoning the Levi's. Jim tore his eyes away from hers and moved them back down to her breasts. Her nipples were hard, pointed and perfect and they quivered as she worked at her pants. His eyes roved down from her breasts and watched what her hands were doing. He smiled and felt the heat of his erection run through him, when the pale pink of her panties peeked through. He returned his gaze to her erotic eyes.

She winked and offered him her half smile, while hooking her thumbs into the pant waist and pulling the Levi's off. She stood and faced him for a few seconds, clad only in pale pink panties, the black vee of her pubic hair clearly showing through.

"She's beautiful. So beautiful," Donna offered. Jim ignored her as Roma slipped the panties off and kicked them out of the way.

"We were made for each other." Roma faced him, nude, with her arms at her sides and tears in her eyes. "If you only knew how much I need you right now."

"I need you too," he said, meaning it like he'd never meant anything before. All his troubles seemed to fade away. At that moment he only had eyes for Roma. She was the beginning, middle and end of his life. "And I love you."

"I love you too." The half smile turned full as she approached. She eased onto the bed, snuggled up next to him, reached between his legs, taking him in her hand, gently squeezing.

"Oh my, that feels sooooo good, don't let her stop."

But Jim wasn't listening to Donna. After a few minutes he rolled Roma onto her back and kissed her breasts, before moving up to her mouth and covering her lips with his. He tasted the salt from her tears and started to pull away, when she wrapped her arms tightly around him, drawing him to her. He entered her and they made love, slowly at first, feeling each other out, then gradually they increased the tempo till they turned into a runaway train.

They climaxed together, silently, holding on to each other, not like it was the first time for them, but like it was the last time for forever. When it was over they hugged like young lovers, fiercely and tenderly and Jim lay lost with the wonder of her and wondered how differently things would have turned out if he'd married her instead of her twin.

"I'd love to stay and spend more time with you, but I gotta get next door before Edna gets back." She laughed. "Listen to me, I'm acting like she's my mother and I might get in trouble." But she got out of bed and started dressing.

Too quickly he was alone with his thoughts, then he closed his eyes and the last thing he remembered before he fell asleep was Donna in his head, saying, *"So that's what it's like for a man. It's so wonderful."*

CHAPTER SEVEN

HUGH WASHINGTON WALKED through the hospital lobby with a spring in his step. Walker had surprised him. The man had given him a new lease on life. Maybe this was the shot in the arm that would put his marriage back together. He hoped so. He was tired of being a weekend father. Tired of sleeping alone. Tired of eating alone. And tired of begging Jane to come back.

He'd been separated a long time. He'd changed. The gray moods were gone. Mostly he owed that to Glenna and her perennially positive attitude. Amazingly, she handled the rape and shooting of her attacker much better than her parents had. They blamed each other. She lay all the blame on the doorstep of the dead rapist.

Maybe it was the superb counseling, maybe it was just her make up, but whatever it was, she hadn't gone through that period that most women go through after a rape. She never blamed herself. Even though she had lied to her parents about where she was that day. Even though she had invited the young man into her home. Even though she should have known better. Even after all those "even thoughs," she had no blame left over for herself. As far as she was concerned the incident was closed. The guy got what he deserved. Justice was done. Life was living for the present and the future. The past was dead and gone.

He was halfway through the lobby when he realized he didn't have a car. He turned to the information desk and asked a young receptionist where the phones were. He flashed her a grin when she pointed down a corridor and felt his heart flutter a little when she smiled back. Then he went to the public phones and called a cab.

Thirty minutes later, as he was paying the cab driver, he remembered that he had a lunch date with his daughter. He silently cursed himself for almost forgetting. Glenna had been out on her own for the last month, living with a girlfriend in a small apartment on the north side of the Long Beach State campus. She worked full time and went to school nights. She was proud of her independence and he knew that she was looking for a chance to show it off by buying him lunch.

The Jim Monday investigation would have to put itself on hold, because nothing was ever going to come between him and Glenna.

He took the steps up to his bachelor apartment two at a time. He had an hour and a half before he was supposed to meet her. Plenty of time. He shucked his suit jacket onto the sofa bed and finished undressing, tossing the rest of his clothes in a heap on the floor.

He felt good in the steamy shower, so he stayed under the spray until it started to turn cold. Then he turned it off and got out, drying as he padded from the bathroom back to the living room. He thought about folding the bed back into a couch, but what was the point, he'd only have to take it out again tonight. Besides he hadn't planned on company. So, for the twenty-first day in a row, he ignored the sofa bed and dressed.

He donned a pair of Levi's, running shoes, his spare shoulder holster with his off duty weapon and a faded blue Cal State sweat shirt with cut off sleeves. He wasn't going to eat in the shore and embarrass Glenna by showing up in one of the old suits from his detective days. Especially not that beat up brown job he was wearing this morning. He was going to look young and hip, like he belonged. Casual.

Dressed, he started for the door, then turned back toward the bathroom for his dose of Skin Bracer to set his face tingling. He looked in the mirror, touched the bandage on his forehead and winced. It hurt. Then he opened the medicine cabinet and reached in for the after shave, when a gecko scurried from the top shelf, jumped onto his bare arm, ran up his sleeve, over his shoulder, brushed along his neck, then dove five feet to the floor and dashed out of the bathroom.

He jumped back and slammed into the wall behind, banging his head. He pushed himself away from the wall, catching his breath and feeling foolish, while he tried to calm his raging heart.

He hated surprises.

"What the hell," he muttered. "First the hospital and now here."

It was unusual, almost impossible and under different circumstances he would have worried about it, but he had other things on his mind. A new job, finding Jim Monday and lunch with Glenna. He wanted her to be the first to know that he was finished with the department. No more gray moods and never being there when he was needed. From now on his family came first. Jane, Glenna and himself—family.

He checked his watch on the way out the door. He had plenty of time to take the bus down Ocean to get his car. At the station he crossed the parking lot to where *Power Glide* lay, parked between two newer Chevrolet relatives, a Corvette on the left, a souped up Z28 on the right. They may be sporty and fast, he thought, but his Impala captured all the eyes. She was old and sometimes hard to start and maybe even harder to keep running, but she looked like the day she came off the showroom floor, waxed and new.

He ran his hand along the hood and flecked some bird droppings off the windscreen with his index finger.

"No shit on you." He unlocked the door, got in. She started immediately, a good sign.

Since he was early, he figured he might get in a little work before lunch, so he drove to Dr. Kohler's clinic on Lakewood Boulevard.

Bernd Kohler's Clinic de Beauté was a modern three story structure near the Traffic Circle, where the old Circle Drive In Theater used to be. He was one of those plastic surgeons that advertised in TV Guide. His ads pictured naked young women, hidden in shadow, always under the caption, "*We can make you look the best you can be.*" Not very good English, but effective. Kohler was a rich man.

He parked in the clinic lot, locked the car and made his way to the reception, where he was confronted by a beauty that looked like she stepped straight out of a centerfold. A perfect advertisement for Kohler's practice.

"Do you have an appointment?" she asked in the kind of voice that made men stammer.

"I'm a police officer." He showed his badge. "I'd like to talk to Dr. Kohler about what happened yesterday morning."

"He's not here, won't be for the next two weeks."

He was about to ask the next most obvious question, when she answered it without his asking.

"He's at his place up north. He has a summer home in Tampico."

"Really? I grew up in Palma. A stone's throw away."

"Dr. Kohler's place is on Mountain Sea Road. Do you know it?"

"I know it well." Washington smiled, putting the woman at ease.

"You'd love his house, everybody does," she said. "It has the woods in front and a cliffside view of the ocean from the rear. I love sitting on that deck and listening to the waves."

"Sounds like a neat place," Washington said.

"Gorgeous, but only from the inside. It looks like a prison from the outside. Gray, with bars on the windows. He has to keep it that way to keep the thieves away, because he's not there all that much."

"Can't be too careful these days," Washington said.

"Would you like me to get him on the phone?"

He told her it wasn't that important. He would see the doctor when he returned and she lit her face up with a smile. He thanked her and made his way back to the car.

It was time to put the Monday-Kohler business out of his mind. He hadn't seen Glenna in two weeks and he was looking forward to lunch. Especially since they were eating at *Armando's,* his favorite Italian restaurant. He smiled at the thought of the rich food. He was hungry.

Thirty minutes later he was sitting in a back booth bursting with anticipation. He wanted to let it all flood out, but Glenna had started in as soon as they were seated.

"What happened to your head?"

"Bad guy hit me. He got away."

"But you'll catch him, won't you," she said, pride evident in her voice.

"I'll catch him, because that's what I do," he said, bragging a little.

"I'm changing my major to police science," she said. "There's no future in psychology, unless I go on to a masters or a doctorate." Her words were like a slap.

"Honey, I want you to do whatever you want. I'll always stand behind you, you know that. But, police science, there's no future there, except the police force."

"Exactly. That's what I want. I want to be a cop, a good cop. Like you."

Emotionally he was torn. Glenna wanting to follow in his footsteps caused a sudden welling up of pride, but the danger of police work brought up fear as well. If anything ever happened to his daughter again, he wouldn't be able to live with himself.

"Darling, are you sure it's what you want? You know cops don't make any money. Not compared to the white collar guys. Heck, even the crooks make more than we do."

"Dad, you're not going to try and talk me out of this, are you?"

"When have I ever been able to talk you out of anything?" He saw the determined set of her jaw. It was true, when her mind was made up, it was locked and there was no key.

"Well, I'm glad, because I really want your support."

"You have it. You'll always have it." Then he went on to tell her about the events of the last two days. How he was only still a policeman by a mere thread, but that he didn't care, because he was finally going to use his law degree. He told her about the hit and run death of David Askew, the shots in the alley, the murder of the two attorneys and the policeman in the jail, the attack on himself and Walker in Huntington Beach, the wounding of Walker, how he banged up his head and skinned his hand and Walker's offer of a job.

"I'm sorry about Walker, but glad that you're going to be doing something you want to be doing," she said when he'd finished, "but that means if I want to follow in your footsteps, I'll have to go to law school," she said.

"You should ask yourself a serious question. Do you want to be a cop, because you want to be a cop, or because I'm a cop, because if it's the latter I really think you ought to reconsider. Don't get me wrong, for years it was good to me and I suppose if I could just knuckle under and do things by the book, it would keep on being good to me, but I can't. I have to do things my way."

"I thought I knew what I wanted. I'm not so sure now. I just know I hate psych."

"Then find something you like, or better yet, take a break, drop your classes while you still can, without being penalized and go to Europe for the rest of the summer. I'll pay for it."

"Dad, you're the greatest, but I don't want a break. I want a direction and I like to finish what I start. I may hate psych and it may only be summer school, but I'll finish the classes. Besides, a little training in psychology might be good for a policewoman." She laughed.

He laughed with her and wondered if he would be laughing as easily with Jane tonight. With the department no longer between them, they might be able to work everything out. He should have realized it sooner, maybe then they wouldn't have separated, but now everything was going to be okay. They'd be together again.

Then his dreams of family were shattered as he saw Jane, arm and arm with a well dressed man in his late forties or early fifties. They were laughing as they made their way to the exit, talking easily, like two people used to being together, like two people familiar with each other. He had forgotten that this was Jane's favorite Italian restaurant, too.

He must have scowled, or maybe the pain in his eyes had shown through, because Glenna sensed that his mood had changed and she turned her head to follow his gaze.

"I'm sorry," she said. "I didn't know they'd be here."

"I didn't know she was seeing anybody," he said, but he should have known. Jane was still attractive and they had been separated for a long time. How long did I expect her to wait before he got his act together.

"Really? It's not a secret. Everybody knows how serious they are."

"I didn't, but I guess I haven't been paying much attention lately."

"She's going to ask you for a divorce. They want to be married. He's very nice and I'm happy for her."

Her words cut like a straight razor, but he did his best not to let the blood show.

"I have an idea," he said. "Can you take a week off work and school?"

"I guess they'd give it to me and I can make the school work up easily. Why?"

"I just thought with Walker in the hospital and me quitting my job today, that maybe I could use a partner on this Jim Monday investigation. It wouldn't be dangerous and you could get a close up look at how boring an investigation really is. See if this is the kind of work you want to do for the rest of your life."

"Oh, Dad, I'd love that, love it, love it, love it." She scooted out from her chair, came around the table and hugged him. "I'll go and call in right now," she said as soon as they broke the embrace.

"It can wait till after lunch," he said.

"Oh, no it can't. I'm not going to give you a chance to change your mind."

Forty minutes later—after a lecture about how ninety-five percent of investigative work is research, four percent informants and one percent luck—they were walking up the stairway to her second floor apartment.

"Hey, before I pack a bag," Glenna said, "why don't I do a Google search on our Dr. Kohler?"

"Why didn't I think of that?" Washington said, impressed.

"If I don't find anything there, I'll check the index to the L.A. Times." She booted up her laptop.

"Pay dirt," she said after only a few minutes. "Look at this obit in the Milestones section. It happened ten years ago, but I think it's relevant."

Washington looked over her shoulder, read on the screen:

Died. George J. Greenwald, 53, Plastic Surgeon; from injuries received in a hit and run auto accident; in San Diego, California. Dr. Greenwald, known as the plastic surgeon of the stars was a prominent figure in California politics and society. His death follows that of his wife, Lillian and oldest daughter, Margot, only a year ago, in a similar hit and run accident, in Del Mar, California. The gruesome coincidence is nothing more than that, a coincidence, say the police. His surviving daughter, Jill, married to Greenwald's, young assistant Dr. Bernd Kohler, is the only heir to a fortune estimated to be in the millions.

"Isn't that curious?" he said. "It seems that our good doctor has been the fortunate beneficiary of an unfortunate hit and run in the past. I wonder what happened to the wife?"

A few minutes later Glenna found out.

She died in a fire, but not before leaving the bulk of the estate that she had inherited from her father to the Foundation for the Junior Blind.

"Her father isn't dead a year and his wife goes to bed with a cigarette and accidentally burns herself up."

"What else?" he asked, a grin on his face.

"Dr. Kohler didn't get the money."

"And what does that tell you?"

"That she didn't want him to have it."

"And why not?"

"Maybe she didn't love him?"

"Or?"

"Maybe she suspected he had something to do with the accident that killed her father?"

"Why?"

"Maybe she thought that it was a little fishy, her father dying the same way her mother and sister did."

"And maybe he tried to kill Jim Monday the same way," he said.

"Then you have him. This is all the proof you need."

"Not by a long shot," he said. "All we have here is tragic coincidence, not proof."

"Then what are we going to do?"

"Get the proof. That's what an investigator does." He printed out the story stuffed the printout into his pocket and said, "I think it's time we called Walker."

Washington picked up the phone and called the hospital. He glanced at his watch while the switchboard operator put him through. When he finally got Walker on the line he spoke quickly, telling him what they had learned.

"Good work." Walker sounded tired over the phone. "Have you seen the news?"

Washington said he hadn't and Walker told him about the latest developments. Two new dead men, attributed to Monday. His wife's twin and a woman, named Edna Lambert, missing. The media calling Monday a serial killer.

"Find him," Walker said. "Find him and clear him before someone puts a bullet in him."

"I'll do my level best," Washington said.

"And take care, Hugh," Walker said before hanging up.

"What do we do now?" Glenna asked.

"We drive to Lakewood and pay a visit to Jim Monday's mother-in-law."

"Why?"

"I'll fill you in on the way."

He finished the telling just as he was nosing into the driveway of a quiet house in a quiet residential neighborhood. The front yard was surrounded by a two foot hedge, there was a tire swing hanging from a giant shade tree in the front yard. The house was white, the shutters orange, the color of flames. It was a cheerful looking place and with a park across the street, a good place to bring up children.

He opened the door and got out, wondering, as he always did, how to handle the questioning. Glenna followed as he mounted the front porch. He pushed the bell and a tall patrician looking woman answered on the first ring. Her blue rinsed hair and no nonsense makeup told him there was only one tack to take with this lady. The truth. She would see through anything else.

He introduced himself as a police officer and showed her his badge. She introduced herself as Jean Barnes and she kept a poker face when he asked if she had seen the news.

"No, I seldom watch it in the afternoon. A thirty minute dose at six-thirty every night is quite enough, don't you think?"

"More than enough. Too much, probably." He smiled at her, then launched in with his story. "I'm going to be straight with you," he said, "because I don't have time to beat around the bush. Right now I'm a police officer. Tomorrow I probably won't be. And this young lady is my daughter, Glenna."

"I don't understand."

"Just let me finish."

"I'm all ears."

"My partner and I were across the street when David Askew was killed." He went on to tell her everything he could think of concerning the events of the last two days, including how Walker had employed him to clear Jim Monday.

"You know," she said, when he finished, "Jim and I have never been close. A personality conflict, I guess, but I know him well and I'll tell you one thing. He didn't do any of what you say he did."

"That's what we're trying to prove. That's why I need to talk to him."

"Why don't we go in and call him?"

"You know where he is?"

"Of course, Roma called me about an hour ago. We talk almost every day. Right now they're in Collinga, half way to San Francisco. They're staying at that beef ranch, the one with a little airport. I can't remember the name.

"Harris Ranch?" Glenna asked.

"That's the one."

Hugh looked at his daughter with raised eyebrows.

"Mom and I drove to San Francisco last month. We stopped there for lunch. They have the world's best beef."

"I thought you were a vegetarian?"

"Most of the time," she said with a wink.

"Let's go inside," Jean Barnes interrupted, "and I'll call him up."

They followed her into the neatly kept house and stood by as she dialed. She reached the Inn but there was no answer in their rooms.

"They're probably in the restaurant," she said.

"Mrs. Barnes, I think it's best if I go up there and I think Glenna should stay with you till I get back."

"No way. I'm going with you," Glenna said.

"Do you think it's dangerous?" Jean Barnes asked.

"No, and no," he said. "I want you here in case she gets through to Monday," he told his daughter. And I don't think it's dangerous. They're far out of harm's way out there in the middle of nowhere."

"Young man," Jean Barnes said, "I'm perfectly capable of getting a hold of my son-in-law. I'll call every half hour if I have to. Take your daughter with you, if it's not dangerous. You said you wanted to show her what it's like to be a cop. Well, show her."

"I was just afraid—"

"I know," she cut him off, "you were afraid that after he talked to me, he'd run away. Well don't worry, he won't. We may have our differences, but he knows I'd never lie to him. I'll tell him you're trying to help. He'll be waiting for you when you get there. Gratefully, I'm sure."

"I'm sorry, it'd be better if you didn't call. If you're wrong and he bolts, it could be catastrophic."

"How do you figure?"

"If he runs into another cop, one who doesn't believe he's innocent—and right now I'm about the only one looking for him who thinks he is—and that cop shoots first—" he let the sentence hang.

"I understand. I won't call."

He wanted to stay longer and question the woman further. He wanted to find out everything he could about Jim Monday, but there wasn't time. He wanted to leave Glenna with her, because he was afraid that it might, indeed, be dangerous. Trouble seemed to be following Monday, but he wanted to justify Walker's faith in him as quickly as possible. He needed that job. It would allow him to quit the department with dignity. So he agreed with her and took his daughter, when he knew he shouldn't.

CHAPTER EIGHT

JIM MONDAY WAS RIPPED FROM SLEEP by a rapping that knocked through him like gunfire. Someone was at the door.

"What?" He jumped out of bed, fighting to see in the dark and losing the battle. The rapping continued. "Who is it?" he said loud enough to be heard on the other side of the door, half expecting the police.

"It's Edna." Jim heard urgency in her voice.

"Just a second." He jumped into Turnbull's slacks, threw on his shirt and opened the door, allowing in the light and a pale Edna Lambert, followed by Roma.

"It's all over the television," Edna blurted out. "They're calling you a mass murderer. Every policeman in the state is looking for you."

"Slow down."

"Turn on CNN," Roma said.

"Slow down, tell me." He flipped on the light.

"My son came by the house, "Edna said." When I didn't answer, he let himself in and found the bodies. He called the police. It's all on the news."

"Wait a second," he went to the nightstand, picked up the remote, turned on the television, going through the channels until he found CNN's *Headline News*. He didn't have to wait long for the story.

The stiff looking newscaster finished a story on Eastern Europe, then went to a commercial. After the break he led with the Jim Monday story.

"And now more on the late breaking story from Long Beach, California. CNN has learned that, Jim Monday, ex-congressman and millionaire developer is also suspected in yesterday's early morning hit and run death of the famous Los Angeles Attorney, David Askew. That brings to six the number of people Monday has allegedly killed. And still missing are Miss Roma Barnes and Mrs. Edna Lambert. Their fate is unknown, but in light of Monday's killing spree, the worst is expected."

Jim hit the power button on the remote as his picture was shown on the screen and the television flicked off. He didn't want to hear anymore.

"How did they know about you?" he said to Roma."

"They found the car, wrecked."

And when Eddie, that's my boy," Edna said, "found the bodies and called the police they assumed, since Roma's car was near my house and since you had just killed three people in the police station less than an hour earlier, that you might be connected with the two dead men in my living room, so they checked for your fingerprints."

"How do you know all this?"

"We didn't turn it off before the end of the story," Roma said.

"I keep getting in deeper."

"Well, I can damn sure set them straight about the dead men in my house. I'll just ring up the police and tell them what happened. I'll tell them that I'm still alive, too."

"What do you think, Jim?" Roma said.

"I think Edna's right, you two should go back and explain it all to the police. Once they see that you're still alive and you explain about the two dead men in Edna's living room, and how it was self defense, they'll know I'm no serial killer. And once they find out those two attorneys were fakes, they'll know they came into the police station to kill me, and that would be self defense, too."

"What about the dead policeman?" Roma asked.

"If you can make them believe someone is trying to kill me, then they'll believe those men killed the policeman."

"So all we have to do is go back and tell our story and everything will be okay?" Roma said.

"Should be."

"Then why don't you come with us?" Roma said. "That seems the smartest thing to do. If you're guilty, you'd never turn yourself in. With us as witnesses and your surrender, they'd have to believe us."

"I'd like nothing better, but someone sent those men after me and he'll do it again. I believe it was Bernd Kohler. I can't prove it and until I can, I'm not turning myself in."

"He's right," Edna said, "but you're still going to need help."

"I have to do this on my own. I would never forgive myself if anything happened to you either of you."

"I know one way I can help," Edna said. "I can get you some identification and credit cards. You don't look that much like my son, but you have the same nose and you both have blue eyes and he has that bushy beard. It might work." She went to the phone.

"Who are you calling?" Jim asked.

"Why Eddie of course," she twinkled. "He'll come right up with his passport, drivers license and credit cards."

"How do you know he won't call the police?"

"For the same reason that I'm helping you. He got home because you stayed on the ground, alone, covering that chopper. Like me, he owes you a debt that can never be repaid."

Jim didn't try to stop her as she made the call, because he knew she was right. Without ID he wasn't going to get very far. He sat on the bed next to Roma as Edna made the call and watched a gecko dart across the wall.

"It will be all right," he told Roma, as Edna Lambert talked in the background.

"I hope so," she said. "I really hope so."

"Oh, and Eddie," they heard Edna say, "bring a spare eye patch." She hung up and faced the couple sitting on the end of the bed. "He's leaving right now, he'll be here in four hours."

They spent the next hour going over all their options, but in the end they agreed that Jim was right. The best thing would be for the women to return to Long Beach and try to clear him. Once it was decided, there was nothing more to be gained by discussion. The women went back to their room to rest and wait for Eddie Lambert.

Jim lay on his bed and stared at the connecting door. He half wanted Roma to come through it and he half feared she would. Twice he got up and started for it and twice he went back to the bed.

He could only imagine what was going through her mind. Was she eager and afraid, or did she regret what had happened. Was she watching the door from the other side, like him, and, like him, was she thinking about her twin sister.

He closed his eyes and tried to get some sleep.

"*Go to her,*" Donna thought.

"*I can't,*" he thought back and then he shut Donna out of his mind.

The phone woke him from a restless sleep a few hours later.

"Hello."

"Eddie's here," Edna said.

"I'll be right over."

When he went over he was introduced to Eddie Lambert. His wild hair, beard and muscular build made him giant looking, but he was no taller than Jim and his eye patch gave him a menacing look, till he smiled and the twinkle in his single eye glowed. He dressed in Levi's, running shoes and a flannel shirt, the kind the surfers wore. His handshake was firm and friendly. Jim liked him immediately.

"Mom explained the whole thing." He handed Jim a passport, credit cards, driver's license and an eye patch. "With this on and your short hair, you could probably pass for me. Anybody looking at the picture would have a hard time figuring out what I really looked like under all this hair." He had a low easy voice.

"I hope this doesn't get you in too much trouble." Jim flipped the passport open and agreed. It would be hard, at first glance, to tell that Jim was not the same man in the photo. If he wore the eye patch, he could probably pass all but the most thorough of inspections.

"Naw, if anything happens because of it, I'll just say I thought I left my wallet at work. That's why I didn't report it missing."

"I'll pay you back for anything I might have to charge on your cards."

"It's not necessary. I owe you."

"I appreciate it, but I can afford it and I'd feel better if I could pay you back."

"If it's what you want, but you don't have to."

Jim looked at Eddie's running shoes.

"I've got a pair of shoes that are about a size too tight and they're killing my feet."

"Mine are eights. Sorry," Eddie said, looking at Jim's large feet.

"They looked small, but I had to ask," Jim said.

The group spent a few minutes making small talk, before Jim retold the events of the last two days for Eddie's benefit.

"So if it was you," Jim asked Eddie, "would you go after Kohler or go to the police?"

"Go after Kohler," he said, without hesitation.

"That's how I feel. I just wanted to hear somebody else say it."

Fifteen minutes later, after having decided that Eddie would take the girls back at first light, Roma asked Jim to take a walk with her.

"Where to?"

"To the mini market other side of the highway. I've got a sweet tooth that I very rarely indulge, but tonight I feel like a candy bar."

A walk across the highway in the tight shoes was the last thing he wanted to do, but Roma was going to be spending the remainder of the night with Edna and he was going to be bunking with Eddie, so it was probably the last time they'd get to spend together till this was all over.

"I feel kind of like I'm having sex behind my momma's back," Roma said as soon as they started out.

"We could get our own room."

"No, then I'd feel cheap."

He put his good arm around her and felt a little rebuffed when she shrugged away, laughing like a little girl.

They walked across a grassy lawn to the main building, where they cut across the parking lot to the access road, then about a hundred yards to the highway, then they crossed on the overpass and then on to the all night mini market on the other side of Highway 5. A quarter mile in all. A silent quarter mile.

They entered the market and Roma picked up two Snickers Bars while Jim went to the magazine section and flipped through Business Week. Roma held up the candy bars for him to see and beamed a smile at him. Then she screamed and jumped back as a gecko went scurrying across the floor.

"I've never seen anything like that in here," the girl behind the counter said, screwing up her face and accenting her pimples. "Looked like a slimy lizard."

"I saw one in my room, over at the Inn," Roma said.

"Wait till I tell Dad," the girl said. "He thinks he knows everything there is to know about every kind of animal we've got out here, but I bet he's never heard of slimy lizards."

"It's only a gecko." Jim, having spent part of his life in Southeast Asia, was used to them, so when he saw one earlier, he didn't think much about it, but it was strange, seeing them where they weren't supposed to be.

"Let's go back," Roma said, clearly embarrassed by her outburst. Jim paid and she put the candy bars in the handbag she'd gotten from Edna, next to the gun.

They walked back over the interstate, stopping to watch the late night travelers and truckers tunnel through the night below. White headlights approaching, headed toward San Francisco, red tail lights receding, going south to Los Angeles.

Jim moved closer to Roma, looked up as the full moon found a hole in the clouds, briefly brightening the night.

"You know I've always loved you," Roma said as she gently pushed him away, so she could see his face lit up by the passing headlights. Then she asked, "Were you happy?"

"I thought we were. I loved your sister with all my heart, like I used to love you so long ago. We wanted the same things, enjoyed the same friends, shopped, spent money. I honestly don't know where it went wrong."

"I want you, Jimmy," she said.

"Right here?" he smiled.

"No, not here. I want you forever."

"We have to give it time."

"No, I don't want to give it time."

"What about Julia?"

"She's got her doctor. She can't have you."

"She's your sister."

"And she loves me and will understand."

"There's so much happening right now. I really do need some time," he said. "Time to find out what's going on. Who's trying to kill me and why. Right now I believe it's Kohler, but what if it isn't?"

"Dammit, I don't want you out there risking your life. Come back with us. Let the police handle it."

"I can't run away," he said.

"Then come back with us and work with the police. That makes more sense. I don't want to lose you. I need you."

Part of him wanted to go back with her. But the common sense part of him knew it would never work. The press would have a field day. They would hound him unmercifully about marrying his wife's twin. There would always be talk. Heads would always turn, then turn away. They would become the fodder for gossip magazines and tabloids. It wasn't the kind of life he wanted to lead. His privacy would be over.

"They would never leave us alone. They'd make our lives miserable."

"We don't have to let them. We can go away. Someplace where they've never heard of you. Spain, maybe, or an island in the South Pacific, or Greece. There's lots of places where they don't watch the news or read the *Times*, places where the sun always shines and it's safe to go out after dark."

She hugged him tightly and he kissed her long and slow and his heart cried out to her.

"All right," he said, breaking the kiss, "I'll go back with you."

"Oh Jimmy!" She squeezed him like a little girl on Christmas morning with her first puppy. "It'll be okay. I just know it. Together we can face anything."

He smiled at her through the dark and they started back for the motel. Roma, planning a new life and Jim already missing his old one. He loved his country and the thought of living someplace else made him feel like a traitor. He'd fought and paid dearly for America and he didn't begrudge his country the price she asked. It was worth it and if she asked it again, especially in light of what happened on Nine-Eleven, he would pay it again.

But if he had to decide between his country and Roma, he would have to take Roma and make a life somewhere else. In Europe, England probably. He was too old to learn a foreign language.

"We could live in England or Scotland. Maybe in a small town," he said.

"I'd like that." She leaned into him as they walked under a dark, starless sky.

They stopped again, halfway between the motel and the interstate and hugged.

"Listen!" Donna interrupted Jim's thoughts.

"Don't move." Jim tensed up as he whispered in Roma's ear.

She froze, sensing the urgency in his voice. She clutched the handbag, looping her finger through the hole and onto the trigger and she remained perfectly quiet. She didn't have to be told twice.

"Something up ahead, between you and your motel, can you hear?"

He listened.

"Yes." He heard a faint breathing sound, like a man with asthma, trying to hide a wheeze, and it was coming closer, and the wheeze was getting deeper.

"Time to move on. Now!" Donna urged.

Jim squeezed Roma's arm to get her attention and they backed away from the wheezing, back toward the sounds of the interstate and the brightly lit up mini market on the other side.

The wheezing moved off to their left and away from them and for a second Jim thought about making a dash for the motel. But he didn't want to run, to put his back to whatever was out there. He wasn't afraid of the animal, it was probably only a stray coyote. It sounded sick. It wasn't anything he couldn't handle, even without the gun and Roma's deadeye aim. But it only seemed prudent to move out of the dark and into the light.

Then the sound faded all together.

"I feel like a frightened child," she said. "Like I'm standing in the hall, by the fire alarm, in school and the big kids are coming for my lunch money. I want to break the glass and call the firemen, but I'm too afraid."

"Don't worry, you've got the fire extinguisher in your purse."

"I know," she said, clutching the gun.

"All of a sudden I want a cigarette," he said, leading the way back toward the overpass and the mini market beyond.

"But you don't smoke?"

"I do tonight." He didn't know why he needed to smoke, he never had, but the desire was strong and now the mini market was closer than the motel, presenting a safe haven.

"It's me, I want the cigarette."

"But I don't smoke," he thought.

"You want to go to the market anyway, I can tell, and I really need a cigarette."

He cut her thoughts off and stopped as Roma's fingers dug into his good arm. The wheezing coyote was ahead of them, still cloaked in darkness, blocking their path. Stalking them.

Her grip tightened as it moved around to their left and moved in closer, still in the dark, but Jim could tell by the sounds it was making that it was no coyote.

"Come on." He led her north, parallel to the interstate, but separated from it by a drainage ditch and a chain link fence. There would be no mad dash across the highway.

"What is it?" she asked, fright beginning to creep into her voice.

As if hearing her, the animal responded with a deep throated sound, a cross between a raspy roar and a baby's cry, that brought the fright rushing full force into her voice.

"Come on, quick," she urged, picking up the pace.

He hesitated. They had a gun. It made more sense to stand. There was nothing up ahead except cattle pens a good quarter mile away. No, the sensible thing to do was stand and if the animal attacked, shoot it.

It roared its crying-baby-lion roar again, louder and Jim changed his mind. Maybe the gun wouldn't stop it. Maybe it was rabid. There would be someone at the cow pens ahead. There would be light. He matched Roma's quick walk.

The animal stayed behind, out of sight, until the smell of thousands of cows assaulted them. The raspy roars came closer together as they got closer to the pens, and it quickened its pace, forcing the pair into a jog and finally into a run.

It picked up speed, starting to close in on them. It let out a roar that ripped into the night, waking the cows, causing them to stir silently, resembling large ghost like animals in the murky night. And Jim knew the animal, whatever it was, was going to charge, to come for them, to kill them.

It roared again, closer. They were running flat out toward the pens, but Jim saw they would never make it.

"*Jump!*" Donna's thought-scream ripped through him, a lightning-warning. He grabbed Roma's hand, pulling her with him as he jumped feet first into the ditch that ran along the highway. They landed in the bottom vee of the ditch, Jim on his feet, Roma on her rear, six feet below the beast above and they both shivered as it roared again and moved off. Jim helped her up and they hugged in the dark—cut off from the highway, the cows, the pens, the beast and reality—by the sides of the ditch.

The dark closed in and the fresh-grave atmosphere of the ditch offered no safety. It would only be a matter of seconds before their stalker came in after them. He took her by the hand and led her, limping and falling in the wet dirt, toward the pens.

Above and behind them, they heard the sound of sliding dirt and tumbling rocks. It was sliding down the side, coming in after them. They heard it hit bottom and Jim wished they could see, so that Roma could get off a shot. But all he could do was pull her away from the steady machine-like wheezing that was down in the coffin-like enclosure with them.

When Jim judged they were below the pens, he started to climb, pulling Roma up with him. The animal was coming fast. Roma jerked her arm free from Jim's grip and turned, with her finger through the hole in the hand bag, on the trigger and waited. The wheezing increased its tempo and lowered its pitch. They felt its strength steamrolling toward them. Then they saw its wide set yellow eyes, glowing fire-bright in the night and Roma fired the weapon.

The moon peeked through a hole in the clouds, but Roma didn't need the light, because the flaming yellow eyes presented her with a target too close and too terrifying to miss. She fired three shots between the two glowing yellow orbs and was rewarded with a roar that shook the night. The thing stopped, the light in the eyes dimmed, but didn't go out.

Jim grabbed her arm and hand in a Viking grip and jerked her up and out of the ditch. They ran toward the pens, visible now in the full moonlight. He felt the weight of the cast on one arm and the drag of Roma on the other. He was afraid he wasn't going to make it. Then he heard the thing scrambling out of the ditch behind them. He forced heart and muscle to give a little more, got his second wind and pulled her with him toward the wooden fence as the clouds aloft again blacked out the moon. The gunshots had slowed, but not stopped the beast.

The cattle, agitated now and afraid, began milling and bleating as Jim and Roma reached the fence. In tandem they hit the ground, rolled under and they were instantly covered in manure and in danger of being trampled by the nervous cattle.

They got up and started to make their way through the fenced in herd, each step burying their feet in manure as they climbed a mountain of the muck. They instinctively headed toward the center of the fenced in pen, dodging between the animals like they were winding through a maze. Then the animals began to settle down and Jim felt a tug on his good arm as Roma stumbled and fell.

He helped her up and for what seemed like the thousandth time that night, they tried to hug their fright away. Then, with the cattle quiet, they moved through them toward the other side of the pen. He wanted out of the enclosure before the animals panicked.

When they slid under the fence the danger outside far outweighed the danger inside, but now Jim was acutely aware of what could happen inside and had no desire to be crushed. He was glad when again the clouds allowed a hint of light through the dark and he saw the other side of the pen only feet away.

He made for the fence, confident that the animal with the yellow eyes had gone. The cattle were quiet, sensing no danger and that was a good sign. He allowed himself to breathe a sigh of relief as he reached his hand out to the fence.

Another roar ripped the night apart. It must have circled around, upwind. Now it was among the herd. The cattle started to panic, bleating, wailing, pushing against each other and them. Roma's hand was ripped out of his as she was trampled by a frightened cow. She screamed and he turned to help, when another roar hurled forth and he saw the beast, a giant lizard-like animal, leap onto the back of a frightened cow, then dive on Roma, mouth wide, showing razor teeth in the moonlight. He watched in horror as it dragged her among the swirling cattle. Then he lost sight of her, as clouds again covered the moon, plunging the cattleyard into blackness and dark night.

He started toward her, screaming, but in the dark he ran into one of the frightened animals and was knocked down. Something banged him in the head and his world went as black as the cattleyard.

CHAPTER NINE

HUGH WASHINGTON AND HIS DAUGHTER rode in silence on their way to the freeway and the beginning of their four hour drive to Collinga. He broke the quiet as they entered the on ramp.

"I lied when I said it wouldn't be dangerous. It could be."

"I know."

"So I want you to stay well out of the way until I see how it's going to go."

"Dad!"

"Promise me or I'll turn the car around and take you home right now."

"Okay."

"Okay, what?"

"Okay, I promise I'll stay out of the way until you make sure it's safe."

"That's better," he said. "When we get there you wait in the car till I question them. Once I make sure everything's all right, I'll come and get you."

"I'll feel like a kid." She pouted. He always bent when she pouted. She could get anything she wanted out of him. But this time he remained firm.

"My way or no way," he said in his policeman's iron voice.

"Your way," she said and the subject was closed. For the rest of the trip they talked about her school, her friends, her job and police work in general. It was almost like they were on a holiday drive. She liked being with him. She liked how he was intensely interested in anything she did. He was her dad and she loved him.

Because of the rush hour traffic leaving Los Angeles, the normal four hour trip took six. Six hours that went by like twenty minutes, with *Power Glide* delivering a smooth, air conditioned ride. Father and daughter had a way of talking, laughing and kidding each other that moved time aside and the forty-five-year-old Chevrolet helped to keep it away.

It was nine-thirty and the night was cloud covered and dark, when he took the Collinga off ramp and steered the car toward the Harris Ranch Inn. He turned into the parking lot, picked a spot opposite the driveway and backed in.

"You still position yourself for the quick getaway," Glenna said.

"I'm not the only one," he said, indicating a white Ford Explorer with a nod of the head.

"Think he's a macho man, too?" Glenna teased.

"I don't think I'm macho, just prepared."

"Okay, Dad, I'm sorry." She was trying to keep a straight face, but her stomach muscles were shaking involuntarily. She was silently laughing at him. He smiled, then jammed his finger into her stomach and tickled her like he did when she'd been a little girl. She burst into laughter and he laughed with her. It felt good.

We'll check into the hotel," he said. "I'd feel better if you were tucked into a warm room, behind a locked door, than sitting out in the car."

She didn't argue.

They approached the reception desk, tired, but full of energy. They seemed to be charging each other. He was close to his quarry, she was with her father, her hero, and they felt the electrons in the night air.

"We'd like two rooms," he told the young man behind the desk. Then he screwed up his nose. "Jeez, what's that?"

"Wind shifted. Usually it goes the other direction, but when it blows south, we get the smell of thousands of beef cattle. You get used to it," he said.

"I don't know if I ever could," her dad said.

"You have the greenest eyes," Glenna told the man. She was direct and disarming.

"Yeah," he said, "if my hair would have been any other color, maybe they wouldn't stand out so much, but it's red and they do."

"My father and I are supposed to meet some friends of ours here," she said, laughing. "Could you tell us if they've checked in?"

"I just got on, but I'll be glad to check. What's the name?"

"Barnes," she said, "Jim and Roma Barnes." She wanted to show her father that she had a flair for detective work and she figured there was a pretty good chance that Monday and his sister-in-law might be using her name, because no way could they use his.

She knew she'd done good and she felt an inner glow when she saw her father's smile of approval.

The desk clerk punched a computer keyboard, stared at the screen for a few seconds, then said, "Nope. I got a Lambert, two doubles. A Holiday, a double. And a Ross, two doubles. No others, it's a slow night. Looks like you beat them in. Want me to tell them you're here when they arrive?"

"That would be nice." She was upset that her gambit hadn't succeeded in finding Monday, but it had, she just didn't know it.

Five minutes later she was sitting on her father's bed, the door to their connecting rooms open. He sat down next to her.

"Why don't you pick up the phone and see if you charm that clerk into telling you what room Edna Lambert was in," he said.

She wondered who Edna Lambert was, but she called the clerk as he'd asked and though that red-headed kid probably wasn't supposed to give her the information, he was more than happy to. Sometimes being young and pretty paid off.

"She's in Room 221," Glenna said.

"And that's where we'll find our man."

"How did you know about this Edna Lambert person?" she asked.

"Walker told me. It was on the news. I'll go right over and talk to Monday. Tell him that I'm on his side. Then we'll see where we go from there."

"I'm going with you."

"No, I let you come this far, but first I want to talk to him alone. I'd never forgive myself if he did something stupid and you got hurt."

"Dad, I'm not a little girl anymore. I'm going."

"No, that's final. Please don't make me regret bringing you."

"Okay, I'll wait here till you call, like a good girl." Usually she had him wrapped around her little finger, but there was that occasional time when he drew the line in the sand and she knew better than to try and cross it.

She watched him cross the manicured courtyard to the building opposite. Since the back of the main building faced the courtyard, he would have to walk through the lobby to get to Edna Lambert's room. She watched his back till he disappeared into the lobby, then she reached into her purse for a cigarette. Three left, she would have to go easy. She lit up and inhaled the blue smoke and tried not to worry.

* * *

When Hugh Washington went through the lobby, he felt that old chill run through him—the goosebumps on his arms, the tingling skin—these were the caution signs. He slipped his hand under the sweatshirt and withdrew the thirty-eight from the shoulder holster. He held it easily in his right hand as he slid both hand and pistol behind his back. Better safe than sorry.

He took the stairs to the second floor, silent as a cat burglar. He stepped on the walkway, looked out across the flatland, inhaled the cattle smell and thought about becoming a vegetarian. Then he snapped back to the task at hand and started toward Room 221. His stomach tightened as he approached the room and he tightened his hold on the gun. The door was ajar, sending a sliver of light into the dark night. He listened for a few seconds. Not a sound. He eased it open and was assaulted by the coppery smell and the attacking sight of blood.

He jumped back and grabbed the railing to keep from falling over the side. He caught his breath, groped for command of his senses. His heart was racing, sweat ran down the back of his neck. He was going to have to go in there.

He steeled his mind, flexed the muscles along the curve of his back and rocked his head around in two quick circles, hearing the creak at the base of his skull. Calm down, he told himself, you've done this before and you can do it now. Damn good thing you made Glenna stay back. He entered the room, fighting to keep his Italian lunch in his stomach.

Never in all his years on the force had he seen anything like this. The four walls, the carpet and the ceiling were covered in splashes of blood, like a giant child had slopped red paint throughout the room. The bedclothes were soaked in red and his reflection through the red tinged mirror looked like a photo from hell. There were no bodies, just the blood—buckets of blood.

He had to check the bathroom for bodies. He picked his way across the room, doing his best to avoid the wet bloodstains on the carpet. He looked down at his new, now red tinged, running shoes and wished that he had worn the old pair. He eased a shaking hand toward the bathroom doorknob, opening it with two fingers. The sound of the door creaking was like a knife blade to his heart, but the sight inside the bathroom mitigated some of the blade's pressure. No bodies, no blood, just a normal bathroom, clean and white, a stark contrast to the room he had just crossed through.

Quick thought, call Glenna. Second thought, call the police. The first thought was the most paramount. He went to the phone, called his daughter and told her what he found.

"I'll be right over," she said.

"No!" he said. "Stay where you are and lock the door. Under no circumstances are you to open that door for anyone but me. Do you understand?"

"Yes, Dad," she said.

"I'll be here a while, so don't worry. I'm gonna call the cops and I'm sure they're not gonna pat me on the back and say, 'Good job, you can go now.' No ma'am, they're gonna nail my black ass to the wall once they find out I was chasing a suspected murderer into their ballpark without informing them."

"So don't call them."

"I have to. I want to know who or what did this and the quickest way is for me to be on the inside. Don't worry, I can handle it. I've been there before. Now I gotta go. Lock the door, okay?"

"I'm locking it now," she said. Then she added, "I'll see you when you get here."

"Love you," he said.

"Love you too, Dad."

* * *

On the one hand she understood why he wanted her out of the way. He was her father. Protecting her came natural to him, but dammit, she didn't want to be left out. She wasn't a little girl. She was living on her own, earning her own income. She lit a cigarette. Life is so unfair, she thought.

Maybe she should just go on over there. What could he say? He'd have to let her stay, to let her see the murder scene and the investigation first hand. But she knew if she disobeyed him, he would pack her back to Long Beach on the first bus out of town. No, she would have to do as she was told and earn his respect.

She decided to take a bath. She took the last drag off the cigarette, then stubbed it out in a crystal ashtray. She went into the bathroom and turned on the hot water, checking it with her hand under the flow. When it was hot, she added the cold. She let the water run while she undressed. Then she padded into the bedroom and picked up her pack of cigarettes off the nightstand.

Only one left. Damn. She loved to sit in the tub and smoke and think and this was definitely a three or four cigarette bath coming up. She went back to the bathroom, checked the water. Too cold. She turned off the cold and turned the hot down to a slow trickle.

Then she remembered her father always had a spare pack in the glove compartment. She smiled as she jumped into her Levi's, ignoring her panties. She pulled on her tee shirt, leaving the bra where it had fallen on the bathroom floor. She thought about the shoes, but it was a warm night and she liked going barefoot. She went through the connecting doors, picked up her father's keys from the nightstand. Then she started for the door. She would have her four cigarette bath after all.

She left the room, smiling as she felt the cool tile of the walkway on her bare feet. The rock tile stairs sent little shivers of feeling from her feet to her shins. It felt good. At the bottom of the stairs she started for the car, then thought, one peek, from a distance, what could it hurt. Her father need never know.

She walked through the parking lot, glanced at *Power Glide* and kept walking. She didn't want to go through the lobby, so she walked around the main building, trying to see which room her father was in. The sound of a distant siren pierced the night, getting closer. She ran from the motel part of the complex to the restaurant, where she hid by the side of the building. She didn't have to wait long.

Two black and white cruisers pulled into the parking lot, sirens blazing, lights flashing. She watched as two officers emerged from each car. They talked for a few seconds, then all four went up the steps. Two held back at the top of the stairs, just in case, she thought. Just in case her father came out shooting. But before the other two reached the room, the door opened and her father came out, hands well away from his body.

"I'm a police officer." He said, showing his shield in his right hand.

"Then you'll understand when we tell you to step away from the door, turn and face the wall, put your hands on the wall and spread 'em." Her dad tossed the uniformed officer his shield then did as he was told.

"I have a thirty-eight, in a right shoulder holster," he said to the officer frisking him. The policeman removed it and stepped back.

"Give him back his piece. This is the guy that called it in," the other officer said.

Glenna stood silent and still, seeing and hearing everything, afraid to move, afraid to breathe, until her father and the four officers entered the room. They didn't close the door, but she was confident they couldn't see her through the cloud covered, dark night. She was about to make her way back to the parking lot when she felt something on her bare left foot. She looked down and stifled a scream as she jerked her foot up, shaking the gecko off, sending it flying into the night.

Shaken, she shivered. She needed a cigarette. She walked across the cool grass next to the brick walkway, preferring the feel of the grass on her bare feet. She covered the distance from the restaurant to the parking lot in quick, lengthy strides. She wanted the cigarettes and she wanted to be back up in her room in a nice peaceful bath, soaking in hot-as-could-be water. She wished she had some bubble bath.

She slowed her pace when she reached the parking lot, taking short, shallow steps toward the car. She'd skinned her feet when she was a little girl, pushing a new bicycle down their asphalt driveway on a cold Christmas morning. Ever since, whenever she walked barefoot on asphalt, chills ran from the balls of her feet to the back of her neck.

She was fifteen strides into the parking lot and halfway to the car, when the winds aloft opened a patch of sky, showing the full moon and removing the veil of darkness that covered the ground. Her spirits lightened and she anticipated the taste of one of her father's stale Marlboros. She picked up her pace and stubbed her toe. Damn. She stopped. It hurt. There was blood. She started limping toward the car. She heard something. She stopped, cautious, like a deer that had just heard a twig snap.

She heard it again. A scraping sound. Still she didn't move. The sound stopped and for a full fifteen seconds she stood stock still. She heard it again. Something scraping along the asphalt, for only an instant, then it stopped.

"Is somebody there?" she queried, in a small, soft voice.

A low animal sound answered. A rumbling sound, a bass sound—halfway between a giant cat-purr and a rough, dog-like growl. She reached into her pocket, took out her father's keys. The animal sound was moving behind the parking lot, to her right. If she could get in the car and lock it, she would be safe. Oblivious to the pain in her foot she started slowly, carefully toward the car. The sound got louder and she picked up her pace. All of a sudden it was in front of her, coming from somewhere close to the Chevy. Her safe haven was cut off.

She stopped, backed up two paces, then stopped again. The moving clouds partly covered the moon, cutting off most of the light, but not all of it. She strained her eyes, willing them to see through the night. The animal growled again. She wanted to run, but didn't. It's a dog, she told herself. A dog, nothing else. Probably a watch dog. She wasn't afraid of dogs. She had a way with them. Even when she was a little girl, she had been able to tame the meanest, mangiest dog in the neighbor hood, Mr. Howard's German Shepherd, with her soothing voice and her lack of fear. Dogs sensed fear and she was never afraid. Not of dogs. Her father said that she must have been a golden collie in another life and, when she was a child, she believed him, because dogs, all dogs, seemed to love her.

"Here boy," she said, "I won't hurt you."

Silence.

She made a clicking sound, encouraging the animal to come forward.

Silence.

Her fear contained, her confidence returned, she started toward the car, taking six inch, oh-so-slow steps, with her hand outstretched, palm down. "Easy, boy. Easy. I won't hurt you."

The animal growled, a deep, raw, throaty sound. She stopped. It didn't sound like a dog. But what else could it be out here in the middle of nowhere. A coyote, maybe? Unlikely, they stay away from people. Something bigger? A bear? No, there were no bears here. In the mountains maybe, but not here. No, it was a dog, nothing else, nothing to be afraid of.

She made the clicking sound again.

"Come on out, I won't hurt you."

It answered with another deep growl, a bottomless sound, a train deep in a water well, rumbling out of the dark and the wet. It was a dog, it couldn't be anything else.

But it sounded like it might be hurt. Would her magic work on an injured animal. Maybe it was hungry. Hungry and hurt. Maybe it was a wild dog. No, that didn't make sense. There were no wild dogs out here. Were there? Maybe. There were people, a town, there could be wild dogs. But she had never heard of a wild dog attacking people. No it had to be a watch dog and she could deal with a watch dog.

She started to call out again, when the animal growl turned into a tiger-like roar. A quiet roar, but a roar nonetheless. It wasn't a dog. She wanted to move, but couldn't. Some invisible force was pressing down on her. Holding her feet planted to the ground. She was a tree and her feet were roots, betraying her by clawing into the asphalt. She was helpless. Her body shook, she could feel the sweat under her arms. She tried in vain to quell her quivering thighs. She tried to control her quick shallow breaths, but her racing heart was in charge, she was panting, like a dog on a hot summer's day. She wanted to scream, but the invisible force turned her scream into a whimper.

She heard the scraping again and her eyes were glued to the direction of the sound. They were glued to her father's fifty-nine Impala. Glued through the dark. The clouds stirred above and again allowed the moonlight to chase away enough of the dark to allow her to see clearly. There was something under her Dad's car and it wasn't a dog.

It slithered forward, till its head was under the front grill. Its bright yellow eyes centered between

Power Glide's headlights. Its reptilian head reminded her of a giant gecko, till it opened its mouth and she saw the scissor-like teeth. Teeth that more rightly belonged in the mouth of a thresher shark. This was a bad thing.

It was crouching under the car and she knew why. It was waiting for her. As clear as a winter dawn, she knew that this thing was connected some way with the gecko she'd shaken from her foot earlier. Somehow that gecko was a warning, a warning she'd failed to heed. She was being warned away, but from what. Her mind raged and her heart raced. If she knew, if she only knew, she would stay away. Oh God, she would stay away.

The thing thrust clawed feet in front of itself and pulled its way from under the car, making the scraping sound she'd heard earlier. She watched as it emerged, like a dragon from its den, till it was standing, a giant gecko with shark's teeth, breathing steam on a hot night, captivating her with its glowing yellow eyes, the yellow moonlight reflecting off its smooth green skin, giving it an iridescent, radioactive glow.

It looked slimy.

She was too stunned to scream. Too stunned to run. Her root-like feet refused to obey. The thing inched forward, opening and closing its bear trap jaws, slamming its shark teeth together with the finality and fury of a jail door.

The thing came at her fast. She could do nothing. She was helpless. She was going to die and there was nothing she could do about it.

Then she heard the sound of tires spinning, smelled the smoke of rubber burning and saw the white Ford Explorer come leaping forward.

The reptile thing was less then a yard from her, jaws open wide, the stench of its foul breath stinging her nostrils, its eyes tearing through to her very core, when the Explorer struck it square in the side, sending it flying away from her. It turned, yellow eyes glazed, and let out a roar that ripped through the night and made her flesh crawl.

"Get in!" The driver flung the passenger door open and she sprang to life.

The slimy lizard thing with the hot breath roared again, only momentarily stunned. It started for her, but this time her feet had wings and she dove into the open door and slammed it shut as Jim Monday put his foot to the floor and once again she heard screeching tires as the back end of the Explorer fishtailed out of the parking lot.

CHAPTER TEN

HE SPUN THE CAR TO THE LEFT, in the direction of the slide, and tightened his hands on the wheel, until the tires bit into the road. He concentrated on the ramp ahead. The speedometer read forty when he entered it, heading toward San Francisco, sixty when they shot out onto the interstate.

He let the needle climb to seventy-five, thought about passing the semi ahead, then decided against it. He didn't want to be stopped for speeding. He settled back, slowed to sixty-five and rode in the wake of the big truck.

Then the girl screamed.

"Please stop." He glanced over at her. "I'm not going to hurt you."

She screamed louder. She was shaking, hands pushing against the dash for support.

"Please!" He raised his voice more than he wanted.

She stopped. He grabbed another quick look. Sweat ringed her forehand. Small spasms seemed to be running through her body, but the violent shaking had stopped.

"You're safe now. That thing can't get you here."

She was quietly sobbing.

"Are you all right?"

She nodded, wiping a tear from her eye with a bent finger.

"I'm Jim Monday." He glanced at her when he said it, saw a flicker of understanding. "You must know who I am. I saw you when you arrived with that policeman. I was hiding in the shrubbery, by the parking lot. I snuck in the car after you went to check in. I needed sleep. Then I saw that thing creeping out from under your car before I had a chance to nod off. How did Washington know where I was?"

She didn't answer and he put her out of his mind as he followed the big truck north.

Ten miles later she said, "You stink."

He was covered in wet cow manure. It was in his hair, on his face, neck and arms. It was seeping through his clothes. He was surprised that it didn't repulse him, surprised that he'd adjusted so quickly.

"Compared with that thing back there, a little cow shit is the least of my problems."

"They'll catch you pretty quick looking and smelling like that."

"Where's your shoes?" he asked, looking down at her bleeding foot.

"I only went to get cigarettes from the car. I should have listened to my father and stayed in the room."

"Washington is your father?"

"Yes," she said. "My name's Glenna and he's my dad."

"And he brought you along after a killer?"

"He doesn't think you're a killer. He wants to prove you're not."

"I am," he said, knuckles white on the wheel.

"No, my dad wouldn't try to clear you if you were guilty." She was running her hands through her hair now, pulling it back. Then she wiped the sweat from her forehead with the back of her hand.

"I didn't say I was guilty. I killed two of the ones in the police station. Not the cop." He relaxed his fingers, now holding the wheel like it was a thing to be caressed.

"And the ones at the motel?" she asked.

"What are you talking about?" He white-knuckled the wheel again as a chill whipped up his spine, lightning-quick, but glacier-cold.

"My Dad went to Edna Lambert's room to find you. He said the walls were covered in blood."

"And the Lamberts?"

"There were no bodies," she said with a lost little girl voice. She was still very frightened.

"That thing killed Roma."

"Your wife's twin," she said. It wasn't a question.

He nodded and they rode the next ten miles without speaking.

"You know," she said, breaking the silence, "you still stink. Don't look very pretty either."

"I'm in a hurry."

"For what?"

"To get to Tampico."

"You're convinced Kohler is behind the attempts on your life?"

"You know a lot."

"Dad and I talk."

"Yes, I believe Kohler's trying to kill me."

"Why?"

"That's the question, isn't it? He already has my wife. She'll get half my money. So why? It doesn't make sense. But it's him. I believe it and if you'd been through what I have, you'd believe it too."

"I didn't say I didn't believe you."

"What about your father?"

"He's trying to prove you're innocent." She sat back in the seat, sighed. She sounded more like a woman now, her voice soft and sure. She didn't seem afraid anymore.

"I wish I could believe that," Monday said, again relaxing his hands on the wheel. Earlier he was afraid she'd go ballistic on him. Scream, rage, maybe go into shock. She was past that now. She'd adjusted quickly. She was stronger than she looked.

"It's true," she said.

"Then I wish him luck."

"So you're on your way to Tampico to confront Kohler and fight to the death?"

"No, yes, I don't know, something like that, maybe."

"How far do you think you'll get smelling like that?"

"Far enough."

"And when is the last time you had some sleep? You look dead behind the wheel. You'll never make it another three hundred miles without rest."

"I'll make it."

"And what about me? What are you going to do with me?"

"I'll let you go at the next city."

"You can't."

"Why not?"

"I could talk. I know where you're going."

"You said your father is trying to clear me."

"But what if he isn't? You acted like you didn't believe me."

"I don't have any choice. I'm not a kidnapper."

"You didn't kidnap me, you saved my life. And you do have a choice. You can take me with you."

"No."

"I want to go. Look at it this way, I can tell the police how you saved my life. I'll be a great character witness. And I can be useful."

"How?"

"You can't rent a motel looking like you do. And you're going to need one, or you'll collapse on the road. You will. You'll fall asleep at the wheel, but if you don't want to stop to rest, you could sleep while I drive."

"Why?"

"My dad is working to prove you innocent. I want to help. I love him, but I want to show him that I'm not a little girl anymore."

"Okay, you can stay. I need all the help I can get."

"What was that thing back there?" she asked without thanking him.

"I don't know, some kind of weird animal. It killed Roma," he repeated.

"And you're running away from it? That doesn't sound like you."

"It'll be back."

"How do you know?"

"You wouldn't believe me."

"Try me."

"It's too fantastic, impossible to believe. You'd think I was crazy."

"That giant gecko was impossible, but I believe in it. I'll believe you. Tell me."

"I'll have to start from the beginning."

"That's the always the best place to start."

He looked ahead, keeping his eyes glued between the semi's taillights, forcing his mind back to yesterday morning. God, was that all the time that had past. One day and it seemed like forever. The story was hard to tell, but he told her. Everything, starting from when the voice in his head told him to jump back, till he saw the shark-like teeth drag Roma among the cattle.

That was the hardest part to relive. He tried to get to her. He slid back under the fence, swallowing dirt and cow shit. He screamed. Something struck him on the head. He was nauseous. He fought to stay conscious, but he must have blacked out. He woke about an hour later, according to his watch, and vomited. Then he cried.

"Stop it. You have to move. It'll come back. It's after me." Donna had thought.

In his grief, he tried to ignore her.

"Don't shut me out. Talk to me."

"She's dead," Jim had thought. His grief weighed him down, like he was covered in lead.

"And I'm sorry, but you're alive, and I'm kind of alive, and if we don't move out of here we won't be."

"I'm not sure I want to live."

"Well I do, so move it!" She forced her will on him. Made him get up. Made him walk back to the car.

"I don't know what to do now," he'd thought.

"You go on with your life till we figure how to get me back."

"Back where?"

"Back where I belong and out of your head."

He started for his room.

"No! Don't go back up there," she'd thought.

"Why not?"

"Let's not get any other friends killed."

"I don't understand?" He'd thought.

"That thing is after me. I know it. It will do anything to keep me from getting back, kill anyone that will assist me. It killed Roma. It will kill the Lamberts if we let it. And it will kill you. It wants you most of all, because you have me."

"Then why didn't it kill me back there?"

"It has to feed on its kill before it can go after another."

"Oh God, Roma."

"Don't go up there, get out of here."

"I need rest. So tired."

"Then get in the car. Rest a few minutes, then we go, we have to," she'd said.

Listening to himself tell it made him realize just how insane it sounded.

"That's when I saw you," he said, finishing the story. "You know the rest."

She was silent for the twenty miles it took him to tell the story and now he sat back, eyes ahead, still on the semi's taillights, waiting for her to denounce him as crazy.

"You slept with you wife's twin sister? How could you?"

"It wasn't like that."

"Don't you have any control?"

"I loved her."

"Look out."

He tightened his grip, brought the car back under control.

"You almost drove us off the road," she said.

"I'll be okay."

"I'm sorry. I'm not one to judge. I've never had a lover."

"You mean—"

"No, I'm not a virgin. I was raped when I was sixteen. My one sexual experience." She told him about the rape and what her father had done. "I've learned to live with it. I'm not afraid of sex or anything like that, I'm just waiting for Mr. Right to come along."

"Why tell me?"

"You told me something that must have been hard to tell. A deep secret. I thought I'd tell you one. Fair is fair. Besides, I needed to tell someone."

"Why hasn't she asked about me?"

"Why haven't you asked about Donna, the voice in my head?"

"Do you want to know, or is that her asking?"

"It's her asking, but I'd like to know too."

"Because I believe you. You don't seem crazy. There's plenty of things out there I don't understand—that lizard thing back there, God, Satan, war, famine, why we can't all get along, what makes an airplane stay up. Donna in your head is just one more."

"Then I should send you back to your father, before that thing comes back." He glanced over at her. She was too young to be caught up in something like this. She belonged on a quiet college campus somewhere, enjoying life as only college kids know how, not here, with him, running from who-knows-what in the middle of the night. She didn't need this and he shouldn't involve her.

"I won't go. I'm staying with you. My dad would never respect me if I walked away."

"But?"

"Ask her if we can kill it?"

"Burn it," Donna thought.

"She says to burn it."

"Then that's what we'll do." Glenna crossed her arms. "You're almost out of gas."

"Five miles to the next town." He checked the gauge. "We'll get gas there. You'll have to do it. I can't be seen like this." He was having trouble keeping his eyes open. He thought about his wife and Kohler. Whoever said life was fair. His thoughts pierced his heart.

"There it is, slow down," she said.

He tapped the brakes, slowed the car as he took the off ramp on the right. He was sorry to lose the steadying comfort of the big truck that had been leading him through the night. He turned right at the top of the ramp and drove by the all night Mobil station. It was one of those places where you went inside, paid, then pumped your gas. Nobody trusted anybody anymore.

There was one car at the pumps, a brand new looking yellow Porsche Boxter, and a young teenager pumping gas into it. He saw a girl in the car. Must be bringing her back from a date. She probably had to be in by midnight. Christ, where did a boy take a girl out here? Necking somewhere, probably.

He pulled over and parked in the dark, a little past the station.

"I'll pull in when they leave. You'll have to go in and pay, then pump the gas. I'll stay in the car." He handed her two twenties.

Jim watched while the boy finished filling the tank. That car looks like it can fly, he thought. Boy probably has rich parents. It was the kind of car every teenage kid ever wanted. The boy replaced the pump when he finished, got back in the Boxter, started it and Jim heard the unmistakable rumble of a car that was more at home at a hundred on the highway then thirty in the city.

He envied the kid. Then he saw the red lights in the rear view mirror. He shut the engine off.

"Now what?" she asked.

He reached into the side pocket of Turnbull's filthy jacket and withdrew the eye patch. Which eye, he thought, the left or the right? Have to take a chance. He slipped it on and covered the left eye.

"*Right eye,*" Donna thought, and he moved the patch over.

"Step out of the car please." An amplified voice said from the police car.

Glenna opened her door, stepped out and was caught in the spotlight. Her long curly hair caught the light rays giving her an angelic appearance. He blinked and his heart fluttered. She was stunning. He opened his door, without taking his eyes off of her, and hesitated. He had to think of something to say. Would Eddie's license work? Would it fool a pair of small town cops? How to explain his appearance? He was in the shit now, both figuratively and factually. He spent another five seconds drinking in her face, smiled, then slid out of the car.

He felt the spot moving from her to where he stood. In another instant the light that made her glow would rake over him and his filthy appearance and it would be all over. He had no story to explain away how he looked. He might as well just call it quits. He was too old to be running around like a TV private investigator bent on revenge. Better to give up, get a warm bed in a quiet jail, and sleep. Let the authorities handle it.

He started to raise his hands, but the Boxter squealed out of the gas station before the light played over him, rear wheels smoking like a dragster's, the roaring engine cutting up the night. The car slid out of the driveway onto the access road, laying a hundred foot strip of black rubber on the pavement as it shot toward the interstate and the spotlight stopped its arc.

The police car screamed into life and bolted after the hot rod. In a flash of an instant both pursuer and pursued were out of sight, swallowed up by the Interstate.

"Let's get out of here!" Glenna jumped back in the car.

"We won't get very far without gas." He eased himself back in the car, felt the sweat on his palms as he slid his hands over the wheel. It had been a close call. If the youth in the Boxter would have waited a second longer before stomping on the gas, he would have been caught in the spot and he might have intrigued the police more than a spoiled teenager on a hot Friday night.

He started the car, pulled up to a pump. Glenna ran into the office, laid down the forty dollars, came out and pumped the gas. The Explorer ate twenty-seven dollars and seventy-six cents worth of fuel. They left without going back for the change.

"Turn right," she said. "Let's see what this town has to offer."

He looked at her, but said nothing.

"You need something to wear as soon as possible," she said. "Oh my gosh, I think I just felt my heart slip." She turned and locked onto his eyes. "What I'm about to say goes against everything I believe in. I'm a policeman's daughter. I believe in the law, right and wrong. But difficult times require difficult solutions, so we're going to see if we can't get you some clean clothes."

"At this time of night?"

"We're going to steal them. There, I said it and lightning didn't strike."

He turned right and a mile from the Interstate the two lane road turned into the main street of a small town. Two blocks of small shops surrounded by a residential community of less than a thousand. The street was poorly lit, two out of three street lights out, and poorly kept, a third of the stores were vacant. Jim Monday wondered if the town had ever seen better times—was it a dream waiting to happen or a dream that died?

"Look, there!" Glenna pointed.

He drove slowly past a Men's store called, Today's Man. It was dark, like the rest of the town. The street was bare. Doors were barred. Blinds were drawn over locked windows. A tumbleweed blew across the street in front of them.

They rolled past a used clothing store, Yesterday's Clothes, on the right, a pharmacy, The Doctor's Drug Store, on the left, past a shoddy Chinese restaurant, a shoddier Mexican restaurant called Francisco's, which blared the slogan in faded yellow paint, *La Comida Mas Fina*, and between Francisco's and The Handy Dry Cleaners, was a small dirt parking lot.

"Pull in there." She pointed and he obeyed.

"We have two choices, the used clothing store or the men's shop. Me I prefer the used clothing place. Less chance of an alarm."

"You've done this before?" he asked, nervous.

"No, never." She sat and stared at Francisco's fading yellow sign, like she was looking for courage. After a few seconds she found it. "Scared?" she asked.

"A little. You?"

"Terrified. Let's go."

They got out of the car, walked half a block back to the used clothing store. He scratched his head, then his side. They stopped, looked in the window, straining to see in through the dark, but all he could see was the reflection of the barren street with its ghostly shadows and it sent a tingling feeling through him.

"Let's go around back," she whispered.

She led the way, squeezing between the store that sold used clothes and the Chinese restaurant. He didn't like being cramped between the two buildings. The weeds and loose dirt crunching under his shoes only served to remind him how tight they were and how much his feet hurt.

"Look." He pointed, once they were at the back entrance. "Alarm tape on the windows."

"Do you know how to get in without setting off the alarm?" she whispered.

"No."

"Let's try the men's store."

"Let's get out of here." He was in enough trouble, serious trouble. It would be plain stupid to get picked up for breaking and entering in a dump like this. If they got caught, they'd probably be shot on sight. Everybody in this kind of town had a gun and knew how to use it.

"As long as we're back here, let's try the men's store." Once again she led and once again he followed, scratching himself along the way.

He felt like he was back in Vietnam, with lice crawling around his body. He itched between his legs. He could feel the dirt underneath his nails and the sweat pouring under his arms. A hot wind blew by and he felt nauseated by his own smell.

He hurried to catch up to Glenna. She was at the back door of Today's Man by the time he caught up to her, staring at the silver alarm tape around the back window and the sign that said, *Protected by Signal Security.*

"Time to go." This time he took the lead. "I don't know why I let you talk me into this. We can check into a motel. You can get the rooms, so nobody has to see me, and tomorrow you can go out and simply buy me some clothes." The answer was obvious, he should have seen it earlier.

"Of course," she said, obviously ignoring him, "a dry cleaners. It was staring us straight in the face." She took off at a slow jog and as much as he wanted to scream at her, to tell her they could get clothes and shoes tomorrow, he didn't. He followed.

"No alarm," she said, panting and staring at the cleaner's back door, "and no bars on the windows."

It figured, he thought. Who in their right mind would break into a dry cleaners in a small town. Can't wear anybody else's clothes, because not only does everybody know everybody else, but everybody knows everybody's clothes as well.

Centered in the top half of the back door was a screen covered sliding window. The screen was weatherbeaten, rusty and worn. It came apart in her hands. She lifted the window, it wasn't locked. She reached in and unlocked the door from the inside. Not even a dead bolt. Just a simple lock.

"Come on," she whispered as she opened the door and went in.

He followed her inside, closing and locking the door after himself. Then the dark room started blinking on and off with the red glowing light coming through the front window from the flashing lights of the police cruiser that pulled up and parked out front.

"Down!" he said, and they dropped to the floor, hiding behind the counter.

"It's that Explorer from earlier." A not very friendly voice from outside said.

"What's it doing here?" A less friendlier voice answered.

"Dunno."

"God that girl was something else, wasn't she?"

"She was, did you get a look at the other one?"

"Couldn't tell if it was a man or a woman, but I'm thinking it was a girl."

"Give me a break."

"Coulda been."

"Well, we got 'em now. Where do you suppose they are?"

"Dunno."

"Think they're robbing the town?"

"Get serious J.D. If you stole all the money in every store on this street, you might could buy a cup of coffee, if you was lucky. No, more 'an likely they're meeting someone here in one a the homes next street over. Selling drugs, I'd guess."

"Then why park here?"

"So the car won't be right in front of the house, stupid."

"Oh."

"Sometimes I wonder about you, J.D."

"What're we gonna do Mike? Wait till they come back?"

"No, dummy, wait here. I'm gonna go and call Jeb down to the Mobil and have him tow that Explorer outta here. Ain't no way them babes are gonna get outta this town on foot. We'll get 'em all right."

"But, Mike, we don't know for sure they done anything wrong."

"Anytime someone sneaks into town in the middle of the night, they're doing something wrong."

Jim and Glenna lay side by side on the floor, suffocating in the silence and the smell of manure. An hour later they heard the sounds of a tow truck as it pulled into the parking lot next door. It hooked up to the rented Explorer and towed it away. The police car followed, leaving them basking in the black night, huddled behind the counter, taking shallow breaths and wondering what to do next.

"I'm going to call my father," Glenna said after they'd gone, "and let him know I'm okay." She pulled the phone off the counter and sat on the floor.

"I don't think that's a good idea." He sat next to her.

"Relax, I won't tell him where we are. I just want to let him know that I'm okay, so he doesn't worry."

She called information, got the number for the Harris Ranch Inn, then called it.

"Can I have Hugh Washington's room please?" she said in a pleasant voice. "Just a second," she said, after a pause. She cupped her hand over the phone and said to Jim, "He's not there. Must still be tied up with the local cops. They want to know if I want to leave a message. I want my father to know I'm with you, but I don't want to mention your name."

"Say you're playing Monopoly with a friend."

"I don't understand?"

"Your father will."

She removed her hand from the mouthpiece.

"This is his daughter, remember me? Please tell him I went out to play Monopoly with a friend and that I'm okay." Then she hung up.

"That cop was right about one thing," Glenna said in a weak whisper. "Ain't no way we can walk out of here without getting caught." Then she shut up as the flashing lights went by and she stifled a scream as something ran across her bare arm in the dark.

CHAPTER ELEVEN

HUGH WASHINGTON LUMBERED through the lobby with sagging shoulders and hooded eyes. Only four hours ago the log cabin motif and big game trophies conspired to make him feel at ease, comfortable. He didn't feel that way now.

He was drained and needed rest. He was almost to the other side of the big room when the red headed kid with the green eyes called out to him.

"Sir, Mr. Washington. I have a phone message from your daughter. You just missed her."

"What?" He swept the cobwebs from his head. Glenna was supposed to be in her room, asleep, not on the other end of the phone. He steeled himself.

"She said not to worry about her, she's playing Monopoly with a friend."

"She say where she was?"

"No, sir."

"She sound like she was okay?"

"She sounded fine. She asked if I remembered her. I told her I did and then she gave me the message. Is everything all right?"

"Yeah, thanks. She didn't say when she'd be back?"

"No, sir."

"Okay, thanks again." He continued his trek through the lobby and went straight to his room, his mind working on the possibilities. Either Monday kidnapped her and she was in extreme danger, or somehow she ran across him and went with him on her own accord.

He voted for her going on her own accord. She had disguised her message so that anyone else, the clerk or the local police, for example, would accept it at face value, but anyone who knew about Jim Monday's wartime nickname would see the real message buried beneath. She was with Monopoly Jim Monday. Christ, what did she think she was up to?

And what about Monday's sister-in-law? And the Lambert woman? Whose blood was splashed all over that room? So much blood. When he called the locals he was convinced they were dead. Some cult group had done them in, drained their blood and splashed it around the room, but he calmed down after the police arrived and let his training take over. The room was covered in blood. It was torn apart. The furniture was broken and ripped. It looked bad, but there were no bodies. So for now, no bodies meant no murders.

They could be alive, though he doubted it. He thought Edna Lambert and Roma Barnes were dead. He thought it was their blood on the walls and he thought Jim Monday might possibly know who killed them. He didn't want to think about the possibility that Monday was the killer everybody seemed to think he was. The thought was unbearable. Glenna was with him.

But even if Monday wasn't responsible, he had to find him pronto. People around him had a nasty habit of winding up dead. Either way, guilty or innocent, Glenna was in danger.

He went to the nightstand where he'd left his keys and cringed. They were gone. He swept the room with his eyes, no keys. He started for the door, but was stopped by the ringing of the phone. He turned, lunging for the instrument.

"Glenna?"

"No, Washington. It's me, Hart."

"How did you know where I was?" Washington was stunned.

"Don't be stupid. You don't think you can dial 911, report a possible murder, identify yourself as a police officer and not have the boys up there check with us?"

"I guess not. I wasn't thinking."

"Damn straight you weren't thinking. Do you know where I am?"

"No?"

"I'm in my office, that's where. It's midnight and I'm not home with my wife and kids. I got called on the carpet, because one of my ex-detectives is off seeking fame and glory, so he can get off the street and worm his way back into Homicide."

"That's not the way it is."

"I don't want to hear a word out of you. If you're not back here first thing in the morning, you're through. You got that? And don't think you can go to your captain, he wanted to toss you to the wolves. It's only because of old times that I talked him into giving you this one last chance. You be here at 8:00." And that was the last word, because the captain hung up.

Damn. That wasn't the way he wanted to leave it. They were his friends, all of them, even Hart. He wanted to leave with a party, a barbecue maybe, everybody wishing him well, patting him on the back, plenty of beer, a few tears. The last thing he wanted was for them to think he was a glory hound. He wasn't that way, never had been.

He half wanted to go back, but he couldn't. Monday had Glenna. He should call Hart back and tell him. Hart was pretty upset though, better to wait till morning and give the man a chance to cool down.

He picked up a pillow, threw it against the wall. A harmless way to let off a little frustration. He mentally kicked himself, then he hurried out the door and down the walkway to the stairway, taking the steps two at a time. He was afraid that no keys meant no *Power Glide*, but when he got to the parking lot, the car was there. The only car showing headlights and grill. The only car positioned for the quick get away. All the others faced in, the white Explorer was gone.

Breathing a sigh of relief, he grabbed his breath and approached his car the way an antique dealer approaches a Ming vase. He rubbed his hand along the smoothly waxed right fender, continuing the caress till his hand was on the right side of the front bumper. He reached under and pulled out the small magnetic Hide-A-Key, opened the case and took out the spare key.

Monday was on his way to Tampico, after Kohler in the Explorer, Glenna with him. He had no choice, he had to follow. His daughter's life was at stake. He'd call Hart tomorrow from Tampico and explain. He'd tell him he was quitting too.

Power Glide started, first try. Thank you, God, he prayed, as he rolled out of the parking lot and turned toward the Interstate.

He stayed on Highway 5 until he turned west onto 805 toward San Francisco three hours later, listening to Smokey Robinson the whole way, until even Smokey couldn't keep him awake any longer. He ejected the CD and pulled off the Freeway at Livermore, where he checked into a motel. He asked for a wake-up call at 5:00, allowing himself two hours sleep. He flopped fully clothed onto the bed, pushed his worries out of his mind and fell asleep.

The wake-up call was on time. He took a quick shower and was on the road by 5:15. Normally he enjoyed early morning driving, when he had the road to himself, but not today, because he was sick with fear for Glenna.

The sun had been up for an hour when he turned off California's Highway 1, and took the road into Tampico. He knew the area. Palma was only a few miles away. He'd grown up here and had nothing but fond memories. He prayed that Glenna was all right, that her memories of the Palma-Tampico area would be fond, too. She had never been up before. He'd always wanted to take her, but he'd always been too busy.

He turned off Kennedy Road onto Mountain Sea and decided that he needed to stretch his cramped body before he went any further. He parked across from the beach, got out and took a couple steps when he spotted a small boy reach into a gunny sack and toss a pigeon into the air.

He smiled. He had pigeons when he was a kid. Racing homers, like the boy had. He caught the kid's eye, waved, then watched as the kid released the birds, one at a time, five in all, then he saw him shout and wave to a woman down the beach gathering shells. His mother, Washington thought. Beyond he saw a homeless beggar approaching the woman. Just another of America's forgotten.

If he wasn't in such a hurry, he might have worried about the woman, but the homeless were harmless, for the most part, and he had lingered too long already. He was in a hurry, so he got back in the car and continued on.

The road paralleled the ocean and he remembered how he used to scamper among the dunes when he was a boy. Then it veered off into the pines and climbed up fifty feet above the sea.

He found Kohler's house, an extravagantly large cliffside home. There had been no homes like this up here when he was a boy. Nothing ever remains the same, he thought. He wanted to stop, but to park across from the isolated house would be to advertise his presence and to announce what he was. He continued slowly by, burning every detail of the place into his mind.

It was set back from the road, a meticulous yard in front, a cliff behind. Bars covered heavily curtained windows. The doctor didn't want the outside looking in. A stone gray home, with dark gray shutters and trim. A cold, forbidding place. The centerfold-receptionist had been right, it looked like a prison. He could imagine a dungeon, cave-dark and damp, complete with rack and hooded torturer. He shuddered as a drafty freeze seemed to settle on him. He wondered if Monday's wife was the ice queen ruler of the roost or if she was the innocent maiden, caught under a sorcerer's spell.

The pine forest was across the street and the nearest neighbor was a quarter mile away. Dr. Kohler had a secure mansion, sitting atop a modest size town.

Was he the big fish in a small pond, splashing his weight and wealth around, or was he the secretive mad scientist, never seen, sending servants down to town to deal with the peasants. Washington wondered which. He needed to know.

He was almost past the house, when he saw a silver-gray Mercedes in the driveway, parked in front of a two car garage. He didn't see the white Explorer and he wondered if he'd arrived ahead of Monday and Glenna. He drove on till he rounded a curve, made a Y turn and headed back. This time he didn't slow down and he didn't look. He'd seen all he needed to see.

He drove back into town and took a room at the Tampico Motel. Then he went shopping. First stop, Pacific Sporting Goods, where he purchased an M-1 carbine, two thirty round clips, five boxes of ammunition, a camouflage military shirt with large inside pockets and matching pants, hiking boots and a backpack. At the camera shop next door he bought a pair of ten power binoculars and a flashlight. At the local mini market, where he was waited on by a turbaned Sikh, he bought enough junk food and powdered donuts to half fill the backpack. Almost as an afterthought he grabbed a couple cans of Dinty Moore Beef Stew, a can opener and a case of plastic spoons.

"This will not be very healthy eating," the Sikh said.

"It's what I've been eating since my wife left," Washington said, warming to the Sikh's smile.

"You are not eating well and I am being a bad business man. I should be shutting my mouth and taking your money."

"And I should follow your advice, but I probably won't. My name is Hugh Washington." He held out his hand.

"And I am Jaspinder Singh." He offered Washington a handshake as firm as the one he received.

"The gray house up the hill, the one with all the bars, you know who owns it?" Washington asked.

"I don't like to be getting in anyone's business."

"I can understand that." Washington showed his badge. "But my daughter is missing."

"Oh my, I should like to help you even if you are a long way from home. Not because you are a policeman. I have been on the wrong side of many policemen in my life. I was born in South Africa, so you see American policemen are not threatening to me."

"I don't mean to threaten you."

"Oh yes, I know. I am only explaining myself, more for my benefit than yours. It is hard for me to inform on another."

"I'm not asking you to inform on anyone."

"Oh, but you are. You are asking who owns the big house. Then you will be asking what do I know about him and I do not like what I know. I would like to remain silent and say I know nothing. But you are asking as a father and not a policeman. A policeman I could turn away. A father, I cannot."

"I don't like the way this sounds."

"And I am sorry to be telling you. A doctor owns that house. A rich German doctor. A man who has a parade of young girls come and go. He thinks we don't know, but we are a small town, and even though he keeps to himself most of the time, we see his people bringing them in and taking them out."

"His people?"

"He has some very rough looking people working for him. Doing what, I do not know. Drugs maybe? There is a lot of that up here. Marijuana fields, California's illegal cash crop."

"What does he do with the girls?"

"Who knows?" The Sikh spread his hands, palms up. "But if he was involved with my daughter, I would most certainly want to know." Washington thanked him, paid, and on his way out the door the Sikh asked, "Will you be wanting to see the sheriff?"

"No. It's something I have to handle myself." He smiled at the man.

"I understand and if anybody ever asks me, you were never here and we never talked."

Understanding lit up Washington's face. If he were to harm Kohler, or even kill him, this man would say nothing.

"I appreciate that," he said.

"Think nothing of it. I too have a daughter, and besides, I don't like that man. I think he would have been more happy in Hitler's Germany than in this free country, where a man like me can own a store and a man like you can be a policeman. He was in here once and in his eyes I saw the hate he had for me. He does not know me, but he hates me. He would hate you more, because you are a policeman and have some power. I pray for your daughter."

Washington thanked him again and left the store. Kohler sounded like a bad man, who employed bad people, who did bad things with young ladies. Maybe Walker was right about Monday and maybe Monday was right about Kohler.

He took his purchases to his room, changed, loaded the backpack and made a mental note to buy a warm jacket. He remembered how cold it got up here at night, even in the summer. On his way to the door it dawned on him that he was late for a meeting in Long Beach.

He went to the phone and a few seconds later he had Hart on the line.

"Where are you, Washington?" Hart asked.

"I can't tell you that, sir."

"Don't give me that. You still work for this department and if you want to keep working for it you'll answer me."

"I quit."

"You what?"

"I quit."

"Have you lost your mind? You can't quit."

"I just did."

"You're working on this Jim Monday thing, aren't you?"

"What I'm doing is personal, sir."

"Well, why didn't you say so. We can arrange some personal time. Just tell me everything you have on Monday and we'll forget this whole thing. You can take all the time you want for your personal problems. You're trying to work things out with your wife, right?" There were a few seconds of silence then Hart said, "Oh shit, we got an earthquake here. I have to go. Call me back in an hour."

The line went dead and Washington's heartbeat started to race, his pulse keeping time like a strobe light, his eyes seeing things in snatches, like time lapsed photography. He tried to take deep breaths, to keep himself from hyperventilating, but images of shaking buildings crashing down on terror stricken children flashed before his mind.

Ever since he could remember he'd been afraid of earthquakes, and even though the temblor was over five hundred miles away, the fact that he was connected to it, even by telephone, was enough to chill his nerves and stampede his heart.

It took him two full minutes to regain control. He was surprised. He had done better in the midst of the San Fernando Quake, a six point five that brought down the VA Hospital. He wondered what was happening to him? It was almost like a seizure. I'm getting old, he thought, once his breathing was regular again.

He thought about calling Walker, but he loathed the thought of calling him in that hospital. The man had enough to worry about right now. Washington shivered. He hated hospitals almost as much as he feared earthquakes. They were places for lying and dying. He didn't envy Walker.

He scooped up the backpack, went out to the car. His plan had been to go up to Kohler's as soon as possible, drive by, find a place to hide the car, walk back and find a spot in the woods across from the house to hide and stake out the place. The best strategy was often the most simple. He would sit and wait. Sooner or later Monday would show up and then he'd get Glenna back.

He'd worry about dealing with Monday after Glenna was safe. If Monday was innocent, he'd move heaven and earth to prove it, but not till his little girl was out of harm's way.

He unlocked the trunk and tossed the backpack on top of the carbine. He was closing it when the silver Mercedes with the dark tinted windows drove by. He scooted around to the driver's side and out of sight as the Mercedes parked by the diner across the street from the motel.

He watched as Kohler got out of the car. The doctor walked around the vehicle with a straight backed gate, like he had a pipe up his ass,

Washington thought. He continued watching as Kohler opened the passenger door and Julia Monday slid out, smoothing her skirt. Then Kohler and Jim Monday's wife walked arm and arm into the diner.

Hugh Washington decided that he was hungry and started across the street. He stopped in the middle of the road, swore at himself for being so stupid and turned back to the motel. I'm the one that put her husband in the police car and took him away. How could she forget me and my ugly face? I remember her. And even if those gorgeous eyes passed over me, Kohler would remember. He didn't look like the kind of man that forgot anything. He stopped at his car, opened the trunk and took out the backpack, closed it and went back into his room.

From inside his room he had a clear view of the diner across the street. He moved a chair to the window, opened the curtains and sat. He opened the backpack and took out the binoculars. They brought the diner ten times closer.

Kohler and Julia Monday were sitting at a table for two, by the window. Washington could see the shaving rash on Kohler's neck that edged up to his trimmed beard. He could see the corners of the forced smile on Mrs. Monday. It looked like she might have been crying. He looked back at Kohler, his thin lips, not well enough hidden by the manicured mustache, were moving rapidly, almost snarling.

A young waitress brought them water and took their order. Kohler ordered for both. He continued talking after the waitress left. Mrs. Monday continued listening. Something wasn't right, she seemed listless, dead on her feet. The shoulder length hair that had been vibrant and fresh two days ago had lost its luster. The sparkle in her eyes was gone. She had that blank look Washington had seen so many times in his career. A combination of sudden shock, loss and grief. It was usually worn on the face of a surviving wife whose husband had been recently murdered.

A third man joined them. He pulled a chair out from an empty table and sat facing the window. Washington had seen his type before. *Weasel* was the first word that came to mind. He was the sly type that all policeman know, the kind that make good informers because they're afraid. Afraid of the police, jail, the streets, themselves. Usually they were junkies and this man looked the type, darting eyes, shaking hands, rounded shoulders and nodding head. The hair on the right side of his scalp was exceedingly long and combed over a bald top. The Weasel was vain. He wore a Polo shirt and had a salon tan. He reached into his pocket and took out a brown cigarette. Designer cigarettes, Washington called them. He started to light up when Kohler knocked the cigarette out of his hand with a sudden slap. The Weasel was afraid of Kohler.

Then the Weasel started talking. He punctuated his words with his hands. An excited man. But his excitement wasn't transferred to Kohler. Mrs. Monday appeared bored. Washington got the impression that the Weasel was always excited. The food came and the Weasel shut up. Pancakes and bacon for Kohler and Monday's wife. Nothing for the Weasel.

Kohler ate deliberately, Mrs. Monday picked at her food, and the Weasel shifted to and fro, openly leering at Mrs. Monday's breasts. Washington followed the Weasel's eyes. Julia Monday was wearing a white silk blouse without a brassiere. Her nipples were visible through the material and she was clearly uncomfortable wearing it and even more uncomfortable with the Weasel's stare.

He moved the binoculars back to Kohler's face. The man was aware of what the Weasel was doing and how uneasy it made Mrs. Monday. The bastard doesn't care, Washington thought. He's enjoying it. Lady, it looks like when you left your husband, you fell into a bucket of shit. Washington got the impression that if the slimy bastard were to reach out and grab one of those breasts, the doctor would only smile. He was one cold son of a bitch.

"Glenna, you don't want anything to do with this man," he muttered, wishing he hadn't had lunch with his daughter yesterday, hadn't told her about his new job, hadn't allowed her to come with him. If he gets anywhere near her, I'll kill him.

He put down the binoculars and called Hart back. The thought of the earthquake in Long Beach caused a slight earthquake in his own body as he dialed the number.

"It's about time you called back," Hart said, after he finally got him on the line.

"You said an hour. It hasn't even been thirty minutes."

"Did you think about what I said? You give us all you got on Monday and all is forgiven. You come back like nothing happened."

"Do I come back on the street or do I get back in Homicide?"

"You get Homicide, if you want it."

Washington knew the man was lying. He might have believed him if he said they would allow him to work to his retirement in a uniform, but he knew there was no way Hart would take him back in Homicide. He understood they wanted Monday awful bad, but they shouldn't want anything bad enough to lie to a fellow officer. The man was playing with his life. It wasn't fair.

"I've given you my decision, Captain. I'm quitting. I'll find another job. One where they don't think they have to lie to you to get you to perform the way they want."

"Hold on a minute, Washington. You owe us. You owe me. We cleaned that mess up after you and kept you out of jail and your daughter out of court. I saved your ass. You can't walk out on me." Hart spat the words down the wire.

"So this is what it comes down to. You using that to whip me into line."

"If I have to."

"I told you, Captain, I'm through, finished, I quit."

"You son of a bitch! You'll be sorry. I can charge you as an accessory."

Washington hung up.

That was that, he thought. No going back now. The only thing left was to make it official. He would have to call personal, turn in his badge, fill out the forms. It hurt, turning his back on the department that had been his life for so long, but he had a bright future to look forward to with Ron Walker. And he was a man that believed in the future. The past was for losers, the future for winners.

He picked up the binoculars as Kohler was counting out change. He wasn't leaving a tip. What a swell guy. How do you feel about him now, Mrs. Monday, him and his Weasel pal. They got up from the table, the Weasel leading the way to the door, followed by Mrs. Monday. Kohler brought up the rear.

He lost sight of them for a few minutes as they made their way through the restaurant, but picked them up as they came out the door. He followed them to Kohler's car, where Kohler went to the driver's side, unlocked the door and climbed in. The Weasel opened the door for Mrs. Monday, but before she could get in, he placed himself between her and the car and ran a hand along her buttocks, giving her a firm squeeze. She didn't pull away, didn't yell, or slap him. She got in the car like nothing had happened, the same blank look on her face.

The Weasel closed the door after her, laughing, turned and walked away. Washington had never seen anything like it. Kohler couldn't have missed it. The man didn't care. And from the looks of things, Mrs. Monday was beyond caring. The doctor started the car and Washington put down the binoculars.

He didn't have to follow them. He knew the way to the doctor's house. He could afford a few minutes to take care of his personal business. He picked up the phone and called Long Beach. He asked for Captain Roberts. Time to tell his boss what he'd already told Hart.

"Robert's desk," a voice he didn't recognize said.

"Is he there?" Washington asked.

"No, he's not. Who's calling please?" It wasn't 9:00 yet. He was always there till 9:00, rain or shine. He never took a vacation. He never got sick. He was there every morning, six days a week from 8:00 to 9:00. Office hours for his men, he called it. That was when he took complaints, solved problems, listened to worries. Only something important would drag him away. A major crisis. An officer shot. Washington felt his chest tighten.

"This is Washington, I won't be in today."

"Hugh Washington?"

"That's right."

"God, I'm sorry about your partner, he was a great guy. Everybody liked him."

"What are you talking about?" Hugh felt the lump welling up in his throat. Not Walker, not him. He was young, with a family. He sat on the bed, the phone still at his ear, waiting for the inevitable words he knew were coming next.

They came.

"Walker died early this morning. I'm sorry, I thought you knew."

He dropped the phone, buried his head in his hands. He blamed himself. If he would have played it by the book and turned everything over to Homicide, or better yet, stayed out of it all together, Walker would still be alive, but instead he went off half cocked, ignoring all the rules, and Walker had paid.

And he didn't know where Glenna was.

CHAPTER TWELVE

"WAKE UP," GLENNA SAID, "It's almost 9:00. You've been asleep for over eight hours." She was backlit against the early morning sun coming in the front window. It basked her hair in a halo, reminding him of how she looked the night before, when she had been lit up by that spot. "We're going to have to find some clothes for you and get out of here before someone comes."

He looked down at what he was wearing and last night came flooding back. It was real, Roma was dead. The car was gone. They were hiding in a dry cleaners and he was sleeping on a pile of clothes in a stranger's shorts and tee shirt. After they'd decided they had to spend the night, he went foraging through the piles of blue paper covered laundry and struck pay dirt—underwear, tee shirt and shorts.

He took his find into the small toilet, stripped and gave himself a whore's bath at the sink, using a roll and a half of paper towels to clean the manure off himself. He grimaced when he remembered holding his head under the faucet, smelling and seeing the brown muck being washed out of his hair and down the drain.

"Where do you plan on going?" he asked.

"I don't know. Out of here."

"We won't get ten feet before the cops pick us up. I don't know about you, but I don't want to sample the bill of fare in the local jail."

"I don't care what bill of fare I sample right now. I'm starving." She pointing at her chest, stared into his eyes. "We have to get out of here. It'll be just as bad if they catch us in the cleaners or on the street. Either way, we're caught," she said.

"I think we should stay here for awhile."

"What are we going to do when Mr. Dry Cleaner shows up for work?" she said.

"It's Saturday."

"Oh yeah." She sighed, closed her eyes, crossed her legs into a full lotus and started to breathe, pulling the air deep into her lungs, holding her breath, then exhaling.

He watched, fascinated. She was serene, her face as worry free as a child's. The rise and fall of her breasts, erotic. Her hands on her thighs, peaceful. She was contradiction personified.

He left her meditating and went looking for clothes. He found two pair of Levi's that fit and stuffed them into a white drawstring laundry bag. He added two denim work shirts, four pair of boxer shorts, two white tee shirts, a Levi Jacket, a pair of dark brown slacks and a white dress shirt. He carried his booty back to where Glenna was sitting in her yoga position and laid it down. He sat next to it.

She opened her eyes.

"What have you got there?"

"Clothes, a couple pair of Levi's, underwear, socks."

"You're gonna take them? More than you need?"

"This from the girl who wanted to break and enter last night." He was having a hard time understanding her.

"But not to take one thing more than we needed and I would have sent the money for what we took when I got home."

He dug under the pile of clothes that he had used for a pillow and pulled out Eddie Lambert's wallet. He took out a hundred dollar bill, reached up and put in on counter. "There, does that make you happy?"

"A nice gesture, but it's pretty stupid." She arched her eyebrows with a twinkle of laughter in her eyes. "We might need the money. No matter how much you have in that wallet, when it's gone we might wish we had that hundred bucks. Take it back. We'll send the money later, when we know we can afford it."

"You're saying *we* an awful lot when it's really just me. Once we're out of here, you go home, back to your family. They're probably worried sick right now."

"No way. My mom has a new boyfriend and they're both somewhere off the coast of Baja on the Love Boat. My dad knows I'm okay. I left a message, remember?" She crossed her arms around her chest.

"A message that probably scared him out of his mind. I'm a wanted murderer, remember that? Even if he thinks I'm innocent, he has to be worried about what might happen to you if the police catch up to us. You could get seriously hurt or worse, killed. No, you're going back as soon as we're safe." He hoped he sounded firm.

"You're gonna need me," she said. "I'll bet every cop in the state is looking for you. I'll bet your picture has been plastered over the news all night long. You think that stupid eye patch you put on last night will fool anyone? And who's gonna buy food? You? Who's gonna find a place to spend the night? You? Who's gonna get us a car? You? And who's gonna get us out of here? You need me and you know it."

He stared at her with clenched fists. It was true, he needed someone. Not her though, not a child, and not a girl. He had friends he could call. He looked up at the phone.

"Don't even think about it," she said.

He remained silent, caught in her deep brown eyes.

"You're thinking you can call someone. Well, you're wrong. The police have already talked to everyone you know. Probably the press, too. I can see your friends on CNN, 'He was such a quiet man. Friendly, always said hello. He's the last man in the world you would think would ever do such a thing. It must be because of the war. Come to think of it he always was a little strange. His wife leaving him like that must have pushed him over.' You call someone like that, they'll go for the fame and the glory. They'll turn you in. We're all you have, me and my dad." It was her turn to look up at the phone.

She was right and he knew it and even if she wasn't, he didn't want to involve his friends. They had families, kids. The last thing they needed was a call from him. "Okay," he said, "call your father."

She scooted next to him, pulled the phone off the counter, started pushing the buttons.

"You remember the number?"

"Yeah, I'm good with phone numbers. Tell me once and I have it for life. Go figure. It's ringing."

She asked for her father's room and frowned. After a few seconds she hung up.

"They said he left during the night without giving them notice, but since he paid by credit card, it was okay. Now what?" She didn't seem as confident as she'd been only a few seconds ago.

"Get a laundry bag and stuff a few day's supply of clothes into it," he said. "Then we'll see."

He watched as she made her way through the clothes. It took her almost an hour and she went through every article of clothing, both the dry cleaning and the laundry, before she found two pair of Calvin Klein Jeans, two blouses, two men's tee shirts, white, size small. She refused to use somebody else's underwear. "I'll buy some when I get some shoes," she said, and he thought about that pair of shoes in the bathroom. He bent over and rubbed his feet, he never wanted to put them on again.

"Okay, again I ask, now what?" She tossed her bag next to his and returned to her position next to him, behind the counter.

"I need shoes too," he said.

"And we need food. And a car would be nice."

"Yeah, breakfast would be good, but there's nothing we can do about food till tonight."

"You mean we're going to wait here all day? In the cleaners?" she said.

"It's ten o'clock and it feels like a sauna in here," he said, starting to sweat. "It'll probably reach into the nineties today. Our feet would burn up on the pavement, and even if we had shoes, we still couldn't leave before dark, because we'd get picked up before we got out of town. We can't leave till tonight."

"Then what?"

"I don't know. I haven't planned farther than going out the back door after dark."

"Great."

"That voice in your head, is it still there?" she asked after a few minutes of silence.

"Donna, are you there?" His thought went unanswered. *"Are you there?"* he asked again and again there was no answer.

"No, she seems to be gone."

"Oh."

"I was starting to get used to her." He leaned back against the counter. "I think I'm going to miss her."

"That's natural. Now you have to deal with your problems yourself." She was wringing her hands in her tee shirt.

"You don't believe me." He looked at her and laughed. "You think I'm hearing voices." He bored into her eyes, looking for a sign and finding none. "Well, I can't blame you. If I were you, I wouldn't believe me either. Anyway it's a moot point, she's gone." The sound of his knees creaking filled the silent room as he got up.

"I'm going to the bathroom." He went into the small bathroom, urinated, flushed the toilet, looked in the mirror, splashed water on his face. His reflection told him he needed a shave. He hated the way his beard was starting to come in gray. Turning away from his own bloodshot eyes, he left the bathroom.

"I'm going to check the office and see if there is anything we can use. Should have done it earlier."

He went into the office adjacent to the bathroom. There was a small wooden desk, scratched and covered with papers, an electronic calculator, a matching chair and nothing else. He sat at the desk. The papers were last week's receipts, apparently the proprietor used the shoe box method of accounting, gather all the receipts, make a pile, throw them in a shoebox and figure it out later. The top two desk drawers filled the shoe box function.

He found a personal phone book in the bottom drawer. It appeared to list the names, addresses and phone numbers of the cleaner's patrons. He also found blank paper, pencils and extra rolls of paper tape for the calculator. And in the back, behind the calculator tape, a forty-five automatic.

"Are you a welcome sight," he said. Then he remembered the guns in the trunk of the rented Ford. If the police find those they'll get real excited, he thought. They'll call in reinforcements and tear this town apart looking for me. They'll do that anyway, once they connect the rental car to Edna.

He picked up the gun, checked the clip and found it full. Eight in the clip, one in the chamber, the safety off. A loaded cannon, ready for action, tucked away in the back of a drawer. A gun out of reach didn't need the safety off. If you're going to take the chance of killing yourself with a weapon ready to fire, he thought, it should at least be accessible in an emergency. People didn't make sense.

He put the gun back. No point in telling Glenna about it. He would get it later. He pushed himself away from the desk, picked up the phone book, leafed through it a second time, then dropped it on the desk amid the pile of receipts and left the office.

"Find anything?" she asked.

"Just a phone book with his customer's names."

"Nothing else?"

"No." He sat down next to her. "I'm going to try and sleep before it gets too hot." It was a long time since he had to force himself to sleep in adverse conditions, but he still knew how. He closed his eyes and took himself back to the bad days of the POW camp. He drifted off to sleep before he had time to set up the Monopoly board, leaving Glenna alone, meditating in front of an imaginary candle.

He woke in a hot sweat at noon. Glenna was asleep on a pile of clothes. It was good that she was able to sleep, he thought, because they would probably be up all night. He closed his eyes, sleep took a little longer, he almost made it to *Park Place*, he didn't get to pass *Go*.

He opened his eyes again at two-thirty.

"I'm glad you're awake." She was in a half lotus now, but as he stirred, she straightened her right leg in front of herself and touched her head to her knee and held the position for over a minute. She repeated the exercise with her left leg, then went back into the half lotus. "I can handle being by myself. I've had practice, but I prefer people. Maybe I just haven't had the life experience to spend prolonged periods in meditation. I can do it, but I don't enjoy it as much as conversation."

They talked, getting to know each other for the next six hours.

She told him about her old boyfriends, not too many, her girlfriends, some now married with children. How she had been a cheerleader in high school her junior and senior years. What it was like to be homecoming queen. How devastated she was when she brought home that one B in third semester Spanish, shattering her 4.0 grade point average. The difficulties of being both class president in her senior year and head cheerleader.

He told her about the war, the POW camp, the VA hospital, the Marine Corps. What it was like to get the medal of honor. What it was like to make his first million. How he loved real estate with a passion. It was a way of making a lot of money without hurting anyone. When he bought a property, he made the seller and his family happy and when he sold something, he made the buyer and his family happy. Until two months ago he had the perfect life. Then his wife met Kohler.

She confessed that her high school career hadn't been all that stellar. She'd never gotten over being the homecoming queen who hadn't gone to the prom. No one asked her. She was stiff on a date. She knew that. She didn't like petting in the back seat. She didn't like being pawed. She was working on it. She was getting better. She was going to be okay.

He told her about Roma and how he fell in love with her and how she moved to Miami. How he was heartbroken and married Julia. He thought he was in love with her, but now he had to admit, maybe he married her on the rebound.

"I have an idea," she said. It was 8:30. The sun had been down for about an hour and a half. "Why don't we get the cleaner's phone book and call the customers. If someone answers we hang up. If we don't get an answer, we know they're not home." She had a satisfied smile on her face.

"I'll get the book." He pushed himself off the floor, picked up his laundry bag and headed for the office. "I'm going to change out of these shorts, while I'm at it." Once in the office he closed the door, took off the shorts and put on a pair of the faded Levi's. Then he opened the bottom drawer, took out the gun, dropped it in his bag. He picked up the phone book as she opened the door.

"Did you get the gun?" she asked.

"How did you know?"

"I checked the office while you were asleep."

"Why didn't you tell me?"

"I wanted to see how you would handle it. You didn't want me to know about the gun? I like that. You were trying to protect me from the harsh reality of the situation. Not very smart, but I like it. Please don't do it again. We should trust each other." She went to the desk. "Do you want to call or should I?"

"You can do it," he said.

She sat down and started pushing buttons, calling numbers in the book at random. It took ten calls before she was blessed with no answer.

"Here we are," she said. "Mary Mckinna. 13 Church Street. Great, look at this." She showed him the phone book. Under the address were the words, *Next to the Cemetery.*

"I was afraid that even if we found someone not at home, we wouldn't be able to find the house. Guess I worried in vain. We should have no trouble finding a cemetery in a town this size."

"No," she echoed, "no trouble at all."

"Let's go," he said.

"I'll get my gear." She went back to their place behind the counter, picked up her laundry bag. "You know," she said, "I'm going to miss this place. I feel like I've entered a new stage in my life." Then she walked to the back door, opened it and they stepped out into the hot night.

Five minutes later they found it.

"The Rio Dulce Cemetery," he read off the sign.

"Think there was a river here?" she whispered.

"Must have been."

"Where's the house?"

"You don't have to whisper, nobody can hear us."

"What about them?" She pointed into the cemetery.

CHAPTER THIRTEEN

"IT HAS TO BE THAT WHITE HOUSE over there." Jim pointed through the cemetery.

"Let's go." Glenna started walking down the street.

"Where are you going?"

"Around. Church Street must dead end into the cemetery. We'll go around the block."

"Car coming." He grabbed her arm, pulled her into the graveyard. They huddled behind a hedge while the car passed.

"It's the police," she whispered. The black and white cruiser rolled on by without stopping. "I didn't tell you something," she said, lying next to him. They were sandwiched between the hedge, shielding themselves from the street, and a row of tombstones.

"What?"

"I felt something crawl across my foot last night. Just before I went to sleep."

"So?"

"It might have been a gecko."

"You think?"

"Could have been, have you seen any?"

"Yes, in my room at the motel and at the mini market on the other side of the Interstate."

"Well, I've been seeing them, too. I shook one off my foot just before you-know-what came creeping out from under my father's car. You think there's a connection?"

"I hope not, but maybe."

"There are no geckos in California. They live in the tropics," she said.

"I know that."

"Just making conversation." She desperately wanted to believe there was no connection. She was sorry she brought it up. Sorry she even thought about it. This wasn't the place to think about slimy things with big teeth that creep in the night.

"We'll cut across the cemetery. It's safer than the street," he said.

He took her by the hand, led her through the sea of tombstones, toward the clean white house. She felt the strength in his hand as she shivered. The clouds let through enough light to cast opaque shadows from the gravestones.

"I feel like the shadows are reaching out for me," she said.

"It's a little scary," he said.

"I'm twenty years old and I've never been in a cemetery before. I don't like it." She heard something, a scraping sound. She tightened her grip on his hand. He froze. "Did you hear it?" she whispered.

"Yeah," he said. She felt his palm, as sweaty as hers. "Did it sound like that thing last night?"

"I don't think so." They remained in place, two statues, ears tuned to the night, but they heard nothing more.

"Must have been the wind blowing some of these across the grass," he whispered, bending down and picking up a bunch of artificial flowers. He tossed them back on the grave. "Come on." He continued leading her through the graveyard.

At the side of the cemetery they found two obstacles between them and the house at 13 Church Street. A shallow drainage ditch and on the other side of the ditch, a four foot wooden fence. They found a plank across the ditch and beyond, a two foot gap in the fence. The Church Street residents must cut across the cemetery as a short cut to downtown Rio Dulce, she thought.

He stepped onto the plank, pulling her along behind. Then he squeezed through the gap, still holding her hand. Once through, they found themselves between the fence and the back of a two car garage. The fence was about three feet from the garage. They were in a dark area, perfect for one of those homeless beggars to hide in, she thought—or a slimy overgrown lizard.

She felt as trapped as the dead neighbors next door in their coffins. Her heart was pounding. She felt like she was being drawn out of a long dark tunnel when he led her away from the dark space. Then they were at the back door of the house.

"At least we don't have to worry about the neighbors calling the police," he said.

"Look at that." She was looking at a new Red Mazda Miata, the price sticker still in the window. The car was parked in front of the garage. "I really wanted one of those, but I couldn't afford one. I hope we find the keys." She looked from the car to the back door. "How do we get in?"

He took the steps up the back porch and tried the door. It was locked.

"That window is open," she said.

He came off the porch and followed her pointed finger. It was open because of the heat, she thought, or maybe there aren't too many burglaries in small town Rio Dulce.

"I'll get down on my hands and knees." He started for the window. You can stand on my shoulders and see if you can get the screen off."

"Careful," she said, "don't trample the flowers." There was a flower bed along the side of the house. He stepped between two small rose bushes, careful not to cut himself on the thorns. Then he dropped to all fours. She stepped onto his back and tried to pry the screen off.

"I can't do it," she said, stepping off. "I need a screwdriver or a knife." She walked along the side of the house. "Aha!" She bent down in front of the flower bed and picked up a rusty garden trowel. "This will work." Then she was on his back again, using the pointed end of the trowel to pry the screen off. "I've got it." She tossed the screen onto the grass. Then, with a feeling of danger and accomplishment, she pulled herself up into the window.

Inside she found herself on the kitchen sink. She squeezed on in. She tried to turn once her rear end was through, but she slipped and landed on the tile floor with a quiet crash that echoed through the quieter house. She pushed herself up and opened the back door. Then she went straight for the refrigerator, pulled open the door and bathed the kitchen in a murky light full of hidden shadows.

"Tupperware." She took out a plastic container and checked the contents. "Tuna casserole." She resealed the lid. "We'll take this with us for later." She took her laundry sack from Jim, dropped the leftover casserole into it.

"Close the fridge. I found a flashlight," he said, closing a drawer next to the sink. He turned it on as the kitchen lost the gloomy light from the refrigerator. "Let's find the car keys and get out of here," he whispered.

She nodded and they went through the kitchen. There was a key rack by the back door, but no keys.

"We need shoes," she said and he followed her out of the kitchen, through a living room. Redneck values at their finest, she thought, looking at the cheap sofa and chairs gathered around a large screen television and stereo rack. The walls were bare white, no art, no bookcases, no books. A sewing machine in the corner, positioned so the lady of the house could sew and watch the big screen while her husband lay on the couch.

Past the living room, they entered a dark hallway. He used the flashlight. The first door on the right was a bathroom, the door opposite, the master bedroom. He followed her in, lighting the way as she went to the closet and opened it. He lit it up for her as she looked through several pair of shoes, men's and women's. She settled on a well used pair of white tennis shoes and slipped them on her bare feet.

"Tight, maybe a half size too small, but better than nothing." She laced them up, then paced the bedroom twice. "They'll do."

"At last." He picked up a pair of new running shoes. "No more screaming feet. You might settle with half a size small, but I've been living with tight shoes for too long." He stole a pair of running socks out of a bureau drawer and slipped them on, then the shoes. "Perfect," he said standing.

The next door on the right opened on a second bedroom. A guest room, she supposed, and the one opposite was a bedroom turned into a sewing room. A large sewing table, with a second sewing machine, a quilting rack and piles of material filled the room. "She probably shuts herself in here while her husband drinks beer and watches football," Jim said, "and when she has to watch with him, she has that sewing machine in the living room."

"I gotta pee," she said.

"What? Here?"

"Can't help it. Gotta go. Gimme the light."

He handed her the flashlight and she went into the bathroom, closing the door after herself.

"It's spooky in here." She unzipped, lowered her jeans, sat on the toilet.

"Hurry up," he said, from the other side of the door.

"I'm going as fast as I can." She finished, dried herself and flushed the toilet. She shined the light across the bathroom, illuminating the wash basin. She went to it and washed her hands, then started for the door, then she turned back toward the sink. She was thirsty.

She turned the tap back on, held the light pointed down at the sink and lowered her head, putting her mouth under the faucet. The cold water tasted good. The water at the dry cleaners had an aftertaste.

She sensed something by her cheek, the water didn't seem to be going down the drain. She turned her head while still drinking. A gecko, less than an inch from her right cheek, its tiny beady eyes staring into her single wide right eye, was half out of the drain, clogging it and paying no attention to the water flooding around it.

She screamed.

The door burst open.

"What is it? What's wrong?"

"I saw one of those geckos, coming out of the drain." She was shaking, the flashlight was on the floor where she dropped it. He picked it up and pointed it at the sink.

"Nothing there."

"I saw it. I did." She was shaking.

"It's gone now," he said.

"What's going on? What's happening?"

"Get a hold of yourself. You've got to keep it together, okay?"

"Okay, okay. Just give me a second." She caught her breath, then did a few deep breathing exercises. Part of her yoga training. "I'll be all right now. Let's get on with it and get out of here."

"Now you're talking." He squeezed her arm in a friendly gesture. "Let's check out the room at the end of the hall." The room turned out to be a den. A man's room. Two oak chairs covered in brown fabric. A single bookcase full of magazines, no books. There was a large oak desk between the bookcase and the chairs. He went to it. The only thing in the top drawer was a forty-five automatic.

"Does everybody in this town have one of those." Then she saw the photo. "Hey, look at that." She pointed and he trained the light on it.

"Wouldn't you just know it," he said. It was a picture of a man and woman holding hands. The woman was wearing a blue formal dress and the athletic looking man smiling down at her was wearing a police officer's uniform.

"Think it's one of the ones from last night?" she said.

"That would just be our luck." He reached into the drawer to pick up the weapon, when a set of headlights swept through the window as a car pulled up in front. He flicked off the flashlight and closed the drawer. "Quick, we gotta move."

They jumped into action.

"Close the doors on the right," he said, closing the door to the den as they went through it. She closed the door to the master bedroom and the guest room. He got the bathroom and the sewing room.

In the kitchen he picked up both laundry bags.

"No time for argument. Take these, and wait behind the garage. I'm going to hide in the den till they go to sleep." He was perspiring heavily.

"But?"

"Do it. I have to stay, we need those keys. And get that screen out of sight." He forced the laundry bags into her hand and herded her toward the back door. "Wait for me, with luck I won't be too long." Her lips were quivering, he brushed the hair out of her eyes. "I'll be okay," he said. "I've had a lot of training. They'll never know I'm here."

She dropped the laundry bags and grabbed him behind the head with both hands. She felt his surprise as she pulled him to her lips and gave him a passionate kiss, full of longing and promise. She broke the kiss and picked up the laundry bags with trembling hands.

"I'll wait for you, as long as it takes."

"Be silent and careful," he said.

She went out, taking both bags. She dashed to the screen, picked it up and took it with her as she headed for that dark place behind the garage.

She made her way along the garage to the back. She'd never been afraid of the dark, but she was afraid of this place. With the overhang of the garage roof, the area between the cemetery fence and the back of the garage seemed a dark tunnel to nowhere. Once in she dropped the bags and leaned against the garage.

It was quiet. No crickets. No night sounds. The sound of her breathing echoed in the dark, bouncing off the fence, then off the garage, making eerie sounds that skyrocketed her heart. Easy, she told herself, sit down and do your exercises. She sat in a half lotus and imagined a flickering candle. She took deep breaths and forced her heart to slow down.

Then she heard something.

She opened her eyes and her pulse screamed.

A scraping sound.

Sweat trickled under her arms.

Another sound, like a snake's hiss.

A cold chill ran from the cold ground, from her buttocks to her tail bone, shooting up her spine like cold lightning blasting into the back of her neck. It felt like her hair was covered in snow. Then it felt like it was on fire.

A low growl.

She lost control of her bladder and wet her pants.

Another low growl. It was coming from inside the tunnel, coming toward her, coming for her. She whimpered, a lost little girl sound, and forced herself out of the lotus. She scooted on her rear, away from the thing creeping toward her.

Another growl. Louder. She wanted to turn away. To get away. To run. But she looked. She couldn't help herself. She thought she saw something, its lizard shape in the dark. For a flash of a second the eyes lit up. A quick bright radioactive flash of yellow, then it was gone.

With her hands behind herself, legs in front, she scooted backwards, crab-like, dragging her backside on the ground. It came closer. She tried to go faster, but it was like she was caught in slow motion. For some reason the thing wasn't moving any faster than she was. It scraped along the ground, toward her, and she scraped along the ground, away from it.

Then she was at the gap in the fence. The gateway into the cemetery.

The thing growled, louder. She could smell and feel its hot breath.

Diving deep within herself, she summoned up the will to move. She dove through the fence as the yellow-eyed thing dove for her. She went across the wooden plank on her hands and knees, crawling fast. She started to get up, but she hadn't been paying attention to where she was going, more afraid of what was behind than ahead, and she smacked her head into a gravestone.

Stunned, she looked behind herself and saw the slimy green thing, halfway through the hole. It hissed at her, its yellow eyes burning bright. It growled and hot steam escaped from around its shark teeth. But it didn't come through the hole.

She wanted to get up, but couldn't. She was trapped, held down by those glowing yellow eyes. But the thing didn't come for her. And looking at it halfway though the opening in the fence, she was reminded of the gecko with those tiny staring eyes, halfway out of the drain in the bathroom sink, and she knew that they were one and the same.

But still it didn't come for her and some instinct carried down from ancestors long dead told her why.

It was afraid of the cemetery.

"Daddy, where are you?" she cried. Then she passed out.

CHAPTER FOURTEEN

HUGH WASHINGTON RUBBED HIS HANDS in front of his mouth, but blowing on them was no help. Last night had been hot, tonight cold, but then he was much farther north and he was by the ocean. He should have know better. He should have remembered.

His breath was no match for the cold night breeze coming in off the sea. He cursed himself for not buying a warm jacket, but the shock of Walker's death tore straight to his heart. That, piled on top of his worry about Glenna, cost him his sense of priorities. Five minutes after Kohler and crew left town he was in *Power Glide* and driving after them. It was like the old days, he was hunting again.

He sat in a thicket across from the gray house, eyes vigilant, ignoring the occasional bug crawling along his arms or down his neck. He hoped the car was okay. When he saw the gravel road a quarter mile past the Kohler house he turned onto it without thinking. He parked out of sight of the main road and locked the car. Now, sitting in the dark, he missed the car's warmth and he wondered if anybody ever used that road.

Earlier, during the walk back to Kohler's, he tried to push all thoughts of Glenna and Walker out of his mind. If he was going to find her, and avenge Walker's death, he needed to keep full concentration on the job at hand. Time enough to mourn Walker after Glenna was safe and warm and Kohler, if he was responsible, was dead and buried. He tried to push his worries about his car away. Either the car would be okay or it wouldn't.

He had been sitting in the thicket since morning, over twelve hours. He'd been cold for four, very cold for two, and still no sign of Monday or Glenna. Maybe something happened to them, an accident. Maybe Monday had been caught. It didn't matter, the smart thing for him to do was wait. He'd give it the night. If they didn't show by morning, he would go to the police.

He opened a can of the beef stew, keeping his eye across the street as he ate with a plastic spoon. He was on his third bite when the porch light came on and the front door opened. Kohler, Mrs. Monday, the Weasel and a third man, big and stupid looking, came out, framed in the light. Big and Stupid locked the door and all four got into the Mercedes. Stupid and the Weasel in back, Mrs. Monday and Kohler in front.

He wondered where Stupid had come from. Had he been in the house all along? Was there anybody else in there? Where were they going now? Dinner?

Following them was out of the question. He hadn't counted on them leaving. What to do now? Sit back and wait. Or?

Or what? Go in, that's what. Go in and see what's what.

He stood, stretched and brushed the dirt from his clothes. He reached under the flap of the unbuttoned camouflaged shirt and checked the gun, an involuntary reflex, and started across the street toward the house.

The front was well lit and the windows were barred. It would be foolish to try and enter that way. The windows on both sides were barred as well. In back he found a large wooden deck set back about ten feet from the cliff. The doctor had a spectacular view. He took the stairs up the deck and found the rear windows barred also. The back door was deadbolted shut.

He wondered how he'd get in, maybe from below. He went back down the stairs. The house might have a basement, accessible from under the deck. The cloudless, star filled sky afforded him plenty of light. Enough to see that there was no basement once he was under the wooden deck. Nothing but a pile of wood and an ax.

"Fuck it." He picked up the ax.

He took the stairs back up two at a time. He swung the ax in a great arc, smashing it against the deadbolt. It was a good lock. It took five solid hits to bust the door open.

Enough light came in the windows so that he didn't have to use the flashlight and it was a good thing, because he'd left it across the street, snugly tucked away in his backpack. Thinking of the forgotten flashlight brought his hand to his gun again. At least he hadn't forgotten everything.

He spent a few seconds admiring the rich kitchen. Cobalt blue tile on the floor and counters, lots of brushed stainless steel. Professional range, oven, microwave and refrigerator. Tiled preparation area in the center, with a small flat digital television mounted on the wall for easy viewing while cooking. Every chef's dream, he thought, leaving the kitchen. He wasn't sure what he was looking for, but he knew he wasn't going to find it among the pots and pans.

The living room was a designer's nightmare. Plush white carpets, top of the line contemporary furniture, lots of oak. A giant Hitachi digital screen mounted above the fireplace, and in the center of the room, a steel and glass coffee table, looking very out of place.

The dining room was also covered in plush white carpet. The center of the room was taken up by a large oak table, surrounded by eight chairs, but what caught his eye was the Hitachi television mounted on the wall, the twin of the one in the living room.

He checked the half-bath off the dining room and found a toilet, shower, and a small digital Sony, mounted on the wall for viewing while sitting. He chuckled, then went up the stairs. He found three bedrooms and a master bedroom. All with televisions, all Hitachi gas plasmas. The master bath had one too. the bathroom that served the other bedrooms, a smaller one. Odd he thought, every room a television, but no DVD players.

He went back down the stairs, sliding his hand along the oak banister. He had more rooms to check. It was a big house. He went back through the living room, through a short hallway and opened one of the two doors.

"Holy shit!" he exclaimed, staring wide-eyed. A large king-sized bed was positioned in the center of the room. A professional video camera was mounted on a wheeled tripod on both sides of the bed. An array of professional track lighting and microphones were hanging from the ceiling. A four by eight soundproofed window was cut out of the wall opposite the bed. Beyond the window, in the next room, he saw a soundboard that would put any recording studio to shame, a rack of state of the art sound equipment and a rack of Macs and DVD recorders.

"Mrs. Monday what kind of man have you gotten yourself involved with?" he mumbled as he backed out of the room. He went down the hallway to the recording studio. The door was locked. He tried to kick it in. He gave it a good blast but the lock didn't give. He took a closer look. Although not a double deadbolt like he'd encountered on the back door, it wasn't the cheap interior lock he assumed he was facing.

He got the ax. The first blow caved in the lock. He went through the door.

On a desk next to the soundboard was a stack of DVDs in plastic cases. He went through them, read the titles written on the cases with a felt pen. *Jim and Jenny, Carrie and the twins, The twins and Linda, Bill and Bill, Carrie and Linda.*

Pornography? That didn't make any sense. You don't kill for that. Not anymore. That stuff flooded the internet and it was free, well free for the most part anyway.

He saw a short stack of CDs on the soundboard, picked them up. Under the stack was a letter printed out on plain bond paper.

Mohammed,

I think you'll find this one to your liking. She's just turned forty, but watch the discs, I think you'll approve. She's seventy percent off because of the age. A bargain and I think you'll agree after seeing her in action that she still has several good years left.

Best regards.

It was unsigned.

"Son of bitch," Washington muttered. The bastard was selling people. He picked up the discs, read the labels. *Julia M #1* through *Julia M #7*. "Oh, Mrs. Monday," he said, feeling genuine pain, "your lover boy is about to ship you off to some guy named Mohammed." Washington could just imagine what the rest of her life would be like.

He took out disc number three and stuffed it in his inside jacket pocket. Then He turned to get a closer look at the recording equipment and the Macintosh computers. Expensive. Professional. He raised the ax and brought it down on the soundboard. Not necessary, but it made him feel good. It only took him five minutes to demolish every piece of equipment in the room. After the equipment, he started hacking up the discs. Then he went next door and took care of the cameras. Normally he wasn't so destructive, but Kohler was turning out to be the kind of man that he really didn't like.

On the way out of the place, he took care of all the flat screen panels and on the walk back to his car he reached the inescapable conclusion that Monday was innocent. Walker had been right. Glenna was safe. He didn't have to call the police in the morning.

All he had to do was what Walker wanted. Prove Monday innocent. That would be easy, all he had to do was prove Kohler guilty. He would enjoy that.

He stopped, ears tuned to the night. There was a cricket chirping up ahead. It stopped. He heard an owl hoot, once, then it went quiet. The only sound was the wind rustling through the trees. Something was out there. He heard movement behind the brush on his left. Something was there. He saw a dog-like shape in the moonlight, heard a growl, then saw a pair of canine red eyes glaring at him from through the brush. He went for his gun and the animal disappeared, like a ghost dog. Somebody's stray, he thought, big one. It put him on edge.

He put the gun away and continued his trek up the dark road toward his car. Twenty minutes later he was back at the motel. He rented a movie and a portable DVD player in the office and listened with feigned interest while a young man with an asthmatic cough tried to explain how to hook the player up to the television.

He was glad to be out of the cold. The walk back to the car had tired him more than he cared to admit. He resolved to get up early and take a brisk jog in the woods. From now on, he decided, he would jog every morning and get back in shape. He had made these promises to himself before and every time, without fail, he quit jogging within two or three weeks. But this time, he promised himself, he would stick it through.

He set the DVD player and the disc on the bed, then shucked off his shirt, shoes and the army pants. He didn't know if the itchy, crawling sensations he felt all over his body were real or imaginary bugs. Either way, he needed a shower and clean clothes.

The clothes he would get in the morning, the shower he would get right away.

He liked taking showers in motels. The hot water seemed to last forever. He luxuriated in the steam, letting the hot water pour over his head and down his back, soothing the cold away.

He did his best thinking in a hot shower. He thought about Jane. His marriage was over. He knew that. He didn't know if he could find someone else, or even if he wanted to. He shivered, despite the steam, at the thought of being alone for the rest of his life. He shivered more at the thought of dating again. Some things were not meant to be, and Hugh Washington dating was just one of those things.

His thoughts wandered to Walker. Without Walker he was without work, unless he called Long Beach and ate humble pie. They would take him back, but he couldn't do it. He wouldn't be able to live with himself. He was too old, too set in his ways, and too much of a man to come sniveling back like a snot nosed brat. No, he told himself, you have to lie in the bed you make. He moved his head under the spray and watched the water run off his body, wishing his problems would follow it down the drain, but knowing they wouldn't.

He turned off the shower, thinking about Monday. How would he react when he found out what kind of man Kohler was and what he had planned for his wife? He'd probably kill the son of a bitch, but he was probably going to kill him anyway, Washington thought, as he wrapped himself in a towel.

He left the bathroom and went to the bed, where he picked up and shook out the camouflaged clothes, trying to rid himself of any little creepy crawlies that might be left over from his stint in the woods.

Satisfied, he folded them and stored them in the closet. Then he dropped the towel and put on his street clothes. He wanted to be ready to leave at a moment's notice. After he was dressed he remembered that nobody knew where he was.

He drew the curtains, hooked the DVD player to the TV, popped in the disc and lay back on the bed to watch.

She stared out at him, from the screen, as striking as he'd remembered her. She was sitting on the edge of that king-sized bed. The one in the room with the cameras and the lights. She turned and looked over her shoulder at the camera and smiled. She thrust out her lower lip and blew the hair out of her eyes, the way he'd seen his daughter do countless times.

It looked like she was cold, the way she was shivering, and his heart went out to her. She turned away from the camera and stretched. The camera followed her shaking hand to the center of the bed, where it locked around her purse. A small leather handbag. She pulled the purse to herself, then opened it.

She withdrew a small mirror, then a tiny glass jar, a vial. She unscrewed the lid. His heart ached as she dumped the white powder onto the mirror, trying to hold it without shaking. She took a credit card out of the purse and started chopping up the small chunks of cocaine into a fine white powder. Finished, she used the card to build the powder into two lines, two inches long. It took a few minutes. She was methodical. He noticed her hands were no longer shaking as she rolled up a crisp hundred dollar bill.

She turned toward the camera, smiled a million dollar smile, winked, pursed her lips and threw a kiss. The camera moved in for a close up as she turned back toward the white powder. She put the bill to her nose, leaned over the cocaine and inhaled, making one of the small white snakes vanish. She repeated the motion with the other nostril, killing the other line.

She sat for a moment, eyes closed. She rolled her head and sighed. Then she turned toward the camera, cupped her breasts, squeezed, and sighed again. He had never seen anything like this. He wanted to take out the disc, but couldn't. He was frozen, mesmerized. He had forgotten about why he was here, there was only him and the seventeen inch color screen. The rest of the world didn't exist.

She scooted off the bed, stood and faced the camera. She had a little girl pout on her lips and she batted her eyes like a whore.

"Get on with it," the doctor ordered, his voice coming from off camera.

"Play some music," she said.

Hugh was shocked, but he couldn't stop watching.

"What do you want to hear?" another male voice out of camera range said.

"*Light My Fire*. Play, *Light My Fire*." In a few seconds the music of the Doors played in the background and she started to sway when Jim Morrison started to sing. The combination of the cocaine and music seemed to put her into a trance.

"I'm going to be oh so good. You'll see," she said. "I'm going to fuck and suck you till you're sore and dry and then I'll make you beg for more." She spread her legs and ran her hands between them. "Oh it feels so good, can't you see," she said in a sultry voice as she masturbated through her silk skirt. Then she moved her hands up to her breasts and massaged them.

GECKO

"Soon you'll each have one of these in your mouth. Think about it." She continued the upward motion of her hands till the fingers found the button at her collar. She unbuttoned it. "One down, four to go." She swayed with the rhythm and found the second button, her hands were shaking again as she slipped it out of the button hole. "Three to go," she said, then she looked at the camera and pleaded. "Do we have to do this?"

"Just take it off and make it look good. We don't have all day." Kohler's voice from off camera again.

Her hands, shaking now, found the third button, then the fourth, then the fifth. She closed her eyes, like she was shutting out the world, and took off her blouse, dropping it at her feet. Her hands went behind her back, for the clasp, but then she dropped them to her sides and let the music rule her as she slow danced with the rhythm. She started masturbating again, moving her right hand with a frantic cadence, undulating her hips with the beat of the music.

She continued like that till the pleasure chased away the shame. She opened her eyes, winked, reached behind her back and said. "I'll bet you boys want to see my titties." Then she undid the clasp and the skimpy bra sprang free. She curved her shoulders forward, shucking it off, and the bra joined the blouse on the floor at her feet. She cupped her breasts in her hands, pointing them at the camera.

"One for each of you." She squeezed the nipples. "Oh, I hope your lips can make them feel this wonderful." She tweaked the buds, pinching herself. She moaned and Washington wondered if she was hurting herself on purpose.

She ran her hands from her breasts down to her skirt, hooked a thumb in each side, slid it down and stepped out of it. She resumed her dance clad only in sheer white panties.

"Come take them off me," she said toward the camera.

"No. Take them off yourself. Then stand and face me and make yourself come," the doctor ordered.

Washington thought he saw her flush a little as she dropped the panties, but he couldn't be sure if she was humiliated or excited. He gasped as she faced him on the screen, legs spread like she was riding a horse, masturbating. Her screams of pleasure filled the room. She wasn't faking.

Without realizing what he was doing, Hugh slipped open the buttons on his Levi's and stuffed his hand in his pants, stroking himself. Soft and slow, keeping perfect rhythm with the woman on the screen. And to his amazement when she screamed, "Oh my God, I'm coming," he came, shooting hot sticky fluid over the inside of his underwear.

"Shit! Shit, shit, shit!" he said, immediately ashamed of himself.

He pulled his hand out, trying his best to keep the sticky stuff away from his Levi's. He wiped his hand on the bed cover, unbuckled his belt and carefully eased the pants off. Then he got up and went back to the bathroom, pulling his sweatshirt off on the way. He took his soiled underwear off in the shower and scrubbed them with soap. Once he was convinced all of the telltale evidence was off the shorts, he opened the shower door and tossed them into the plastic covered wastebasket. Something else to buy tomorrow, he thought. He spent another five minutes letting the heat and steam wash away the shame and guilt he felt.

When he finished with his second shower of the evening, he toweled off, then went naked out of the bathroom. He bent over to pick up his Levi's as she moaned in ecstasy. He turned his head to the screen.

Julia Monday was on her hands and knees. The Weasel on his knees behind her, fucking her from the rear. Stupid was standing at the edge of the bed. Her mouth was wrapped around his cock. Kohler must have been working the camera. The Weasel was pumping furiously and Stupid's face was flushed red. Stupid looked like he was going to explode as she worked on him. It looked she was enjoying herself.

Washington felt disgusted, he jabbed his right arm out, index finger extended, and turned the set off. Then he ejected the disc and got dressed. He didn't trust himself to sleep naked tonight. He sat down on the bed and pulled on his shoes and socks. The canned beef stew hadn't dented his appetite. His stomach was growling as he walked out the door. It was only 10:00, something should be open.

Something was, the diner across the road. He rubbed his arms against the cold night and crossed the empty street. He didn't notice the gray Mercedes in the parking lot. The hostess smiled shyly and asked him if he wanted smoking or nonsmoking. He said he didn't care. Something by the window.

It was smoking. He inhaled the tobacco fumes from the booth behind and wished he had a cigarette. He was about to raise his hand and call the waitress, when he heard the clipped German accent that followed the tobacco smoke. He hadn't been paying attention. He wondered if they had seen him and if they had, if Kohler had recognized him.

He saw the waitress approaching. He wished her away, but she kept coming. He wished harder. She kept coming. He buried his face in the menu, wishing she would walk on by.

She did.

"Here's the damage, thirty-four fifty," he heard her say to Kohler's party in the next booth. She was a middle aged woman who had probably worked the night shift for twenty years. When she saw Kohler was going to stiff her on the tip, she said, "Big spender, think you can afford it?"

"You're wasting your time," a high squeaky voice said. Washington placed the voice with the Weasel. "He's heard it all before and he doesn't care." He laughed.

"Please, don't bother coming back," she said.

"Lady," Kohler said, "you do your job and I'll do mine. If you don't like it, I can always talk to the manager."

"You're looking at her, and like I said, please don't bother coming back." Hugh glanced up. Her jaw was set tight. Her right hand was balled into a fist, the knuckles white. She was rubbing the thumb against the index finger, hard, chasing the blood away. She looked like she wanted to belt Kohler. Washington figured that Kohler got that reaction from a lot of people.

"Then I will go to the owner," Kohler said.

"You're looking at her too. And it still goes. Don't come back."

"It's your loss." Kohler got up. Hugh pressed his face further in the menu as the doctor stormed by, followed by Mrs. Monday, the Weasel and Stupid.

After they left the waitress turned to Washington. "You look like you didn't want that asshole to see you."

"You don't miss much."

"No I don't, Hugh." At the sound of his name he looked up into the big woman's smile.

"I know you," he said.

"You better, you bastard." She broke out into a laughing smile, showing lots of teeth.

"Four Eyes," he said. Now he was laughing. "You're Susan Spencer."

"I never really liked that name," she said.

"And I liked Metal Mouth?" he grinned back at her.

"I guess I was pretty cruel to you boys, you little wimp." She laughed.

"Not so little any more," he said. "And we deserved it, always making Johnny's big sister and her friends miserable. We really did love to torment you guys," he said.

"And we kind of liked it. Little boys chasing after us. It was cute." She lost her smile for a minute. "Seeing you here like this reminds me of Johnny. I haven't thought about him in a long time. When I first heard he was killed, I blamed myself. I thought that if I'd have been a better sister, understood him more, maybe he would've stayed in school. It was years before I figured out it was just the times. Sex, drugs, rock 'n' roll, and the war. He chose war. Karma. There was nothing anyone could do."

He saw a gecko dart across the floor and was reminded of the one he'd seen in the hospital. And the talk of a dead friend brought Walker to mind. Something wasn't right. He hadn't been hurt that bad. He shouldn't have died.

"Look, I have to go. I'll come by before I leave town."

"You're a policeman now, I hear."

"That's right and if you'll excuse me," he said, sliding out of his seat, "right now, I'm trying to figure out a way to put that German son of a bitch away for a long time."

"I wish you luck." She gave him a great bear hug. "If you need anything while you're here, you call me."

"Count on it," he said and then he left.

He hurried across the street, oblivious to the gray Mercedes still in the parking lot, but even if he would have seen it, he wouldn't have been able to see Kohler's hate filled eyes staring at him through the dark tinted glass.

Back in his hotel room, he called the information operator in Orange County and got the number for Hope Hospital. He asked for Patti Hamilton and was put on hold. After a long wait, which he occupied by pacing the room with the phone at his ear, she came on the line.

"This is Patti Hamilton." She sounded as pretty as she looked in the hospital.

"This is Hugh Washington. Do you remember me?" He crossed his fingers.

"Of course I remember you, Hugh Washington," she said. "How did you know my name?"

"Are you still wearing that name tag?"

"Oh yeah," she laughed. Then her voice dropped as she changed from light banter to deep concern. "I'm sorry about your friend."

"That's why I called. I saw another one of those gecko things and was reminded about the one I saw in the hospital, and I got to thinking there was something funny about Ron dying like that. He seemed pretty healthy to me."

"They didn't tell you?" He heard her gasp.

"Tell me what?" His hand tightened on the phone.

"You're friend was murdered."

"Murdered?" He knew something wasn't right. But he hadn't suspected murder.

"And not just murdered," she said, her voice cracking. "He was torn apart. Ripped to pieces. I was the one who found him. It was horrible. It was like some big animal tore into him. The walls were covered in blood. It was even on the ceiling. They're trying to keep it quiet, but I figured you would know. You were his partner." There was a long silence between them. Then she said, "And you know what else? Just before I went into that room, just before I found him, one of those geckos came running under the door, tearing out of that room like it knew what was inside. It scared the holy be Jesus out of me."

He saw movement across the room, on the ceiling. He looked up and it stopped and sat there, mocking him. A small green gecko, on the ceiling, upside down. Still.

"Shit," he whispered into the phone. "I gotta go. There's one on my ceiling, right above my head." He hung up the phone leaving her wondering and worrying.

"Glenna, dear Glenna," he said, as he made his way toward the door. He felt foolish. They were harmless, but still they were out of place here. He eased the door open and stepped out into the parking lot. He unlocked the Chevy, got in and relocked the door, started it and drove off into the night, hoping that Glenna was okay and that there were no geckos wherever she was.

CHAPTER FIFTEEN

GLENNA SHIVERED IN HER SLEEP. She was cold and she had to go to the bathroom. She hated getting up at night, getting out from under the warm blankets, leaving a friendly dream. When she was a little girl and wanted the light off, she would lay in bed and wish her father into the room. He usually came, but when she had to pee, no amount of wishing in the world could make it go away. She just had to get up and take care of it herself.

She reached for the blanket. She didn't have to go that bad. She would wait a while longer. She wanted to sink back down to that wonderful place in the sun. She was reliving a vacation in Honolulu with her parents. She loved the beach, the night life, the Hawaiian attitude, but most of all, she loved the hot climate. She shivered again and moved her hand farther down, looking for the covers, but they weren't there.

She opened her eyes. Just for a peek. She wasn't in bed. Not safe at home. She was cold. She had to pee. She was in the cemetery.

The dark clouds were gone and the moonlight dancing off the tombstones made them appear ghostly and forbidding. She was laying across a grave, facing a silvery slab. *John Thomas Tanaka, Taken by accident on his fifteenth birthday, August 1, 1959, Walking in a Better Place*, she read, and her heart went out to him. Fifteen. He hadn't even started to live. Were you a good boy, John Tanaka? Did your parents call you Johnny? She noticed the fresh flowers and wondered about such devotion after all this time.

She touched her forehead and winced. She was already getting a welt. How long had she been asleep. Not asleep, the thought assaulted her, she had passed out. She turned away from John Tanaka's tombstone, toward the gap in the fence, expecting to see those glowing yellow eyes, but the slimy lizard thing was gone. She breathed a sigh of relief.

She felt the cool wetness between her legs and she shivered again. She wanted to get up and pee. She wanted a dry pair of pants, but they were in one of the laundry bags on the other side of the fence, behind the garage. No way was she going back through that gap. I'm going to stay right here with you, Johnny Tanaka. Safe in your arms. I'm not moving till Jim Monday comes through that fence. And like when she was a little girl, she wished her dad would come.

* * *

He crushed his opponent, a North Vietnamese colonel, with his three hotels on Park Place. The imaginary game was one of the long ones, about three hours, he figured, and still he heard the television set in the other room. Would they never go to sleep?

He was cramped in a tight sitting position, in a dark closet, in the den. The sound of the television filtered through as a steady drone, reminding him of the constant barrage his North Vietnamese captors blared through their loud speakers.

He wasn't able to escape from that prison, he hadn't even tried. That was the hardest thing for him to live with, the not trying. He was able to stand up to them. Able to resist their torture. Strong enough not to sign anything. But not brave enough to try and get out. No man was as courageous as they had painted him. He had been afraid. He hadn't tried to escape, because he was more afraid of what was outside the wire than inside.

Outside was the terrifying war. He started fighting his fear before he even got to Vietnam. Everyday something more to be afraid of. Everyday. Everyday he fought fear and did his job. He was an excellent soldier. Distinguished in battle. Decorated by his superiors. Demanding of himself. First to fight. Last to retreat. Always afraid.

When he was captured and he knew the war was over for him, the fear fled. He was flooded with an immense feeling of relief. His captors never understood that. They expected another whimpering dog. Monday didn't cry out when tortured, but he didn't resist either. After awhile, they left him alone. Maybe he could have escaped, but he didn't try. And here he was all over again, cringing in a kind of prison cell, not trying to escape.

No, he told himself, not again. He was not going to sit and wait. He was going to escape and wipe away the memories of all those nights when he was forced to turn inward. He went deep into his mind and found a can of gas and a book of matches. He poured the gasoline on the Monopoly board, struck a match and imagined the flames. He'd played his last Monopoly game. Glenna was counting on him. He had cowered in the closet long enough.

He stood in the dark and opened the door. The sky had cleared and the moonlight filtering in the window reflected off the glass enclosed photograph on top of the desk. He went to the desk, opened the top drawer and withdrew the forty-five, sticking it between the small of his back and his Levi's.

He hoped the television would cover whatever noise he made. He breathed a sigh of relief when the door to the hallway opened without a sound. To get to the kitchen and the key rack, where he hoped he would now find a set of car keys, he would have to go though the dining room at the end of the hallway. The dining room was open to the living room, where somebody was watching a late movie.

He reached down and slipped his new shoes off. Clad now in stocking feet, shoes in hand, he tiptoed down the hallway. The bedroom door was open. There was someone sleeping inside. He tiptoed past.

The sound of the television was like a freight train moving through his head. The volume had increased and the chords ripping off of Bruce Springsteen's guitar pierced him like daggers. The TV watcher was channel surfing, now settling on MTV.

He peeked around the corner at the end of the hallway and saw the back of a head rising out of the armchair, facing away from him, staring at the big screen. Bruce was dancing on stage, guitar in hand. He took the plunge and started a quiet walk across the dining room, hoping any sound he might make would be covered by the E Street Band. He saw an arm rise out of the chair, remote in hand. A finger hit a button and Bruce vanished, replaced by a black and white Charlie Chan movie. The head started to turn. Jim took a quick step and slid into the kitchen. He stubbed his toe on a kitchen chair and the sound seemed to echo through the kitchen like a cannon shot.

"That you, Honey?" a male voice said from the living room. He stood, silent. He saw a set of keys in the rack. He took them and stuffed them in the front pocket of his Levi's. "Honey, get me a glass of water," the male voice said.

"All right," a female answered, as the channel changed again. Bruce and the Band were back. The woman was coming toward the kitchen, he felt it. Five quick steps and he was in the laundry room. Two more steps, at the back door. He opened the door with sweaty hands and was out in the night, closing the door when the kitchen light went on. She would have her snack and get her husband a glass of water and never know he had been there.

Thank you Bruce, I'll buy one of your CDs someday, he promised as he hurried across the yard and alongside the garage. He found the laundry bags behind it, but not Glenna.

He sat and waited for his heart to slow down. He rubbed the dirt off his socks and put on the shoes. Where was she? She promised she would wait. He couldn't believe she took off. She'd promised. He remembered the kiss. She'd promised. He felt the dark closing in and he smelled something stale. He didn't like it back there, maybe Glenna didn't either.

He got up and made his way to the gap in the fence and poked his head through.

"I knew you would come," she said, rising into a sitting position. "I knew it." She was a battered angel leaning on a tombstone, basking in the moonlight. He pulled himself through and dashed across the plank to her side.

"The lizard thing was back there," she said, quivering and wide-eyed, "but it was afraid to come into the cemetery." She was saying more, but he was unable to hear. A searing pain shot through the base of his skull. He felt like his head was being ripped apart. He collapsed at her side, falling across John Tanaka's grave.

* * *

He didn't know how long he had been out, but when he came to he was in a hospital bed. He looked up at the white ceiling through hazy eyes. His head turned and he saw the clear bag hanging on the silver stand. He was being fed intravenously. He wondered what was in the IV.

His head turned again, he was alone in the room. His eyes moved back toward the IV and cold fear washed though him. He was laying in a hospital bed. Helpless. Motionless. Watching. His head was turning, his eyes were moving, but he wasn't doing it. Something or someone had control of his body.

He tried to talk.

"Where am I." He felt the words but they made no sound.

"Is that you, Jim Monday?" It was a female voice, soft, with an accent, not British, almost Australian. "Did you come to help me?"

"Who is that? Where are you?" He had seen enough when his eyes involuntarily swept the room to know that he was alone.

"It's me, Donna." Her words had weight, they hung in the air—not in his head. They had sound. *"But this is how you're used to talking to me, isn't it?"* She thought.

"You're back."

"No, I'm not. Not the way you think."

His head moved again and he stared down the length of his body. He was in a hospital bed, wearing a white gown, restrained. Strapped in, like a common criminal. Feet and arms strapped to the sides of the bed. He was immobilized. His eyes moved and locked on his breasts, jutting toward the ceiling, nipples visible through the gown's thin cotton.

"Get the picture?" He heard her voice again. Soft. Silky. Smooth. She lapsed back into thought, *"You're in my head now."*

"How?"

"I don't know, but we are in heaps of trouble."

"Why are you in the hospital? And why restrained?"

"I don't know. I've only been conscious for a few hours. A man came in earlier and I tried to talk to him, but he ignored me. I don't think this is a real hospital."

"Why not?"

"No nurses, no noise, no TV, no patients, no windows—things like that."

"How are you doing?" a voice coming from the doorway asked.

"Where am I?" Donna asked, "And who are you?"

"You're in my clinic, and I'm—" He let the sentence trail off. "You don't really need to know my name."

"What am I doing here?"

"Getting better I hope. You gave me quite a fright when you went into the coma. I thought I was going to lose you, but you hung in there and pulled through. That was good for me, because virgins are getting harder and harder to find."

"What?"

"I checked. If they're not virgins I use them for a few days, then kill them. Virgins I have to save. And you're not just any virgin, you're special." He started to unbutton his shirt.

"What are you doing?" she asked, voice squeaking.

"I have to keep you intact, orders, but I am allowed to play. I just can't break anything, so to speak."

The shirt was hanging open, showing a hairy chest and a fat belly. He rubbed the beer pot with his right hand, pulled a rolled cigarette out of his pocket with his left. He lit it and the pungent smell of marijuana filled the room. He took a deep drag and held his breath. After exhaling with a long sigh he held the joint to her lips.

Donna clamped her mouth shut.

He reached into his pocket and brought out a switchblade. He flicked it open.

"Very sharp." He leered at her. "Either you suck smoke like a good little girl, or I'll slit your throat and find a new virgin. You decide."

"Easy decision," she thought, *"I smoke the joint."*

"He'll probably kill you anyway. Don't do it if you don't want."

"I don't want, but I'm too young to shoot through." She opened her mouth and took a long drag on the joint. She was no stranger to marijuana. Almost everybody she knew had tried it. It was the Northland's largest, though unofficial, cash crop.

"That's better." He took another long drag. Before the joint was half finished, she was more stoned than she had ever been with her friends at the mall. Despite her terror, she closed her eyes, and for a brief few seconds she imagined she was sitting on the concrete benches of the small outdoor mall in downtown Whangarei on a hot December night, passing a joint back and forth, laughing and giggling with the girls, teasing the boys. When she opened her eyes he was taking off his shirt.

"What are you going to do?" Her head was swimming. Waves of pleasure and terror ran the course of her body. Pinpricks of joy and pain. She was riding a black stallion called fear. Dread filled her every pore. She felt both wonderful and terrified.

"Nothing you won't like. I'm just going to play a little." He held the joint between his lips while he bent over and took off his shoes and socks. He took a drag, then put it back to her lips. She inhaled, drawing the smoke deep into her lungs. She held her breath as he took off his pants. Maybe, she thought, if she held her breath long enough, she would pass out and he would go away. He pulled his boxer shorts off and stood before her, hairy and naked.

She continued to hold her breath. He sensed what she was trying to do and poked her in the stomach, forcing her to exhale.

"Naughty, naughty, trying to miss all the fun."

She gasped, her lungs screaming for air. He shoved the joint to her lips and she drew in more of the acrid smoke, and it threw her into a coughing spasm. He stepped back and watched till she settled down and was able to breath.

"The way I look at it," he said, "we can do this one of two ways." He walked naked to a rolling metal chest of drawers and withdrew two objects. "In my left hand I'm holding a standard battery operated vibrator. It can be the source of much pleasure. In the right I'm holding a standard Los Angeles police issue taser, capable of sending several thousand volts of electricity though your nervous system. It can be the source of much pain. Which is it to be?"

She didn't answer.

He pushed a button on the taser and she saw a bolt of blue electricity jump between the two terminals.

"It's very painful," he said.

"The vibrator," she whispered.

"Good. Very good." His hands went between his legs and he started to play with himself, making himself hard. He rolled the chest of drawers to the bed and withdrew a jar of oil. She wanted to struggle, but she was bound to the bed. She screamed and continued screaming as he used the switchblade to slice away the hospital gown, leaving her bound and naked. He poured some of the oil on her breasts and started to massage them. She stopped screaming.

He worked slowly with expert hands on each breast. She closed her eyes and watched the colors on the inside of her eyelids pulsating with the raging beat of her heart.

The massaging hands stopped for a minute and she opened her eyes. He turned out the light and lit a candle. The flicking flame cast him in an evil shadow. Satanic was the word that flashed across her mind as he returned with the oil and worked on her feet, sending waves of pleasure shooting up her legs. She closed her eyes in a state of terrified ecstasy.

"I'm here, Donna," Jim thought. *"We can get through this."*

"Can you feel it? Can you feel what I feel, like I felt what you felt?

"Yes. You have to fight this. Be strong. We can fight it together."

"Come on Jim, just enjoy it."

"How can you say that?"

"It's out of our control. Right now I am completely in that man's power. The last thing I want is the knife slicing across my throat. If that son of a bitch wants me to moan and enjoy what he's doing, then I am going to moan. I'm going to keep my eyes closed and let him do whatever he wants and I'm going to do my level best to enjoy every bloody second, because right now my body is the only weapon I have, and I'm going to use it to try and keep myself alive."

"I'm sorry. I wasn't thinking."

"Well now that you are, enjoy yourself, you just might learn something."

He took her advice, joining himself to her and they let the naked man send oceans of pleasure through her body.

"Just a little Demerol in the IV. To make you enjoy it more. Demerol and marijuana, a wonderful combination, don't you think? Nobody can resist it."

"Hmmmm," she moaned.

His hands were back on her breasts. Jim quivered along with Donna, wanting more as badly as she. She arched her back against the restraints when he took a nipple into his mouth, offering him more. Every fiber of their entwined consciousness tingled in anticipation when they heard him turn on the vibrator.

And Jim moaned with her when he slid it between her legs. They arched her back, her body, and their twin desires wanting, needing more. They started thumping her buttocks against the bed, fighting the restraints, the two of them soaring to a sexual high neither had thought possible. Jim was with her, every pulse of the way, matching the thrust of herself against the vibrator, and he yelled along with her, a loud devil yell, "Yes, yes, yesssss," when the orgasm finally struck, sending sonic booms of pleasure from her core through to their very essence. They were bound as no two had ever been bound. And they both knew that it was forever.

"I think you might have enjoyed that even more than me."

She opened her eyes.

He was still naked. He put down the vibrator.

"You know," he continued, his slitted eyes gleaming, "what Manfred is going to do to you when he gets here?"

"When?" she whispered. She was exhausted. She could have asked, what? But she could well imagine. She was more concerned with when. How long did she have to win this man over? To get him to loosen her bonds. To get him to make a mistake, so she could get away.

"Next Sunday, at midnight. He doesn't want to see you before the sacrifice." They watched as he picked up the taser. "You see he's going to fuck you, burn you alive, then feed you to his pet." He pressed the taser against her breast and they screamed, this time in pain, then everything went black.

* * *

It was quiet, when he opened his eyes, once more in control of what he saw. A cool breeze bathed his sweat soaked face. He was spent.

"Are you okay?" Glenna asked. He saw the concern in her eyes.

"I think so. It feels good to be back." Out of Donna's body, he no longer felt the combined effects of the two drugs. He just felt used. Raped and used.

He was ashamed for having enjoyed it. He had been degraded. He vowed to find and kill that man, if it was that last thing he ever did. And, Manfred, whoever he was, the man that pulled the strings, he would kill him too. Slowly and painfully.

"Sometime before next Sunday at midnight, I hope," Donna thought.

"You're back?"

"You didn't think I wanted to stay with that maniac alone, did you?"

"I thought you were going to die," Glenna said, holding his damp head in her lap. "First you passed out, then you started moaning, and the moans started to get kind of loud, so I had to hold my hands against your mouth. I was afraid I was going to suffocate you. Then you started bouncing and moaning like you were having great sex. Then you tried to scream, but I held my hand tight, and then you went limp. I thought you were dead."

"She's back." He sat up, then told her everything that had happened while he had been away, leaving nothing out.

"And you're sure it wasn't a dream? A strange nightmare? You've been through an awful lot."

"Tell her I know what it feels like to be tied down and abused. I'm not under the influence of any drugs now. Tell her how degraded I feel."

He told her.

"I want to believe you, I really do, but it's all too fantastic."

"I think I know what he meant, when he said Manfred was going to feed her to his pet," Jim said.

"What?" Glenna gasped. "You mean—"

"Yeah, that thing with the big teeth. I think that somehow it's connected to her, or me, or both of us. It knows where we are. It can follow us somehow."

"That's crazy talk, but I believe you. That thing is for real. That I know. And it followed us for over a hundred miles. It followed us and found us, but it was afraid of the cemetery. It wouldn't come in after me. It's not all powerful. We can find a way to kill it."

"Burn it. It's the only way."

"She said it again, we have to burn it."

"How does she know?"

"My mother told me stories about giant geckos and the underworld. They're evil, and the only way to send them back to where they come from is to burn them."

"And you believe your mother's stories?" Jim thought.

"She's Maori, she wouldn't lie."

"She says she's Maori and that her mother told her about giant geckos from the underworld. If you burn them, it sends them back."

"Then we'll burn it," Glenna said. "Us sisters have to stick together."

"Sisters?"

"She's Maori, that makes her black as far as I'm concerned. She's a sister."

He sat up and let the cool night breeze wash over his sweat drenched body.

"We have to find my father," Glenna said. "If anyone can find where she is and save her, he can. He's the best."

"Isn't he just an ordinary police officer?"

"Would just any police officer have found you at that motel so fast?" She went on to tell him about her father and how he was the best homicide detective that ever lived. She thought a lot of him and if only part of what she said was true, then Jim wanted his help.

"We need this man," Donna thought.

"I agree."

"How do we find him?"

"He'll go for Kohler. He'll watch and wait. If we find Kohler, he'll find us." She stood up and offered him her hand. He gave it and she helped him up. "Did you get the keys?"

He nodded.

"I can't go back behind that garage, could you go and get my laundry bag? I have to change."

"Here? Now?"

"I peed my pants when that thing was after me."

He was gone less than half a minute. She took a pair of the jeans out of her bag.

"Turn around," she said, "so I can change."

He turned away from her.

"Okay, I'm ready," she said after less than a minute. "Let's go."

"We have to go back through the fence to get the car."

"But not behind the garage?"

"Not behind the garage."

"What if it comes after us?"

He reached into his laundry bag, withdrew the forty-five and handed it to her. "Do you know how to use this?"

"Of course. Daddy's a cop and I'm Daddy's little girl."

He reached behind his back and brought out the other gun.

"You took more than the keys?"

"Yes I did." He stood, listened to the night for a few seconds, then he walked the plank over the drainage ditch and went through the gap in the fence, holding the gun in front of himself, the bag behind. She followed, copying his moves. They slipped along the side of the garage, like ninjas in the night, both aware that there were people in the house.

There were two cars in the driveway now. The red Miata and a Chrysler LaBaron. He dropped his gun in the bag and went through the key ring till he found what he was looking for.

"We'll take the Miata," he whispered. He unlocked the door and they put their bags behind the passenger seat. "We can't start it here. We'll have to push it down the street." He was still whispering. "You get behind the wheel and I'll push."

Five minutes later they were roaring out of town, headed toward the interstate, with Glenna driving. He was thinking about Donna. Donna back in his head again. Donna strapped to a hospital bed halfway around the world. She was part of him now. However evil the intent of the man that abused them, he had fused them. They were one. He could no more live without her than he could his heart. He still loved Julia, but like a sister. What he felt for Donna was what great poets wrote about. And he didn't even know what she looked like.

"*I'm terribly pretty and I love you too,*" she thought.

"*Hey, those thoughts were private.*"

"*I love you,*" she thought.

"*I love you too, more than anybody's ever loved anything,*" he thought back.

"*I want to be with you always, Jim Monday, always. Come to New Zealand. Come and get me and make me yours.*"

"*Not even death itself could stop me. I'll leave first thing in the morning.*"

"*No. First you must confront this man that killed your friend. I've felt your grief, this man must pay.*"

"*We only have a week to find you. I can deal with Kohler later.*"

"*No, if he's the one responsible for your friend David's death, your wife is in danger, too. If something happens to her and we could have stopped it, we couldn't live with ourselves. Find this Dr. Kohler you hate so much and do what you must, but let's do it quickly, because this man, Manfred, is coming soon. And who knows what else his wicked servant has planned for me."*

"I hope her father's half the detective she said he is and I wonder where he is now?" Jim thought, as Glenna braked for the stop sign by the Mobil Station just before the Interstate.

"Penny for your thoughts?" Glenna said, interrupting his conversation with Donna.

"I was thinking about your father. Wondering where he is right now."

"He's in Tampico. I'm sure of it." She popped the clutch, smoking the tires as she flew through the gears like a pro, making the Miata scream as they sped onto the freeway.

CHAPTER SIXTEEN

HUGH WASHINGTON RUMMAGED in his pocket for his room key, his head still spinning from the drink. He keyed the door. The blast of hot air from inside caused him to flush. He'd left the heat on. He turned it off, flopped down on the bed and watched the ceiling move. He hadn't sat in a bar till last call since before he was married, and the way he felt, it would be another twenty years before he did it again.

When he left the motel five hours earlier, he hadn't intended on getting drunk, hadn't even intended on going to a bar. Seeing Susan Spencer again after thirty years made him homesick, so he took the ten minute drive down Across The Way Road and found himself back in Palma.

The lazy main street of thirty years ago now sported two bars, three restaurants, a sporting goods store, two pharmacies, a bookstore, two banks, two gas stations and a few other small businesses. Not a big town by anybody's standards, but not the one bar, one gas station town that he'd grown up in.

He parked in front of the bookstore. He wanted to walk the street. A few minutes wouldn't hurt. Plenty of time to get back and watch Kohler's place. Besides, he still needed a warm jacket, though he doubted he'd find anyplace open.

He moved up the street with an easy stride, curious as any vacationing tourist. He was reminded of the many vacations he'd gone on with his family and how he and Jane used to love window shopping, looking at things they couldn't afford. He'd sense the longing in her heart and he'd say, 'Someday I'll buy you one of those,' and she'd always answer, 'You're all I want. You and Glenna.' But he always suspected she wasn't being completely truthful, because she stared at the new dresses and the jewelry with a kind of burning intensity, like she was carving the image into her mind. If she couldn't possess it physically, she would posses it mentally.

He was feeling sorry for himself and he hated it. He stopped in front of Dewey's Tavern. A drink might help chase the blues away and some of the cold as well. He went in. The tavern might have been transported from London. Even the smell was authentic. He bellied up to the bar and ordered a Guinness. When in Rome.

"Mr. Washington, we are meeting again." Hugh recognized the voice of Jaspinder Singh even before he turned around. He shook his hand. Singh was drinking a coke.

"You live in Palma?" Hugh asked, making conversation.

"Eleven years, since I bought the market Tampico side." Tampico was on the north side of the bay, Palma the south.

"You work Tampico side, live Palma side. You must know everybody in the area?"

"Are you wanting more information?"

"A little. I was wondering if you could help me put a couple of names to a couple of descriptions."

"I could try."

"The first fellow is a skinny little man, losing his hair, combs it over, right to left," Washington swept his hand across his head to show what he meant, "slanty eyes, reminds me of a weasel."

"And the other," Jaspinder Singh said, "Looks like an ape?"

"Yep."

"They are Frank and Bobby Markham. Frank is the older brother, Bobby is as stupid as he looks. Not retarded. Just stupid."

"You can see it in his eyes," Hugh said.

"Yes, in his eyes. I am thinking these are not nice men. Very bad. As you must know, they work for Dr. Kohler. Where he found them, nobody knows, but many people are wishing he would send them back."

"Have they been into any trouble?"

"No, I don't think so. You would have to ask Sheriff Sturgees. It's just that they look at you with contempt, like you're beneath them. I could well imagine them as Gestapo working under a man like Kohler. They seem well suited for that kind of work."

"You wouldn't happen to know where they live, would you?"

"They live at Kohler's."

"That's cozy."

"The doctor is away most of the time. When he's out of town you can find the Markham brothers

Tampico side, drinking at the Long Bar, or here. When the doctor is in residence, they stick to him like shadows."

"One more question, not related. When I was a boy my dad used to take me Tampico side, to Dewey's Men's shop. It was the only place you could buy Levi's. This Dewey related?" He made a sweeping gesture with his hand.

"His son."

"And old man Dewey? Is he still alive?"

"Very much so and still selling Levi's in the same location."

"It's good to see that not everything has changed." Washington took a long pull on his beer.

"Much here has, like the murders this morning."

"What murders?"

"A woman was attacked on the beach early this morning, right in front of her son. Fortunately an alert passerby was swift thinking and ran the homeless beggar down in his jeep."

Hugh felt sick. He was a trained cop. He should have stopped and made sure that woman was all right.

"Is she okay?" he asked.

"Oh yes, the man was stopped before he could cut her."

"He had a knife?"

"Oh yes, a big knife, a Bowie knife."

"Very bad," Washington said, glad the woman hadn't been hurt.

"But it looks like he killed a young family earlier, before he attacked the woman. We are getting too much like the big city. Soon I fear I will have to look for another place to bring up my children."

"Where? It's getting to be the same all over."

"Out by Victorville maybe, the high desert, not much crime there?"

"What kind of life can kids have out there?" Washington wanted to know.

"I just want them to have a life."

"I understand that," Washington said, thinking about Glenna and what America's violent society had done to her.

"I went to a lot of trouble to become an American," Jaspinder Singh said, as if reading his mind, "but I want my kids safe. I might leave. Maybe Canada or Australia," he paused for a few seconds, "or New Zealand. Someplace safe."

He sat with Jaspinder Singh through three more beers, before bidding the man goodnight. He should have gone too, but he stayed, sipping beer and feeling sorry for himself, till last call. Never again, he told himself, as he went into the bathroom to splash cold water on his face.

Knowing he couldn't sleep and feeling that he'd let Glenna down by not being on station in the thicket across from Kohler's, he decided to go out there now. He changed back into the camouflage clothes he'd bought earlier, having to struggle into them. He wasn't drunk, he thought, just a little tight, but deep down he knew that if he would've pulled himself over, he would've taken himself to jail. He grabbed his keys and went out the door.

He cranked the ignition, the starter motor whirred, but the car didn't start. He tried again, nothing. The car was trying to tell him something, but he wasn't listening. He pumped the gas three times, held the pedal to the floor, cranked the ignition a third time and the car sprang into life. He drove out of the parking lot, making a left turn on Mountain Sea Road, toward Kohler's and that dirt road a quarter mile beyond.

It was a quarter to three when he turned onto the dirt track and parked the car. Once the headlights were off he was bathed in black. It was a dark night, the moon and stars hidden under a low, cloud-covered sky. Like last night, he thought, when he'd found the blood all over the walls. He had the unshakable feeling that the overhanging clouds and the bloody walls in that room were intertwined and he shivered, but he was too drunk to be afraid.

He fumbled the keys out of the ignition and stumbled out of the car. He wondered how he made it out here and how he was going to get the trunk open with his unsteady hands in the dark, but he did. He took out the carbine, the extra clip and the flashlight, then closed the trunk.

"Prepared, like a boy scout," he mumbled, as he flicked the flashlight's switch. The light stayed dark. "Some boy scout," he said, still mumbling. "No batteries." But through the fog haze he vaguely remembered buying some. Again he fumbled with the keys, struggling with the trunk. Once it was open, he ran his hands around the interior, like a blind beggar searching for a dropped quarter.

He found the batteries and fought another dark struggle with the plastic bubble wrap and another getting them into the flashlight, but still it wouldn't light. He took the batteries out and reversed them. Still no light. He slumped over and started to fall, but he threw out his hands and held on to the car for support.

He stayed like that, fighting nausea and trying to hold down the vomit that wanted to come. He lost the battle and threw up. His stomach muscles clenched as great gobs of viscous vomit seemed to tear his insides apart. He fought for air, wanting it to stop, hoping it would stop, but still he heaved, spewing out the contents of his stomach and continuing on, dry heaving.

Finally it stopped, leaving him gasping for air, his body demanding oxygen. He used the car for support, bending over the right front fender, holding on to good old *Power Glide*. He took deep breaths, the way he'd seen Glenna do when she was doing her yoga exercises and after a few minutes he felt better.

He stood up, backed away from the car, faced into a cool breeze, forced his shoulders back and took one last, deep breath. The wind cooled his face. He felt better, less drunk and he wanted a cigarette. The stale Marlboros were in the glove box.

He slid into the passenger seat, popped the glovebox, grabbed the cigarettes and his gold Zippo. Normally he didn't smoke in the car, but it was his rule and he felt like breaking it. He flipped a smoke into his mouth and flicked the lighter.

He inhaled deeply, sat back and closed his eyes. What was he doing out here in the middle of the night? By now Kohler had surely called the sheriff. If he was caught out here like this, it wouldn't be hard for even the most incompetent of small town cops to stick him with the crime. It was stupid for him to have broken in that way. Even dumber to go at the video and sound equipment with the ax. It was a weakness, that kind of stuff made him go out of control.

He took another drag, held the tobacco in his lungs, exhaled the blue smoke, and didn't feel any better. The cigarette wasn't any help. He stubbed it out.

He should go back to the motel. Shower and sleep it off. He almost started the car to do just that, but as he was about to crank the ignition a picture of Glenna flashed through his mind and he knew he wasn't going back to the motel. He cursed himself for drinking when his daughter was in danger, but he was confident he had purged himself from the worst of the alcohol's effects. He got out of the car.

The dark clung to him like a second skin, blocking his vision and chilling his soul. There was just enough light for him to see the road at his feet and two arm lengths ahead, not any more. A good boy scout would have checked the flashlight and made sure it worked before embarking on such a fool's errand, but boy scouts didn't go on fools errands. A cop might—fathers do.

Clutching the carbine, holding it in front of himself, at the ready, he started his trek toward the gray house. He had almost made the twenty feet up to the road, when he heard the sound. A movement in the brush. He stopped and listened, more sober by the second. But he heard only silence.

He started again, eyes down, on the dirt road. He let out a sigh of relief when he reached the pavement. Easy sailing now.

A deep throated growl came from up ahead, blocking his way. Washington stopped, moving his eyes off the road, willing them to reach out through the night and bring him a picture of whatever was blocking his path, but the night armor was too strong for his vision's arrows. Something threatening was there and he might as well have been blind.

He stopped again, tuned his ears to the dark as he chambered a round. He pointed the carbine ahead, where he thought the sound had come from, and pulled the trigger.

The gunshot ripped through the silent night followed by an agonizing howl, then by the sound of something thrashing through the thick brush, scraping and tearing along the ground, bellowing as it fled away from Washington. And the night went silent again and as if nothing had happened, he forced his eyes down to the paved road and continued his trek. Kohler's place was a quarter mile away and at the rate he was going, it would be dawn before he arrived at the thicket.

Watch dog, wild dog, child's pet or bear, he didn't know or care what it was he'd shot. His only thought was of Glenna. If he wanted to get her back, he would have to be at Kohler's when she arrived with Jim Monday. He had delayed too long already. His resolve was firm. Nothing was going to stand in his way, not animal, nor man, but his resolve was quickly tested. He heard something twisting and turning in the brush and it was no longer tearing away from him in desperate flight. It was moving toward him with deliberate caution.

He put his nose in the wind. The thing coming for him had a smell all too familiar. He had been assaulted by it before, once following a freeway accident, once when he helped a fireman drag a burning woman from a blazing building. It was impossible to guard against. There was no protection from the smell of burning flesh. This thing coming for him was no dog, or bear.

He sensed that it was hugging the ground, forcing the brush aside like some kind of great snake. He used his ears, forced himself to concentrate on the sound and not the odor, which threatened to make him sick all over again. He was alert now, the adrenaline forcing all effects of the alcohol away. And in his new state of awareness, he reasoned that the thing was using the odor to misdirect him. Odor is carried with the breeze which twists and turns through the woods. It lies. He had to depend on his ears, they would give him the animal's true position.

He listened as it drew closer, clawing and scratching on the ground. He closed his eyes and let the sense of sound take over. Again he used his instincts and fired into the night. And again the thing screeched, thrashed and moved away. Two shots and two hits, but this time it didn't move as far. It hissed, like a snake hisses, but sounded more like a giant boiler releasing pent up steam, and he was overpowered with the pungent burning smell. He was tempted to shoot again, but he held his fire. He was a veteran and he wanted to make every shot count.

Something in the back reaches of his mind said run, but somehow Washington knew to run was to die. He waited, motionless. And it moved in closer, stalking him. It might be tough, Hugh thought, but it couldn't be silent. He waited till he heard it leave the brush. It's on the road. It thinks I can't hear if it advances along the blacktop, but it's wrong, I can. The thing was unable to mask the sound of its claws sliding on the smooth road and Hugh's excellent hearing guided the direction of his fire like radio guided lasers.

Five quick rounds filled the night like explosions and the roar of the beast followed like an erupting volcano. Hugh fired the last three rounds of the ten round clip, ejected, jammed in the fresh clip and, while the animal still roared, he fired five more shots into the screams, still failing to silence the howling beast.

Fighting temptation he held his fire. The animal was directly in front of him, raging and screeching, clawing and scratching, but it wasn't getting any closer. He shot his hands into his pocket and came out with the gold Zippo. He flicked it and for a flash of a second saw the thing that had been stalking him.

Big, reptilian, cringing from the Zippo's light, bleeding from scores of wounds, foaming at the mouth, a baseball-sized eye on both sides of its lizard-like head, eyes glowing yellow against the Zippo's flame. It hissed foam and steam at the light and moved away, slinking on its belly, backwards, away from the fire.

Holding the Zippo in his left hand with his arm extended forward, Hugh tucked the carbine into his side and fired the last five shots into the head of the beast. All direct hits, causing it to spasm and jerk with each shot. The last shot jerked it onto its back, but it quickly righted itself and roared, blaring like an elephant, showing Hugh the hatred in its flaming yellow eyes, daring him to put out the flame.

Hugh dropped the carbine, grabbed his pistol from the shoulder holster, and advanced on the reptile.

"You're going to eat shit, motherfucker."

* * *

Badly wounded, it tried to back away from the advancing human with the fire. It was confused. Humans always ran. They were prey. Prey didn't fight back and prey never attacked. But this human was something new. It was changing the rules. And, having never been hunted, the beast didn't know what to do. It had never run from prey. But this wasn't prey anymore. This was something different. This was a hunter.

It opened its wide mouth, showing jagged teeth, then growled, hissing blue steam into the cool night. This never failed to frighten humans, usually paralyzing them with fear. But the prey, that was no longer prey, extended an arm, and flame leapt out from the human's hand, and great pain flashed in its throat as three quick explosions smashed into its mouth.

It hissed again, gurgling blood. If only the human would drop the fire it could attack, but the arm that dealt pain stiffened and the reptile backed off as the arm jerked and something smashed into its left eye making everything on its left side go dark. It turned, and for the first time in its long life, it fled.

* * *

That's it, Hugh thought, I'm going for the law. He had faced the beast and driven it back. But he was under no illusions. It had taken several fatal hits and had not gone down. He had only two shots left, if he encountered it again, he would lose. It was time for the horse soldiers.

He turned back to the side road, holding the Zippo high as he walked. Hugh Washington's mother didn't raise a dumb boy. He'd noticed the effect the flame had on that thing and he wondered how long since he'd last put fluid in the lighter. If it failed now, he was a dead man. But the flame held till he reached the car and Hugh again gave thanks that there were some things you could always count on. Some things that never let you down.

He breathed a sweat-chilled sigh of relief as his hands sought out and opened the driver's door. A second sigh escaped him as he moved into the car, positioning himself behind the wheel. He flicked off the lighter and put it away. He searched his pockets for the keys, found them, and was sliding the key into the ignition when a voice in the back said. "Out early, aren't you, Mr. Washington?"

Hugh froze.

"That's a good idea. Don't move. I have a small, but very effective pistol pointed at the nape of your neck. Killing you now would give me great pleasure, but the doctor wants a word. I trust you'll be willing to oblige."

"Take me to your leader, Mr. Markham." Hugh tried to sound more confident than he felt.

"Ah, you know me. Excellent. Doc said you must be sharp to find him here so quickly."

"Just lucky."

"Unlucky is more like it," the Weasel said, "especially when he finds out how you treated his little darling. He's gonna be real mad. Shooting up a poor defenseless creature like that. Oh yeah, he's gonna be mad."

Five minutes later Hugh piloted *Power Glide* into Dr. Kohler's driveway, wondering if they were going to let him get out alive.

"That's good," the Weasel said. "Now turn it off."

Hugh obeyed.

"You know, Washington, if you woulda just come by the house and asked your questions, you mighta lived through all this, but breaking up Doc's equipment that way and destroying his discs like you did, real stupid that was. Did you destroy the one you stole, too?"

"I don't know what you're talking about," Hugh said, hoping he'd get a chance to use the thirty-eight and those last two shots.

"Don't waste it on me. Get out of the car."

Hugh opened the door and was greeted by Dr. Kohler.

"How are you this morning, Officer Washington?" His German accent was short and still clipped.

"Been better."

"Yes, I'll bet you have."

"I'll be better again."

"No, I don't think so."

The shadows cast on the doctor's face by the porch light behind didn't do him any favors. Hugh was reminded of B-grade, black and white horror movies with bad casts and bad endings. The flaring nostrils jutting out from Kohler's sharp nose, inflating and contracting with each angry breath told Hugh that the doctor had the worst of all bad endings planned for him. He knew hatred when he smelled it.

"Julia, come out here," Kohler snapped.

Washington's heart skipped when she stepped into the lighted frame of the open front door. She was nude, with her hair blowing in the night breeze. The sight of her standing there like that took his breath away and his heart went out to her.

"You wanted to look," Kohler said. "Look."

"I don't know what you're talking about," Hugh said.

"Oh, come now. You broke in here. Rather crudely done, I might add, and you destroyed some very valuable things. And you took something of mine. Now you see her in person. You see, all you had to do is ask, you didn't have to take the disc."

"I still don't know what you're talking about."

"Julia, take him inside."

Hugh stood breathless as she approached. She smiled at him with misty eyes, took him by the hand and led him into the house. He was helpless, caught in the web of her beauty and the sadness of her eyes. He could do nothing else but follow.

"Sit," Frank Markham commanded, pulling him away from Julia and indicating a chair. Hugh sat. "Hands behind your back." He complied and Frank Markham, the Weasel, tied him to the chair. Hands behind and legs to the front, while Kohler held the gun. He was helpless, unable to move.

"You've done this before," Hugh said.

"Yes." He paused. "A bullet to the back of the head usually follows, but I think Doc has something more interesting planned for you."

"I asked you not to call me that." Kohler glared at the Weasel.

"Yes, sir. Sorry, sir," Frank Markham said.

"Bobby, get out here," Kohler called.

Bobby entered the room, a glint in his stupid eyes. He smiled blankly at Washington and leered at Julia Monday. The bulge in his work pants told everybody in the room that her naked body excited him.

"Get the razor," Kohler said.

Bobby Markham left and returned, holding a straight razor. Kohler moved over by Washington and stepped behind him. He put his hands on Hugh's shoulders and started to massage them. Kneading hard, hurting him. He moved up to his neck and pressed his thumbs roughly into his wind pipe, choking off his air. He released them and Hugh gasped, sucking air.

"I was going to have the boys perform for you. With Julia. But then you've already seen the three of them perform together, haven't you?"

"I said, I don't know what you're talking about."

"So I had to come up with something to top what you've already seen," Kohler went on, ignoring Washington. "And all you have to do is sit back, watch, enjoy and die."

"You can't kill a police officer in your own home and get away with it. You've got to be crazy."

"On the contrary. I'm very sane. A little crazy tonight perhaps, because you've ruined both my chances of selling Mrs. Monday and at getting her husband's millions."

"You did murder Askew? You were behind it?"

"Of course, but you'll never tell anyone, because by the time anybody finds your body, I'll be miles away with a perfect alibi."

Washington shivered, the man was insane.

"Bobby," Kohler said, a curt command.

Bobby Markham approached Julia and moved behind her. She stood facing Washington. Naked and alluring. Bobby reached around from behind her with his right hand and massaged her breasts.

"Okay, Bobby, that's enough, he's seen it." Kohler turned to the Weasel. "After I've gone, torch the place, but make sure he's not tied to the chair when the place burns. Make it look like an accident."

"Can do, boss."

Again Kohler moved behind Washington and again he wrapped his hands around his neck and slowly choked his air off.

"Stare into her eyes," Kohler said. "There's something I want you to see."

Washington obeyed, lost in those lovely liquid eyes and his heart started to crack when Bobby Markham brought the straight razor to her neck, and it broke when he slit her throat. She never took her eyes off of him. He watched her die and he felt his own life ebbing, knowing he had only seconds left. His last thought was of Glenna. He hoped she wouldn't come here.

Then the earthquake hit.

CHAPTER SEVENTEEN

JIM HAD BEEN DRIVING for just under two hours when the road started to shake. He jumped on the clutch with his left foot, moving his right from the gas to the brake, slowing the speeding car. They were half a minute off Highway 1, less than five minutes from Tampico.

"What is it?" Glenna asked.

"Don't know. Flat maybe." He maneuvered the car to the side of the road. The road continued to shake.

"Earthquake," Glenna said.

Without a word they hopped out of the car and moved away from it. They were both Californians and earthquake-wise. If possible, get away from buildings, cars, electric wires, anything that could become a large falling object.

She lost her footing and fell.

"Shoes too tight," she said, but he knew it was more than shoes, because he was having a hard time keeping his footing himself. He offered her a hand, started to pull her up when a strong tremor shook the earth and he found himself on the road beside her. They rode out the quake like that, sitting in the middle of the road, in the dark, hands, feet and buttocks on the pavement, clawing for balance.

"The big one?" she asked, when the shaking had stopped.

"I don't think so." All Californians lived in the shadow of the big one.

She scooted next to him and he put his good arm around hers. It was over as suddenly as it had begun and the night was quiet again. The only sound, the purring of the Miata's engine. The only light, the twin beams shooting off the headlights into the black. Then the Miata's cat-like engine was drowned out by a great rumbling scream, followed by a bellowing hiss that sent shockwaves to their souls, dwarfing the terror caused by the earthquake. Together, their eyes followed the beams of light and like macabre spotlights they landed on the reptile thing that had been with them since Collinga.

The lights seemed to dance over it as it twisted and thrashed in obvious pain. Only one radioactive eye reflected the Miata's light back at them and is wasn't as bright as before. Its slimy green surface was covered in sticky bright blood. A darker kind of blood oozed around its mouth, hiding most of its teeth and filtering a kind of blue smoke that carried a carrion smell and a sense of impending death.

It marked them with its one eye and wailed into the night. Glenna screamed. He held her tighter. It started to come for them. The guns were in the car.

They were powerless, paralyzed, at its mercy. It closed half the distance between them with a slow deliberate movement, half crawl, half slither, wheezing and coughing blood, the blue smoke with its powerful smell of death engulfing them.

It moved directly into the light, between the beams, toward the front of the car. They were in the center of the road, behind and to the left of the Miata, witnessing the slow movement. It inched its front legs forward, trying to sink its claws into the black top, fighting for a purchase, squirming, twisting and clawing, closer, ever closer.

It stopped five feet from the front of the car, bathed in the headlights. It fixed them in its eye and was quiet. It raised its great head and turned it slightly to the right, almost as if it knew something was coming and in the distance, behind the beast, Jim Monday saw the high beams of an approaching car, speeding toward them, the sweet sound of its high performance engine, cutting through the night.

The sight of the car snapped Jim out of his paralysis and he pulled Glenna out of the center of the road as the speeding car bore down on them. He turned back to stare at the beast and gasped as it let loose a gut wrenching roar, followed by spitting blood and blue steam. Then the oncoming car was on them, the bright lights momentarily blinding them. When the car had passed the beast was gone. Almost like it had been sucked up into the exhaust of the gray Mercedes.

And the night was silent and dark.

"Is it gone?" She wrapped her arms around him and held tightly.

"I don't know." He listened to the night and the soft purr of the Miata's engine. He heard an owl off in the distance. A cricket chirped and was answered.

"Yeah, I think it's gone." He got up, dusted off, offered her his hand and helped her up.

"Did you see it? It looked like it had been in a fight. It looked hurt."

"Good," he said and started for the car.

Fifteen minutes later, after filling the tank at an all night service station, he asked the night clerk for directions to Dr. Kohler's.

"Just follow Kennedy out to Mountain Sea Road and turn left. Big gray house on the right. Bars on all the windows, you can't miss it. No point going by though, he ain't home," the youth said.

"How do you know?"

"Cuz he just gassed up, not ten minutes ago. In a hurry. And he didn't head home. He was going out of town and he was going fast."

"You sure it was him?"

"You don't forget a man like that. You had to have passed him coming in. Big gray Mercedes."

"Was he alone?" Jim asked. "Was there a woman with him?"

"Hard to see through those tinted windows, but I think he was alone."

"How do you know?"

"Cuz he pumped his own gas."

Jim thanked him and paid him.

"Do we take off after the Mercedes or do we check out his house?" Glenna asked after they were back in the car.

"The way he was driving, he's on Highway 1 by now. We'd never catch him."

"Do we go by the house now or later, when it's light?"

"We know he's not there now. Besides, I'd like to see my wife as soon as possible and make sure she's all right. And I have to tell her about her sister."

"Do you want to go alone? Should I wait in a motel?"

"No, we're still looking for your father. And if he's any kind of father at all, he'd never forgive me if I left you alone after everything that's happened. We stay together till we find him."

He stopped before turning onto Mountain Sea Road.

"When we get there," he said, "we're not going to be as stupid as we were back there." He reached behind her seat and picked up both laundry bags. He reached into hers and withdrew the forty-five and handed it to her. "One for you," he said, "and one for me." He withdrew the second pistol and set it on his lap.

"You think we might need these with Kohler gone?"

"I wasn't thinking about Kohler."

"Oh yeah, our yellow-eyed friend might still be lurking around."

"Right." He tossed the bags back behind her seat, turned onto Mountain Sea and headed up toward Kohler's house. It had been a long night and daylight was still over three hours away. He downshifted into third as they approached the house.

"Look, it's my father's car!" She pointing to an antique Chevrolet parked in the driveway. Monday continued on, slowing, but not stopping. He pulled over when he was safely past the house and parked.

"Come on, let's go! My father is back there."

Jim grabbed one of the forty-fives, got out of the car and started for Kohler's at a run.

"You die, motherfucker!" a voice boomed out as he was going up the porch and Jim knew someone had a gun pointed at him.

But before the man pulled the trigger, a skinny man came running out the front door. "It's gonna blow," he shouted, and the night was rocked by an explosion coming from the back of the house and the place erupted in flames.

Jim knew there wasn't enough time to bring his own gun to bear on the man behind him, but he had to try.

Another blast lacerated the night. Jim turned and saw a big man jerk forward his finger squeezing the trigger, sending still another explosion out into the dark, the shot going wild.

Glenna stepped out of the thicket, a look of horror on her face as she watched the man jerk and dance, a stringless marionette out of control, finally collapsing, face down on the driveway.

Jim stared at her standing in the middle of the road, holding the smoking gun at her side. Her sweat soaked skin reflecting bronze from the rising flames. She was an avenging angel and he was sure he had never seen anyone so beautiful.

He heard movement behind, spun around toward the skinny little man who had come screaming out of the house. And he saw into the eyes of a demented soul.

"You killed my brother," he wailed. Then he turned away from Jim and fled into the house.

"My father's in there," Glenna screamed.

If there was a chance Washington was still alive, he owed it to Glenna to try and get him out.

He dashed through the front door holding his breath. He almost tripped over his wife's nude body. He was heartsick. Smoke filtered in from the back of the house. He bent low in a search for breathable air. He went to his wife, threw down the gun and dropped to his knees. Her throat had been cut. She was dead and there was nothing he could do for her.

It was too much, first David, then Roma, now this. The despair was total. He was lost in a black sea of agony, sinking under waves of heartbreak and anguish, the raging fire of his grief, as real as the fire raging around him. He rocked his head back and stared up at the smoke running along the ceiling and wailed one long, loud word, "Noooo."

He felt the smoldering heat on the back of his neck, but didn't care. It was over, he couldn't go on. Sweat dripped off his forehead, stinging his eyes and blurring his vision. It was hard to breathe and getting harder, but it didn't matter anymore, nothing mattered anymore. The sooner it was over the better.

"Stop it! Get a grip on yourself."

"Go away," he thought.

"No, you can't do this. She's dead, you're not. I need your help. I need you. Glenna's father needs you."

"Glenna's father?" she had his attention.

"Over there. Do something!"

Washington was on the other side of the room, tied to a toppled chair.

"He might be alive, you have to check!" Donna ordered. *"You can't feel sorry for yourself and let that man die."*

He slid along the carpet to the police officer, staying under the rising smoke, fighting to ignore the heat. Washington was unmoving and looked dead, but Jim had to be sure. Using his index finger he felt his neck for a pulse and found one.

"He's alive." Donna thought.

"I've got to get him out of here." Jim tried to untie the ropes, but his hands were sweaty and slippery and the bonds too tight. He only succeeded in frustrating himself and wasting time.

The back of the house was covered in flames, but the fire hadn't reached the living room yet. Flames were licking their way down a hallway, advancing like an invincible army. In seconds the living room would be engulfed, the heat already intense, and the more Jim struggled with the binding rope, the closer the fire came.

He stopped struggling with the knots. He wasn't going to get the rope untied in time. There had to be another way. He looked around the room for something sharp and found nothing. His eyes settled on his wife's body and again he felt a pang of grief, but it was replaced with a shot of hope. The straight razor that had been used to kill her lay by her side, bright, bloody and evil.

Staying low, he slithered along the plush carpet back to Julia. He had to reach over her body to get the razor. He did it quickly, his hand brushing against her breasts. She was still warm. His hand locked on the open razor and he felt her blood on the blade, hot, alive. He jerked his hand away and cut himself. His blood mingled with hers on the sharp silver blade and he turned away from her body, his eyes squeezed closed, and fought down the bile that raged to come up.

"Hurry!" A voice screamed through the heat.

Jim opened his eyes and stared into the deep brown eyes of Hugh Washington, laying on the opposite end of the room.

"If you don't pick it up, we're both gonna be toast," Washington said, not so loud now that he had Monday's attention.

Jim snaked his arm over Julia's body again, picked up the razor and started to slide back toward the bound police officer, when he heard a booming explosion, and something slapped the floor near his face. He looked up frantic, pulse racing and saw the little man standing in the hallway, shirt on fire, feet slightly apart, both arms extended, right hand firmly holding a pistol, left hand around the right wrist. There was nothing he could do. In seconds he would be dead, but as the man started to pull the trigger the flames leapt to his scraggly hair and face. He screamed as they danced over his body. In his death throes the man pulled the trigger again and again and again, but he was firing blind, his shots going wild.

Covered in flames, the man screamed louder, chilling the night with his wild death yell. For an instant it looked like he was going to make a flaming dash through the living room to the front door and the cool night beyond. But he spun around, a burning ballerina, and dashed back down the hallway, into the flames, his screams spurring Jim into action.

He crawled toward Washington and sliced through the ropes that bound him to the chair. Once free, Washington pointed toward the door.

"Let's get out of here."

Jim nodded and together they crawled toward safety.

"Dad," Glenna shouted, when they came thorough the door. She jumped onto the front porch, started pulling her father away from the flames.

"Easy, daughter, I can do it." Washington stood and together, father and daughter, they helped Jim Monday get to his feet. Then to Jim, Washington said. "Police?" It was more question than statement.

"No," Jim answered.

"Want them?" Washington asked.

"No."

"Then we gotta go." He stopped, pointing. "What's that?" He was looking at Bobby Markham, dead on the ground next to his car. "Did you do that?" He was asking his daughter with his eye on the forty-five tucked into the waist band of her jeans.

She nodded.

"Give me the gun."

She obeyed, handing it to him, butt first the way he had taught her. He wiped her prints off with his shirt, then he tossed it through the front door into the blazing house.

"Hopefully when they sift through all this, they'll think these two shot each other. Now we really gotta go." He looked at Jim, "You got a car?"

"Down the road." Jim pointed.

"Okay, we go." Washington looked in the car, checking to see if the keys were in the ignition, they were.

Five minutes later Jim Monday drove into the parking lot of the Tampico Motor Inn behind Washington, two and a half hours before dawn. Another ten minutes and Washington had secured two more rooms, one upstairs for Monday and one downstairs, next to his, for his daughter. It was another five minutes, as they were entering the all night diner across from the motel, before they heard the sirens.

"Feel the earthquake?" Susan Spencer greeted him.

"Saved my life," Hugh said.

"How so?"

"Someone had their hands around my throat and the earthquake frightened them into letting go." He paused. "What are you still doing here?" He asked.

"Two girls called in sick. One of the drawbacks of being the owner."

Washington laughed and said, "I'd like you to meet my daughter, Glenna."

"Any daughter of Hugh's is a friend of mine." Susan shook Glenna's hand like a man. "And I know who you are," she said. "Your picture has been all over the news."

"It's not true," Jim said, "none of it."

"I know that, otherwise I would have called the sheriff the second you walked through the door." She wore her smile wide and she winked at him. "Hugh wouldn't be bringing you in here if you were guilty."

"I appreciate your trust," he said.

"I'm not trusting you. I'm trusting Hugh. We go back a long way."

"Thanks Susan," Washington said. "We'd like some coffee, quiet conversation and a poor memory."

"How poor?"

"If anybody ever asks, Glenna and I came in alone and we got here an hour ago."

She looked up at a Felix the Cat shaped wall clock, with a swinging tail, counting the seconds.

"Yeah, I remember now, you came in at three o'clock, I remember it was three, because that's the time I was supposed to get off, but Clara and Ellie didn't come in and I had to stay. You were here from then till whenever you leave." She smiled at Hugh and asked. "Will you be leaving town in the morning?"

"Yes."

"Well, I wish you all the luck." Then she took their order.

They sat in silence, tired, tense and hungry. When the order came they wolfed it down quickly and quietly.

"Why did you need to establish an alibi?" Monday asked when they were finished and drinking coffee. "It would have been easier and less risky to say nothing. Nobody need ever know we were up there."

"Ah, my felon friend," Washington said, "once it comes out that I was up there talking to Kohler, then I might need an alibi."

"Why tell anyone?"

"Because while I was up there he confessed to being behind Askew's murder. Of course, I can't tell anyone that, because the next logical question would be, why didn't I arrest him, and I'd have to tell the whole story. I don't want to do that. I don't want Glenna involved in any of this. But what I can do is say that I was up there earlier this evening, say around ten, and your wife told me she found out Kohler was behind Askew's death. I'll say I planned to inform the police when I got more proof. It's believable. I'm known for running an investigation close to the vest. After I left Kohler's I went over to Palma where I had too much to drink. I came back to the motel sloshed and Glenna dragged me over here and started pouring coffee down my throat."

"That way," Glenna interrupted, looking Jim directly in the eyes, "you're off the hook for David Askew's death and once Kohler's name is brought up, Dad should have no trouble connecting the phony lawyers at the jail to him and—"

"And the two I killed at Edna Lambert's," Jim finished the thought for her.

"You got it," Washington said. "Once I say that Mrs. Monday told me Kohler was behind Askew's murder it, gives me a valid reason to investigate the doctor It might take a week or two, but I'll prove your innocence. You can count on it."

* * *

Jim lay in bed, staring at the ceiling as sunlight danced in through the top of the curtains. The swaying shapes of shadows on the ceiling, caused by sunlight filtered through a shade tree outside the window, reminded him of the black and red ant wars he used to watch when he was a child. He always cheered for the black ants, the red ants always won. Life wasn't fair then, it wasn't fair now.

David was dead. Roma and Julia were dead. The Lamberts, whose only crime had been trying to help him, were dead. Kohler, who should be dead, was gone and Washington wanted Jim to come back to L.A. with them and give himself up.

"It would look better," he'd said, and Jim agreed, but he had other problems. Donna was still strapped in a hospital bed somewhere in New Zealand, about to become part of some macabre sacrifice. He had a week to get halfway around the world to find and save her.

For the fifth time in the last hour he sat up and looked at the picture on Eddie Lambert's passport. With his long frizzy hair, bushy beard and that eye patch, he looked like a wild man. Jim slid the eye patch over his eye and looked at himself in the mirror above the bureau. The patch was the same. They both had blue eyes, but there the similarity ended. Eddie's face in the photo seemed harsh, like he had a permanent chip on his shoulder. The face in the mirror had a satisfied, self made look about it, even with the patch. The man in the photo had a bag under his good eye, the man in the mirror did not. But still, Jim decided, if an immigration officer didn't look too closely, it might work.

There was a gentle knock on his door.

"Jim, it's Glenna."

"What are you doing here?"

"Can I come in?" She spoke in a soft, halting voice. She was smiling.

"Sure." He opened up and she came in, walked over to the double bed and sat down.

"You're not going back with us. You're going to try and find her, aren't you?"

"Yes."

"Is she there now?"

"Yes."

"Have you been, I don't know how to say it, talking, I guess?"

"No. Not since earlier tonight. Since she made me snap out of my grief and cut your father loose."

"Then how do you know she's still there?"

"I just know."

"Would you ask her a question for me?"

"Sure."

"Ask her if it's okay if we make love."

"What?" Jim was shocked. Her question was the last thing he expected. She was a nice girl, but that's what she was, a girl. And even if she wasn't, he'd just lost his wife, her throat cut and her body still smoldering in that gray house. Even if he wanted to, he probably couldn't.

"*Tell her it's okay,*" Donna thought.

"*No, I won't. It's not okay.*"

"*She needs you. You owe it to her.*"

Glenna watched the struggle going on inside of him. The back and forth written on his face. There was nothing she could do except sit on the bed with her hands folded in her lap and wait. Wait and count on Donna to understand.

"*No, I don't, and how can you think I do?*"

"*She saved your life and now she's asking you to save hers. It's fair. A life for a life.*"

"*What do you mean?*"

"*Ask her.*"

"Why? Why me? Why now?" he asked Glenna.

"What did she say?"

"It's not relevant."

"What did she say?" Glenna insisted.

"She said it's okay, but that's not the point."

"I knew she'd understand."

"I don't understand." Jim was perplexed.

"When that man raped me he took something from me and I haven't been able to get it back. On the surface I pretend I'm this superwoman that can handle anything. It's out of my mind, I tell myself. I'm over it, I tell myself. All men aren't like that, I tell myself. But dammit, it's not out of my mind. I'm not over it and part of me thinks that all men are like that. I've never had real sex and I'm afraid that I never will. Now I've met you, another man besides my father who I can believe in. I need help. I want you to help make me whole."

"Even if I wanted to, I don't think I can."

"Let's see," She said, her liquid brown eyes on the verge of tears as she lifted off her tee shirt. Her bare breasts were caught in the early light, copper globes casting perfect shadows. He knew he'd be able to do what she wanted and he knew that it was right.

Once again he was entwined with Donna as they watched Glenna kick her shoes off. He felt Donna sigh as Glenna slipped down her jeans and he felt Donna's strong sexual desire as Glenna opened her arms and beckoned them. For the next hour the three of them made slow gentle love. They kissed and touched and embraced and when finally Glenna started to move her body beneath him, approaching her climax, they were brought along with her, riding a roller coaster though a carnival of delight.

"I'm there," she thrilled, wrapping her arms around Jim and squeezing tightly. "I'm there and it's wonderful."

CHAPTER EIGHTEEN

FRANK MARKHAM, THE WEASEL, turned and ran back down the hot hallway. The house was on fire and he was trapped like the bees he used to put in jars and burn when he was a boy.

He felt the fire at his back. His clothes were burning now. He smelled meat cooking and realized it was his own burning flesh. He dashed to a side window. It was barred. Frantically he sought the safety release. Found it and pushed. The bars popped out and he threw himself out the window, his fall cushioned by the roses below, their thorns slicing through his charred flesh.

He screamed as he rolled through the bushes, further cutting and ripping himself, his body a searing mass of pain, his mind wailing against the injustice. Everything was going so smoothly, it wasn't fair. It wasn't fair. Out of the roses, he rolled on the cool grass toward the cliff, struggling to get away from the fire. Through it all he clutched the gun, like a lifeline. He was still clutching it when he climbed over the back fence and jumped over the cliff.

In his crazed, pain filled world all he wanted was an end to the hurt. But instead of a beautiful ride into the night sky with the release of a quick painless death on the beach below, he went bouncing and screaming down a steep, jagged incline. More cuts, abrasions, ripped flesh and torture. The loose dirt on the bouncing ride down doused most of the flames, but the loose rocks rolling with him continued to batter against his bruised body on his slipping, sliding, dropping ride toward the bottom.

And still he held on to the gun. His mind screamed, but it didn't shut down. If he was still alive when the carnival was over he could use the gun. A quick blast from the cannon and no more hurt.

He slammed into a large rock jutting out from the earth. The wind was knocked out of him as he went up and over it, only to land again on the sloping earth, face first. He felt his nose break, tasted his blood, mingled with dirt, sweat and burnt skin. He wailed as his body bounced and flipped over, his head pivoting on the hard surface, leaving facial skin and scalp in his wake.

He landed on his back and continued the slide, feet first as the mountain ripped into his legs, buttocks and back, his skinny thin shoulder blades acting like twin rudders, keeping him on a straight track down to the dark sea below. Then he hit bottom, still breathless, and he rolled in the sand, killing the remaining flames, but not the hot, ice pick pain. He scrambled to his feet and made a mad dash for the sea, his flesh blistering, charred skin combining with polyester and cotton to form a putrid puss.

He knew he'd made a mistake as soon as he hit the water. The saltwater engulfed his legs. The stinging torture sent a banshee cry from his lips, telling the night that a pain that couldn't get any worse—got worse. He tried to stop his forward momentum. He had to get out of the ocean. He failed, stumbled and fell in the surf. He fought the oscillating ocean and somehow managed to get a purchase on the bottom. He moved his feet like a swimmer that had seen a shark. He struggled against the waist deep water, frantic to get out.

Back on the beach, he collapsed on the wet sand, a blistering, bleeding, blob of pain, still clutching the gun, but his tortured mind had thrown away all thoughts of suicide. He got up like a rummy drunk on a Saturday night and stumble blundered toward town. Two or three agonizing steps, then he fell. He picked himself up, took a few more steps and fell again, but he continued on that way, a long, screaming, walking crawl toward town and the motel where that big, black, bastard cop was staying—and revenge.

* * *

Washington woke to the sun's rays streaking through the blinds and thought about the fish bowl he lived in. People crammed next to each other, seeking privacy by not knowing their neighbors. That was no kind of life.

He should have moved back north years ago. This was the kind of place he should have brought Glenna up in, but Jane was an L.A. girl. She would have been lost without malls, perfect year round weather and a thousand and one different movie theaters. To move up here was to lose Jane. But eventually he lost her anyway and still he lived in the city, where your neighbors didn't want to know you. Where if you were a little too loud on a Friday night they called the police, called him. He set his jaw and made a decision. He was home. He wasn't going back.

He had a little money saved. After he split it with Jane he might have enough for a down payment on a small cottage outside of Palma or Tampico. One with a brick fireplace, where he could sit at night and listen to Bob Dylan or Billie Holiday in front of a roaring fire. He wouldn't have a television. No outside influence, no cop shows, no news about politicians stealing tax dollars and making senseless wars, no game shows, no sitcoms, just good music and a hot fire.

There must be some kind of job up here for an ex-cop. He would ask Susan. She'd know and she'd help. They went way back and they didn't come any better. Where else could you walk in on someone you hadn't seen in over half a lifetime and ask them to alibi you, like he'd asked her, and know they'd do it, no questions asked? That's the kind of people he remembered. That's the kind of people who live up here.

Robert Frost was right, 'Home is where, when you have to go there, they have to take you in,' but he could go Frost one better, 'Friends are people who, when you have to ask, have to help.' This was his home, it always had been. He had friends up here, friends like Susan Spencer. He'd look them up and he'd start today.

He pushed the covers off, sat up, reached toward the ceiling and yawned. He swung his legs out of bed, forcing his body to gingerly follow. He groaned, stood, stretched and yawned again. The morning was cool, but he knew the day would be hot, that's the way it was in the Pacific Northwest in the summertime.

He had no need to tell anyone he wasn't going back, well Glenna, but no one else. Jane had apparently found happiness with another, his job was kaput and if he never went back to that apartment it would be too soon for him. He thought about it on the way to the shower, he would have Glenna pack his things when she got back, give the required thirty day notice on the apartment, turn off his utilities and send his stuff up on the bus. He was staying. Now and forever. He wanted to finish out his life in this place. He wanted to die in this place.

He stepped out of the shower and toweled off, happier than he'd been in years. He went to the window and peeked out at the day. The sun was up, bright and orange. The town was starting to come to life. The fog was lifting. Everywhere he looked—green. Green, green and more green. He brought his eyes from the trees beyond the town, looked across the street and frowned. He spied Jim Monday and Glenna coming out of the diner. They were walking arm and arm. Monday was smiling, she was too, and she had the kind of smile on her face that he hadn't seen since that horrible day. She was happy and it looked like she was in love.

His first impulse was to run outside with nothing on but the towel and wipe that shit eating grin off Monday's face. Who did he think he was messing with Glenna? But he pulled back the reigns on his temper and studied his daughter's face as they waited for a car to pass. She was radiant and who was he to judge. She was a smart girl, old enough to know her own mind, and if he had any doubts, all he had to do was run down there with his mouth flapping and she'd damn well tell him. That's the way he'd raised her.

He shifted his gaze back to Monday as they stepped into the street. He was happy too. And the way he had his arm around her was more protective than possessive. Had Glenna told him about that horrible day? The way he held her, looked both ways before stepping off the curb, watching the big man get out of a beat up brown Ford Granada on the other side of the street, like any unknown man might be a threat to her, and the way his eyes crinkled when he looked at her, told him that maybe Monday wasn't so bad for her after all. True, he was older, he was white and he was a lousy dresser. Washington laughed to himself, but he was a man and despite how hard Glenna had tried to hide it, he didn't think she would ever be happy with any man.

"Take what you get and make the best of it," he told himself out loud. But he was her father and he was still concerned. So he jumped into his Levi's. What could it hurt, a little talk. He'd be calm, not lose his temper, he thought as he laced up his running shoes. Problem, how to bring it up? He could say he saw them arm in arm leaving the diner, but what if they said, 'So what? That doesn't mean anything. We've been through a lot together the last two days and we've grown close, nothing more.' Of course, he knew there was more, but he could hardly say she was wearing the look of a happy, satisfied woman, could he?

No, better to say nothing. He would wait, he decided, slipping into his shoes. With his mind made up he went back to the window and peeked out in time to see them walking away from the motel, arm and arm, like lovers out for an early morning stroll.

He jammed the room key into his pocket, strapped on his shoulder holster, pulled on his sweatshirt and hustled out the door and down the stairs, following. He saw them down the street, turning the corner at Kennedy, heading toward the beach. What's wrong with you, he thought, they're going to the beach, not eloping. Mind your own business. But he couldn't help himself, he continued to follow, allowing them a generous lead.

Kennedy ended at Mountain Sea Road which paralleled the beach beyond. The pair stopped for traffic, then crossed the street. They weren't arm in arm now, not even holding hands. Just two people out for a walk on the sand. Why couldn't he leave it alone? Obviously he'd read the signs wrong.

They started up the dunes beyond the road. Soon they would be going down the other side and be out of sight. He should go back. It's wrong to chase after her like this. He turned and took a few steps away from the beach, but he changed his mind. He couldn't continue to follow, because once he crested on the top of the dunes they would see him. But what if he got ahead of them. He could run along the road for a couple hundred yards and climb up a sand dune and wait. If they did happen to see him, he could say he'd been out walking for some time and fancy meeting them here.

But which way? Left or right, north or south? He picked south and took off at a slow trot. Two hundred yards and he crawled to the top of the dunes to see if he could see them coming. He saw them going. They had left their shoes behind and were jogging on the wet sand. He had come up behind them.

He slid back down the dune and started running south, the dunes between him and the couple he was following. He poured it on for another quarter mile then climbed to the top of the dunes again, only to find them even with him and still jogging. Damn, Monday couldn't be in that good of shape. He'd have to quit sooner or later, preferably sooner, Washington hoped, huffing like a locomotive.

Now it was a matter of pride, he was determined to get ahead of them. He started jogging along the street for another quarter mile, till Mountain Sea Road turned and wound up into the hills. He kicked off his shoes. He could pick them up on the way back. Now he was jogging barefoot on the sand, still keeping the dunes between himself and them. Dismissing any thought of climbing back up the dunes to check their progress, he kept on, heart racing. He knew Glenna. She would want to prove she could stay with Monday, and Monday's male pride wouldn't let him quit till she did. Washington was afraid that he was in for quite a workout.

He continued running for another quarter mile, till he didn't think he had anything left, then he put on a burst of speed that reminded him of his track days in college. He was running toward an imaginary tape and when he passed it he raised his arms in an imaginary victory. But like his college victories, this one had taken its toll. His heart was thumping. He was sweating up a storm. He bent over, hands on his knees, sucking air and looked up at the sand dune.

Then he started up it, hands pushing on his knees, feet slipping in the sand, sand oozing between his toes. He huffed his way to the top and vowed he'd never smoke again. The beach was farther away than he'd remembered. The bay curved away from the road and the straight track he'd been running along. There was no sign of them, just another sand dune, and after that, another.

He should go back, he told himself, but to have come this far and to have to admit he hadn't been able to keep up, that he was out of shape, that he was too old, no, he couldn't do it. So he slid down the dune, then climbed the next and slid down it, and climbed the next. He was rewarded with a cool ocean breeze coming off the sea when he reached the top of the fourth dune. He lay down on top of it and smiled. Jim and Glenna were coming toward him, walking and talking, two friends, not lovers, Washington thought. He'd been such an old fool.

* * *

Frank Markham stumbled and jerked along the beach, holding the gun in a charred claw that used to be a hand. Shards of suffering shot to his brain from all points on his body, interrupted only by blasting bolts of pain.

The fire had scorched off his scraggly hair. His left ear had been removed in the slide down the cliff. He had third degree burns on most of his body. His clothes had either been burned or ripped off. It was impossible for him to walk upright. He had no sense of direction. He had been wandering back and forth, fighting to stay alive for over three hours. It had taken a super human effort, supported only by steaming hate and sizzling stabs of agony.

He was reaching the outer limits of his malice-fueled strength. It was time for the raging animal in him to admit defeat. To lie down and die. To let the worms reclaim him for the earth. The thought of worms eating at his eyes sent him the determination to lumber along for a few more agonizing minutes, but even hate can't carry a body along forever. He straightened up in one huge electric shock of shooting pain and tried to rage at the sky, but his vocal chords had been burnt out and no sound came.

Struggling to see, forcing his eyes open, he saw the ocean and remembered how, instead of helping him ease the pain, it had hurt him. He wasn't going to let the ocean claim him, better the worms. He turned toward the dunes, higher ground, away from the grasping sea. Still standing straight, he forced his blistered feet to carry him to the base of a sand dune, where he collapsed.

Sand worked into his bleeding blisters, causing a new, much worse, sensation of pain-filled torment, but despite the torture, he crawled upward on hands and knees, still clutching the gun, till he was halfway up the dune. He rolled onto his burnt back, no longer suffering. Nature had finally removed the pain. His brain was shutting down. He felt good, like after bedding a fine whore. He was king of all he could see. He opened his eyes to take a last look at his domain. And he saw them.

The bitch who'd shot his brother and the bastard who he'd tried to kill just before he'd run into the fire.

An animal thing in him raged. He could not be king, could not enjoy this absence of hurt, could not, would not even deserve to die and face hell while they lived. The pain came back and racked his body with convulsions. Everything hurt. He was burnt, cut and bleeding. He had suffered like no one had ever suffered, felt what no man had ever felt. And he would be denied admission to the gates of hell as long as those two lived.

He stood erect and pointed the gun.

* * *

Hugh Washington lay atop the sand dune and watched the pair approach. Glenna walked happy. She bounced along, smiling at Monday, her hands weaving and punctuating her words. Laughing, she bent down and picked up a shell and handed it to him. He inspected it, smiled, and dropped it into his pocket. She picked up another, held it up against the sun, bent down again and held the shell under the approaching surf, to clean it. Her jeans were wet to the knees, but she didn't seem to care. She handed the wet shell to Monday, who laughed and put it in his pocket with the others.

Hugh heard her squeal with delight and saw her jump into Monday's arms. She planted a long kiss firmly on his lips. So they were lovers after all. They broke the kiss and continued their walk, again arm in arm, like when they left the diner. She looked so happy. Could anything that made her look like that be wrong?

He felt the hairs on the back of his neck bristle, a chill rippled down his spine. Somebody was behind him. He turned and saw Frank Markham, burnt, blistering, bleeding and holding a gun. Washington acted without thinking, screaming as he came sliding down the dune, clawing at his shoulder holster for the thirty-eight.

* * *

The thing that used to be a man, held its fire and spun its head around. With only one working ear it couldn't tell what direction the sound came from, but it didn't have to depend on its ear because the huge black cop was moving like a freight train, trying to get between him and his targets, and he was raising a pistol as he ran.

* * *

Hugh Washington screamed again, trying to distract the thing with the gun. He raised his thirty-eight and started shooting. The first shot missed.

* * *

Bobby Markham fixed his eyes on the big cop and moved his gun to follow his line of sight and pulled the trigger only a fraction of a second after Hugh Washington's second shot blew half his head away, ending his pain forever.

* * *

Markham's shot ripped past Washington's left ear, whizzing like an angry bee.

"Dad," Glenna screamed, running toward him.

Washington grunted a smile and sank to his knees in the sand, out of ammunition and exhausted.

CHAPTER NINETEEN

HE LEANED BACK IN HIS SEAT and his old fear of flying crawled up out of the dark. He'd been worried they'd spot the difference between the picture on Eddie's passport and his face, especially in the light of all the security they supposedly had in these days of Homeland Security and their seemingly never ending terrorist alerts, but a guy with half a brain took a quick look at the passport, then asked him to remove his shoes. He'd been sweating a bit through that ordeal, but nothing like this.

He wasn't afraid, he told himself, but when he turned his palms over, his hands were damp. He brushed the hair from his eyes. It was slick with sweat.

"Are you all right, sir?" A pretty blonde flight attendant asked.

"I'll be okay." He met her eyes, tried to concentrate on her freckles.

"There's nothing to be afraid of, we're quite safe."

"Do I look afraid to you?"

"A little." Then, "You have flown before, haven't you? And survived?" She smiled.

"Yes, barely, but I lost my eye." He laughed as he pointed at the eye patch.

"Seriously?"

"No, just kidding, but I am a little bit afraid of flying."

"Like I said, it's perfectly safe. I've been doing it for years."

"I'll be okay."

"If you need anything, just ask." She started to move down the aisle, stopped, turned back. "Really, any problems at all, just give me a call. That's what I'm here for."

"I can't believe it. You're afraid of flying?" Donna thought after the flight attendant had moved away.

"Where have you been?" he asked, surprised at himself for not missing her earlier.

"I've been here all along, I just thought you needed time to get over everything that happened."

"Maybe I did. But I think I'm going to need your help getting through the next ten hours."

"I suggest sleep."

"Not a chance."

"When I was a little girl and couldn't sleep, my mother would tell me stories, and the way she told them made them so real that they took away all my problems and worries, better than the movies, better than TV. When she finished I would lay in my bed, sometimes happy, sometimes sad, sometimes scared, depending on the

story. But happy or afraid, I always forgot about not being able to sleep as soon as she finished with the telling."

"That's nice."

"Why don't I tell you one of my mother's stories and we'll see if it works."

"Really, Donna, I don't think there's any way I'm going to sleep."

"Let's try. Put your seat back, close your eyes and listen to me. We have a word in Maori, Ngaarara, that can mean many things, like insect, reptile or even monster. And we have a sort of legend, or maybe tale is a better word, about a kind of monster that my mother, and her mother before her called Ngaarara, for want of a better name.

"This doesn't sound like it's going to be a bedtime story," Jim thought.

"But it's the story I'm going to tell you," Donna thought, *"so please listen, because it's important."*

Then Donna told her story.

* * *

Long ago two girls climbed a tarata tree to pick the leaves to scent their oils, because they wanted to smell as pretty as they looked. The tree grew on a hill and when they saw the village in the valley below, the girls felt like birds, at one with the sky. The oldest was seventeen, the youngest, a girl named Mahina, was barely fifteen and she wanted to climb as high as she could, because she wanted to touch the clouds.

Mahina was very happy that day, but her happiness was quickly chased away by the sound of a man below, calling up to them.

"Which one of you will come and be my bride?"

The girls looked down and were frightened at the sight of him. He was old and withered, with stringy hair and slits that hid his eyes.

"Not me, sir," the older girl said. "because I am going to marry my sweetheart in three days time."

"Then it will be you." The man pointed a bony finger at Mahina.

"Not I," Mahina answered, "for I have no wish to marry for many years."

"I am sorry, but you cannot refuse."

"But I do refuse," Mahina said.

Then, all of a sudden, they were covered in a cloud of blue smoke and when it had cleared away the man was gone, but in his place was a giant green tree gecko. And it was laughing.

The girls shuddered at the laughter, because if you hear the laughter of a green gecko, it means someone close to you will die. The only way to avoid the curse is to catch and burn the reptile before death comes to the village.

Again there was smoke and, quick as a wink, the man was back and the girls knew at once that it was no ordinary old man on the ground below them, it was Ngaarara, the evil Gecko Man.

"I have come searching for a bride." He pointed that bony finger again. "And I choose you, Mahina."

"But I don't choose you." Mahina looked straight into his slitted eyes, trying not to be afraid. "So go away."

"You have heard my pet's laughter. If you refuse, death will meet your family before your feet touch the ground. All will die, your mother, father, brothers and sisters. Even your little niece, who I know you love very much."

Mahina knew this was true, so with sadness in her eyes and a heavy heart, she nodded her head, climbed down from the tree and Ngaarara, the Gecko Man, took her away.

The older girl ran back to the village and told Mahina's family and they were overcome with grief, but *there was nothing they could do, because the evil Ngaarara was already gone.*

However, after some time Mahina was able to convince Ngaarara that she had accepted her fate and one day she told him that she wanted to take him home to meet her family. The Gecko Man agreed, because he had fallen in love with her and he wanted to make her happy.

So the very next day he took her back to her village. He remained at the outskirts, while Mahina went to her father's house to make arrangements for the meeting and a feast to follow. After awhile she returned and told Ngaarara that he was to be received in her father's house and that he would be accepted as a son. This made Ngaarara happy and he walked tall and proud when he entered the village, puffing up like a peacock when he was greeted by Mahina's father and brothers.

"Where are the women?" the Gecko Man asked.

"They are doing what women do while we men eat and drink," Mahina's father said and he sent Mahina away.

Ngaarara was delighted. It was the best meal he'd ever had and for the first time in his life he felt like he belonged, like he had a family.

"Now," Mahina's father said when the sun started to go down, "you wait here while we go and bring the women and a special surprise."

"Go, go." Ngaarara was ecstatic, a special surprise for him. "Get it and hurry back and when you return, I'll tell you my secret."

But the surprise the men had for Ngaarara was not to be to his liking. Mahina's father and brothers barred the door and piled firewood under the windows. Then they burned the Gecko Man alive, because everyone knows the only way to really kill a being like Ngaarara is to burn him until he's nothing more than ash.

After the fire burned itself out, the villagers sang and danced throughout the night. Mahina was back and Ngaarara was dead.

* * *

"That's the traditional end of the story. Mahina returns to her village and everybody lives happily ever after, but there's more," Donna thought.

"Ngaarara's secret," Jim thought.

"Precisely," Donna thought. "The Gecko Man's secret."

* * *

Mahina and all the villagers thought that her husband had the power to turn into a giant gecko whenever he wanted, like she'd thought he'd done in the smoke that day he'd come to take her away. But that afternoon, when she'd come to fetch him from the outskirts of the village, Ngaarara told his young wife his secret and it was this. The giant gecko and the man with the slitted eyes, were one and the same, but not the way she had thought. They were two parts, bound to each other, the same and different, never far apart.

Kill the man and the gecko finds a replacement by anointing another, whose mind is then taken over. Kill the gecko and the man finds a replacement by anointing a small green tree gecko which is transformed into a man-sized giant. This way the evil pairing goes on forever.

Unfortunately Mahina didn't get a chance to tell her father this before they burned Ngaarara. He was not one, but two. They hadn't killed him. They just made him angry. Very angry.

* * *

"You see, Jim Monday, I know this to be true, because that young girl stolen by Ngaarara was my grandmother's *grandmother. This story has been handed down on the female side of my family for generations, because we know that someday he is going to come back and seek his revenge."*

"And you think that thing that killed Roma is the Gecko Man coming after you."

"I do."

"Your mother told you that story to put you asleep?"

"Among others."

"Was she trying to scare you to sleep?"

"No, she was trying to make me aware," Donna thought. *"Now lay back and think about what I have told you.*

* * *

"Excuse me sir." He felt a squeeze on his shoulder and almost screamed.

"You'll have to raise your seat for the landing." It was the stewardess with the freckles. "Did you enjoy the flight?"

"You're kidding. I've been on edge ever since we left L.A."

"I guess I was kidding. I did see that you were pretty anxious, but you made it."

"Yeah, I did." He smiled. "The plane didn't fall out of the sky, I didn't flip out. All in all, I guess I'm pretty pleased with myself." Then he asked, "What's the local time?"

"It's 10:45." She squeezed his shoulder again. "I hope you enjoy your stay in New Zealand.

"Me too." He started to adjust his watch.

"Oh, and it's Wednesday. We lost a day when we crossed the date line."

He thanked her and she continued down the aisle, checking seatbelts and seatbacks.

"We lost a day," he thought. *"I hadn't counted on that."*

"And I don't know anything about Whangarei. It seems so hopeless."

"I thought you were from there?"

"No, I'm a city girl, from Auckland. Never been to the North Country, till this."

"Why did you go and what's the last thing you remember?" He asked, trying to keep his mind off of the descending plane.

"My older brother lives in Whangarei. He and his fiancée just moved up, and they were getting married. We came up for the wedding. We arrived Tuesday night and we stayed at the Park Side Motel. I had my own room. I remember going to sleep. I don't remember waking up."

"Your parents must be sick with worry."

"I know. I thought about asking you to call them, but that would only complicate things."

"It seems the logical place to start looking is the motel. It's the only clue we have."

"You'll find me. I just know it."

"First we have to get through customs," he thought, and they both began to worry.

The plane bucked and he grabbed on to the armrests with white knuckles.

"Just a little turbulence," the stewardess said as she made her way back down the aisle, "nothing to worry about." But Jim worried all the way to the ground. He was still worrying when he was in line at Immigration and Passport control.

"I don't look a bit like Eddie Lambert," he thought.

"It feels like your heart is going to beat right out of your chest. If you don't calm down, you're going to have a heart attack."

He tried to control his breathing.

"And stop sweating. It feels like I've just stepped out of the shower."

"Next," a voice called.

Jim looked up. He was at the head of the line. The voice wanted him. He walked ahead, presented his passport. The man opened it, glanced at the photo, turned to a middle page, stamped and returned it.

"Next," he said again, through with Monday.

"He barely looked at the picture," Monday thought, as another control officer passed with a sniffer dog. The dog passed his nose over Jim's carry-bag and kept going. *"The dog even okayed me."*

"Let's go," Donna thought.

Fifteen minutes later they were driving out of the airport in a red Toyota, rented with Eddie Lambert's Visa Card. The eye patch was back in Jim's pocket.

"Get over!" The thought was a screech going through his brain. *"You're on the wrong side of the street."*

"Forgot." He jerked the car to the left side of the road.

It was two hours later and two o'clock in the afternoon when they stopped at a Mobil Station just outside Whangarei for directions to the Park Side Motel and petrol. Jim remembered the last Mobil Station he'd stopped at, just outside of another small town, and he thought of Glenna. He was glad she was going to be okay. Then he looked in the side mirror and watched as the attendant put petrol in the car. The last time a gas jockey put gas in his car in California was sometime back in 1975.

Five minutes later he shut off the engine, grabbed his bag, locked the car and entered the lobby of the Park Side Motel.

"Do you have a room for a few days?" he asked the man behind the desk.

"Sure do, we're mostly empty. It's early." The man had a nervous tick in his left eye and he smelled like fresh earth. "Excuse the clothes." He handed Jim a registration card, "but I'm the gardener too."

"I'm looking for someone who checked in last Tuesday." Jim noticed the dirty corner on the card as he filled it out. He used Eddie Lambert's name.

"And who would that be?" the man asked as Jim watched him pick at the dirt under his nails with a clean card.

"I'm looking for some friends that came up for a wedding."

"The Tuhiwais?" The man set the folded card aside, tick going crazy.

"Yeah. I was supposed to meet them here four days ago, but I missed my flight," Jim lied. "I called their home in Auckland and there was no answer. I was wondering if they're still in town?"

"You don't know?"

"What?" Jim thought he knew, but he wanted the man to tell him.

"Their daughter Donna went missing the night they checked in. At first they thought she might have been kidnapped, but the parents don't have much money. Now they think she ran off."

"Ran off?"

"Who knows why kids do what they do today. If you want to know anything more, you'll have to ask the police."

"I'll do that." Jim thanked the man, whose eye was batting up a storm now.

"Here's your key. You have her room." The man was trying to force his eye to stay closed and not having much success.

"Her room?"

"The same room Donna Tuhiwai was in last week."

"Coincidence, or did you do that on purpose?"

"Just coincidence," the man said, struggling to keep his eye slammed shut. Jim didn't believe him.

He flopped on the bed as soon as he entered the room, stared at the ceiling and tried to think. Donna went missing from this room less than a week ago. She was being held in a windowless room somewhere, strapped to a hospital bed. There had to be more, something he was missing.

"You need rest," Donna thought.

"I'll be fine," he thought back.

"Nonsense, take a couple hours. You're dead tired."

"Maybe you're right. But just a few minutes." He closed his eyes and in seconds was asleep.

He woke with a steady knocking on the door.

"Don't answer it," Donna warned.

"You're being paranoid." He sat up and stretched.

"I'm not."

"Who is it?" Jim called out, getting out of bed.

"Linen service," a male voice on the other side of the door answered.

"See, you were worried about nothing." He turned the knob.

The door burst open and Jim had a quick look at a small man with rugged features. He staggered back from the door, but he wasn't quick enough. A fist shot into his stomach, doubling him over, then something came down on his head and the lights went out.

He woke slouched in a chair as cold water was splashed onto his face. He sputtered and spit to keep from gagging. He tried to bring a hand to his face to wipe away the water, but his hands and arms weren't obeying his commands.

"How do you feel?"

Jim turned his head to the direction of the voice and found the small man seated in a chair by the door.

"You can stop trying to move your arms, your hands are handcuffed behind your back."

"Why? Are you the police?"

The man laughed.

"How'd you get the cuffs over the cast?" Jim asked, remembering how he showed the cast to Washington to get him to leave the cuffs off.

"With difficulty."

"Why are you doing this? I'm not a criminal."

"Hey, that's enough. I'm the one that's supposed to be asking the questions here."

"Okay, ask."

"You came around asking questions about the missing girl."

"I did not," Jim said, playing for time.

"Phil, the desk clerk, called and said you were asking."

"I was not."

The short man got up from his chair, walked to the bureau, picked up a tourist magazine, rolled it, and smacked Jim in the head.

"I need better answers."

The slap stung, but Jim had faced a lot worse. There was nothing this little man could do that could make him say something he didn't want to.

"I'm not a brave man," Jim said. "If I knew what you wanted me to say, I'd say it."

"Why were you asking about the girl?"

"When the guy at the front desk handed me the key, he said I was in the room the girl went missing from. He made me curious, so I asked. I didn't know I was committing a crime." He hoped the man would buy his story.

"You didn't come here looking to meet someone?"

"Yes I did," Jim lied. "My fiancée, she should be here around eight." He looked out the window. It was dark out, he'd slept longer than he'd planned.

"If what you say is true, why would Phil call and say different?"

"Why don't you go get him and ask? I'm not going anywhere." Jim was beginning to enjoy confusing him.

The man grabbed the phone, pushed buttons. After a few seconds he began speaking,

"Tell Manfred we have a problem. I think Phil was a little anxious to earn some extra money." A few seconds silence. "No, Phil told this American that he had the same room as the missing girl, so the guy asks a few curious questions, and Phil reacts like he's from Interpol." More silence. "Okay," the man said and hung up.

"The boss will be here in ten minutes, then we'll figure out what to do with you."

"Are you going to arrest me?" Jim tried to sound afraid. "Because if you are, I have something to say to you."

"What's that?"

"If this was Chicago, half the money in my wallet would be gone, these cuffs would come off and your wife would have a new dress tomorrow."

"Are you trying to bribe a police officer?" The man was smiling, apparently amused at being mistaken for a policeman.

"No, sir," Jim said. "I was just saying what would happen if we were in Chicago."

"How much do you have in that wallet?" the man asked.

"Over a thousand American dollars."

"Cash?"

"You can buy your wife a nice dress with half of that and have change left over."

"What keeps the cops in Chicago from taking it all?"

"Leave a man broke and he might go crying to your boss. Leave him half his money and he says, thank you very much, and forgets it ever happened."

"And that's what you would do? Forget this ever happened?"

"I just want this over before my fiancée gets here. Can't we make a deal? Call off your boss, take the money, and everybody goes away happy." Jim tried to sound like he was pleading. However, he knew the man wasn't going to let him go. When his boss arrived, they would question the desk clerk and more than likely it would be big trouble for Jim Monday.

"Let me see the money." The little man was greedy.

"All right." Even though his hands were cuffed, Jim had little trouble pulling Eddie's leather wallet out of his hip pocket. The little man came close, reached behind Jim to take it, but before his fingers touched the leather, Jim kneed him in the face. The little man with the rugged features was dead before he hit the floor.

Jim scrambled out of the chair, sat next to the body on the floor. Any minute he expected company and he didn't want to greet them with his hands behind his back. He faced away from the body and tried to maneuver his hands into the dead man's jacket pocket as the glare of headlights streamed in through the front window, playing across the wall, followed by the sound of a car pulling into a parking place out front.

He jammed his hands deep into the pocket only to find it empty. He looked up at the front door and wondered if it was locked. The chain wasn't drawn and he couldn't tell if the lock was engaged or not. If it was locked, would the dead man's boss break it in? No, of course not. He'd get a key from Phil. He worked his hand into the other pocket as he heard the engine shut off.

No key there either. He only had seconds left. He scooted toward the man's midsection, fishing in the left front pocket of the man's jeans as he heard the car door open. He wondered if the man outside had a gun. The dead man didn't, at least he hadn't seen one. Maybe he should have looked. He heard the car door close.

No key in the pocket. He quickly checked under the man's leather jacket for a shoulder holster and found none. One front pocket left. Last hope. He had to slide up onto the body to get at it. He straddled the dead man's waist and with his hands behind himself, he eased his right hand into the man's pocket. There was a knock on the door.

Loose change and no key.

The knocking resumed, louder.

"Hey, Tony, it's us." The boss man wasn't alone. There were at least two of them, three, counting Phil, the desk clerk, and he was trapped.

"See if there's a pocket on the inside of the jacket," Donna thought.

Jim spun around, still straddling the dead man, so that he was facing the feet. He cringed when it sounded like he pushed air out of the corpse. The body still felt alive. He hurriedly ran his hand inside the jacket and breathed a sigh of relief when he found a pocket there.

"Get Phil and get a key to this room," a squeaky voice whined from the other side of the door.

Not much time left. Bingo, the key was there. He fumbled it out of the pocket, fumbled it into the keyhole and felt a sharp wave of pleasure as the handcuffs unlocked.

He looked around the room for a weapon and realized that even without the handcuffs he wouldn't be a match for three men. He was still trapped.

"The window, there's a park out back." Once again it was Donna to the rescue.

He hurried around the bed and opened the window.

"Hurry up," he heard from outside the front door.

The wallet. He dropped the wallet when he kicked the man in the head. He had to get it. And his bag. He had to have it. The passport was in it. Without them he'd have no money, no credit, no ID, and no place to go.

"It's about time," he heard from out front. He didn't have time to go back for the wallet or bag.

He pushed the screen off, stepped out the window and into the night as he heard a key being inserted into the front door. He ran across the park toward a group of bushes about fifty yards from the motel and he slid into them like he was sliding into home, trying to beat out a throw from second base.

CHAPTER TWENTY

HE WOKE, KISSED BY THE SUN and fighting for breath. Thursday, he thought, exhaling into a violent coughing spasm. He gasped air between the racking coughs and jerked himself into a sitting position, slapping dirt from his face. He struggled for a breath, exhaled, took another and the coughing subsided. He recognized the symptoms. He was having an asthma attack. His last one had been over forty years ago.

The grass was wet with frost. His clothes were damp. The seasons, like his life, were upside down. It was winter in July and the cold night spent outside had brought back the dreaded asthma of his youth. He needed to see a doctor. He couldn't go all day fighting for air, not if he wanted to find Donna.

He looked through the bushes to the park beyond and a profusion of bright flowers. Across the street were middle class homes with middle class lawns, and on the corner, a café. He watched as people came and went, knowing he wouldn't be one of them. He had no money. He gasped again and again was racked by a coughing spasm. He would have to do something. He had to see a doctor.

He crept out of the bushes and stood to greet the dawn. He looked around, making sure he was unobserved, and brushed off. He wished he had a coat hanger to scratch under the cast and he wished he had some warm clothes.

He started across the park, hoping a walk would warm him. Every other breath was punctuated with a cough and every other cough, punctuated by a sharp spasm, his stomach muscles clenching and jerking, forcing him to bend over, hands on his knees, till it passed.

"I'm back."

"You were gone?" He hadn't noticed she'd been away.

"I went away just as you were going to sleep. I remember the police were still over in the motel room when you closed your eyes. When I opened mine, I was back in my body. And I was on a boat."

At the mention of the police, memories of last night came flooding back. From his hiding place in the bushes he'd been able to see into the room he'd fled. The two men who'd entered were not the kind of people Jim wanted to cross sides with. Both big, wearing black woolen sweaters and seaman's caps. They'd looked like a body building advertisement.

He'd watched as they came to the window and looked out. It seemed as if they'd been looking right at him and he'd been tempted to get up and run, but he knew they couldn't see him through the dark and the bushes. When they turned away from the window he had half expected them to come around the motel and look for him. Instead, they'd left.

He'd hidden in the bushes, shivering for another fifteen or twenty minutes and, seeing no activity, decided to crawl back in the window and get his things. He was halfway across the park, when the front door opened and the police came in. He'd turned, darted back into the bushes. They were still there an hour later when he'd drifted off to a cold, fitful sleep.

Now awake, with a wheezing cough that seemed to be getting worse, no money for a doctor or even breakfast, he was fast running out of ideas and the asthma attack had sapped his strength.

"We could go by my brother's, he'll help," Donna thought.

"Do you know how to get there?" He thought. Any idea was better than no idea.

"No, but I know the address. 1737 Norfolk Street and I remember from one of his letters, he said it was a two minute walk from the center of town. So it can't be far."

He stopped a jogger and asked directions to Norfolk Street. Five minutes later he was standing on the front porch of a small home with a trimmed lawn, surrounded by a white picket fence. He could have been in any small town in America forty years ago.

He rang the bell and doubled over, coughing and gasping for air.

"Can I help you?" Jim heard a soft woman's voice, but couldn't straighten up to see the face.

"In a second." He waited for the spasm to finish.

"Come in." She took him by the hand. "What is it? Asthma?" The concern in her voice was real and he was impressed that she would invite a stranger into her home. Not in America, he thought. Not anymore.

"I think so, hasn't affected me since I was a teenager." It was a struggle to force the words out.

"You're American?" She led him to a sofa.

"Yes." He looked into her deep brown eyes, clear, wide and honest. Then he bent forward and coughed his way through another attack.

"Here, this will help." She put a blue inhaler to his lips. "It'll relax your bronchial tubes and let you breathe."

He inhaled the medicine as she released it and within seconds he was breathing.

"Now this," she said, handing him a brown inhaler, "the blue one helps to stop it once it has started and the brown one contains a steroid that helps keep it from starting."

He took three puffs from the brown inhaler and handed it back to her, feeling better.

"It's my mother," Donna thought. *"What's she doing here? Ask if Daddy is here?"*

"Is Daddy, excuse me," he mumbled, "I mean is Mr. Tuhiwai here?"

"What did you say?" The woman looked him in the eye.

"I asked if Mr. Tuhiwai was here?"

"You called him Daddy. Only Donna calls him that. Do you know where she is?" She was speaking in a rapid staccato and her eyelids hooded over. She balled her tiny hands into fists, bit into her lower lip, then shouted, "Mohi, come in here!"

"What is it?" A short, well built man answered her call. He looked like a bantam weight ready to fight.

"I think this man knows something about Donna."

"Just a minute." Jim coughed, but not as badly as before, the medicine was starting to work. They waited, glaring. When he was able to breathe, he said, "I don't know where she is. I'm trying to find her and I need help. I came here looking for her brother."

"He's dead," Mohi Tuhiwai said.

"Oh no." Donna's thought was filled with despair.

"How?" Jim asked.

"Why should we tell you? We don't even know who you are," Mohi Tuhiwai said.

"Because something very bad is going to happen to your daughter, Sunday at midnight, unless I can find her and stop it. And right now I'm sick, hungry, tired, out of money, my passport and clothes are gone, some bad men want me dead and the police want me for murder, both here and in America. I need help. Donna told me to come here."

"Then you know where she is?"

"No. Only that she's on a boat, she doesn't know where it is."

"I don't understand," Mohi Tuhiwai said.

"I don't have much time and I need you to believe me. It'll be a lot easier to explain if you each ask me a question. Something that only you and your daughter would know."

"If you're trying to pull something—"

"Please, sir, there isn't much time. Just do it."

"Donna was bit by our neighbor's dog when she was four years old. Where did it bite her?" Mrs. Tuhiwai asked.

"The dog's name was Phoenix, it belonged to Mr. Hoeta and it bite me behind the left knee, I still remember how much it hurt."

"Behind the left knee, its name was Phoenix, she still remembers how much it hurt." He paused for a second. "Now you sir."

"I don't know what you're playing at." His face was flushing red as he advanced on Jim.

"Ngaarara has her," Jim said.

"Stop, Mohi," Donna's mother said, her voice quiet, but commanding. Mohi stopped.

They stared at him and electric tension filled the room.

"I need your help," Jim said, breaking the silence. "I've seen it. It tried to kill me. It's killed people I love. I want to help Donna and I want to kill it."

"How can you know this?" Mrs. Tuhiwai sat next to him on the sofa.

"She came into my head four days ago, in California. My life hasn't been the same since." And he told them everything. When he finished he lay his head back and closed his eyes.

* * *

When he opened them he was in a small wooden room. He felt the gentle rocking and he knew at once he was with Donna, on a boat.

They roved their eyes around the room. Knotty pine paneling covered the walls and ceiling. It seemed out of character. Boat makers usually used hard woods, like teak or oak. The knotty pine would quickly swell and warp in an ocean environment. The cabin was comfortably warm, on a warm day it would be hot and on a hot day, a sweat box.

Cheap pine cabinets, with cheap pine doors, still smelling of fresh sawdust, adorned the wall at the foot of the bed. Those doors, once exposed to humidity, would cease to function. No boat builder was responsible for this.

They turned her head to the bulkhead at the left side of the bed. It was covered with a large mirror, giving the room an illusion of being larger than it was. The mirror was held in place by cheap plastic brackets, the kind made for a small bathroom mirror.

It would come crashing down at the first hint of high seas.

A young woman stared back at him from inside the mirror. She was naked. Her breasts grabbed his eyes and held them in their grasp, firm, with perfect amber nipples.

"Take your eyes off my tits and look at me," she ordered, and he moved his gaze. She had the kind of face that could start a war. Smooth bronze skin, silky dark hair, full eyebrows and lashes, high cheek bones. And her perfect face was set on a body that would turn the head of even the most senile. She was every man's dream woman, radiating that strange mixture of childlike innocence and sexual desire.

She was a girl in a woman's body. Dark amber eyes, matching her nipples, shined at him and drew him into her very being. He allowed them to swallow his soul and in them he saw his life race by and he knew that his life was nothing without this girl-woman.

He heard a large diesel starting. The engine fired, ran for about thirty seconds, then died. It fired again, ran a minute, then died again. So, he thought, they were working on the engine. How long before they came to check on their captive.

He might be a coward in the air, but he loved the sea and was a fearless sailor, veteran of over a hundred races. He knew boats and it was time to put his knowledge to use. From the new pine paneling and cabinets and the amateur way the mirror was mounted, he deduced that the boat was being refitted by someone who didn't know what he was doing.

He heard the steady sound of a forklift purring by. They were in a shipyard. Another forklift told him it was a busy shipyard. From the way the boat rocked gently in the water, he knew it had a deep keel, a sailboat.

Someone jumped onto the hull with a solid thud. Not the sound of deck shoes on teak, more the sound of work shoes on iron. An old iron sailing ship decked out in cheap pine.

They heard the sound of heavy footsteps coming toward the cabin. They braced themselves for the worse, but he felt himself slipping away.

"Don't leave me," she pleaded.

"I can't help it."

"Come back for me. Save me. Take me away to be your bride forever and ever."

"I will." He felt himself being tugged, a rope around his soul, jerking him away and he was powerless to do anything about it.

"Promise."

"I will find you and we will be together. I swear it." And the world turned black.

* * *

He woke on the Tuhiwai's sofa, the midday sun streaming in the living room window, shining in his eyes. He blinked and turned away from the light, its warmth welcome. He was covered in a soft quilt and his head rested on a down pillow. He settled his eyes on a wall clock and felt a pang at the loss of time. He had been asleep, or unconscious, for over three hours.

"You're awake," Donna's mother said. "One minute you were talking and the next you were out."

"You didn't call the police?" he said, thankful, but wondering why she hadn't. He would have.

"Mohi wanted to, but I wouldn't let him. If Ngaarara has her, there is nothing they can do."

The cough attacked him again. His stomach muscles seized as he started gasping for air.

"Here." She handed him the blue inhaler.

"Thank you." He took three puffs and caught his breath. "I don't know what my problem is."

"It's asthma," she said. "We have a lot of it in New Zealand. Nobody knows why."

"You're kidding?"

"No. I work in a medical office in Auckland, so I see a lot of it, especially in immigrants from America and England. It happens a lot to people that had it when they were young. They come here and it comes back."

"Does it go away?"

"Sometimes yes, sometimes no. I've had it all my life. I use the inhalers to control it. It's not so bad, the brown one before going to sleep and in the morning when I wake up. The blue one if I get congested."

"Isn't there a pill you can take?"

"Yes, prednisone, it's a steroid. It usually works, but we generally don't like the side effects."

"Which are?"

"Weak bones, enlarged head." She made an oval with her thumbs and index fingers around her head. "And a hump on your back." She held her right hand over her shoulder, just below the neck to indicate where the hump would be.

"Three things I don't want," he said.

"I believe your story," she said, changing the subject back to her daughter.

"You believe me?"

"Nobody, except the females in my family, knows the end to that story. It's something that's been handed down from mother to daughter throughout the generations. We've been waiting a long time for Ngaarara to exact his revenge. Now he's come."

"And your husband, does he believe me?"

"He doesn't know what to believe."

"Where is he?"

"Not far, I sent him out when you started to wake, so that I could talk to you alone. He doesn't believe in the old ways, like I do. Is my daughter's spirit still in you?"

"No."

"Taawhiri-maatea, the god of the winds, carried Donna's spirit so far, halfway around the world, to find you. It's almost too much for even me to believe, but who knows the ways of the Gods. The only thing I can think of is that the connection binding you and my daughter must be great for her spirit to be drawn over the seas like that."

"Okay, Linda, what did you find out? Mohi Tuhiwai came through the front door. His strong stare bore into Jim. His patience was clearly worn.

"If we want Donna back, we should help this man," Linda Tuhiwai said.

"I think we should call the police."

"Then we'll never find her, can't you just this once admit that there might be something in this world you don't understand," she said.

"Listen," Jim interrupted, "I want her back as badly as you, but if we go to the police, they'll put me in jail and we'll lose any contact we have with her."

"Are you sure she's not still with you?" Linda Tuhiwai asked again.

"Yes."

"Why not?" Mohi wanted to know.

"How do I know. I don't know anything about this kind of stuff. But while I was asleep I was with her, where she is."

"Give me a break," Mohi said.

"Listen to him. We've already lost Danny, I don't want to lose Donna, too."

"I think they're going to burn her, Sunday, at midnight."

"Midnight, Sunday morning or midnight, Sunday night?" she asked.

"I don't know, but I'm guessing Sunday morning. He wants his revenge. He wants her to burn, like he did. I can't swear that's his plan, but I feel it."

"Like Danny," Linda Tuhiwai said, and she told Jim that her son and his new bride burned to death when his car went off the road and struck a lamp post. "Maybe it wasn't an accident, the car going out of control, and the fire. Maybe it was Ngaarara."

Mohi Tuhiwai still looked skeptical.

"I know you want to call the police, but there's nothing they can do. We're her only hope. There is no one else. Until I came you were just sitting around waiting for news. If you keep that up, the only news you're going to get is going to be bad. I don't want bad news for her, not now, not ever. I need your help."

"Listen, darling," Linda said to her husband, "he's right, at least we'd be doing something. He wants to save our daughter and he needs our help."

Mohi Tuhiwai was silent for a moment, then said, "He'll have it."

"She's on a boat that's being refitted, in a port somewhere. An old iron sailboat, probably big, the refit is being cheaply done. They're using pine where they should be using teak. We find the boat, we find her. Also there is a man working at the Park Side Motel that might know something."

It had been dark for almost an hour when Jim Monday and Mohi Tuhiwai drove into the parking lot at the Park Side Motel. They had spent a discouraging six hours checking out the sailboats in and around Whangarei and found only two that looked like they might be what there were looking for. One, *the Sundowner*, an iron clipper in the marina, hadn't seen a refit in the last ten or fifteen years and the other, the *Reptil Rache*, an old iron Dutch schooner converted into a cruising boat, but it had a new teak deck, a new paint job and new sails. It looked first rate, a very expensive refit. Not the cheap job he had witnessed earlier. Either the boat he was looking for wasn't in Whangarei or it had sailed earlier in the day.

Jim felt he was missing something.

Mohi shut the engine off and they got out of the car. It was raining hard and he held his hand above his forehead in a futile attempt to keep some of the rain out of his eyes. Jim, with a quick dash from the car to the office, didn't bother.

"Remember me?" Jim asked, shaking water from himself.

"You were here yesterday. You left without paying."

"If you think I came to settle my bill, you're mistaken. I want to know who you called."

"I don't know what you're talking about." The left eye started flapping, but only for a few seconds, because before he could say anything else Mohi's left hand shot forward like a striking cobra, grabbing the taller man by the hair. He pulled down in a swift jerking motion, bouncing Phil's head off the counter with a thud that sounded like a handball coming off the wall. Phil started to scream, but before sound could escape his lips, Mohi, with his left fist still balled firmly in Phil's hair, held his head up and slapped him in the face, causing Phil to flush red. That out of control left eye stopped flapping.

Jim was stunned at the smaller man's speed, but there was more to come. Mohi's hand shot into his jacket pocket and came out holding a scaling knife. He slammed Phil's head back onto the counter and held it there. He flashed the sharp steel in front of the frightened man's eyes.

"I will end forever your nervous little tick if you don't answer, my friend." He held the knife a mere centimeter from the left eye, which was flapping again, "Then I'll give you a second chance. If you still don't answer I'll put out your right eye. Then I'll pop your eardrums and leave you blind and deaf."

"They'll kill me," Phil squeaked.

"I'd rather be dead than the way I'm going to leave you, but then I'm Maori."

"I have the number taped to the cash register," he said. Jim saw it and pulled it off. "It's a mobile phone, on a boat somewhere. I don't know where. That's all I know, I swear."

"I think you lie." Mohi lowered the knife from Phil's eye and ran it lightly along his cheek. Phil shivered, and Mohi continued playing with him, running the knife along Phil's jaw, bringing it to rest under his chin for an instant, then moving it down his neck, over his Adam's apple and down to his throat, where with an easy flick, he pricked the neck, causing a droplet of blood and a quivering gasp from Phil. "What else do you know?" Mohi asked.

"They have a place ten minutes out the Tutikaka Road. Big house, secluded, lot of land, several acres."

"How will I know it?"

"The entry is right before a sharp bend in the road. There's a red mail box on a post by the entry. You can't miss it if you know what you're looking for."

"How can I believe you? How can you know this?"

"My brother delivered parts there. He recognized them from the description I gave him."

"What description? What parts?

"German, they're German. Boat parts."

"That's quite enough, Phil." A man entered, pointing a gun at Mohi. One of the men Jim had seen through the window from his hiding place in the bushes. He was still wearing the black seaman's cap and wool sweater "You can drop the knife, little man."

Instead Mohi did the opposite. He thrust the knife through the soft flesh under the chin up into Phil's brain. Then he whirled toward the man with the gun, lunging toward him, screaming like a man charging into battle.

The man in black fired and Mohi spun backwards, but before he could fire a second time, Jim kicked him in the groin. He screamed and doubled over. Jim smashed his fist into his face, sending the man sprawling to the floor. He wanted to stop, but he had been hounded and terrorized beyond his limits. He was filled with anger and hate and he finally had somebody he could vent his rage on. As the man struggled to get up, Jim kicked him savagely in the head, killing him. Only then did he turn to see if Mohi was still alive.

Jim feared the worst and his thoughts were racing ahead. How could he tell Linda Tuhiwai her husband was dead? She trusted him and he repaid her trust with more grief, as if she hadn't already suffered enough.

"We have to get out of here," Mohi groaned from the floor. "Help me up." Jim obeyed, bending to help the man to his feet.

"How bad is it?" Jim asked, thankful the man was still alive, but cringing at the sight of so much blood covering Mohi's left shoulder. He had seen worse, Mohi would live.

"Get the gun and let's go," Mohi said, ignoring Jim's question. Jim scooped up the gun and helped Mohi hobble to the car. They were a full kilometer away when they heard the sirens. Jim Monday was still one jump ahead of the law.

"Hospital?" Jim questioned.

"No, I have someone I can call," Mohi said. The words were an effort. He was losing a lot of blood.

"But—"

"No, it's better this way. No report, no questions."

"Can you trust this someone?"

"Yes, he's Maori. Some of us still stick together."

"Can you drive?" Jim asked.

"Sure."

"Can you direct me to Tutikaka Road? Would you be able to drive back after you dropped me off?"

"Yes, but I don't want you going after them alone."

"You can come back with reinforcements as soon as they patch you up, but I want to go now. Time's running out.

* * *

Jim was cool and damp as he moved through the trees. Moving through the bush at night reminded him of night patrol in Vietnam. He didn't like it then. He didn't like it now. He rubbed his arms against the cold as he started up a small hill. On the top he looked to the heavens. He was directly under the Southern Cross. Its five stars had guided sailors for centuries and he hoped they would bring him luck and guide him tonight.

He started down the tree-covered hill, moving silently, every lesson he'd learned in Vietnam guiding his footsteps. Halfway down the hill he saw the house. It was built into the side of the next hill. A three story wooden home that ran along the side of the hill, each floor surrounded by a balcony that ran the length of the house. A river ran through the small valley between the two hills, sending up pleasant sounds of running water.

The house was nestled in its own little world.

He continued down the hill and was relieved to see that the river was nothing more than a shallow stream he could jump across. A twig snapped behind him and he forgot about the stream, throwing himself to the ground and hugging the damp earth. He lay quiet as something moved by in the bush to his right. He strained his eyes, but saw nothing. Whatever it was, it didn't appear interested in him as it moved on.

He started to rise when he heard the sound of voices approaching the stream from the other side. He moved away from the stream to the cover of the bush. An insect crawled along his arm, but he let it be. The men were too close for him to risk even the slightest movement.

The arm under the cast begged to be scratched and another insect crawled on his neck and moved under his shirt, inching its way down his back, but he remained still. The voices were speaking German and were coming closer, making no effort to hide their presence. Jim willed himself to blend with the bush as they came into view on the opposite side of the stream. He held his breath as they both bent over and set their beer cans on the ground, before undoing their flies and urinating into the water. They were talking and laughing, not like they were drunk, more like they were having a good time.

He coughed and the laughter stopped. The sound of their twin streams of urine, splashing in the stream, cut through the night. Jim clenched his stomach muscles, fighting to control the spasm, while the two men finished and zipped up. They stood at the edge of the stream, ears tuned to the night, listening for a sound that didn't belong. After thirty seconds that seemed like forever, one of them laughed and bent down to pick up his beer can. The other returned the laugh, said something in German that made his companion laugh louder and stooped to pick up his beer. Jim held his breath as they turned and headed back into the bush, glad the two Germans were not outdoorsmen.

He allowed himself a series of muffled coughs after he was sure they were gone. He started to rise when the spasm finished, but checked himself. He heard something. He remained flat, face on the ground, senses aware and he felt sick as the familiar smell of the Gecko's putrid breath danced along on the breeze.

It was here. Out there somewhere. And he knew what he had heard earlier. It had been here all along. Waiting for him. Then he was blinded by light.

"Don't move." The command was meant to be obeyed. "Stand, hands on your head, or die where you lay. Your choice." The voice was thick with its German accent.

Jim stood, slowly, with his fingers laced on top of his head.

"Come forward, toward the light."

CHAPTER TWENTY-ONE

PAIN SHOT DOWN HIS SPINE. His eyes were open but he was encased in black, unable to move. Paralysis was the first thought that struck him. The lights went on. He squinted against the intense white and his eyes gradually grew accustomed to it. The powerful light was directly overhead, its rays, reflecting off the bare white walls, showered the room.

The large clock on the opposite wall was the first thing that grabbed his attention. One-fifteen. He hoped it was 1:15 in the morning. Even so that left him less than forty-eight hours to find Donna.

He tried to get up and couldn't. He dropped his chin to his chest, looked down the length of his body. He was naked, his arms spread down from his shoulders in an inverted vee and they were tied to the side of the bed. His legs made the same vee and were lashed to the bottom corners of the hospital bed. He was bound in the same way Donna had been earlier.

He tugged at his bonds, but they didn't give. He was at his captor's mercy. He remembered the feeling and he didn't like it. His back was screaming. He had to fight for every breath. His head felt like it had been split open. His broken arm throbbed and itched under the cast. He was horribly thirsty and he had to piss, but none of this equaled the terror he felt at being confined again.

The door on the opposite side of the room burst open and one of the men in black walked in, dragging an IV stand. The man set it up by the side of the bed and grinned at Jim as he ripped the seal off the needle and held it up to his eyes, inspecting it. Apparently satisfied, he attached it to the plastic tube running off the clear bag.

"I would have killed you last night, but Manfred wants you alive. He wants her to see you die before she burns. Great guy, don't you think, Mr. Monday?" The man's thick accent reminded Jim of all the concentration camp movies he had ever seen and he remained silent as the man slipped the needle into his left wrist.

"Demerol and a little heroin, a special cocktail, to make you feel good and keep you quiet." The man stayed in the room, watching until the drug started to work its magic. In minutes his back no longer hurt, his head felt fine, the itching stopped and he was beyond caring as he floated on a cloud of pleasure. The man in black could slice his leg off and he wouldn't care.

"I'll see you in the morning. The lights are on a timer. They come on at seven sharp." The man turned off the lights and closed the door. Jim heard the sharp sound of a bolt clicking into place on the other side. He was locked in.

Overkill, he thought, because it was impossible for him to untie the ropes that bound him to the bed. And why would he want to? He felt pretty good right where he was. But there was a small part of him still resisting the drug, a part that remembered Donna and the danger she was in, a part that tried to fasten onto something the man in black had said, something that didn't seem right, and then he drifted off, to sleep, and to dream.

But his dreams were not the drug induced dreams of well being and pleasure his captors counted on, instead they were dreams of concentration camps and terror. Even in sleep, he fought the drug, and in his tortured dreams he struggled with the problem. What did the man say that wasn't right? He said something. A clue. He gave a clue. It was something for Jim to hang his mind on as he fought the drug and when the lights went on he was already awake and he knew what it was.

His name. The man knew his name.

And with the lights on he was able to study the room. As promised the clock said seven. His time was running out. He looked up at the clear bag and noticed it was still dripping the drug into his arm.

Movement. He spied movement, and he fastened his eyes on the far corner where the wall at the foot of the bed met the wall to his left. And on the ceiling, a blob of black. A blob of black that moved. It couldn't be, but it was—a black widow.

It bounced up and down on its eight legs, a small black marble bouncing on the ceiling. Odd, he thought, black widows were native to the United States. What was one doing here, on a ceiling, indoors, in a warm room? They liked to be on the edge of things—in the dark, but near the light—in the dry, but near the damp. They were seldom seen and they seldom bothered anyone, but he had been bitten in the past and he couldn't forget it as he watched the spider settle into the corner.

He had to piss like a race horse now, he wasn't going to be able to hold it much longer.

"Can anybody hear me?" he shouted. Nobody answered, nobody came. He shouted again and from the way the walls seemed to absorb the sound, he gathered the room was soundproofed. Since all the rooms in the front of the house had windows that opened onto the small ravine opposite, he figured that the room he was in, was built into the side of the hill. He could shout forever, nobody would hear.

He would hold it as long as possible, but if somebody didn't come soon, he was going to piss himself. If the intention was to degrade him, it would fail, he had been degraded before, this was nothing.

More movement and he turned his head as something slid up the wall toward the spider. A small green gecko looking for lunch. The gecko stopped inches from the black spider and made a tiny sound, a kind of chattering laughter. The spider backed away.

The gecko moved forward an inch—and stopped. The spider backed an equal inch away—and stopped. The gecko moved up the corner toward the ceiling, but the spider held her ground. The gecko issued another chattering challenge, but its laughter had no affect on the spider, she still held her ground. The gecko inched closer and the spider jumped forward, attacking, but the gecko was a blur as it backed down the wall, the widow's poison fangs missed by inches.

The gecko darted back, chattering and goading. It made no sense. The spider was no match for the reptile. It should have been over in an instant. Instead the gecko darted up the wall and on to the ceiling, coming close to the spider, then backing off. Jim didn't understand, but the fight above captivated him and, as it drew closer, he found himself silently rooting for the spider.

When they reached the center of the ceiling, the spider backed up to the copper-colored light fixture, looking like she was going to make a final stand, and the gecko stopped, still chattering and snapping at it. The spider, with her back against the fixture, raised her front two legs and bared her deadly fangs, daring the gecko to come closer. The gecko remained only a sliver out of reach, like it was uncertain about its quarry, like it knew a head on rush could be fatal.

They stood facing each other, two lone soldiers locked in a fight to the death, each waiting for the other to make the mistake that would cost it its life. Jim wondered if the giant gecko with the shark's teeth was hovering over Donna like the one above was hovering over the spider. Were they to be devoured like the black lady with her back against the light fixture? Was their fight as hopeless as hers? But the spider hadn't given up yet, one second she was standing, back protected, fangs bared, facing her enemy, the next she was scooting around the light fixture, faster than Jim thought possible. The gecko took the bait and cautiously inched after her, but the spider had gone all the way around the fixture.

She came at the gecko's back, front legs raised, but at the last instant the gecko darted across the ceiling. One second she was a breath away from victory, the next the gecko was five feet away. The spider moved back around the light fixture, like she thought she could hide from the monster that had been nipping at her legs, but the gecko was having none of it. It rushed the spider, then backed off, always dancing a whisker away from the deadly fangs, forcing her away from the fixture and back on her journey across the ceiling above. Jim watched fascinated and then he figured it out. The reptile was herding the spider the way a sheep dog does sheep.

And he knew why the gecko didn't go in for the kill. It had no intention of finishing off the spider. It was herding the spider toward him. That's why the black widow was here, half a world away from home, it was brought here by his captors, to terrorize him. That meant they had been expecting him and he had fallen into their trap.

He pulled at his bonds, but only succeeded in digging the ropes into his wrists. Fortunately he didn't feel the pain, thanks to the drugs dripping into his arm. He tore his eyes away from scene on the ceiling and looked at the plastic bag hanging on the chrome stand. No help there. He ran his eyes along the plastic tube to his arm. No help there either, but maybe he could pull out the needle.

He bent his wrist and tried to remove the tape, but he couldn't bend it enough. He twisted his hand around and pinched the plastic tube with his thumb and forefinger. At least he could stop the flow of the mind numbing drugs, but how long could he keep the tube pinched off? Fifteen, maybe twenty minutes? And what good would it do? The gecko would have the spider directly overhead before then.

He studied the plastic tube for a second time, his eyes following along its clear surface to where it buried itself into the tape covering his wrist. The needle was inserted into his wrist downward, facing toward his open palm. If he could work it out, he could use it to cut through the rope binding his hand. If he tugged on the tube, maybe he could pull it out, if the tape would give, and if the tube held fast to the needle. Four big ifs.

He pulled on the plastic tube with thumb and forefinger and winced. Even with the pain killing drugs flowing through his body, he felt the needle dig into his wrist. He grit his teeth and gently tugged on the tube a second time as the gecko moved the spider still closer. A stabbing pain shot from his wrist along his forearm. Each time he pulled up on the tube, the tape across his wrist forced the needle downward into it. The pain was excruciating.

He relaxed the pressure and watched the battle on the ceiling. The spider wasn't submitting to the gecko's wishes willingly. The gecko, chattering and snapping, would herd the spider two or three inches toward the space above where he lay, but the spider would move an inch or two aside, forcing the gecko to move around her and try and move her back on course. Sort of a three steps forward, two steps backward kind of situation and all the while the hands on the clock were ticking away. Time was running out for Donna.

He bit his lip against the pain he knew he was going to cause himself and silently screamed as he pulled on the tube. The silent scream turned into a belly wrenching wail as the needle dug into his flesh, but still he pulled on the tube and suddenly it pulled free.

The steady drip of the fluid hitting the floor echoed throughout the silent room, reminding him of leftover rain splashing down a rain gutter after a summer rainstorm.

He thought about giving up. It would be so easy to lie back, piss himself and go to sleep. He looked up at the spider just as she moved to the side. The gecko again moved around her to put her back on course, but instead of complying with the reptile's wishes, like she'd been doing, she attacked, almost catching it with her fangs. She hadn't given up yet. His bladder felt like it was going to burst, but in his drug induced state he equated wetting himself with giving in. He would hold it as long as possible. If the black lady above could hold on, so could he.

The steady patter of the dripping solution picked up an echo. Stereo, he thought, craning his head around to look. The clear drops were being matched drop for drop by the red liquid drops of his blood as it oozed out the tiny tunnel the tube had left in the tape. Great, he thought, if he didn't do something, he would slowly bleed to death.

The thick red liquid covered his wrist and hand, making it impossible to see how bad the wound was and how fast he was losing blood. He wanted to know. The clear tube was hanging less than an inch from his grasp, so he stretched his bloody hand against the rope, hooked it with his index finger, and twisted his hand around, so that the drip landed on the bloody tape. He planned on the slippery liquid washing away enough of the blood to give him a look at the place where it flowed from the tape, but the blood was too thick and the drip too slow.

He stared at the clear liquid mingling with his blood and for a few minutes was lost in the clear splotches among the red ooze. Then he saw the gold band he still wore and wondered how slippery the red ooze was. He let go of the tube and watched it swing away. He had taken a vow. Till death do us part. Julia was dead, he was no longer married. He bent his wrist and moved his thumb behind the ring on his ring finger and pushed it over the knuckle. He was surprised how easily it slipped off.

The soft pinging sound the ring made as it bounced on the tile floor sent shivers of grief and regret through him. He shouldn't have done it. He wanted the ring back. He stared at his bloody hand with his thumb still folded under his ring finger and an idea struck him. He had seen Julia fold her hand like that every time she slipped off a bracelet. With the slippery goo covering his hand, maybe he could slip it out from the rope tied around his wrist.

He looked up and saw that the spider was directly overhead, with the gecko moving around it, snapping at its legs. It was too fast for the confused spider, snapping first at its front, then an instant later at its back, keeping the spider spinning in a vain attempt to defend herself. Any second it would fall.

Gritting his teeth, he pulled his hand against the rope and came up against an unexpected obstacle. The needle. If he tried to slip his hand through the rope, he'd drive the needle further into his wrist and that would really hurt. He looked up at the spider bravely defying the gecko and made his decision. He let out a yell as he jerked his hand against the rope.

The defiant scream turned into an agonizing cry. The needle, pushed by the rope, dug into his wrist. His hand slipped further through the loop. The rope caught under the needle, pulling it up and ripping it through skin, tendon and muscle. He clamped his mouth shut, biting back a second scream as the room echoed with the crack of the needle snapping. His hand slipped through the rope as the spider fell, landing on his naked chest with a quiet plop.

His first impulse was to swat the spider off with his newly freed hand, but he bit his lip against the pain shooting from his wrist and watched the spider sitting on his belly button. This time he wasn't frozen with fear. He felt a certain empathy with the deadly spider. They had the same enemy. He looked up at the chattering gecko above and, as if the spider knew what the man was thinking, it side stepped away from his belly, slid down his waist, walked across the bare mattress, dropped a web to the floor and slid down, away from Jim.

He grabbed the chrome IV pole with his bloodied hand, pain shooting from his wrist as his fingers closed on it, but he was a man with a mission. He lifted it an inch off the ground, testing its weight and balance. Then he turned his attention to the noisy gecko, set his mouth in a tight grin and looked away. But instead of setting the pole back on the floor, he shot his arm upward sending the pole flying to the ceiling like a spear.

He missed the gecko by over six inches, but the clear plastic IV bag flopped up, hitting the reptile like a water balloon, stunning it and sending it falling with the chrome tube, and the clear bag. The metal pole made a clanging sound when it hit the tile floor. The half full IV bag made a loud pop as it broke open, spilling its gooey liquid contents. The gecko hit with a tiny thud.

He saw movement out of the corner of his eye, turned his head to see the spider, a black blur, dart across the room toward the fallen reptile. She was on its back as it came to life. She sank her fangs into its flesh repeatedly as it twisted and tried to throw her off, but she held on with all eight legs, riding the gecko like a cowboy rides a bronco. She stayed with it until it quit its death throes and lay still.

When she was satisfied her enemy was dead, she hopped off its back and did a little dance around the fallen reptile. Despite everything, Jim smiled when she spun around, and he watched as she moved across the floor to the door and began to climb back toward the ceiling. She paused when the wall ended and the ceiling began, but after a few seconds she started her trek along the ceiling. She didn't go far. She stopped over the doorway. Stopped and waited.

Jim swung his bloody left hand over and untied his right. Once it was free, he pulled out the rest of the broken needle with a tight grimace. He was weak and still bleeding. He pulled the sheet from the bed and tore a strip off with his teeth. Then he wrapped it tightly around his wrist. Only when he was sure the bleeding had stopped did he untie his feet.

He still had to piss. He looked around the room and settled on the farthest corner. He climbed off the bed, made his way to it, where he lay his cast against the wall for support and urinated. Finished, he stumbled to the door and wasn't surprised to find it still locked from the outside. He went back to the bed, picking up the IV stand along the way. A five foot long chrome tube would make a good weapon. He propped it up by the bed, then sat and massaged his legs. The only thing left for him to do was wait—like the spider.

The lights went out twelve hours later and he was still waiting. He was beginning to think no one would ever come. Twice more he stumbled to his corner. Once to urinate, once to squat. The pleasant, drug induced sensation was replaced by a raw, nagging hunger. One arm ached, the other itched, his head hurt. He was naked, alone and fighting for his sanity, when he drifted off to a fitful sleep.

He woke several times during the night, but no one came. When he slept his dreams were peppered with fire and monsters. When he was awake his thoughts were of death and pain. He didn't know which was worse. But awake or asleep, through the fire or the pain, he wondered who'd brought a black widow halfway around the world to frighten him. Everyone that knew about his being bitten by a black widow and how terrified he was that day, was dead.

How did they know? Could they read his mind?

After a time that could have been ten hours or thirty he heard the sound of the deadbolt snapping open. He grabbed the IV pole and moved through the blinding black to where he imagined the center of the room was. He was weak and his grip on the chrome tube sent flaming stabs of white hot hurt shooting up from his mangled wrist, but the clicking of the turning doorknob grabbed all his attention. A man stepped through, backlit by the light flooding through the doorway.

"Hey," Jim heard a startled voice say as he swung the tube at the man's head the way a home run hitter swings at a fat pitch coming down the pipe. He felt himself connect, but the tube slipped out of his hands as his eyes fought against the light.

"Son of a bitch," another voice screamed.

Jim squinted as the overhead light came on.

"Get back or I'll shoot." It was the second man in black. The first lay dead on the floor. His face bashed in, the chrome IV stand at his side. "You killed him." The man pointed a gun at Jim. His pockmarked face was flushing deep red and Jim could feel the heat of his anger. "The boss wants you alive, but I don't think so." He raised the gun and held it away from his body, pointing it at Jim's heart as the black marble fall from the ceiling and landed on the man's face.

The man screamed, because he knew what just bit him on the cheek. The gun flew out of his hand as he flattened both palms to slap the spider off, but before his hands reached his face Jim's right foot connected with his balls. The man doubled over and the spider went flying. Jim moved in, grabbed the bending man by the hair and forced his head down against the cold tile as the spider scooted away.

"Where is she?" Jim demanded.

"Fuck you," the man said. Jim held his head fast against the floor, forcing him to face the retreating spider. The man shivered when it stopped and screamed when it turned and headed back toward him. "Get it away," he bellowed.

"Not a chance."

"You're supposed to be terrified of it," the man whined. "The boss said it'd scare the shit out of you."

"He was wrong. Now where is she?" The spider moved closer. The man's eyes were open wide with fright and they turned cross-eyed as she came to a stop mere millimeters from his crooked nose.

"She's on the boat," he croaked, an instant before his heart exploded. He died before he could say which boat. Frightened to death.

"Jim, Jim Monday, are you in there?" Jim recognized the voice of Mohi Tuhiwai.

"Here," he called out. "I'm here."

Mohi Tuhiwai burst in the room as he collapsed.

"Get away old girl," he whispered and the black widow scooted under the bed to lay her eggs and found a dynasty.

"It's ten o'clock, we only have two hours," Mohi said, breathing hard.

"No, we have a whole day."

"It's Saturday night," Mohi said, and Jim was crushed. He had been asleep and under the influence of the drugs for a whole day. He was almost out of time and he wasn't any closer to finding Donna than before he'd been captured.

"I know where she is," Mohi exclaimed, breathless. "*Reptil Rache*, Linda figured it out. It means, *Reptile Revenge*. In German!"

CHAPTER TWENTY-TWO

JIM CHECKED HIS DAMAGED WRIST in the light. It was already starting to scab over. He turned to Mohi. "I need clothes."

"The one without all the blood looks your size."

They stripped him, leaving the body clad only in underwear.

"The wool itches," Jim said.

"New Zealand wool doesn't itch." Mohi looked at the black sweater. "Comes from Germany, not New Zealand. That explains it."

Jim finished dressing by putting on the dead man's work boots, thankful that they fit. It was time something went right. Then he picked up the gun, a thirty-eight police special.

"This thing is older than God." Jim jammed it between his belly and the pants, under the sweater.

"Guns are hard to come by in New Zealand," Mohi said.

"Apparently." Then, "What took you so long?"

"I got home okay," Mohi said, "but I passed out in the driveway. Linda dragged me into the house and called an ambulance. I'd lost a lot of blood and when I came to I was delirious. They took me to the hospital, gave me blood and antibiotics. I've been drugged up for the last twenty-four hours." He grimaced. "They got the bullet out, but they kept me on pain killers. It took me a whole day to remember what that guy at the motel said about this place, then I called Linda and snuck out of the hospital. Sorry, I did my best."

"You did good enough, we still have time. How's the shoulder now?"

"Not bad. I'll be all right." But the sweat running down his forehead told Jim that he was in serious pain.

"Linda's outside, in the car," Mohi said. "Follow me."

"How did you get in?"

"Door wasn't locked." Mohi led him through the house to the dark night outside. Linda Tuhiwai was waiting in the parked car out front. She got out when she saw them coming.

"I was getting worried," she whispered.

"It's okay, you don't have to whisper anymore," Mohi said.

"How did you know to translate the boat's name?" Jim asked Linda as he climbed into the backseat.

"Mohi told me the man at the motel said they were German." Linda got back in and started the car. "German bad guys, boat with a German name, it wasn't hard to put together. After I figured out the

Reptil Rache was the boat we were looking for, I went down to the port and did a little asking around while Mohi was in the hospital.

"But the boat we're looking for is fitted out with cheap pine. We saw that boat. It's first rate," Jim said.

"On the outside," Linda said. "The inside is pretty, but not practical."

"How do you know?"

"I talked to the man who installed the new air-conditioning unit below," Linda said. "He's married to a friend of mine. He told me the boat had been completely refitted last year. That's why she looks so good. A German named Manfred Penn bought it two months ago and gutted the inside. He didn't like the boat toilets and showers. He wanted the kind he was used to, never mind that they'll flood as soon as he hits rough seas. The plumber tried to tell him, but he doesn't listen. He also wanted larger staterooms and he didn't like the look of teak. He wanted light, knotty pine. He thinks it's prettier. The carpenter tried to tell him you need hard wood on a boat, but he doesn't listen. After a while people stopped trying to tell him."

"That sounds like the boat," Jim said.

"There's more," Linda said. "The boat sails with the dawn. Nobody seems to know for where."

"You learned a lot," Jim said.

"She's a smart woman," Mohi said.

"What's this Manfred Penn look like?"

"Bald and ugly as my husband's mother."

"Linda!" Mohi chastised.

"Uglier," Linda said.

"We're here." Linda parked the car at the end of a pair of long twin piers. The pier on the left had a small oil tanker tied to its left side. There was nothing tied to its right. The pier on the right had a cargo ship moored to its right. Pallets of bagged cement, six feet high, were stacked on the twenty-foot wide pier, four abreast and over thirty deep.

Two forklifts were busy scooping up the pallets and delivering them to a crane that bent down from the cargo ship. On the left side of the right pier was the old Dutch schooner, *Reptil Rache*. She was a hundred and twenty-five feet long, but sandwiched between the cargo ship and oil tanker, she looked small.

They got out of the car.

"Keys?" Mohi asked and Linda tossed them to him. He went to the trunk and opened it. "Take one of these." Mohi handed Jim a fishing rod. "Maori men fish here every night, even some *pakehas*, white men. We can get close without them suspecting anything."

Jim followed Donna's parents out onto the left pier, where they sat a few feet away from three old Maori men who were fishing in the moonlight. They dropped their lines into the water and stared at the boat. The three fishermen didn't comment on the fact that Jim and Mohi weren't using bait.

The sails were tied on. There was a rough looking man sitting on the deck, watching the forklifts and the crane do their work. The *Reptil Rache* was ready to sail and they had posted a guard to keep off unwelcome visitors. It would be impossible to sneak aboard.

"How come the diving ladder's still down?" Jim wondered aloud, referring to a stainless steel ladder hanging over the side of the boat and extending into the water.

"It was delivered today," a Maori man from the group to their right said. I guess they wanted to see if it worked."

"If we can distract the guard, I could swim over and climb on board."

"The water is dirty, polluted and awful cold," the Maori said. The two others in his party nodded their assent as the three moved over to join them.

"I think my daughter's on board." Mohi explained the situation to them.

The Maoris wanted to storm the boat, but Jim told them if they did, the men onboard might kill the girl. He didn't tell them they might get hurt themselves. These kind of men wouldn't think of their own safety.

"I need a way to keep this old thirty-eight dry," Jim said.

One of the fishermen went to his lunchbox, took out two sandwiches and removed them from a Ziploc plastic bag. Jim zipped the gun into the bag and nodded his appreciation when the fisherman offered him the sandwiches and a thermos of coffee. He didn't have to ask. These men were Maori, they knew when a man was hungry.

With his hunger and thirst partially satisfied, Jim was ready to go into the cold water.

"There's a ladder at the end of the pier," Mohi said.

"Okay." Jim tucked the gun back into his pants, then took off the sweater and the work boots. "I'm ready." He turned to Mohi, "If I'm not off by midnight, assume I'm dead and burn the boat."

Linda gasped.

The old men's eyes popped open.

"If Donna's alive, we'll be off. If we're not, it'll mean I found her dead and it won't matter what happens to me."

"I won't burn it if she's not off," Mohi said.

"We'll need a fire in front of both entry ways and under the windows on that doghouse," Jim said, ignoring Mohi. "If I do find her alive, we can leap through the flames into the sea. If that thing is on board, the fire will hold it back."

"I won't burn it if she's not off," Mohi repeated.

"Start the fire." Jim looked him in the eyes. "If we get away, I don't want that thing coming after her ever again. If she's there and alive that fire might be the only chance we have of getting off."

"He's right, Mohi," Linda said. "We have to do what he says."

"I have gasoline in my trunk," one of the old men said.

"Can I count on you?" Jim asked, standing in the ladder.

"You can," Mohi and Linda said as one.

"You can," the three fishermen echoed.

"You might need this." The fisherman who had given him the sandwiches held out a scaling knife. "It's very sharp, skin a man easy, if you want."

Jim put it between his teeth, climbed down the ladder and slipped into the cold, dirty water.

* * *

Donna struggled against the ropes, but only managed to chafe her wrists further. The brass seaman's clock on the wall read thirty minutes to midnight. Not much time left. She remembered when she was a little girl and used to count down the days till Christmas. Time seemed to take forever. The night before she would lay awake and watch the second hand on her lighted bedroom clock creep ever so slowly around the glass enclosed circle. The second hand facing her now seemed to be racing.

She gasped as someone opened the cabin door.

"Ah, did I startle you?" She heard the German accent before she saw the face. Long thin nose, beady gray eyes, hollow cheeks, and hairless. No eyebrows, barely any eyelashes, no hair, not balding, but shaved. If there ever was a living Death's Head, this was it. If ever a head belonged on the shoulders of a Gestapo uniform, this was it. If ever evil flashed from behind a grin, she was seeing it now. "Someone will come and untie you in just a minute," he said.

Donna caught the gleam in his eye and was afraid.

"By the time you finish your shower, we will have some clothes ready for you and after a quick examination to make certain you are all right, a policewoman will drive you home."

"Shower?" Donna said through parched lips.

"Yes, you've soiled yourself and besides, your hair is a mess." The man attempted a laugh, as if he had made a joke. Donna didn't find it the least bit humorous. Then it hit her, what the man had said.

"Policewoman?" Donna couldn't believe it. She also couldn't believe she'd soiled herself without noticing. It must have happened while she'd been out. Just a short while ago she'd have been embarrassed about it. Now she didn't think she could ever be embarrassed again.

"I'm here, Doctor." A pleasant female voice drifted into the cabin from behind the man.

"Ah, yes." The doctor turned to face a causally dressed young woman. "Officer, untie this woman and help her to a shower, but first get me a glass of water." The policewoman left and returned almost immediately with a glass. She handed it to the doctor.

Donna looked up into the woman's eyes as she bent over her with a sharp knife and sliced through the ropes that had been binding her to the bed. She allowed herself to be filled with hope. Once the ropes were off, the policewoman massaged her wrists and helped her sit up.

"Feel a little better now?" she asked and Donna nodded.

"Give her some of this, but not too much right away." The doctor handed the policewoman the glass. Then he left and Donna sipped at the water and reveled at the clean, clear taste. It felt glorious as it slid down her throat.

"There is a very anxious man waiting to see you," the policewoman said, "and I know you don't want to see him looking like this."

"Jim Monday?" Donna said.

"Yes." The policewoman smiled. "He's in the salon. It's because of him that we found you." The woman helped Donna stand and wrapped her in a bathrobe. "The shower is at the end of the corridor." She showed Donna the way. "You'll find soap, shampoo and conditioner inside."

"Thank you so much," Donna said and with the woman's help, she hobbled down the hall to the shower. She was too tired and to overjoyed at being rescued to feel humiliated, besides she didn't think she would ever feel humiliated again either.

Once in the shower she allowed herself to finally feel relief. She had been saved. Jim had done it. She would be with him in a few minutes and the horrible nightmare would finally be over. Shivering, she turned on the water, stepped under the warm spray and sighed as the water washed the filth from her body.

She reached for the shampoo and lathered her hair, luxuriating in the soapy suds. She poured more shampoo into her hand and lathered her arms, breasts, stomach and legs. It felt wonderful just to be clean.

Then all of a sudden she felt guilty. Her brother was dead, so many others, but thank God it was over now. Jim had done it. He had arrived with the police in time.

"Are you almost finished?" It was the policewoman.

"Almost." She hated to leave the shower, but Jim was waiting for her. She quickly poured some conditioner in her hand and ran it through her hair. She wanted to look her best for him. She rubbed it in, massaging her scalp and running her fingers through her long hair. She continued massaging as she rinsed it out.

"Hurry up honey," the policewoman said, "everybody is waiting."

She turned off the water and stepped out of the shower. There was a warm towel hanging on the rack. She wrapped it around herself and sighed as it soaked up the water. It was so soft. She was so lucky. Dry, she put on the robe and opened the door.

"This way." The policewoman had been waiting. She led Donna down the hallway. "Everybody is waiting in the salon."

"Go on, honey," the policewoman said when they'd reached the end of the corridor. "Just a little more and it will all be over." She opened the door for Donna.

"Thank you so much." Donna stepped into the salon.

Something wasn't right.

"Come in, we've been waiting," the hairless doctor said. His voice and accent frightened her. She froze. The two men with the doctor were no policemen. They were dressed in the same black sweaters and seaman's caps she had seen through the window of the Park Side Motel.

The only furniture in the salon was a double bed in the direct center of the room. Its clean white sheets glowed, reflecting the rays of an overhead light. There were two video cameras mounted on tripods, one on each side of the bed. This wasn't right. Something was wrong—very, very wrong.

"Get on the bed, bitch," The policewoman smacked her on the back. Donna stumbled and the woman pushed her again, guiding her, so that she fell onto the bed.

* * *

The water chilled him to the bone. The salt in it sent pain stabbing from his damaged wrist up his arm. He fought the urge to scream out. He pushed off toward the boat, conscious of the unnatural weight of the revolver tucked into his belly and the awkward weight of the cast on his right forearm. He decided on the breast stroke, took a deep gulp of air, careful not to lose the knife, shivering as he made his way toward the *Reptil Rache.*

He estimated he had to cover about twenty-five yards at a stroke a yard, five strokes per breath, five breaths and he would be there.

Three strokes, four strokes, five, first breath. He broke the surface, sucking air around the knife. Water seeped under the cast and the jeans he had taken from the dead seaman were heavy and uncomfortable to swim in. Eight strokes, nine, it felt like his lungs were going to burst, one more stroke before the precious air, ten. He took another breath.

Eleven strokes, twelve, he needed air now. He was freezing. His fingers were numb. He felt the cold steel in his mouth and tasted the polluted water as it seeped between his lips to wrap itself around the tip of his tongue as it stuck out and rested below the sharp blade. Thirteen strokes, fourteen, he was light headed, he couldn't make the last stroke, not without blacking out. Yes, yes he could, only one more, the thought raced through him. A short, quick stroke, but a stroke, fifteen.

Suck air.

Sixteen strokes, seventeen, well over halfway. He felt something big glide by. Shark was his first thought. It came within inches. Maybe a dolphin, but he discarded that thought, too close to shore. Polluted harbor, there would be no dolphins here. Eighteen strokes, nineteen, it came by again. This time it bumped him as it swam by. He forced his eyes open and got a quick look at it as it broke the surface. It was no shark. Twenty. He took the scaling knife out of his mouth, gulped air and waited for the Gecko's return.

He held the knife in his right hand, concealed by the cast, as he hung limp in the water, playing the decoy, hoping the reptile would think him dead. He sensed rather than felt its approach, closer, coming closer, but it whizzed on by, forcing him to continue his charade. He wanted to open his eyes, but he knew it would be pointless in the murky water. He would have only one chance at the beast and he would have to rely on instinct.

He tucked the knife to his chest and waited, every nerve tingling with anticipation and cold. He was fully relaxed, allowing himself to become one with the water. He had no need for another breath. He sensed the thing coming for him and he resisted the temptation to lash out prematurely.

He knew he couldn't kill it, but he'd learned that he could slow it down. Something inside him wailed. "*Do it now.*" A new voice, not Donna's. An urgent voice, a commanding voice, his own voice. He obeyed and shoved his right arm forward, like it was spring loaded, slamming the sharp steel into the thing's flesh. He kept a firm grip on the knife, drawing it along the underbelly of the beast. Then he twisted it, slicing back along the direction of his original incision as the thing bucked into his side, bellowing out foul air as it swam away.

Jim kicked toward the surface. The rise up seemed an eternity. Pumping adrenaline had used up his oxygen supply. He didn't know how deep he was and he didn't think he would make it, but he held on, breaking the surface cleanly, taking great gulps of air. He was within an arm's reach of the dive ladder. He didn't know what awaited him above, but he knew if he didn't get out of the water quickly, the gecko would be back.

He slid the scaling knife back between his teeth and grabbed out for the ladder. He was exhausted, but he calmed his rate of breathing and silently pulled his way on up.

* * *

Donna was stunned, but she wasn't submissive. She screamed as she fell forward onto the mattress, started her roll even before she landed on the soft surface, pushed off with her left hand and clawed the false policewoman's face with her right. The imposter screamed, stumbling backward, her face covered in new blood.

Donna struggled to get up, but four strong arms pulled her down and flipped her onto her back.

"No," she shouted, as they tied her arms and legs to the four corners of the bed. She was trussed up, spread eagled, and there was nothing she could do about it, but scream her rage at her betrayal. After a few seconds she stopped screaming.

She glared swords at the two big men. She was in trouble. *"If you're coming, Jim Monday, come now. Please come now,"* she thought desperately, but he didn't answer. The connection had been broken.

"Okay, start the equipment and get out of here." The doctor with the Death's Head said and Donna watched without struggling as the big men fiddled with the cameras, then the men and the false policewomen left the salon, going up through the galley and onto the deck.

"It's just you and me now." The doctor's laughter was a guttural rasping, like a mean dog's growl. "I've waited a long time for this. Generations." He looked at her with glassed over eyes. "We should get to know each other better." He grabbed her robe by the left lapel, balled it into his fist and ripped it off, leaving her naked before him—defenseless.

Her bound hands started to shake as he kicked off his shoes.

"First I'm going to use you," he said through a Nazi killer's smile. "I'm going to have to do it fast, because it's almost midnight." He reached down and pulled his socks off. Then opened his coat, took it off and she saw the shoulder holster.

"Big eyes, I see the gun frightens you." He pulled off the holster, took a gun out of it. "It's a Beretta Cougar. The most beautiful thing I have ever owned." He held the gun up, stroked the barrel. "You want a closer look?"

She shook her head.

"Yes you do." He pointed the barrel between her eyes, touched it to her forehead. "Nine millimeter, fifteen rounds in the magazine, double action, a point and shoot weapon. But not with the safety on." He laughed, then with the gun still on her forehead, still between her eyes, he clicked it off.

"Now it's read to go." He wrapped a powerful right hand around her jaw, squeezed, forcing her mouth open, forcing the barrel in.

"Suck on that." He laughed again, a devil's laugh. "I could blow your head right off." He pulled out the gun and Donna gasped for air as he ran the barrel down to her breasts, first covering one nipple, then the other, then he took it down further, to her sex.

"I'd shove it in, but I've got something else I want to shove in first." He pulled the gun away, eyes glazed. "Almost no recoil with this wonderful weapon. It's because of the rotating barrel."

She squeezed her eyes shut, sickened by the sight of him.

"Ah, you're not interested."

She tried to will him away.

"Open your eyes."

She refused.

"I'll shoot of your kneecaps. It'll be very painful for you."

She opened her eyes.

"That's better. Now we can talk." He tossed the gun on the bed and pulled off his shirt, revealing a dirty tee shirt. His body odor was overpowering.

"It's true I don't bathe much anymore. I suppose it's been the anticipation. I've been wanting you for a long time. He pulled off the tee shirt and leered at her. "Do you like the accent, the Nazis had so much to offer, it's a shame they lost."

"You're not German?" She was confused.

"Of course not, the accent's affected."

"I don't understand."

"Come on, you know me."

"Ngaarara," she whispered.

"Yes."

She squirmed against her bonds, wishing him dead and gone.

"I didn't think you had it in you," he said, changing the subject as he unzipped his pants. "You cast your spirit halfway around the world, even I can't do that." He paused, staring at her. "You cost me a good deal of money and several years of pleasure. I only wish there was some additional torture I could induce to make you pay for your sins, but time is short."

He flipped his erection out of his pants and she flinched as its single eye stared at her.

"It is large, isn't it?" He massaged himself. "I like it when it works out that way. Sometimes I get a body with a small one, they work fine, but they don't frighten the young girls nearly as much as something like this." He pulled on himself.

Her eyes were frozen wide and she struggled against the ropes.

"I will be able to masturbate to your deflowering for years upon years, enjoying you forever." He stopped massaging himself and dropped his pants. He laughed, a devil's rasp, as he stood before her, naked.

"After I fuck you, I'm going to call in my German bully boys. They're going to stuff you in the oven."

She pulled harder against the ropes.

"We have a very modern industrial galley on board, including an oversize stove, perfect for you. You'll be cooked alive and I'll have every delicious scream on video."

* * *

Jim pulled himself up on the first rung of the dive ladder and caught his breath. He transferred the knife from his mouth back to his right hand and quieted his heart by taking long deep breaths. He was in a hurry, but he didn't want to blunder foolishly over the side and get himself killed before he had a chance to free Donna. He climbed two rungs of the ladder and poked his head over the rail.

The man on watch had his back to him. He appeared to be watching the four old Maori men beyond. They were involved in a heated argument of some kind. Jim climbed up over the rail, glad that Mohi was doing his job. If he had any doubt about how to handle the man on watch, the black sweater and seaman's cap he was wearing made up his mind. The last two men he'd met who were dressed like that had tried to kill him. Jim eased up behind the watchman and silently slit his throat.

He saw the Maori men start toward the boat, but he didn't have time to wait for them. He slipped down the open hatch and found himself looking down a long companionway, with cabin doors on each side. He eased down the corridor. Donna could be in any one of these rooms, he thought, but he knew differently when he heard a familiar voice traveling from beyond the partially open door at the head of the hallway, and all of a sudden he knew what the connection between himself and Donna Tuhiwai had been.

"I have so much to get even for, fucking you and burning you doesn't seem like enough. If only I had more time." The voice and the accent almost threw him into shock. Maybe the man called himself Manfred Penn now, but that wasn't the name that Jim knew him by.

He moved quickly down the corridor, taking the plastic enclosed gun out from the front of his wet pants as he walked. He stopped just before the door, took the gun out from the plastic bag, took a deep breath and kicked the door open.

"You?" a bald, clean shaven Bernd Kohler said.

"Me!" Jim pulled the trigger, but a scream filled the night air, throwing a chill through his spine and throwing his aim high and wide. The hairs on the nape of his neck stood on end as Bernd Kohler answered the scream of the gecko with one of his own. Before Jim could fire again, Kohler dashed up into the galley, tore through the hatchway and was gone.

In seconds he would be up the ladder to the pier and away and there was nothing Jim could do about it, because he couldn't leave Donna tied and naked. He moved quickly to the bed.

"What's that? He nodded toward an automatic pistol as he sliced though the ropes.

"A madman's gun." She grabbed it the instant he'd freed a hand. "Mine now."

"We have to hurry," he said.

"Don't have to tell me twice," she said. "Let's get out of here."

Not yet." He took her hand and led her out of the salon, up into the galley. They backed against the wall opposite the hatchway, as far from the hatch and the adjoining windows as they could get.

Donna gasped as the giant reptile shot out of the water, a second scream escaping from its shark-like mouth.

Jim braced himself against the bulkhead as it flopped back into the dark water. A third scream tore through the night as it shot back out of the ocean, again soaring over the rails, but this time it landed on the deck. It was through the hatchway in seconds.

* * *

Kohler cowered and hid at the bow, behind the anchor motor, naked and cold. He heard the Maori men up front when he came out the galley hatchway on the starboard side. He kept low, peered around the galley and saw them. They came down the port side toward the rear and he scuttled forward up the starboard side to the crew quarters. He stayed low and the Maori men went by on the other side of the boat without seeing him.

He wondered what had happened to the crew. They were supposed to be on watch, not drinking down below. He eased himself around the anchor motor and climbed down into the crew's forward cabin. He didn't need the lights to know they were all dead. Even the woman. Those men might have been old, but they were Maori. Kohler respected them. They knew how to handle an enemy.

He pulled a body off a lower berth, tore the mattress off the bed. He smiled to himself—Monday and the girl were going to die. He pulled up the plywood cover, reached inside the hidy hole under the berth and pulled out an M-16 assault rifle.

He was a slave to his anger. He didn't bother putting on any clothes. He climbed out of the crew quarters, keeping low as he moved around the anchor motor. Then he slipped through the forward hatch, down into the corridor below. His pet would get them from the stern, he'd come at them from the bow.

He didn't give a thought to the Maoris on board. After eliminating the girl and Monday, he'd dive naked into the sea. As long as the gecko lived, he'd be safe. This body would die, but he'd get another. It was time anyway, he was tired of being a German.

* * *

"Down! Jim shoved Donna to the right and dove left as the beast came for them. She heard him fire off a round, saw the gecko jerk when it was hit as she slammed into the side of the bed that, until just moments, ago she'd been tied to.

A lightning bolt of pain blasted into her back when she struck and the fancy Beretta Cougar pistol that the doctor loved so much went flying from her hand. She gasped for breath, wrestling for air as she clawed for the gun.

Air, she needed air. Her stomach spasmed, muscles clenching out of control. She couldn't see. Where was the gun? She scraped the varnished floor with her nails in a vain attempt to find it, sweeping her hand back and forth as she battled for breath.

The gecko screamed, a sound somewhere between a baby's bawl and a wolf's howl. A banshee cry. The sound was huge, deafening, a wailing screech that set her nerves afire and ice pricks stinging up her spine.

"It's under the bed!" Jim shouted.

"What?"

"The bed."

The gecko roared, a lion's sound now, an angry hunter's roar that forced her eyes open and drew her in. The beast was mammoth, every bit the size of an African lion. It's eyes were radioactive yellow, it's sabertoothed fangs gleamed as if they were brand new and it's green, lizard like skin shown bright as a palm frond in a brilliant equatorial rain, but it was dripping deep red blood over the brightly varnished deck and from Donna's position, flat on the floor, she saw that the reptile had a deep slit along its underbelly, like the fish her father filleted.

It looked like it was in pain.

* * *

It had been in this life for only a short time and already it felt pain. More than it had ever known in it's long history. It was bleeding, losing its insides all over this smooth and flat place and it's right shoulder felt like it was on fire.

It glared at the prey with the loud pain stick in its hand and roared, but the prey didn't show its back, didn't flee. Again, as in the life it so recently left behind in that place across the ocean, it was faced with prey that was not prey. It was confused. How was it supposed to know the difference.

It turned toward the woman sprawled out only a short leap away. That was prey. It was getting weak. It had to feed. Instinctively it knew the woman had not been selected for nourishment. Ngaarara had other plans for her, but it needed to feed now.

"It's all right, my pet, you can have her." It heard Ngaarara's voice in its head, the way it always did.

"No you can't!" another thought voice. This had never happened before. Who, what, how could this be? It was even more confused now. *"Go away!"* the stranger's thought voice again.

"Take the woman!" Ngaarara screamed the thought.

"No!" the stranger thought.

It turned toward the woman and it knew who the stranger was.

* * *

Something odd was going on and Jim wasn't exactly sure what. Donna and the gecko were staring at each other as if they were communicating. For an instant it looked like the beast was going to spring at her, but now it was holding its ground.

He got up, got into the shooter's position, legs wide, two hands on the weapon. The gun might be old, but he'd hit what he was aiming at while he and his target were on the move, he couldn't miss now. He sighted on one of the beast's large yellow eyes, the one on the left.

Every fiber in his being said, shoot. But Donna seemed to be staring the thing down. He didn't know what to do.

* * *

"Very interesting," the doctor thought and Donna heard him as she'd Jim earlier. *"You are strong."*

"You should just take your pet and go," Donna thought as she smelled smoke.

"But you know I won't," he thought.

"Yes, I suppose I do." And all of a sudden Donna was able to see through his eyes. She saw the rifle in his hand, saw the door she'd seen earlier, the door that led into the salon. He was just on the other side of it.

"I've waited a long time for my revenge, I'll not be cheated when I'm so close."

"Smell the fire." Donna thought.

"What?"

"You're afraid now. I feel it."

"Bitch." Any second he was going to burst into the room, rifle blazing.

"Shoot!" Donna shouted as she rolled under the bed.

* * *

Jim fired and took out the eye.

The beast screamed, the sound of pure torture, as it swung it's single good eye toward him.

Jim fired again and took it out too.

The gecko wailed, a ghastly sound that chilled Jim's spine. Then it charged, mouth agape, but Jim stepped aside and emptied the gun into it's great head. It was blind, but still dangerous as it thrashed around the salon.

* * *

Kohler felt his pet's pain, sensed it's blindness, and for the first time in his long life, he was afraid. There was fire ahead, he'd sensed it though the woman. His pet was blind and had been trapped. He couldn't pass through the fire.

Neither could he.

Better to fight another day. He turned to flee the way he'd come, but all of a sudden there was smoke there. Someone had set fire to the front of the boat.

There was only one way out for him now and that was through the salon and out the rear hatchway or through the windows in the galley. Either way he had to go through that door and he had to do it now.

He kicked it open.

* * *

Donna grabbed the weapon as the doctor burst though the door, rolled back out from under the bed and started pulling the trigger.

The first shot hit the man who called himself Ngaarara square in the chest and sent him flying back into the corridor and somehow, despite the fact that she kept shooting, he managed to kick the door closed after himself. But she couldn't stop, she kept firing, blasting round after round into the doorway until the gun was empty and then the salon was quiet, save for the heavy breathing of the gecko monster, now on it's side in the galley, gurgling blood with every breath.

She grabbed onto the side of the bed, used it to steady herself, then got up off the floor, and all of a sudden she was conscious of the fact that she was nude.

"The boat's on fire," Jim Monday said. "We gotta go."

They stared at each other for an instant, then she ran into his arms and he kissed her.

He pulled away.

"Really, he said, "we gotta go."

The back hatchway, a doorway to the aft cockpit, was open, she saw the flames.

"It's through the fire," he said, "but we'll land in the water if we keep going."

"I'm gone." She dashed through the doorway, felt the fire as she dove over the side and into the cold sea below.

* * *

The Maori men moved away from the galley after they set the fire. They were reluctant to leave the boat. They heard the screams and shooting from below, but these men were not old women, either the pakeha would save the girl, or he would not. They had done everything asked of them. It was in the pakeha's hands now. Mohi was in agony, wondering if he'd done the right thing. The father in him wanted to rush through the flames and find his daughter, but Monday had convinced him not to do that. Monday was a pakeha, but he was Maori-brave and Mohi respected that.

He clenched his fists and tightened his jaw. Then he smiled as he saw Donna burst out the starboard companionway, dashing through the flames, and he grinned wider as Monday followed in her wake, leaping over the side into the cold sea below.

"Quickly." He jumped onto the pier, the three old men followed. "There's a ladder over here," he yelled to Monday, and the old men silently congratulated themselves for a job well done as they helped the pakeha and Mohi's daughter out of the sea. Two of the old men removed their coats and offered them to the shivering couple.

And then they all shivered as one long, agonizing scream roared out from the boat, waking up the night. Then all was silent—the only sound the licking flames and the quiet sea, lapping against the pier.

"Cheeky little bugger," One of the Maori men said.

"What?" One of his mates asked.

"Little green gecko just ran over my foot. See, there it goes."

The Bootleg Press Catalog

RAGGED MAN by Jack Priest
BOOTLEG 001—ISBN: 0974524603
 Unknown to Rick Gordon, he brought an ancient aboriginal horror home from the Australian desert. Now his friends are dying and Rick is getting the blame.

DESPERATION MOON by Ken Douglas
BOOTLEG 002—ISBN: 0974524611
 Sara Hackett must save two little girls from dangerous kidnappers, but she doesn't have the money to pay the ransom.

SCORPION by Jack Stewart
BOOTLEG 003—ISBN: 097452462x
 DEA agent Bill Broxton must protect the Prime Minister of Trinidad from an assassin, but he doesn't know the killer is his fiancée.

DEAD RINGER by Ken Douglas
BOOTLEG 004—ISBN: 0974524638
 Maggie Nesbitt steps out of her dull life and into her dead twin's, and now the man that killed her sister is after Maggie.

GECKO by Jack Priest
BOOTLEG 005—ISBN: 0974524646
 Jim Monday must rescue his wife from an evil worse than death before the Gecko horror of Maori legend kills them both.

RUNNING SCARED by Ken Douglas
BOOTLEG 006—ISBN: 0974524654
 Joey Sapphire's husband blackmailed and now is out to kill the president's daughter and only Joey can save the young woman.

Night Witch by Jack Priest
Bootleg 007 — ISBN: 0974524662
   A vampire like creature followed Carolina's father back from the Caribbean and now it is terrorizing her. She and her friend Arty are only children, but they must fight this creature themselves or die.

Hurricane by Jack Stewart
Bootleg 008 — ISBN: 0974524670
   Julie Tanaka flees Trinidad on her sailboat after the death of her husband, but the boat has a drug lord's money aboard and DEA agent Bill Broxton must get to her first or she is dead.

Tangerine Dream by Ken Douglas and Jack Stewart
Bootleg 009 — ISBN: 0974524689
   Seagoing writer and gourmet chef Captain Katie Osborne said of this book, "Incest, death, tragedy, betrayal and teenage homosexual love, I don't know how, but somehow it all works. I was up all night reading."

Diamond Sky by Ken Douglas and Jack Stewart
Bootleg 012 — ISBN: 0974524697
   The Russian Mafia is after Beth Shannon. Their diamonds have been stolen and they think she knows where they are. She does, only she doesn't know it.

Bootleg Books are Better than T.V.

THE BOOTLEG PRESS STORY

We at Bootleg Press are a small group of writers who were brought together by pen and sea. We have all been members of either the St. Martin or Trinidad Cruising Writer's Groups in the Caribbean.

We share our thoughts, plot ideas, villains and heroes. That's why you'll see some borrowed characters, both minor and major, cross from one author's book to another's.

Also, you'll see a few similar scenes that seem to jump from one author's pages to another's. That's because both authors have collaborated on the scene and—both liking how it worked out—both decided to use it.

At what point does an author's idea truly become his own? That's a good question, but rest assured in the rare occasions where you may discover similar scenes in Bootleg Press Books, that it is not stealing. Writing is a solitary art, but sometimes it is possible to share the load.

Book writing is hard, but book selling is harder. We think our books are as good as any you'll find out there, but breaking into the New York publishing market is tough, especially if you live far away from the Big Apple.

So, we've all either sold or put our boats on the hard, pooled our money and started our own company. We bought cars and loaded our trunks with books. We call on small independent bookstores ourselves, as we are our own distributors. But the few of us cannot possibly reach the whole world, however we are trying, so if you don't see our books in your local bookstore yet, remember you can always order them from the big guys online.

Thank you from everyone at Bootleg Books for reading and please remember, Bootleg Books are better than T.V.

JACK PRIEST
TORTOLA, 2000

Printed in the United States
25567LVS00001B/13-18

9 780974 524641